the ANGEL

CARLA NEGGERS

the ANGEL

DOUBLEDAY LARGE PRINT HOME LIBRARY EDITION

MIRA®

This Large Print Edition, prepared especially for Doubleday Large Print Home Library, contains the complete, unabridged text of the original Publisher's Edition.

MIRA®

ISBN-13: 978-0-7394-9473-8

THE ANGEL

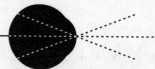

This Large Print Book carries the
Seal of Approval of N.A.V.H.

To Kate and Conor

ACKNOWLEDGMENTS

To Brendan Gunning for all the wonderful Irish and Irish-American stories, and to Myles Heffernan, Paul Hudson, Jamie Carr and Christine Wenger for sharing your knowledge and expertise.

To Sarah Gallick for the help with Irish saints and for sending me early excerpts from *The Big Book of Women Saints.*

To my daughter, Kate Jewell, and my son-in-law, Conor Hansen, for getting us all to southwest Ireland. Conor, I'll never forget standing in the stone house where your great-grandfather was born, or meeting your cousins on the Beara Peninsula.

To Don Lucey for the insight into Irish music and all the great recommendations.

To my agent, Margaret Ruley, and to my editor, Margaret Marbury, for the unwavering patience and support, and to the rest of the fabulous team in New York and Toronto— Donna Hayes, Craig Swinwood, Loriana Sacilotto, Dianne Moggy, Katherine Orr, Marleah Stout,

8   ACKNOWLEDGMENTS

Heather Foy, Michelle Renaud, Stacy Widdrington, Margie Miller, Adam Wilson and everyone who makes MIRA Books such an incredible pleasure to work with.

And to Joe Jewell, my husband, for all the great times in Boston, "our" city, and to Zack Jewell, my son . . . yes, another trip to Ireland is in the works. Can't wait!

Carla Neggers
P.O. Box 826
Quechee, VT 05059
www.carlaneggers.com

⌁Prologue

South Boston, Massachusetts
2:00 p.m., EDT
July 12, Thirty Years Ago

A scrap of yellow crime scene tape bobbed in the rising tide of Boston Harbor where the brutalized body of nineteen-year-old Deirdre McCarthy had washed ashore. Bob O'Reilly couldn't take his eyes off it.

Neither could Patsy McCarthy, Deirdre's mother, who stood next to him in the hot summer sun. Coming out here was her idea. Bob didn't want to, but he didn't know what else to do. He couldn't let her go alone.

"Deirdre was an angel."

"She was, Mrs. McCarthy. Deirdre was the best."

Ninety degrees outside, and Patsy shivered in her pastel blue polyester sweater. She'd lost weight in the three weeks since Deirdre hadn't come home after her shift as a nurse's aide. At first the police had believed she was just another South Boston girl who'd gone wrong. Patsy kept at them. Not Deirdre.

She disappeared on the night of the summer solstice. The longest day of the year.

Appropriate, somehow, Bob thought.

Patsy's eyes, as clear and as blue as the afternoon sky, lifted to the horizon, as if she were trying to see the island of her birth, as if Ireland could bring her the comfort and strength she needed to get through her ordeal. She'd left the southwest Irish coast forty years ago at the age of nine and hadn't been back since. She loved to tell stories about her Irish childhood, how she was born in a one-room cottage with no plumbing, no central heat—not even an outhouse—and how she'd learned to bake her famous brown bread on an open fire.

Bob wondered how she'd tell this story. The story of her daughter's kidnapping, rape, torture and murder.

The police hadn't released details, but Bob, the son of a Boston cop, had heard rumors of unspeakable acts of violence and depravity. He was twenty and planned on becoming a detective, and one day he would have to wade through such details himself. He hoped the victim would never be someone he knew. He and Deirdre had learned to rollerskate together, had given each other their first kiss, just to see what it was like.

"I heard the cry of a banshee all last night," Patsy said quietly. "I can't say I do or don't believe in fairies, but I heard what I heard. I knew we'd find Deirdre this morning."

The fine hairs stood on the back of Bob's neck. A retired firefighter walking his golden retriever at sunrise had come upon Deirdre's body. The police had come and gone, working with a grim efficiency, given Boston's skyrocketing homicide rate. Now they had another killer to hunt.

With the city behind them and the boats out on the water and planes taking off from Logan Airport, Bob still could hear the lapping of the tide on the sand. He'd never felt so damn helpless and alone.

"Deirdre Ita McCarthy." Patsy crossed her arms on her chest as if she were cold. "It's the name of an Irish saint, you know. Saint Ita was born Deirdre and took the name Ita when she made her vows. Ita means 'thirsting for divine love.'"

Patsy was deeply religious, but Bob had stopped attending mass regularly when he was sixteen and his mother said it was up to him to go or not go. He knew he'd go back to church for Deirdre's funeral.

"I've never been good at keeping track of the saints." He tried to smile. "Even the Irish ones."

"Saint Patrick, Saint Brigid and Saint Ita are early Celtic saints. Saint Ita had the gift of prophecy. Angels visited her throughout her life. Do you believe in angels, Bob?"

"I've never thought about it."

"I do," she whispered. "I believe in angels."

It wouldn't strike Patsy as particularly contradictory to say in one breath she'd heard a banshee—a solitary fairy—and in another that she believed in angels. If her beliefs brought her comfort, Bob didn't care. He didn't know what to tell her about banshees or angels or anything else. Her husband had died of a heart attack four years ago. Now this. "The police will find who took Deirdre from us."

"No. They won't. They can't." Patsy shifted her gaze back to the crime scene tape floating in the water. "The police are only human after all."

"They won't rest until they catch whoever did this."

"It was the devil who took Deirdre. It wasn't a man."

"Doesn't matter. If the police have to go to hell to find and arrest the devil, that's what they'll do. If I have to do it myself, I will."

"No—no, Bob. Deirdre wouldn't have you sacrifice your soul. She's with her sister angels now. She's at peace."

Bob suddenly realized Patsy meant the devil literally. He pictured Deirdre with her blond hair and blue eyes, her translucent skin and innocent smile. She was as good as good ever was. She wouldn't have stood a chance with someone who meant her harm. Devil or no devil.

He'd miss her. He'd miss her for as long as he lived.

He pushed back his emotions. It was something he'd need to learn to do if he was going to be a detective and catch people the likes of whoever had killed Deirdre.

"We don't want this cretin to hurt someone else."

"No, we don't." Patsy turned from the water. "But there are other ways to fight the devil."

Two hours later, Bob found his sister, Eileen, reciting the rosary on a bench in the shade of a sprawling oak on the Boston College campus, where she had a summer work-study job at the library.

"I didn't know you still had rosary beads," he said.

"I didn't, either. I found them in my jewelry box this morning." She spoke in a near whisper as she held a single ivory-colored bead between her thumb and forefinger. "I haven't said the rosary in ages. I thought I might not remember, but it came right back to me."

Bob sat next to her. His sister was the smart one in the family. She'd returned two days ago from a summer study program in Dublin. No one had called to tell her Deirdre had gone missing. What could Eileen do from Ireland? Why spoil her time there, when they all hoped Deirdre would turn up, safe and sound?

When news of the discovery of Deirdre's body reached the O'Reilly household that morning, Eileen pretended nothing had happened and left for work.

"I've just come from the waterfront with Mrs. McCarthy," Bob said.

Eileen tensed, as if his words were a blow, and he didn't go on. Her hair was more dirty blond than red like his, and she had more freckles. She'd never thought she was all that attractive, but she'd always been hard on herself—his sister had no limit to her personal list of faults big and small.

"There's nothing the police can do now." Eileen lifted her eyes from her rosary beads and shifted her gaze to her older brother. "Is there?"

"They can find Deirdre's killer. They can stop him from killing again."

"They can't undo what happened."

His sister's left hand trembled, but her right hand, which held her rosary beads, was steady. Bob noticed how pale she was, as if she'd been sick. His smart, driven sister had so many plans for her life, but coming back home from Ireland to Deirdre's disappearance had thrown Eileen right back into the world she was trying to exit.

And now Deirdre was dead.

Eileen's fingers automatically moved to the next bead, and he saw her lips move as she silently recited the Hail, Mary.

He waited for her to finish the entire rosary and return her beads to their navy velvet pouch. She clutched it in her hand and leaned back against the bench.

They both watched a squirrel run up a maple tree.

Without looking at her brother, Eileen said, "I'm pregnant."

Of all the things Bob had anticipated she might say when she'd finished praying, he hadn't imagined that one. Their parents would be shocked. *He* was shocked. She didn't have a boyfriend that he knew about.

He fought an urge to run away. Get out of Boston, away from the aftermath of Deirdre's death, from what was to come with his sister. It all flashed in his mind— Patsy grieving next door, the police hunting for Deirdre's killer, Eileen getting bigger, trying to figure out what to do with the baby.

The baby's father. Who the hell was he?

Bob curled his hands into tight fists. He was young. He didn't have to stay in Boston and deal with all these problems. He could go anywhere. He could be a detective in New York or Miami or Seattle.

Hawaii, he thought. He could move to Honolulu.

"How far along are you?" he asked.

"Not far. I haven't had the test yet, but I know."

"Eileen..." Bob looked at his younger sister, but she didn't meet his eyes. "What happened in Ireland?"

But she jumped to her feet and walked quickly toward the ivy-covered building where she worked, and he didn't follow her.

A week later, a series of calls into the Boston Police Department alerted them to a man who had just leaped from a boat into Boston Harbor.

He was in flames when he hit the water.

By the time a passing pleasure boat reached him, he was dead.

Within hours, the dead man was identified as Stuart Fuller, a twenty-four-year-old road worker who rented an attic apartment three blocks from the house where Deirdre McCarthy lived with her mother. Police discovered overwhelming evidence that tied him to Deirdre's murder.

They had their devil.

The autopsy on Fuller determined that he'd drowned, but his burns would have killed him if he hadn't gone into the water.

That evening, Bob found Patsy on her back porch with about twenty small angel figurines lined up on the top of the wide wooden railing. Despite the summer heat, she wore a pink polyester sweater, as if she expected never to be warm again.

"Deirdre collected angels," Patsy said.

"I know. It made it easy to buy her presents." Bob pointed at a colorful glass angel he'd found for her on a high school trip to Cape Cod. "I got her that one for her sixteenth birthday."

"It's beautiful, Bob."

His throat tightened. "Mrs. McCarthy—"

"The police were here this morning. They told me about Stuart Fuller. They asked me if I knew him."

"Did you?"

"Not that I recall. I suppose I could have seen him in the neighborhood."

She narrowed her eyes slightly. "At church, perhaps. The devil is always drawn to good."

Bob watched her use a damp cloth to clean a delicate white porcelain angel holding a small Irish harp. It was one of the more valuable figurines in Deirdre's collection and one of her favorites. She'd loved all kinds of angels—it didn't matter if they were cheap, cheesy, expensive, ethnic. She used to tell Bob she wanted to buy a glass curio cabinet in which to display them.

"Patsy...do you know anything about Fuller's death?"

She seemed not to hear him. "I have a story I want to tell you."

Bob didn't have the patience for one of her stories right now. "Which one?"

"One you've never heard before." She held up the cleaned figurine to the light. "My grandfather first told it to me as a child in Ireland. Oh, he was a wonderful storyteller."

"I'm sure he was, but—"

"It's a story about three brothers who get into a battle with fairies over an ancient stone angel." Patsy's eyes sparked, and for a moment, she seemed almost happy. "It was one of Deirdre's favorites."

"Then it can't be depressing. Deirdre didn't like depressing stories."

"She didn't, did she? Come, Bob. I'll make tea and heat up some brown bread for you. It's my mother's recipe. I made it fresh this morning. My father used to say my mother made the best brown bread in all of West Cork."

Bob had no choice but to follow Patsy into her small kitchen and help her set out the tea and the warm, dense bread. How many times had he and Eileen and Deirdre sat here, listening to Patsy tell old Irish stories?

She joined him at the table, her cheeks flushed as she buttered a small piece of bread. "Once upon a time," she said, laying on her Irish accent, "there were three brothers who lived on the south-west coast of Ireland—a farmer, a hermit monk and a ne'er-do-well, who was, of course, everyone's favorite..."

Bob drank the tea, ate the bread and pushed back tears for the friend he'd lost as he listened to Patsy's story.

~Chapter 1

Keira Sullivan swiped at a mosquito and wondered if its Irish cousins would be as persistent. She'd find out soon enough, she thought as she walked along the trail to her mother's cabin in the southern New Hampshire woods. She'd be on a plane to Ireland tomorrow night, off to the southwest Irish coast to research an old story of mischief, magic and an ancient stone angel.

In the meantime, she had to get this

visit behind her and attend a reception tonight in Boston. But she couldn't wait to be tucked in her rented Irish cottage, alone with her art supplies, her laptop, her camera and her walking shoes.

For the next six weeks, she'd be free to think, dream, draw, paint, explore and, perhaps, make peace with her past.

More accurately, with her mother's past.

The cabin came into view, nestled on an evergreen-blanketed hill above a stream. Keira could hear the water tumbling over rocks and feel it cooling the humid late spring air. Birds twittered and fluttered nearby—chickadees, probably. Her mother would have given all the birds on her hillside names.

The mosquito followed Keira the last few yards up the path. It had found her at the dead-end dirt road where she'd left her car and stayed with her throughout the long trek through the woods. She was less than two hours from Boston, but she might as well have been on another planet as she sweated in the June heat, her blond hair coming out of its pins, her legs spattered with mud. She wished instead of shorts she'd worn long pants, in case her solo mosquito summoned reinforcements.

She stood on the flat, gray rock that served as a step to the cabin's back entrance. Her mother had built the cabin herself, using local lumber, refusing help from family and friends. She'd hired out, reluctantly, only what she couldn't manage on her own.

There was no central heat, no plumbing, no electricity. She had no telephone, no radio, no television—no mail delivery, even. And forget about a car.

On frigid New England winter nights, life had to get downright unbearable, if not dangerous, but Keira knew her mother would never complain. She had chosen the simple, rugged existence of a religious ascetic. No one had thrust it upon her.

Keira peered through the screen door, grateful that her mother's stripped-down lifestyle didn't prohibit the use of screens. The pesky mosquito could stay outside.

"Hello—it's me, Mum. Keira."

As if her mother had other children. As

if she might have forgotten her only daughter's name since chucking the outside world. Keira had last visited her mother several weeks ago but hadn't stayed long. Then again, they hadn't spent much time together in the past few years, never mind the past eighteen months when she'd first announced her intention to pursue this new commitment.

Her mother had always been religious, which Keira respected, but this, she thought as she swiped again at her mosquito—this isolated hermit's life just wasn't right.

"Keira!" her mother called, sounding cheerful. "Come in, come in. I'm here in the front room. Leave your shoes on the step, won't you?"

Keira kicked off her hiking shoes and entered the kitchen—or what passed for one. It consisted of a few rustic cupboards and basic supplies that her mother had scavenged at yard sales for her austere life. Her priest had talked her into a gas-powered refrigerator. He was working on talking her into a gas-powered stove and basic plumbing—

even just a single cold-water faucet—
but she was resisting. Except for the
coldest days, she said, she could manage to fetch her own water from the
nearby spring.

Winning an argument with Eileen
O'Reilly Sullivan had never been an
easy task.

Keira crossed the rough pine-board
floor into the cabin's main living area.
Her mother, dressed in a flowing top
and elastic-waist pants, got up from a
high stool at a big hunk of birch board
set on trestles that served as her worktable. Her graying hair was blunt cut, reminding Keira of a nun, but although her
mother had turned to a religious life,
she'd taken no vows.

"It's so good to see you, Keira."

"You, too." Keira meant it, but if she
wanted to see her mother, she had to
come out here—her mother wouldn't
come to her in Boston. "The place looks
great. Nice and cozy."

"It's home."

Her mother sat back on her work
stool. Behind her, a picture window
overlooked an evergreen-covered hill-

side that dropped down to a stream. Keira appreciated the view, but, as much as she needed solitude herself at times, she couldn't imagine living out here.

A nearby hemlock swayed in a gust of wind, sending a warm breeze through the tiny cabin. Except for a wooden crucifix, the barn-board walls of the main room were unadorned. Besides the worktable and stool, the only other furnishings were an iron bed with a thin mattress, a rocking chair and a narrow chest of drawers. Not only was the small, efficient cast-iron woodstove the sole source of heat, it was also where her mother did any cooking. She chopped the wood for the stove herself.

The land on which the cabin was built was owned by a South Boston couple whose country home was through the woods, in the opposite direction of the path Keira had just used. She considered them complicit in her mother's withdrawal from the world—from her own family. They'd let her choose the spot for her cabin and then stood back, neutral, until she'd finally moved in last summer.

A year out here, Keira thought. *A year, and she looks as content as ever.*

"It really is so good to see you, sweetheart," her mother said quietly.

"I didn't mean to interrupt your work."

"Oh, don't worry about that."

A large sheet of inexpensive sketch paper was spread out on her worktable. Before retreating to the woods, she'd owned an art supply store in the southern New Hampshire town where she'd moved as a young widow with a small daughter. Over the years, she'd become adept at calligraphy and the tricky art of gilding, supplementing her income by restoring gilt picture frames and mirrors and creating elaborate wedding and birth announcements. Now she was applying her skills to the almost-forgotten art of producing an illuminated manuscript. The same couple who'd let her build on their land had found someone willing to pay her to illustrate an original manuscript of select Bible passages. Other than requesting an Irish Celtic sensibility and choosing the passages, the client left her alone.

It was painstaking work—deliberate, skilled, imaginative. She had her supplies at arm's reach. Brushes, pens, inks, paints, calligraphy nibs, gilding tips, a gilding cushion, polishing cloths and burnishers.

"You're working on your own Book of Kells," Keira said with a smile.

Her mother shook her head. "The Book of Kells is a masterpiece. It's been described as the work of angels. I'm a mere human."

Another wind gust shook the trees outside on the hill. Storms were brewing, a cold front about to move in and blow out the humidity that had settled over New England during the past week. Keira wanted to get back to her car before the rain started.

"Did you see the Book of Kells when you were in Ireland in college?"

"I did." Her mother's tone was distant, controlled. She shifted her gaze to the blank, pure white paper on her desk, as if envisioning the intricate, thousand-year-old illuminated manuscript. "I'll never forget it. What I'm doing is quite different. Much simpler."

"It'll be wonderful."

"Thank you. The Book of Kells consists mainly of the four Gospels, but I was asked to start with the fall of Adam and Eve." Her mother's eyes, a striking shade of cornflower blue, shone with sudden humor. "I haven't settled on the right serpent."

Keira noticed a series of small pencil sketches taped to the birch board. "Those are some pretty wild serpents. It doesn't get to you, being up here all alone drawing pictures of bad-assed snakes and bolts of lightning?"

Her mother laughed. "No bolts of lightning, I'm afraid. Although..." She thought a moment. "I don't know, Keira, you could be onto something. A bright, organic bolt of lightning in the Garden of Eden could work, don't you think?"

Keira could feel the tension easing out of her. She'd moved to Boston in January after a brief stint in San Diego and had trekked up here on snowshoes, hoping just to find her mother alive and reasonably sane. But her mother had

been warm and toasty, a pot of chili bub-
bling on her woodstove, content with her
rigid routines of prayer and work. Keira
had thought living closer would mean
they'd see more of each other. It hadn't.
She could have stayed in San Diego or
moved to Miami or Tahiti or Mozam-
bique—or Ireland, she thought. The land
of her ancestors.

The land of her father.

Maybe.

Her mother's sociability didn't last,
and the humor in her eyes died almost
immediately. A studied blankness—a
sense of peace, she would no doubt
say—brought a neutrality to her expression. She seemed to take a conscious
step back from her engagement with
the world. In this case, the world as rep-
resented by her daughter.

Keira tried not to be offended. "I
came to say goodbye for a few weeks.
I leave for Ireland tomorrow night for
six weeks."

"Six weeks? Isn't that a long time?"

"I'm doing something different this
trip." Keira hesitated, then said, "I'm

renting a cottage on the southwest coast. The Beara Peninsula."

Her mother gazed out at her wooded hillside. A second screen door opened onto another rock step and a small yard where she'd planted a vegetable garden, fencing it off to keep out deer and who knew what other animals.

Finally, she let out a breath. "Always so restless."

True enough, Keira thought. As a child, she'd roamed the woods with a sketch pad and colored pencils. In college, she'd snapped up every opportunity to go places—backpacking with friends out West, jumping on a lobster boat with a short-lived boyfriend, spending a summer in Paris on a shoestring. After college, she'd tried several careers before falling back on what she loved most—drawing, painting, folklore. She'd managed to combine them into a successful career, becoming known for her illustrations of classic poems and folktales. That her work was portable, allowing her to indulge her sense of adventure, was another plus.

"When I was here last," she said, "I

told you about a project I'm involved with—I'm working with an Irish professor who's putting together a conference on Irish folklore next spring. It'll be in two parts, one in Boston and one in Cork."

"I remember," her mother said.

"One of the emphases will be on twentieth-century immigrants to America. I've been working that angle, and I ended up deciding to put together and illustrate a collection specifically of their stories. I have a wonderful one Gran told me before she died. She was from West Cork—"

"I know she was. Keira..." Her mother's eyes were pained.

"What's wrong? I've been to Ireland before. Not the Beara Peninsula, but—Mum, are you afraid I'm going to run into my father?"

"Your father was John Michael Sullivan."

But Keira was referring to her biological father. Her mother had returned home from a summer study program in Ireland at nineteen, pregnant with Keira. When Keira was a year old, her mother had married John Sullivan, a South Boston electrician ten years her senior. He was killed in a car accident two years later, and his widow and adopted daughter had moved out of Boston and started a new life.

Keira had no clear memory of him, but when she looked at pictures of him, she felt an overwhelming sense of affection, gratitude and grief, as if some part of her did remember him. Her mother never discussed that one trip to Ireland thirty years ago. For all Keira knew, her biological father could have been a Swedish tourist or another American student.

She debated a moment, then said, "A woman on your old street in South Boston heard about the folklore project and got in touch with me. She told me this incredible story about three Irish brothers who fight with each other and fairies over an ancient stone angel—"

"Patsy McCarthy," her mother said in a toneless voice.

"That's right. She says she told you this story, too, before your trip to Ireland. The brothers believe the statue is of one of the angels said to visit Saint Ita during her lifetime. The fairies believe it's not an angel at all but actually one of their own who's been turned to stone. There's more to it—it's quite a tale."

"Mrs. McCarthy told a lot of stories."

"Her grandfather heard this one when he worked in the copper mines on the Beara Peninsula and told it to Patsy when she was a little girl in Ireland. The village where the brothers lived isn't named, but there are enough details—"

"To pinpoint it. Yes, I know."

"And the spot where the hermit monk brother lived. You could make a stab at finding it, at least, if you know the story." Keira waited, but when her mother didn't respond, continued. "Patsy told me you were determined to find the village and look for the hermit monk's hut on your trip to Ireland before I was born."

"She's a gifted storyteller."

"Yes, she is."

Her mother lifted a small, filmy sheet of gold leaf to the light streaming in through the window. The use of gold— real gold—was what distinguished a true illuminated manuscript, but Keira knew it was far too soon for her mother to apply gold to her work-in-progress.

"Do you know the difference between sin and evil, Keira?"

Keira didn't want to talk about sin and evil. She wanted to talk about Patsy's old story and magic, mischief and fairies. "It's not something I think much about."

"Adam and Eve sinned." Her mother turned the gold leaf so that it gleamed in the late-afternoon light. "They wanted to please God, but they succumbed to temptation. They regretted their disobedience. They took no delight in what they did."

"In other words, they sinned."

"Yes, but the serpent is a different case altogether. He delights in his wrongdoing. He exults in thwarting God. He sees himself as the antithesis of God. Unlike Adam and Eve, the serpent didn't commit a sin in the Garden of Eden. The serpent chose evil."

"Honestly, Mum, I don't know how you can stand to think about this stuff out here by yourself."

She set the thin gold leaf on the pure white paper. Keira knew from experience that the gold leaf was difficult to work with but resilient, able to withstand considerable manipulation without breaking into pieces. Applied properly, it looked like solid gold, not just a whisper of gold.

"We all sin, Keira," her mother said without a hint of a smile, "but we're not all evil. The devil understands that. Evil is a particular dispensation of the soul."

"Does this have anything to do with Ireland? With what happened there when you—"

"No. It has nothing at all to do with Ireland." She took a breath. "So, how's your work?"

Keira stifled her irritation at the abrupt change of subject. It felt like a dismissal and probably was, but she reminded herself that she hadn't come out to the woods to judge her mother, or even for information. She'd come simply to say goodbye before flying out of Boston tomorrow night.

"My work's going great right now, thanks." Why go into detail when that world no longer interested or concerned her mother?

"That's good to hear. Thank you for stopping by." She got to her feet and hugged Keira goodbye. "Live your life, sweetheart. Don't get too caught up in all these crazy old stories. And please don't worry about me out here. I'm fine."

On her way back through the woods, Keira resisted the urge to look over her shoulder for the devil and serpents. Instead, she remembered herself as a child, and how her mother would sing her Irish songs and read her stories. Every kind of story—stories about fairies and wizards and giants, about hobbits and elves and dark lords, princes and princesses, witches, goblins, cobblers, explorers and adventurers.

How could such a fun-loving, sociable woman end up alone out here?

But Keira had to admit there had been hints of what was to come—that she'd seen glimpses in her mother of a mysterious sadness and private guilt, of a longing for a peace that she knew could never really be hers in this life.

Her mother insisted she hadn't withdrawn from the world or rejected her family but rather had embraced her religious beliefs in a personal and profound way. She viewed herself as participating in a centuries-old monastic tradition.

That was no doubt true, but Keira didn't believe her mother's retreat to her isolated cabin was rooted entirely in her faith. As she'd listened to Patsy McCarthy tell her old story, Keira had begun to wonder if her mother's trip to Ireland thirty years ago had somehow set into motion her eventual turn to the life of a religious hermit.

Another mosquito—or maybe the same one—found Keira, buzzing in her ear and jerking her back to the here and now, to her own life. She swiped at the mosquito as she plunged down the narrow trail through the woods to the dead-end dirt road where she'd parked.

The story of the three Irish brothers, the fairies and the stone angel wasn't about a pot of gold at the end of the rainbow. Ultimately, Keira thought, it was about the push-pull of family ties and the deep, human yearning for a connection with others, for happiness and good fortune.

Mostly, it was just a damn good yarn—a mesmerizing story that Keira could illustrate and tell on the pages of her new book.

"They say the stone angel lies buried to this day in the old ruin of the hermit monk's hut."

Maybe, maybe not. Patsy McCarthy, and her grandfather before her, easily could have exaggerated and embellished the story over the years. It didn't matter. Keira was hooked, and she couldn't wait to be on her way to Ireland.

In the meantime, she had to get back to Boston in time for a reception and a silent auction to benefit the Boston-Cork folklore project that had brought her to Patsy's South Boston kitchen in the first place.

She glanced back into the woods, wishing her mother could be at the reception tonight. "Not just for my sake, Mum," Keira whispered. "For your own."

~Chapter 2

Boston Public Garden
Boston, Massachusetts
7:00 p.m., EDT
June 17

Victor Sarakis didn't let the heavy downpour stop him.

He couldn't.

He had to warn Keira Sullivan.

Rain spattered on the asphalt walks of the Public Garden, a Victorian oasis in the heart of Boston. He picked up his pace, wishing he'd remembered to bring an umbrella or even a hooded jacket, but he didn't have far to go. Once through the Public Garden, he had only to cross Charles Street and make his way up Beacon Street to an address just below the gold-domed Massachusetts State House.

He could do it. He *had* to do it.

The gray, muted light and startling amount of rain darkened his mood and further fueled his sense of urgency.

"Keira can't go to Ireland."

He was surprised he spoke out loud. He was aware that many people didn't consider him entirely normal, but he'd never been one to talk to himself.

"She can't look for the stone angel."

Drenched to the bone as he was, he'd look like a madman when he arrived at the elegant house where the benefit auction that Keira was attending tonight was being held. He couldn't let that deter him. He had to get her to hear him out.

He had to tell her what she was up against.

What was after her.

Evil.

Pure evil.

Not mental illness, not sin—evil.

Victor had to warn her in person. He

couldn't call the authorities and leave it to them. What proof did he have? What evidence? He'd sound like a lunatic.

Just stop Keira from going to Ireland. Then he could decide how to approach the police. What to tell them.

"Victor."

His name seemed to be carried on the wind.

The warm, heavy rain streamed down his face and back, poured into his shoes. He slowed his pace.

"Victor."

He realized now that he hadn't imagined the voice.

His gaze fell on the Public Garden's shallow pond, rain pelting into its gray water. The famous swan boats were tied up for the evening. With the fierce storms, the Public Garden was virtually empty of people.

No witnesses.

Victor broke into an outright run, even as he debated his options. He could continue on the walkways to Charles Street, or he could charge through the pond's shallow water, try to escape that way.

But already he knew there'd be no escape.

"Victor."

His gait faltered. He couldn't run fast enough. He wasn't athletic, but that didn't matter.

He couldn't outrun such evil.

He couldn't outrun one of the devil's own.

No one could.

~Chapter 3

Beacon Hill
Boston, Massachusetts
8:30 p.m., EDT
June 17

Not for the first time in his life, Simon Cahill found himself in an argument with an unrelenting snob, this time in Boston, but he could as easily have been in New York, San Francisco, London or Paris. He'd been to all of them. He enjoyed a good argument—especially with someone as obnoxious and pretentious as Lloyd Adler.

Adler looked to be in his early forties and wore jeans and a rumpled black linen sport coat with a white T-shirt, his graying hair pulled back in a short pony-tail. He gestured across the crowded, elegant Beacon Hill drawing room toward a watercolor painting of an Irish stone cottage. "Keira Sullivan is more Tasha Tudor and Beatrix Potter than Picasso, wouldn't you agree, Simon?"

Probably, but Simon didn't care. The artist in question was supposed to have made her appearance by now. Adler had griped about that, too, but her tardiness hadn't seemed to stop people from bidding on the two paintings she'd donated to tonight's auction. The second was of a fairy or elf or some damn thing in a magical glen. Proceeds would go to support a scholarly conference on Irish and Irish-American folklore to be held next spring in Boston and Cork, Ireland.

In addition to being a popular illustrator, Keira Sullivan was also a folklorist.

Simon hadn't taken a close look at either of her donated paintings. A week ago, he'd been in Armenia searching for survivors of a moderate but damaging earthquake. Over a hundred people had died. Men, women, children.

Mostly children.

But now he was in a suit—an expensive one—and drinking champagne in the first-floor chandeliered drawing room of an elegant early nineteenth-century brick house overlooking Boston Common. He figured he deserved to be mistaken for an art snob.

"Beatrix Potter's the artist who drew Peter Rabbit, right?"

"Yes, of course."

Simon swallowed more of his champagne. It wasn't bad, but he wasn't a snob about champagne, either. He liked what he liked and didn't worry about the rest. He didn't mind if other people fussed over what they were drinking— he just minded if they were a pain in the ass about it. "When I was a kid, my mother decorated my room with cross-stitched scenes of Peter and his buddies."

"I beg your pardon?"

"Cross-stitch. You know—you count these threads and—" Simon stopped, deliberately, and shrugged. He knew he didn't look like the kind of guy who'd had Beatrix Potter rabbits on his wall as a kid, but he was telling the truth. "Now that I'm thinking about it, I wonder what happened to my little rabbits."

Adler frowned, then chuckled. "That's very funny," he said, as if he couldn't believe Simon was serious. "Keira Sullivan is good at what she does, obviously, but I hate to see her work overshadow several quite interesting pieces here tonight. A shame, really."

Simon looked at Adler, who suddenly went red and bolted into the crowd, mumbling that he needed to say hello to someone.

A lot of his arguments ended that way, Simon thought as he finished off his champagne, got rid of his empty glass and grabbed a full one from another tray. The event was catered, and most of the guests were dressed up and having a good time. From what he'd heard, they included a wide range of people—academics, graduate students, artists, musicians, folklorists, benefactors, a couple of priests and a handful of politicians and rich art collectors.

And at least two cops, but Simon steered clear of them.

"Lloyd Adler's not that easy to scare off," Owen Garrison said, shaking his head as he joined Simon. Owen was lean and good-looking, but all the Garrisons were. Simon was built like a bull. No other way to say it.

"I'm on good behavior tonight." He grinned, cheekily putting out his pinkie finger as he sipped his fresh champagne. Owen just rolled his eyes. Simon decided he'd probably had enough to drink and set the glass on a side table. Too much bubbly and he'd start a fight. "I didn't say a word."

"You didn't have to," Owen said. "One look, and he scurried."

"No way. I'm charming. Everyone says so."

"Not everyone."

Probably true, but Simon did tend to get along with people. He was at the reception as a favor to Owen, whose family, not coincidentally, owned the house where it was taking place. The Garrisons were an old-money family who'd left Boston for Texas after the death of

Owen's sister, Dorothy, at fourteen. It was a hellish story. Just eleven himself at the time, Owen had watched her fall off a cliff and drown near the Garrison summer home in Maine. There was nothing he could have done to save her.

Simon suspected the trauma of that day was the central reason Owen had founded Fast Rescue, an international search-and-rescue organization. It was based in Austin and operated on mostly private funds to perform its central mission to put expert volunteer teams in place within twenty-four hours of a disaster—man-made or natural—anywhere in the world.

Simon had become a Fast Rescue volunteer eighteen months ago, a decision that was complicating his life more than it should have, and not, he thought, because the Armenian mission had fallen at a particularly awkward time for him.

Owen, a top search-and-rescue expert himself, was wearing an expensive suit, too, but he still looked somewhat out of place in the house his great-grandfather had bought a century ago. The decor was in shades of cream and sage green, apparently Dorothy Garrison's favorite colors. The first floor was reserved for meetings and functions, but the second and third floors comprised the offices for the foundation named in Dorothy's honor and dedicated to projects her family believed would have been of particular interest to her.

Owen glanced toward the door to the house's main entry. "Still no sign of Keira Sullivan. Her uncle's getting impatient."

Her uncle was Bob O'Reilly, her mother's older brother and one of the two cops there tonight Simon was avoiding. Owen's fiancée, Abigail Browning, was the other one. She and O'Reilly were both detectives with the Boston Police Department. O'Reilly was a beefy, freckle-faced redhead with a couple decades on the job. Abigail was in her early thirties, slim and dark-haired, a rising star in the Homicide Unit.

She was also the daughter of John March, the director of the Federal Bureau of Investigation and the reason Simon's association with Fast Rescue had become complicated. He used to work for March. Sort of still did.

He'd decided to avoid Abigail and O'Reilly because both of them would have a nose for liars.

"Any reason to worry about your missing artist?" he asked Owen.

"Not at this point. It's pouring rain, and the Red Sox are in town—rained out by now, I'm sure. I imagine traffic's a nightmare."

"Can you call her?"

"She doesn't own a cell phone. No phone upstairs in her apartment, either."

"Why not?"

"Just the way she is."

A flake, Simon thought. He'd learned, not that he was interested, that Keira was renting a one-bedroom apartment on the top floor of the Garrison house until she figured out whether she wanted to stay in Boston. He understood wanting to keep moving—he lived on a boat himself and not by accident.

"Abigail's bidding on one of Keira's pieces," Owen said.

"The fairies or the Irish cottage?"

"The cottage, I think."

They were imaginative, cheerful pieces. Keira had a flare for capturing and creating a mood—a part-real, part-imagined place where people wanted to be. Her work wasn't sentimental, but it wasn't edgy and self-involved, either. Simon didn't have much use for a painting of fairies or an Irish cottage in his life. No house to hang it in, for one thing.

Irish music kicked up, and he noticed an ensemble of young musicians in the far corner, obviously enjoying themselves on their mix of traditional instruments. He picked out a tin whistle, Irish harp, bodhran, mandolin, fiddle and guitar.

Not bad, Simon thought. But then, he liked Irish music.

"The girl on the harp is Fiona O'Reilly," Owen said. "Bob's oldest daughter."

Simon wasn't sure he wanted to know any more about Owen's friends in Boston, especially ones in, or related to, people in law enforcement. It was all too tricky. Too damn dangerous. But here he was, playing with fire.

Owen's gaze drifted back to his fiancée, who wore a simple black dress and was laughing and half dancing to the spirited music. Abigail caught his eye and waved, her smile broadening. They were working on setting a date for their wedding. Whenever it was, Simon planned to be out of the country.

"You can't tell her about me, Owen."

"I know." He broke his eye contact with Abigail and sighed at Simon. "She'll find out you're not just another Fast Rescue volunteer on her own. One way or the other, she'll figure out your relationship with her father—she'll figure out that I knew and didn't tell her. Then she'll hang us both by our thumbs."

"We'll deserve it, but you still can't tell her. My association with March is classified. We shouldn't even be talking about it now."

Owen gave a curt nod.

Simon felt a measure of sympathy for his friend. "I'm sorry I put you in this position."

"You didn't. It just happened."

"I should have lied."

"You did lie. You just didn't get away with it."

The song ended, and the band transitioned right into the "The Rising of the Moon," a song Simon knew well enough from his days in Dublin pubs to hum. But he didn't hum, because if he'd been mistaken for an art critic—or at least an art snob—already tonight, next he'd be mistaken for a music critic. Then he'd have to rethink his entire approach to his life, or at least start a brawl.

"In some ways," he said, "my lie was more true than the truth."

Owen grabbed a glass of champagne. "Only you could come up with a statement like that, Simon."

"There are facts, and there's truth. They're not always the same thing."

A whirl of movement by the entry drew Simon's attention, and he gave up on trying to explain himself.

A woman stood in the doorway, soaking wet, water dripping off the ends of her long, blond hair.

"The missing artist, I presume."

Even as he spoke, Simon saw that something was wrong. He heard Owen's breath catch and knew he saw it, too. The woman—she had to be Keira Sullivan—was unnaturally pale and unsteady on her feet, her eyes wide as she seemed to search the crowd for someone.

Simon surged forward, Owen right with him, and they reached her just as she rallied, straightening her spine and pushing a sopping lock of hair out of her face. She was dressed for the woods, but even as obviously shaken as she was, she had a pretty, fairy-princess look about her with her black-lashed blue eyes and flaxen hair that was half pinned up, half hanging almost to her elbows.

She was slim and fine-boned, and whatever had just happened, Simon knew it hadn't been good.

"There's a body," she said tightly. "A man. Dead."

That Simon hadn't expected.

Owen touched her wrist. "Where, Keira?"

"The Public Garden—he drowned, I think."

Simon was familiar enough with Boston

to know the Public Garden was just down Beacon Street. "Are the police there?" he asked.

She nodded. "I called 911. Two Boston University students found him—the body. We all got caught in the rain, but they were ahead of me and saw him before I did. He was in the pond. They pulled him out. They're just kids. They were so upset. But there was nothing anyone could do at that point." Despite her distress, she was composed, focused. Her eyes narrowed. "My uncle's here, isn't he?"

"Yes," Simon said, but he wasn't sure she heard him.

He noticed Detectives Browning and O'Reilly working their way to Keira from different parts of the room, their intense expressions indicating they'd already found out about the body through other means. They'd have pagers, cell phones.

The well-dressed crowd and the lively Irish music—the laughter and the tinkle of champagne glasses—were a contrast to stoic, drenched Keira Sullivan and her stark report of a dead man.

Abigail got there first. "Keira," she said

crisply but not without sympathy. "I just heard about what happened. Let's go into the foyer where it's quiet, okay?"

Keira didn't budge. "I didn't see anything or the patrol officers on the scene wouldn't have let me go." She wasn't combative, just firm, stubborn. "I'm not a witness, Abigail."

Abigail didn't argue, but she didn't have to because Keira suddenly whipped around, water flying out of her hair, and shot back into the foyer, out of sight of onlookers in the drawing room. Simon knew better than to butt in, but he figured she wanted to avoid her uncle, who was about two seconds from getting through the last knot of people.

Simon wished he still had his champagne. "I wonder who the dead guy is."

Owen stiffened. "Simon—"

"I'm just saying."

But Owen didn't have a chance to respond before Detective O'Reilly arrived, his hard-set jaw suggesting he wasn't pleased with the turn the evening had taken. "Where's Keira?"

"Talking to Abigail," Owen said quickly,

as if he didn't want to give Simon a chance to open his mouth.

O'Reilly gave the unoccupied doorway a searing look. "She's okay?"

"Remarkably so," Owen said. "She's not the one who actually found the body."

"She called it in." Obviously, that was plenty for O'Reilly not to like. He sucked in a breath. "How the hell does a grown man drown in the Public Garden pond? It's about two feet deep. It's not even a real pond."

Good question, but Simon didn't go near it. He wasn't on O'Reilly's radar, and he preferred to keep it that way.

The senior detective glanced back toward his daughter, Fiona, the harpist. She and her ensemble were taking a break. "I need to go with Abigail, see what this is all about," O'Reilly said, addressing Owen. "You'll make sure Fiona stays here until I know what's going on?"

"Sure."

"And Keira. Keep her here, too."

Owen looked surprised at the request. "Bob, she's old enough—"

"Yeah, whatever. Just don't let her go traipsing back down to the Public Garden and getting into the middle of things. She's like that. Always has been."

"There's no reason to think the drowning was anything but an accident, is there?"

"Not at this point," O'Reilly said without elaboration and stalked into the foyer.

Simon didn't mind being a fly on the wall for a change. "Does the uncle get along with his daughter and niece?"

"They get along fine," Owen said, "but Bob sometimes forgets that Keira is ten years older than Fiona. For that matter, he forgets Fiona's nineteen. They're a complicated family."

"All families are complicated, even the good ones." Simon moved closer to the foyer doorway just as Keira started up the stairs barefoot, wet socks and shoes in one hand. She was prettier than he'd expected. Drop-you-in-your-tracks pretty, really. He noticed her uncle scowling at her from the bottom of the stairs and grinned, turning back to Owen. "Maybe especially the good ones."

Ten seconds later, the two BPD detectives left.

The Irish ensemble started up again, playing a quieter tune.

Owen headed for Fiona O'Reilly, who cast a worried look in his direction. She had freckles, but otherwise didn't resemble her father as far as Simon could see. Her long hair had reddish tints but really was almost as blond as her cousin's, and she was a lot better looking than her father.

People in the crowd seemed unaware of the drama over by the door. Caterers brought out trays of hot hors d'oeuvres. Mini spinach quiches, some little flaky buttery things oozing cheese, stuffed mushrooms, skewered strips of marinated chicken. Simon wasn't hungry. He noticed Lloyd Adler pontificating to an older couple who looked as if they thought he was a pretentious ass, too.

Simon went in the opposite direction of Adler and made his way to the back wall where Keira's two donated watercolors were on display.

He decided to bid on the one with the cottage, just to give himself something to do.

It was a white stone cottage set against a background of wildflowers, green pastures and ocean that wasn't in any part of Ireland that he had ever visited. He supposed that was part of the point—to create a place of imagination and dreams. A beautiful, bucolic place. A place not entirely of this world.

At least not the world in which he lived and worked.

Simon settled on a number and put in his bid, one that virtually assured him of ending up with the painting. He could give it to Abigail and Owen as a wedding present. Even if he didn't plan to go to the wedding, he could give them a present.

He acknowledged an itch to head down to the Public Garden with the BPD detectives, but he let it go. He'd seen enough dead bodies, enough to last him for a long time. A lifetime, even. Except he knew there would be more. There always were.

Instead, he decided to find another glass of champagne, maybe grab a couple of the chicken skewers and wait for a dry, calmer Keira Sullivan to make her appearance.

⁓ Chapter 4

Beacon Hill
Boston, Massachusetts
8:45 p.m., EDT
June 17

Keira peeled off her hiking shorts and added them to the wet heap on the bathroom floor of her attic apartment. Her hands shook as she splashed herself with cold water and tried not to think about the dead man and the expressions of the two students as they'd frantically checked him for a pulse, uncertain of their actions, desperate to do the right thing even as they were repulsed by the idea of touching a corpse.

"The poor man," she said to her reflection. "I wonder who he is." She saw herself wince, and whispered, *"Was."*

She towel-dried her hair as best she could, expecting a twig or a dead mosquito to fall out, a souvenir from her earlier hike to her mother's. None did, and she combed out the tangles and pinned it up. She'd been looking forward to tonight's auction and reception, but her visit with her mother and then the awful scene in the Public Garden had sucked all the excitement out of her. She just wanted to get the evening over with and be on her way to Ireland.

But for Ireland, she wouldn't have even been in the Public Garden tonight. She'd dropped her car off with a friend in Back Bay to look after for the next six weeks and ran into the students dragging the man out of the pond on her way to the Garrison house. As she'd raced up Beacon Street after the police had arrived, she couldn't shake the notion that her mother's talk about sin and evil had put her in the Public Garden at exactly the wrong moment.

But that was unfair, Keira thought, and

as she returned to her bedroom, she found herself wishing she could call her mother and tell her what had happened.

Everything changes.

She dug through her small closet, pulling out a long, summery skirt and top. The apartment was no more permanent than anywhere else she'd lived, but she liked the space—the efficient, downsize appliances, the light, the view of the Common. It wasn't on the grand scale as the rest of the house, but it had charm and character and worked just fine for now. Compared to her mother's cabin, Keira thought, her apartment was a palace.

In five minutes, she had wriggled into her outfit, put on a bit of makeup and was rushing back down the stairs again. Two deep breaths, and she entered the drawing room. Her cousin Fiona's ensemble was playing a jaunty tune that didn't fit Keira's mood, but she tried to appreciate it nonetheless.

Owen immediately fell in alongside her, and she smiled at him. "I'm okay," she said before he could ask.

"Good."

He had a way about him that helped center people. Keira could imagine how reassuring his presence would be to a trapped earthquake victim. "Who was the man I saw you with earlier?" she asked. "Big guy. Another BPD type?"

She thought Owen checked a grin, but he wasn't always easy to read. "You must mean Simon Cahill. He's a volunteer with Fast Rescue."

"From Boston?"

"From wherever he happens to be at the moment." Owen smiled as he grabbed a glass of champagne from a caterer's tray and handed it to her. "A little like you in that regard. I don't know what happened to him. He was here two seconds ago."

Just as well he'd taken off, Keira thought. She'd spotted him at the height of her distress, and if Owen was a steadying presence, Simon Cahill, she thought, was the opposite. Even in those few seconds of contact, she'd felt probed and exposed, as if he'd assumed she had something to hide and was trying to see right through her.

She thanked Owen for the champagne

and eased into the crowd, realizing her hair was still damp from the downpour. For the most part, people she greeted seemed unaware of her earlier arrival, which spared her having to explain.

Colm Dermott, a wiry, energetic Irishman, approached her with his usual broad smile. She'd met him two years ago on a trip to Ireland, where he was a highly respected professor of anthropology at University College Cork. He'd arrived in Boston in April after cobbling together grants to put together the Boston-Cork conference and had immediately recruited Keira to help.

"The auction's going well." He seemed genuinely excited. "You must be eager to go off tomorrow."

"I'm packed and ready to go," she said.

"Ah, you'll have a grand time."

She'd given Colm a copy of the video recording she'd made of Patsy McCarthy telling her story, but hadn't told him about her mother and her long-ago trip to Ireland.

They chatted a bit more, but Keira

couldn't relax. Finally, Colm sighed at her. "Is something wrong, Keira?"

She took a too-big gulp of champagne. "It's been a strange day."

Before she could explain further, her emotional younger cousin burst through the crowd, her blue eyes shining with both excitement and revulsion. "Keira, are you okay?" Fiona asked. "Owen just told me about the man you found drowned. I wondered why Dad and Abigail left so fast."

Colm looked shocked. "I had no idea. Keira, what happened? No wonder you're distracted."

She quickly explained, both Colm and Fiona listening intently. "It wasn't a pleasant scene. I wish I could have arrived sooner, but it might not have made any difference. He could have had a heart attack or a stroke, and that's why he ended up in the water."

"Do you know who he was?" Colm asked.

Keira shook her head. "No idea."

"I hope he wasn't murdered," Fiona said abruptly.

"I hope not, too," Keira said, reminding

herself that her cousin was the daughter of an experienced homicide detective. "The police are there in full force, at least."

Owen returned and spoke to Fiona. "I just talked to your father. He's going to be a while and asked me to give you a ride back to your apartment—"

"I can take the subway."

"Not an option."

Fiona rolled her eyes. "My dad worries too much."

But she seemed to know better than to argue with Owen. She and some friends were subletting an apartment for the summer that her father considered a rathole, on a bad street, too far from the subway and too big a leap for a daughter just a year out of high school. Keira had stayed out of that particular discussion.

"I'll water your plants while you're in Ireland," Fiona said, giving a quick grin. "Maybe I'll talk Dad into buying me a ticket to Ireland for a week. You and I could visit pubs and listen to Irish music."

"That'd be fun," Keira said.

"It would be, wouldn't it? Right now I guess I should go pack up."

"I'm sorry I didn't get to hear more of your band."

"They were fantastic," Colm interjected.

Fiona beamed and headed across the room with Owen.

Colm turned back to Keira with a smile. "Fiona's more like her father than she thinks, isn't she?" But he didn't wait for an answer, his smile fading as he continued. "If there's anything I can do, you know how to reach me."

"I appreciate that. Thanks, Colm."

He rushed off to speak to someone else, and Keira found herself another glass of champagne. As she took a sip, feeling calmer, she noticed small, white-haired Patsy McCarthy in the foyer.

Keira immediately moved toward her. "Patsy—please, come in. I'm so glad you could make it."

"Thank you for inviting me." Within seconds of meeting almost a month ago, Patsy had dispensed with any formalities and insisted Keira call her by her first name. She nodded back toward

the door. "I thought it'd never stop raining."

"I know what you mean. It was quite a
downpour."

With a sudden move, Patsy clutched
Keira's hand. "I wanted to see you before you left for Ireland. You're going to
look for the stone angel, aren't you?"

"I'll be in the village that undoubtedly
inspired the story—"

"You'll be there on the summer solstice. Look for the angel then."

The summer solstice played a key role
in the story. "I'll do my best."

"The Good People want to find the
stone angel as much as you do. The
fairies, I mean. The angel's been missing
for so long, but they won't have forgotten it. If you're clever, you can let them
help you." Patsy dropped Keira's hand
and straightened her spine. "I'm not
saying I believe in fairies myself, of
course."

Keira didn't tackle the older woman's
ambivalence. "If they believe the angel's
one of their own turned to stone and
want it for themselves, why would they
help me?"

"That's why you must be clever. Don't let them know they're helping you."

"I'll try to be very clever, then."

"The brothers will be looking for the angel, in their own way. They and the fairies all want the tug-of-war over it to resume. It's meant to resume." Patsy tightened her grip on Keira's hand. "If you find the angel, you must leave it out in the open. In the summer sun. It'll get to where it belongs. Don't let it go to a museum."

"I promise, Patsy," Keira said, surprised by the older woman's intensity. "I'll look for the angel on the summer solstice, then, I'll be clever and if I find the angel, I'll leave it out in the sun—assuming that's up to me. The Irish might have other ideas."

Patsy seemed satisfied and, looking more relaxed, released Keira's hand and eyed a near-empty tray of chocolate-dipped strawberries.

Keira smiled. "Help yourself. Would you like to take a look around?"

"I would, indeed," Patsy said, lifting a fat strawberry onto a cocktail napkin. "I have every one of your books, you know. Do you think you'll illustrate my story one day?"

"I'd love to."

"That'd be something. It's a good story, isn't it?"

"It's a wonderful story."

Patsy smiled suddenly, her eyes lighting up. "Irish brothers, an angel and fairies. All the best stories have fairies, don't you think?"

"I love stories with fairies."

With Keira at her side, Patsy ate her strawberry and moved from artwork to artwork, as if she were in a museum, gasping when she came to Keira's two paintings. "Oh, Keira. My dear Keira. Your paintings are even more incredible in real life." She paused, clearly overcome by emotion. "This is the Ireland I remember."

Whether it was an accurate statement or one colored by time and sentiment, Keira appreciated Patsy's response. "It means a lot to me that you like my work."

When Patsy finished her tour of the drawing room, she took another chocolate-covered strawberry and started for the foyer. "Can I see you back home?" Keira asked.

Patsy shook her head. "My parish priest drove me. Father Palermo. Like the city in Sicily. He couldn't find a parking space, so he's driving around until I finish up. Did you know that my church is named after Saint Ita?"

Keira smiled. "The Irish saint in your story."

"It's strange how life works sometimes, isn't it?"

They walked outside together. A simple black sedan waited at the curb. A handsome, dark-haired man in a priest's black suit and white clerical collar got out and looked across the car's shiny roof. "Are you ready, Mrs. McCarthy, or shall I drive around the Common one more time? I don't want to rush you."

"I'm all set. This is the artist I told you about, Father. Keira Sullivan."

"Ah. Miss Sullivan. I've heard so much about you."

Keira couldn't read his tone, but Patsy added politely, "Keira, I'd like you to meet Father Michael Palermo."

He tilted his head back slightly, as if

appraising her. "Mrs. McCarthy tells me you're collecting stories from twentieth-century Irish immigrants."

"That's right. She's been very generous with her time."

Patsy waved a hand in dismissal. "I'm just an old woman with an ear for a good story."

Father Palermo kept his gaze on Keira. "Your mother grew up a couple doors down from Mrs. McCarthy."

"Two," Keira said without elaboration. "A pleasure to meet you, Father."

"Likewise."

He climbed back in behind the wheel, and Patsy got into the passenger seat and smiled at Keira. "Give my love to Ireland," she said with a wink.

After they left, Keira lingered on the sidewalk. The wind had picked up, but after the heat and humidity of recent days, she appreciated the drier conditions that came with the gusts. The puddles that had formed in dips in the sidewalk would be dry by morning.

"So you're off to Ireland in search of angels and fairies." Simon Cahill grinned at her as he leaned against the black iron railing to the steps of the Garrison house. "Do you believe in fairies?"

"That's not what's important in my work."

"Ah, I see. That's a dodge, but whatever. Keira, right?"

"That's right—and you're Simon. Owen's friend. I didn't realize you were still here."

"I have to pay for my painting."

"Your painting?"

"Your watercolor of the Irish cottage. I couldn't resist."

"You bid on my painting? Why?"

He shrugged. "Why not?"

Keira didn't answer. He was obviously a man who could charm his way into or out of anything. And he made her uncomfortable—no, not uncomfortable... self-conscious. Aware. Maybe it was because he was the first person she'd spotted when she'd arrived from the Public Garden. Some kind of weird imprinting that was inevitable, unavoidable.

Finally, she said, "You don't care about a painting of an Irish cottage."

"I care. I just didn't bid on it for myself.

Abigail wanted it, but she was going to lose out. I decided it'd be a nice wedding present for her and Owen. He'll like it because she likes it." The corners of Simon's mouth twitched with amusement. "Don't frown. He thinks you're good, too."

Not only, Keira thought, was Simon dangerously charming, but he was also observant. And frank. "Thank you for bidding on the painting. The proceeds from the auction will be put to good use. You're not from around here, are you?"

"Not really."

"Then where do you live?"

"Direct, aren't you? I have a boat. It's at a pier in East Boston at the moment, but it's only been there since yesterday. Before that, it was in Maine. I met Owen and some other Fast Rescue people at his place on Mount Desert Island after our mission to Armenia."

Keira had read about the devastating earthquake. "That must have been tough."

"It was." He didn't elaborate. "I was in London when it happened. I go back tomorrow."

"What's in London?"

"The queen. Castles. Good restaurants."

The man had an appealing sense of humor, and, in spite of the tension of the past few hours, Keira felt herself relaxing. "Very funny. I meant what's in London for you?"

"I'm visiting a friend. What about Ireland? What's there for you, besides angels and fairies?"

Answers, she thought, but she shrugged. "I guess I'll find out."

His eyes narrowed on her, and she noticed they were a vivid, rich shade of green. "Up for a bit of adventure, are you?"

"I suppose I am."

"Have a good trip, then."

He ambled off down Beacon Street. When she returned to the drawing room, Keira checked with Colm. "How much did my cottage painting go for?"

"Ten thousand."

She couldn't hide her surprise. "Dollars?"

"Yes, dollars, Keira. It was four times

the highest bid. Simon Cahill bought it. Do you know him?"

"No, I just met him tonight. What about you?"

"I talked with him for all of thirty seconds. Well, he must want to support the conference."

"He must. I'm grateful for his generosity."

"As am I," Colm said.

Keira said good-night and headed for the stairs up to her apartment, amazed at how Simon had managed to get under her skin in such a short time.

It had to be because of the intensity of the past few hours. What on earth did they have in common?

She'd be back to normal by morning, finishing up her packing and heading to the airport by evening. At least she wasn't going to Ireland by way of London; there was no risk they'd be sitting next to each other on the same flight.

It was a long way across the Atlantic.

~Chapter 5

Boston Public Garden
Boston, Massachusetts
10:00 p.m., EDT
June 17

Abigail Browning paced on the sidewalk along the edge of the man-made pond where the two college students had discovered the body of Victor Sarakis, a fifty-year-old resident of Cambridge who apparently, even according to the initial take of the medical examiner, had drowned in about two feet of water.

Normally, Abigail found the Public Garden a soothing, pleasant place to be, with its graceful Victorian walks and statues, its formal flower beds and labeled trees, its mini suspension bridge over the curving pond. Technically, it was a botanical garden—a refuge in the heart of the city of Boston.

Tonight, it was the scene of a bizarre, as yet unexplained death. Police lights and the garden's own Victorian-looking lamps illuminated the scene as detectives, patrol officers, crime scene technicians and reporters did their work. By tomorrow morning, there would be virtually no sign of what had gone on here tonight. The swan boats, a popular Public Garden attraction for over a century, could resume their graceful tour of the shallow water.

Abigail stopped pacing, grateful, at least, that she'd worn a pantsuit and flats to tonight's reception. Trees, flowers and grass were still dripping from the downpour. Most likely, it had been raining, and raining hard, when Victor Sarakis ended up in the water. The medical examiner had already removed the body for an autopsy. Anything was possible. Heart attack, stroke, an unfortunate slip in the heavy rain.

Pushed, tripped, hit on the back of the head.

Abigail wasn't ready to jump to any conclusions.

She glanced sideways at Bob O'Reilly, who'd decided, on his own, to interview the two students. Reinterview, Abigail thought, irritated. The responding officers had talked to the students. She'd talked to them. Now Bob was talking to them. For no good reason, either, except that he was a senior detective with decades of experience on her and presumably knew what he was doing. But she wished he'd go back up to Beacon Street and listen to his daughter play Irish music.

The students—summer engineering students from the Midwest—looked worn out. They could have gone back to their dorm a long time ago—they just didn't.

They'd told Bob the same story, about cutting through the Public Garden from a bookstore on Newbury Street, hoping to beat the storm and get to a friend's apartment on Cambridge Street. When the skies opened up on them, they debated going back to the bookstore or pushing on to their friend's place.

Then they'd spotted a body in the pond.

"You could tell he was dead by looking at him?" Bob gave them one of his trademark skeptical snorts. "How?"

"I don't know," the thinner of the two students said. He had a scraggly beard and was shivering as his wet clothes dried in the breeze. "It was obvious."

"He didn't look like he'd been in the water that long," his friend said. He was meatier, and he'd gotten just as wet, but he wasn't shivering.

"Long enough," Bob said.

The students didn't respond.

"You didn't see him before you noticed him in the pond?" Bob asked.

They shook their heads. They'd answered the same question before, maybe twice already. Abigail knew she'd asked it.

Bob gave them a thoughtful look. "How do you like BU?"

The skinny student didn't hide his surprise—and maybe a touch of annoyance—at the personal question as well as his friend did. "What?"

"My daughter goes there. Music major."

"We don't know any music majors," the meaty kid said quickly.

Abigail bit her tongue at the exchange, but Bob didn't mention Fiona by name and finally told the students to go on back to their dorms. This time, they didn't hesitate.

Bob turned to her. His red hair had frizzed up in the humidity and rain, and his freckles stood out on his pale skin. "You look like you want to smack me."

"It's a thought."

He obviously didn't care. She'd never met anyone with a thicker hide. She owned a triple-decker in Jamaica Plain, a Boston neighborhood, with him and a third detective, an arrangement that for the most part worked out well, but tonight, for the first time, she could see the potential for complications.

"Press is all over this one," Bob said, nodding to a camera crew. "Some rich guy from Cambridge tripping on his shoelaces and drowning in the Public Garden swan pond."

"We don't know he's rich, and, actually, it's called the lagoon."

"Lagoon? Lagoon reminds me of *Gilligan's Island*. Why don't they just call it a pond?"

"Maybe it's a Victorian thing." Abigail ran both her hands through her short, dark curls, noticing wet spots where water had dropped onto her head from leaves of the nearby shade trees. "And Mr. Sarakis was wearing loafers. No laces to trip over."

"Figure of speech."

Abigail said nothing.

"This is a straightforward death investigation, Abigail. Guy running in the rain slips or trips and goes flying, hits his head on the concrete, falls into the drink and drowns. A freak accident."

"A good detective doesn't let assumptions drive conclusions," she said, adding with just a touch of sarcasm, "I wonder who gave me that advice when I decided to become a detective?"

"Don't give me a hard time. I'm not in the mood."

She didn't blame him for wanting Victor Sarakis's death to be an accident, considering his niece was the one who'd called 911.

Abigail kept her mouth shut. Normally she would appreciate Bob's insight, his questions. He'd been in Boston law enforcement through some of its most difficult crime years. He wasn't bitter and burnt-out so much as cynical. He'd seen it all, he liked to say, and not much of it had been good. But she didn't want him around right now. It wasn't just because of Keira's involvement with the case, either.

"Never mind my bad mood," he said. "You've been prickly for days."

"So?"

He didn't answer, and she felt him studying her in the same way he had when they'd first met eight years ago. He hadn't believed she'd make a good police officer, much less a good homicide detective. She'd won him over slowly, despite what he considered a lot of baggage. Her father was the FBI director, a liability from Bob O'Reilly's perspective because it brought attention to her. By itself, it was enough for him to rule her out as police officer material. But that wasn't all. She'd quit law school after her husband was murdered four days into their Maine honeymoon, a case that had remained unresolved for seven years, until a break last summer.

Finally, she knew how Chris—her first love—had died, and who had killed him. For seven years, it was all she'd wanted in life. Answers. Justice. The lifting of the burden of not knowing what had happened that awful day.

But the break in the case had changed her life in a way she hadn't anticipated. During her hunt for her husband's killer last summer, she'd also opened herself up to falling in love again.

She could feel Bob's eyes on her and brought herself back to the present. "There's no evidence of foul play," he said.

Abigail chose her words carefully. "So far, no, there isn't."

"He had his wallet in his back pocket."

Indeed, the wallet had made identifying Victor Sarakis easy because it came complete with his driver's license, ATM card, credit cards, insurance cards, bookstore frequent-buyer card and seventy-seven dollars in cash. No loose change, unless it had fallen out of his pants into the water or grass. If it had, the crime scene guys would find it.

But Abigail knew Bob had raised the point about the wallet because it played into his desire for Sarakis's death to be an accident.

"What do you suppose he was doing out here in the rain?" she asked, knowing Bob wouldn't like the question but refusing to let him bulldoze her.

"Movie, play, Starbucks. It's Boston in June. He could have been doing a million different things."

"He's from Cambridge."

"A lot of people from Cambridge cross the river for a night on the town."

She knew that and wasn't sure why she'd brought it up, except that Victor Sarakis didn't strike her as a night-on-the-town sort. He wore expensive, if traditional, clothes—khakis, polo shirt and loafers. No socks. She hadn't found a receipt from a nearby restaurant or shop or ticket stubs in his pockets. Patrol officers were at his house in Cambridge attempting to notify next of kin, but, so far, no one was home.

"Keira arrived at the party late. I wonder—"

"Don't even go there." Bob's tone had sharpened. "You have no cause to push this thing."

Abigail wasn't intimidated. "A dead man. That's cause enough."

He tilted his head back slightly in that way she knew so well. It said that he knew she was deliberately pushing his buttons, that he wasn't saying anything now because he was going to give her a chance to dig a deeper hole for herself.

So she did. "I wonder if Victor Sarakis was on his way to the auction. Maybe he was going to bid on one of Keira's paintings."

Bob rocked back on his heels. He and Abigail had worked together a long time, and she knew her comment would set him off. He could be volatile, or he could be patient. The choice depended on what he wanted, what tactic he thought would work to his best advantage. He wasn't unemotional. He just had his emotions under tight wraps.

As far as Abigail could see, Bob had never known what to make of his niece. At almost thirty, Keira was a successful illustrator and folklorist, but with no roots, no sense of place. She'd been on the move since high school. Bob, on the other hand, had never lived anywhere but Boston.

"I doubt it was the only event on Beacon Hill tonight, but go ahead, Abigail," he said. "Check the guest list. Knock on every door within ten blocks of here. It's not like you have anything else to do, right?"

She had a full caseload. Every detective in the department did. But she shrugged. "I'm trying to remember how I heard about the auction. I don't remember getting an actual invitation. I think it was just an announcement." She sighed. She didn't know why she was antagonizing Bob. "Forget it. I'm getting ahead of myself."

He seemed to soften slightly, but that could be a tactic, too. "It's the time of year. Summer solstice is getting close.

It's worse than a full moon. Too damn much sun, I swear. Brings out the weirdos."

Abigail couldn't resist a smile. "Bob, nobody says weirdos anymore."

He grinned at her. "I do."

"What's with you and the summer solstice?"

"Nothing." He yawned—deliberately, Abigail thought—and did a couple of shoulder rolls, as if he needed to loosen up. "I should get back. When you see Owen, thank him for giving Fiona a ride home for me."

"Sure, Bob. I'm sorry Keira got here when she did. It's not an easy thing, coming upon a body."

"Fiona wants to spend a week in Ireland with Keira visiting pubs and playing music. Can you imagine the two of them?" He wrinkled up his face and blew out a breath. "Fiona keeps telling me I worry too much. Maybe I do. I don't even like her taking the subway alone, never mind getting on a plane to Ireland by herself."

"She takes the subway all the time.

She's a music student. She's got lessons, ensemble practice."

"Plays the freaking harp. You believe I have a daughter majoring in harp?" He rubbed the back of his neck as if he were in pain. "And I have a niece who paints pictures of fairies and wildflowers and collects loony stories people tell by the fire."

"They're both incredibly talented, and Keira's successful in a highly competitive business. Plus, they both get along with you, which is saying something."

Bob let his hand drop to his side. "Wait'll you have kids."

His words were like a gut punch, and Abigail looked away quickly, muttering a good-night and making a beeline for the crime scene guys, thinking of something she could ask them. Anything. Didn't matter what. She didn't want Bob to see her expression, to wonder what demons were haunting her now.

This was private, damn it. Personal. Up to her and her alone to figure out.

Kids.

She pictured herself with a big belly, Owen with a toddler on his shoulders—

the three of them in the Public Garden on a beautiful June day. But it was a fantasy. Reality was so much more complicated. She and Owen weren't even married yet, and babies would change her life, change his life.

Abigail turned her attention back to the pond. What *had* brought Victor Sarakis to Boston tonight? Never mind her mood or Bob's mood, it was a question that needed an answer.

She spotted a crime scene guy she recognized. What was his name? She couldn't remember. He was new. Really young. Grew up on a tough street in Roxbury.

"Malcolm," she whispered, then raised her voice, calling to him. "Malcolm—hang on a second."

"Yes, Detective?"

She glanced back at Bob, who pointed a finger at her and shook it—his way of telling her he knew what she was up to and would be watching.

Malcolm frowned at her. Abigail pointed to the sidewalk. "I just want to make sure we get photos of any cracks in the walks that could trip a guy running in the rain."

"Of course. No problem."

"Thanks."

Bob continued across the picturesque mini suspension bridge over the pond. With a sigh of relief, Abigail studied the spot where Victor Sarakis had come to the end of his life. There was no fence on this section of the pond. If he'd tripped—or whatever—on the opposite bank, the knee-high cable fence could have broken his fall, perhaps kept him from drowning. But the water was so shallow—he must have been unconscious, otherwise why didn't he just get up?

The autopsy would tell her more, but she had to agree with Bob and the medical examiner that Victor Sarakis's untimely death was likely an accident.

In the meantime, she had work to do, and a long night ahead of her.

She touched her cell phone, but decided—no. Owen already knew she had a case and would be back to her place late. He had an early start in the morning for a Fast Rescue meeting in Austin. He was always on the go—Austin, Boston, his place in Maine, disaster sites and training facilities all over the world.

Let him get to bed, Abigail thought, and not worry about her. She wouldn't want him to hear anything in her voice that would tell him she was gnawing on a worry, a problem. Because he'd ask her to explain, and she wasn't sure she could. Whatever was going on with her wasn't about him. It was about her.

And in those long years after Chris's death, she'd grown accustomed to working out her issues on her own.

She wondered if Victor Sarakis had left behind any children, but pushed the thought out of her mind as she joined Malcolm in looking for cracks in the walks.

~Chapter 6

Logan International Airport
Boston, Massachusetts
10:00 a.m., EDT
June 18

FBI Director John March greeted Simon with a curt handshake in an ultraprivate VIP lounge at Boston's Logan Airport. March had flown up from Washington, D.C., that morning specifically for this meeting. He had an entourage of hulking FBI special agents and staffers with him, but they stayed out in the hall.

He was in his midfifties and trim, and although his hair was iron-gray, its curls reminded Simon of March's daughter,

Abigail. But March wouldn't be seeing her today. He wouldn't risk it. Simon knew it wasn't just that March was protecting a classified mission. He didn't want to have to explain his complicated history with the Cahills to a daughter—a cop daughter, no less—who knew nothing about it. It didn't have to be a secret. It just was one.

"Some days, Simon," the FBI director said, "I wish you'd decided to become a plumber."

"If it's any consolation, some days I wish I had, too." Simon had been fourteen, crying over his father's casket at a proper Irish wake in the heart of Georgetown when he'd first met March. "At least when you're a plumber and you're knee-deep in crap, no one tries to convince you it's gravy."

"I've put you in a difficult position."

"I put myself there. You're just capitalizing on it. That's your job. I'm not holding it against you."

"My daughter will." March's tone didn't change from its unemotional, careful professionalism. "I've kept too many secrets from her as it is."

Simon thought he detected a note of regret in the older man's tone, but maybe not. Simon didn't have the details, but apparently John March had known more about the circumstances surrounding the murder of his daughter's first husband, an FBI special agent, than he'd let on. Nothing that would have led to his killer any sooner. But Abigail didn't necessarily see it that way.

"Comes with the territory," Simon said without much sympathy.

He hadn't asked for March's help all those years ago, when the then FBI special agent was wracked with grief and guilt after failing to stop the execution of Brendan Cahill, a DEA agent and friend, in Colombia. But there was nothing March could have done. The killers had videotaped themselves. The video showed them tying up Simon's father. Blindfolding him. Firing two bullets into his forehead. Simon had seen the tape. For years, he thought he'd stumbled onto it—that he'd been clever, outwitting the brilliant, powerful John March. He was over that illusion now. March had arranged for Simon to find the tape and see his father's murder.

Instead of feeling angry, bitter and betrayed, Simon had felt understood. March had known that once Brendan Cahill's young son had realized the tape existed, he'd find a way to see it.

What Simon hadn't realized, until recently, was that March had never mentioned him or his father to his daughter. Not once in twenty years.

He was a hard man to figure out.

March stayed on his feet. "I've told you as much as I know about what comes next."

Simon doubted that, but he shrugged. "Great. I'll be in London cooling my heels."

"We've got him, Simon. We've got Estabrook, thanks to you."

With a little luck, the "thanks to you" part would stay between Simon and March, but Simon had learned not to count on luck. "I'll feel better when he's in custody."

"Understood."

Simon could sense March's awkwardness. Ordinarily he would keep his focus on the big picture and not concern himself with what a mission meant for Simon personally. But this mission was different. Eighteen months ago, Simon had left the FBI and started a new life—volunteering for Fast Rescue, making a living helping businesses and individuals plan for disasters. It wasn't a bad life. He had a good reputation, a decent income and the kind of freedom he'd never had as a federal agent.

Enter Norman Estabrook.

To the public, Estabrook was a thrill-seeking billionaire hedge fund entrepreneur into extreme mountain climbing, high-risk ballooning, kayaking down remote, snake-infested rivers—whatever gave him an adrenaline rush. To a tight inner circle of trusted associates, he was also at the center of a network that dealt in illegal drugs and laundered cash for some very nasty people. Estabrook didn't need the money, obviously, and he sure as hell didn't care about advancing any particular cause. He liked the action. He liked thwarting authority.

In particular, Norman Estabrook liked thwarting John March.

Simon was in the perfect position to infiltrate Estabrook's network, and that was what he'd done. He'd known from the beginning if Norman Estabrook was arrested as a major-league criminal—which he would be—and Simon's role as an undercover federal agent remained a secret, his name would still be associated with Estabrook and his criminal network. Who'd hire him for anything, never mind trust him with their lives?

If he was exposed as an FBI agent, there went that career, too.

Either way, Estabrook would want him dead.

But Simon figured those were the breaks in his line of work. He stayed on his feet and noticed March did, too, the comforts of the lounge immaterial to either of them. They'd simply needed a private place to meet.

Simon grinned at the no-nonsense FBI director. "If this blows up in my face, I can always become a plumber."

"You could do worse," March said.

"Estabrook didn't make a fortune by being stupid."

"You've done your part, Simon. You provided what we needed to unravel this bastard's network. He's a bad actor, and so is the company he keeps." March gave a thin smile. "Excluding you, of course."

"Of course."

"There's nothing more you can do right now. Estabrook's at his ranch in Montana, and he thinks you're visiting a friend and recuperating from the Armenia mission."

Simon shrugged. "I tend to get into brawls when I'm at a loose end."

"You're not at a loose end. You're in wait mode."

"Same thing."

"If there's another disaster—"

"I wouldn't wish a disaster on anyone just to give me something to do. Owen's trying to get me to get involved with Fast Rescue training. Makes my eyes roll back in my head, thinking about training people to do what I already know how to do."

March looked down, and Simon could have sworn he saw him smile. "Just do what a disaster consultant and search-

and-rescue specialist would do between jobs, and you'll be fine."

"Will Davenport's putting me up in
London."

"Ah. Sir Davenport. Or is it Lord Davenport?"

"One or the other. Both. Hell, I don't
know."

March's eyes didn't change. Nor did
his mouth. Nothing, but Simon detected
a change nonetheless. Will Davenport
was a wealthy Brit who believed he
owed Simon his life. Maybe he did, but
Simon wasn't keeping score. Apparently
Will also had a history—a less favorable
one—with the FBI director. Simon didn't
know what it was and wasn't sure he
wanted to.

"I take it Davenport is unaware of your
reasons for going to London."

It was a statement, but Simon responded. "If he is, he's keeping it to
himself."

"That'd be a first," March said, making
a move for the door. "Simon, we've got
Estabrook, and we'll blow open his network and save lives. A lot of lives. You
know that, don't you?"

"I do, sir. I also know Abigail's eventually going to find out my history with you—"

"Not your problem."

It wasn't that March had acted as something of a surrogate father to Simon for the past twenty years that would get to Abigail. It was that she'd never known. At first, Simon was too caught up in his own anger and grief even to notice that March never took him to meet his family. He'd show up at Simon's ball games—a few times at the police station, after Simon got into fights—and stay in touch with the occasional phone call. When Simon headed off to the University of Massachusetts, March paid him a couple of visits each semester, taking him out for pizza, checking in with him about grades. March never suggested the FBI as a career. He wasn't director in those days, and when Simon decided to apply to the academy, he never discussed the idea with him.

March opened the door. "Stay in touch," he said.

"I will. By the way, do you know Keira Sullivan?"

"We've met. Very pretty—talented artist."

"She found a dead guy in the Public Garden last night."

"That was her?"

Simon didn't know why he'd brought her up. "She's heading to Ireland tonight to research some story about Irish brothers, fairies and a stone angel. I don't know. I could forget Will and go chase fairies in the Irish hills—" But he stopped, noticing a change in March's expression. "Something wrong?"

"I'm just preoccupied with this Estabrook thing." He seemed to manufacture a smile. "Keira Sullivan's a temptation you don't need right now, wouldn't you say?"

Simon didn't answer, and March left, shutting the door sharply behind him as he went out into the hall.

With a groan of pure frustration, Simon plopped down on a plush chair and lifted his feet onto a coffee table. He noticed a copy of the morning *Boston Globe* on the table. On the front page was a grainy black-and-white shot of the man who'd drowned in the Public Garden. Well off, middle-aged, no wife or children. The BPD Homicide Unit was investigating, but there was no indication of foul play.

Simon pictured Keira Sullivan bursting into the Beacon Hill house last night after she'd called 911. Pale, soaked, dressed like a lumberjack. Twenty minutes later, she'd floated back into the drawing room looking like a willowy Irish fairy princess herself. He admitted he was intrigued, but March had a point. Without even trying, Simon could think of about a thousand reasons why he shouldn't waste his time indulging in fantasies about Keira Sullivan. Artist, folklorist, flake. BPD detective's niece. Off to Ireland.

She was also friends with Owen Garrison, who was already keeping what he knew about Simon from Abigail and didn't need to worry about lying to Keira, too.

Simon dropped his feet back to the lounge floor.

Who was he kidding? He *was* indulging in fantasies about Keira Sullivan.

Just as well he had the trip to London. Best to find some water and a candy bar for his flight.

As he exited the lounge, he envisioned—as if it were right in front of him—the painting of the Irish cottage he'd bought at last night's auction. It was as if he was there, in Keira's world, and he imagined her with brush in hand, her pale blond hair pulled back, her blue eyes focused on where the next dab of paint would go.

Simon heaved a cathartic sigh. "Get a grip," he muttered.

The hall was empty of FBI agents. His flight would be boarding soon.

He went in search of a candy bar.

~Chapter 7

On her second night in Ireland, Keira indulged in a "toasted special"—a grilled ham, cheese, tomato and red onion sandwich—and a mug of coffee liberally laced with some Irish whiskey. She hadn't specified a brand. She'd told Eddie O'Shea, the owner of the only pub in the tiny Beara Peninsula village where she was to spend the next six weeks, that she wanted whiskey, whiskey from Ireland. Otherwise, she didn't care.

"Another coffee?" Eddie asked her. He

was a sandy-haired, slight man with a quick wit and a friendly nature that seemed tailor-made for his work.

"No, thank you." Keira heard the touch of Boston in her voice, a surprise to her given her wandering lifestyle. She picked up a triangle of her sandwich, melted cheese oozing from the toasted white bread, a bit of onion curling into a charred sliver of ham. Less than two days on the southwest coast of Ireland, and she was settling in fine and looking forward to her stay there. "If I had more coffee, I'd have more whiskey, and then I'd be in a fix."

Eddie eyed her with what she could only describe as skeptical amusement. "You're not driving."

"I plan to take a walk." She picked up her mug, the coffee still very hot, and let it warm her hands. "I love these long June days. Tomorrow's the summer solstice. You never know what mischief you might encounter this time of year."

"Off to dance with fairies and engage in a bit of magic, are you? Well, be careful, or you'll be mistaken for a fairy princess yourself."

"Do you believe in the Good People, then, Eddie?" she asked with a smile.

"I'm not a superstitious man."

She hadn't told him Patsy's story. Investigating a tale of Irish brothers, fairies and a stone angel, Keira had decided, required a clear-but-not-too-clear head. She wanted to be gutsy but not reckless, determined but not insane. She hoped the combination of whiskey and caffeine would do the trick.

Eddie moved off with a tray of drinks, delivering them to a knot of men gathered in a semicircle of spindly chairs in front of a small television. She'd learned they were local farmers and fishermen who'd known each other all their lives. They'd arrived at the pub one by one over the past hour to watch a hurling match and argue good-naturedly among themselves. If they'd been arguing about fairies, magic, ancient rituals and ancient stories told by the fire—that, Keira thought, would have compelled her to eavesdrop, perhaps even to join them. She didn't know much about hurling, except that it was fast, rough and immensely popular with Eddie O'Shea and his friends.

She'd had dinner at the pub last night, too. She'd hit it off with Eddie right away. Nonetheless, she was keenly aware that the locals were beginning to construct a story about her and her presence in their village. She supposed she'd helped by dropping an odd tidbit here and there—not fiction so much as not the whole truth. She'd never once lied to any of them.

They believed she'd come to Ireland in the typical Irish-American search for her roots and herself, and she supposed, in a way, she had.

She left a few euros on the wooden bar and took her coffee with her as she stepped outside into what was, truly, one of the finer evenings of this and her two previous visits to Ireland. A good beginning to her stay, she thought. She could feel her jet lag easing, the tension of her last hours in Boston finally losing its grip on her.

A man in a threadbare tweed jacket, wool pants, an Irish wool cap and mud-encrusted wellies sat at a picnic table next to the pub's entrance. He faced the street, smoking a cigarette. He looked up at Keira with eyes as clear and true a blue as she'd ever seen. His skin was weather-beaten, laced with deep wrinkles. He had short, straight gray hair. He could have been sixty or eighty—or a hundred-and-eighty, she thought. He had a timeless quality to him.

He said something in Irish that didn't include one of the fifty or so words she knew. Her mother spoke Irish—or used to. "I'm sorry—"

"Enjoy your walk, Keira Sullivan." He blew out a cloud of cigarette smoke and gave just the slightest of smiles. "I know you. Ah, yes. I know you well."

She was so stunned, she jumped back, stumbling and nearly spilling coffee down her front.

When she righted herself, coffee intact, the man was gone.

Where had he slipped off to so fast?

Keira peered up the quiet, narrow village street, lined with brightly colored stucco houses. The vivid blue, fuchsia, green, yellow and red could light up even the gloomiest Irish weather. Baskets of lavender and dark pink geraniums hung from lampposts. A few cars were parked along the sides of the road, but there was no traffic. Except for a single dog barking toward the water and the occasional hoots from the men in the pub, the street was quiet.

Keira debated going back into the pub to see if the man was there, or asking Eddie O'Shea if he'd seen him, but as much as she and Eddie had hit it off, she'd known him less than two days and didn't want to stir up any further gossip.

Maybe the mysterious man had over-indulged in Guinness and was staggering up a nearby lane, or he lived in one of the houses on the main street and simply had gone home.

Maybe he'd decided to have a little fun with the American tourist.

She couldn't read anything into what the man—a perfect stranger—had said.

Keira took his spot at the picnic table, and as she sipped her coffee, lukewarm now, she noticed there wasn't even a hint of cigarette smoke in the pleasant evening air.

After she left the pub, Keira shoved her hands into the pockets of a traditional Irish wool knit sweater she'd bought in Kenmare, a pretty village famous for its shops and restaurants. It was located farther up Kenmare Bay, which separated the Beara and the Iveragh peninsulas, two of the five fingers of land in southwest Ireland that jutted out into the stormy Atlantic Ocean.

She turned onto a bucolic lane that ran parallel to the village's protected harbor, gray and still now at low tide, and across the bay, the jagged silhouette of the MacGillicuddy Reeks of the Iveragh Peninsula were outlined against the muted sky. Off to her right, the rugged, barren mountains of the sparsely populated Beara Peninsula rose up sharply, with tufts of milky clouds, or fog, maybe, sinking into rocky crevices.

Keira could hear the distant bleating of the sheep that dotted the hills.

The ancient stone walls along the lane were overgrown with masses of pink roses and wildflowers—blue, purple and yellow thistles, pink foxglove, various drifts and spikes of white flowers.

And holly, Keira saw with a smile, lots

of it. By tradition, cutting down a holly tree was bad luck.

There were tall rhododendrons and the occasional pop of a bright fuchsia that had long ago escaped cultivation. The southwest Irish climate, warmed by the Gulf Stream, was mild year-round, hospitable to subtropical plants in spite of fierce gales.

Her rented cottage was just up ahead, a traditional structure of gray stone that, to her relief, was charming and perfect for her stay. Keira made a mental note to send a postcard to Colm Dermott thanking him for his help in finding it.

She hugged her sweater closer to her and pushed back any thoughts that might entice her to duck into her cottage and pour herself another whiskey and put on music, then tuck herself among her warm blankets and sketch pretty pictures of Irish scenery. It was tempting just to forget her mission.

After another thirty yards, she turned onto a dirt track that wound through the middle of a rock-strewn pasture, marked off with barbed wire and rising sharply. She'd walked up this way yesterday to get a feel for her surroundings. She was surprised at how well they corresponded to the details in Patsy's story.

Sheep grazed far up into the hills, part of the Slieve Miskish Mountains that ran down the lower spine of the peninsula to the Atlantic and the now-defunct copper mines, where Patsy's grandfather had worked.

The track leveled off briefly, and Keira heard a grunt nearby.

A cow. It's only a damn cow.

Then came a shriek of laughter, and a woman's voice. "Oh, no! Look—I stepped in it!"

A man chuckled. "Apparently cows don't care about prehistoric ruins."

The couple climbed over a barbed-wire fence onto the track. They were obviously American, the slight breeze catching the ends of their graying hair as they checked their scuffed walking shoes for cow manure. The woman smiled at Keira. "I suppose if one's going to traipse through a cow pasture, one should expect cow patties. Are you going out to the stone circle?"

"Not tonight," Keira said.

She'd checked out the stone circle yesterday after her arrival. It was one of over a hundred of the mysterious megalithic structures in County Cork, a particularly good example because it was relatively large and missing just one of its eleven stones. Getting to it required climbing over fences and navigating cows, rutted ground, rocks and manure.

The woman gave up on her shoe. "It's incredible—and to see it this time of year..." She beamed, obviously delighted with her adventure. "Such a thrill. We half hoped we'd run into fairies dancing."

Her companion sighed. "*You* hoped we'd see fairies."

She rolled her eyes with amusement and addressed Keira. "My husband has no sense of romance." She gestured broadly toward the harbor and village below. "We're staying in Kenmare. You're American, too?"

"I'm from Boston—I'm renting a cottage here," Keira said, leaving her explanation at that.

"Lovely. Well, enjoy your walk."

"Mind the cow flops if you go in the pasture," her husband said.

Keira wished the couple a good-night, and as they ambled down the gravel track, she felt more relaxed. It wasn't as remote out here as it seemed. She'd come prepared. She had food, water, a flashlight, a first-aid kit and a whistle for emergencies.

"You'll be in Ireland on the summer solstice. Look for the angel then."

The summer solstice wasn't until tomorrow, but Keira figured she'd have a good look around tonight, get the lay of the land. With a little luck, maybe Patsy's story would lead her straight to the hermit monk's hut.

Regardless, it was a beautiful evening, and Keira was enjoying herself on her first full day of what promised to be a perfect six weeks in Ireland.

~Chapter 8

Cambridge, Massachusetts
3:00 p.m., EDT
June 20

Abigail parked her unmarked BPD car on a quiet street off Memorial Drive lined with mature trees and stately homes. Very Cambridge. Victor Sarakis's house was a traditional Colonial with gray-painted shingles and black shutters. He was relatively wealthy, she'd discovered, and also something of an eccentric.

She turned the engine off and scowled at Bob O'Reilly next to her. He'd jumped into the passenger seat at BPD headquarters a half second before she could hit the locks and take off without him. He was getting on her nerves, but wasn't everyone? "Shouldn't you be pushing papers somewhere?"

He opened his door and glanced over at her. "What did you do, sit there stewing all this time and thinking up that one?"

"No, it just popped out."

"Good. I'll pretend it didn't."

Abigail didn't respond. She knew he objected to her coming out to Cambridge. He had good reason. The medical examiner had determined that Victor Sarakis had drowned. There was no indication of foul play, a contributing natural cause or the involvement of alcohol or drugs, illegal or otherwise. A full autopsy report, with the results of more tests, was in the works, but everything still pointed to a bizarre accident. From past death investigations, Abigail knew it was entirely possible they'd never figure out the exact sequence of events that had led to Sarakis's death.

Bob had already made clear he didn't

care what the exact sequence of events was. He wanted Abigail to focus on clear-cut homicide cases. She didn't report to him, but he'd been charged with improving BPD's percentage of solved versus unsolved homicide cases after a withering series of pieces in the media and figured that gave him license to get in anyone's and everyone's face, including hers.

Abigail had hoped to get to Cambridge and back without Bob ever knowing, but that hadn't worked out. A middle-aged man in apparent good health drowning in two feet of water was provocative—worth a bit of follow-up, at least in her judgment. Bob was free to disagree, provided he stayed out of her way.

She got out of the car, shutting her door with more force than was necessary. It was hot—too hot for June. Tomorrow it'd rain, and then she'd be griping about that. Given her mood, she had to admit that Owen had picked the perfect time for a quick trip to Fast Rescue's Austin headquarters.

She went around the front of the car to

the sidewalk. Tom Yarborough, her partner for the past six months, shared
Bob's opinion of the Sarakis drowning
but hadn't made a stink when she'd said
she wanted to head out here on her
own.

Bob motioned for her to go ahead of
him up Sarakis's front walk. "It's your investigation," he said.

Ignoring his sarcasm, Abigail took in
her surroundings. The brick walkway
was chipped. The front door needed a
fresh coat of its dark green paint. The
iron railing was loose on the steps. She
had no cause to look into Sarakis's fi-
nances yet, but she wondered if eccen-
tricity explained the run-down condition
of his place. Everything sagged or was
in need of scraping, paint, a good car-
penter. A termite inspection wouldn't
hurt, either.

She took note of the full attic, one-
story sunroom and attached two-car
garage. "What do you think, Bob—five,
six bedrooms?"

"At least, except they won't all be bedrooms. No wife, no kids. Retired at fifty.
He'll have a library, a game room, a

dead-animal room—you know, to display stuffed birds and deer heads."

"Think he was a hunter?"

"Didn't have to be."

From her years working with Bob, Abigail knew he wasn't being literal. He was sizing up Victor Sarakis as a moderately wealthy, eccentric loner who probably had serious amateur interests—ones that probably didn't include gardening, she thought as she noted the dandelions, crabgrass and bare spots that dominated the small front lawn. His was definitely the ugly duckling house on the street.

She rang the doorbell, the faint sound of a ding inside the house telling her it worked.

"Tomorrow's the summer solstice," Bob said next to her, as if that explained an unusual death in the Boston Public Garden.

Abigail glanced back at him. "Don't start that again. The summer solstice is a happy time. Lots of sun, flowers, bonfires, dancing."

"Too much daylight, people go nuts.

They can't take it. Brings out the worst in them."

She had no idea if he was serious.

"I know what's eating me," he said simply. "The summer solstice, and my crazy niece chasing fairies in Ireland. You, though. What's going on with you?"

"What's going on is that I'm trying to do my job, and you're here interfering."

"That's not what's going on. You're used to me interfering. You know you don't have to be here. You're letting a straightforward death investigation consume you."

"What was Sarakis doing that close to the water? It must have been raining when he ended up in the lagoon." She knew she'd said lagoon instead of pond just to get on Bob's nerves. He deserved it. "You'd think he'd have stuck to the walks and gotten to shelter as fast as possible."

"Maybe he was feeding the pigeons."

Just as she reached for the bell again, the door opened. A trim man with close-cropped graying hair stood on the threshold, looking tired, grim. He wore neatly pressed slacks and a loose-fitting silky sweater. From his expression, Abigail guessed he already knew who they were, but she showed him her badge and introduced herself and Bob.

"I'm Jay Augustine, Victor's brother-in-law." He stood back, opening the door wider. "Please, come in."

"I'm sorry for your loss, Mr. Augustine," Abigail said.

"Thank you." He waited for her and Bob to enter the foyer, then shut the door. "Why don't we talk in the sunroom—"

"That'd be fine," Abigail said.

He led them down a center hall. From what she could see, the interior of the house was immaculate and tastefully decorated, a decided contrast to the ratty exterior. They went through an elegant dining room into a small, adjoining room with windows on three sides and French doors that opened onto a brick terrace. Abigail noticed Bob was paying attention, taking in every detail—habit from years on the job, she thought, if not any real interest in her case.

Jay Augustine stood in the middle of

the sunroom as if he didn't know what else to do with himself. "Victor spent a great deal of time in here. It's the only casual room in the house. He—" Augustine's voice cracked, and he paused, clearing his throat. "Every room in the house is crammed with his various collections. Except this one. Funnily enough, he spent most of his time in here."

"What did he collect?" Abigail asked.

"My brother-in-law had many interests and the time and money to indulge them. He went all over the world. My wife and I are dealers in fine art and antiques, but Victor bought most of the pieces you see here on his travels. He lived a full life, Detective Browning. That's at least some consolation."

Abigail didn't respond.

"Well." Augustine took in a breath. "You're homicide detectives, aren't you?"

She nodded. "It's routine to conduct an investigation when—"

"When a man trips and falls in the Boston Public Garden?"

She noted the slightest edge to his

tone. "Where do you and your wife live, Mr. Augustine?"

"We have a home in Newton. Our showroom is in Boston, on Clarendon Street."

"When did you last see your brother-in-law?"

"I stopped by two weeks ago. Charlotte—that's my wife—was with me, but I can't speak for her. She may have seen Victor since then. They were close, but they didn't live in each other's pockets."

Bob walked over to the French doors and looked out at the terrace, as run-down as the front of the house. "Where's Mrs. Augustine now?" he asked.

"In Boston at our showroom," Jay said. "It's quiet there. Most of our business is done by appointment. She's having a difficult time. Victor was such a vital presence in our lives. I actually met Charlotte through him. We've only been married two years... I'd located an Italian Renaissance tapestry Victor had been looking for. He was different, as you can see for yourselves, but he was a good man."

"Where were you the night your brother-in-law died?" Abigail asked.

"In New York on business. Charlotte was at home." He swallowed visibly, then nodded to the terrace. "Victor had been talking about hiring a yard service and getting repairs done on the house. He'd had complaints from neighbors. He wasn't angry. He was aware that he was oblivious to things like peeling paint, chipped shutters and weeds. He just didn't care, provided the house was keeping out the elements and his collections were protected."

Bob started to pace, a sign he was getting impatient. Abigail moved back toward the dining room, noticed a knee-high wooden elephant, ornate silver, an array of Asian masks, a huge, colorfully painted bowl in the middle of the table. She'd never been one for a lot of antiques and collectibles around her.

"My wife and I are busy, Detective," Jay Augustine said behind her. "We had no warning—we're dealing with our shock as best we can. I could take the time to show you around, but I don't see what point it would serve."

At that point, neither did Abigail. Augustine ducked past her, and she and Bob followed him back out to the hall.

"What do you and your wife do now?" Bob asked.

Jay seemed surprised by the question. "Now? Oh, you mean with this house and Victor's collections. He left a will, thank heaven. Charlotte is meeting with the attorney tomorrow."

Bob bent over slightly and peered at a parade of statues of giraffes on a console. "Guess he collected giraffes, huh? Is your wife his sole next of kin?"

"Yes. Victor never married."

"Did he keep good records of what he owned?"

"Not particularly."

"He have anything a museum might want?"

Augustine inhaled through his nose, as if to rein in his impatience. "Potentially a considerable amount of what Victor collected would interest a museum—and Charlotte and me, too, if that's what you're going to ask next."

Bob didn't respond. Abigail knew he didn't care if he was getting on Augustine's nerves. "Did your brother-in-law spell out what he wanted done with his collections?"

"He left those decisions to my wife. To be quite frank, I'm saddened but not surprised that Victor died the way he did. He was very absentminded. He often lost track of where he was and what he was doing. You're wasting your time, Detective Browning. I'm sure the citizens of Boston have more urgent things for you to do than to investigate an accidental drowning."

"Again, I'm sorry for your loss," she said.

"No, you're not," he snapped, walking briskly up the hall.

As they came to the foyer, Abigail noticed that the pocket doors to a room on her right had popped open a few inches. Just inside was a bronze statue with horns, bulging eyes and a forked tongue.

It was a five-foot-tall statue of the devil.

"Mind if we take a peek in here?" she asked mildly.

Jay regarded her impassively. "As you wish, Detective."

Using two fingers, Bob slid open the pocket doors and gave a low whistle as he and Abigail entered the wood-paneled room. The devil statue was frightening, but it wasn't alone. The walls and the furnishings—large oak library-style tables, smaller side tables, open and glass-fronted bookcases—were jam-packed with items that all appeared to involve, in some way, the devil.

"Ol' Scratch lives," Bob said.

"Victor was a gifted amateur scholar and independent thinker," Jay Augustine said, not defensively.

Abigail noted a stack of books on a small table that all appeared to be about hell, damnation, devils or evil. "Where did he get this stuff?" she asked.

"Various places," Jay said. "Victor was obsessive once he sunk his teeth into something. About three years go he developed an interest in evil, hell and the devil. He considered it no more unusual than someone else's interest in goblins and trolls."

"I like flowers myself," Abigail said.

"Not everything in here is an original." Jay nodded toward a disturbing painting on the front wall of naked men suffering in a fiery hell. "That Bosch, for instance, is a copy. You know Bosch, don't you?"

"I don't," Bob said blandly.

"Hieronymus Bosch was a Dutch painter in the Middle Ages known for his vivid depictions of hell and damnation. He had a fervent belief in the fundamental evil of man. In his world—depicted brilliantly in his work—man was redeemable only by faith in God."

"Doesn't look as if anyone got redeemed in this painting," Abigail said.

"It's called *Hell*. Appropriate, don't you think? It's one in a series of four paintings Bosch did in the late fifteenth century. The others are *Ascent of the Blessed, Terrestrial Paradise* and *The Fall of the Damned*."

"Sounds as if you know something about this collection yourself," Abigail said.

Augustine shrugged. "Charlotte and I saw the originals on a trip to Italy last summer. We helped Victor find a painter to do this copy."

This obviously struck a nerve with Bob. "What for?"

"He wanted it."

Bob moved closer to the painting. "Kind of looks like Mordor in the *Lord of the Rings* movies, doesn't it? I haven't read the books. My daughters have—I got through *The Hobbit,* and that was it for me."

By habit and conviction, Abigail knew, he never used the names of any of his three daughters—Fiona, Madeleine and Jayne. At nineteen, Fiona was the eldest and more or less on her own, but Madeleine and Jayne were just fourteen and eleven. They lived with their mother in Lexington, close enough to visit their father regularly. They were good kids and got along with him, not always an easy task.

But Abigail didn't want to think about kids right now.

She wandered through the room. Sarakis's devil collection included paintings, drawings, illustrations, ceramics, books—and movies, she noted with surprise, from Vincent Price to *The Omen* and *Beetlejuice.*

"This shit gives me the willies," Bob blurted.

Abigail nodded to a locked door at the far end of the room. "What's in there?"

"That's Victor's climate-controlled room," Jay said with a slight, irritated sigh. "It maintains precise temperature and humidity conditions that certain items require for preservation. It's quite small and cramped, Detective."

A noise out in the hall drew their attention back toward the pocket doors.

A bushy-haired man—no more than twenty-five—stood in the doorway in a Harvard T-shirt and baggy shorts. "I thought that was a cop car out front."

Augustine seemed to welcome the intrusion. "Liam, it's good to see you. Detectives, this is Liam Butler, Victor's personal assistant."

"That sounds lofty," Liam said, his cheerfulness incongruous given all the images of hell and damnation around him. "I did scut work for Victor in exchange for a small salary and a suite upstairs. I'm a graduate student at Harvard. Political science— I don't know anything about art or collectibles. This was the perfect job. Flexible hours, decent pay, independence. It's been great." He gave a small moan, ran a hand through his hair. "I still can't believe he's gone."

"How did you come to know Mr. Sarakis?" Abigail asked.

"He and my father worked together— a brokerage firm in Boston. My father's at the Chicago office. He's still slogging away. Victor retired about six months ago." Liam seemed eager to talk. "He had me help sort through and catalog his collections. He's got things stashed all over the house. I swear we're going to find an Egyptian mummy stuffed under one of the beds."

"It's all a legal matter now that Victor's dead," Jay said stiffly.

Abigail looked for a reaction from Liam, but he didn't even seem to notice Jay had spoken. "How long did you work for Mr. Sarakis?" she asked.

"Eighteen months. I'm going to miss this job."

"What will you do now?"

He blew out a breath, shaking his head. "Stay here as long as I can, then find a new place. I can move in with some friends, maybe. Rents are expensive around here, but I saved some cash, thanks to Victor."

"Victor always spoke highly of Liam," Jay said.

Bob eased over to a black-wire sculpture of a particularly vile-looking devil. "Looks like a twisted great blue heron to me. So is Victor's sister into the devil and evil?"

Augustine tensed visibly. "I'm sure that Charlotte will be happy to answer any legitimate questions you have, Detective O'Reilly."

Bob shrugged. "Good."

Abigail noticed Liam backing out into the hall at the testy exchange. "Did you see Mr. Sarakis the day he died?" she asked.

"Just at breakfast. I spent most of the day helping a friend study for her orals—well, not study so much as deal with the pressure."

"What was Mr. Sarakis's state of mind that morning?"

"Preoccupied. That wasn't unusual, though. He was always chewing on some idea, some interest. He was a brilliant, inquisitive man, Detective." Liam choked up a moment. "A gentle soul—a true Renaissance man."

"He was also a little strange," Bob interjected.

"Yeah. So what?" There was no defensiveness or irritation in Liam's tone. He seemed to be asking a genuine question, trying to understand what Victor Sarakis's eccentricities could possibly have had to do with his death.

A fair point, Abigail thought. "What problem was he 'chewing' on?" she asked.

"I don't know. He didn't say, and I didn't ask. It wasn't a big deal. He'd often lose himself in his thoughts. Don't get me wrong. He was a great guy. But you can look around here and see why he retired at fifty, can't you?"

She could, indeed. "Do you know why he went to Boston the night he died?"

"Nope," Liam said without hesitation. "Look, I wish I could help, but I don't know what Victor was doing in Boston or why he drowned. I'm sorry it happened, that's all. If you have more questions, ask away. It'd be good to get all this over with. Otherwise, I'd just as soon go up to my room."

"Go ahead," Bob said. "We'll be in touch if we have further questions."

With a look of relief, Liam departed, disappearing up the stairs as Abigail joined Bob in the hall.

Jay stepped past them into the foyer and pulled open the creaky front door. "I appreciate your thoroughness, but if there's no reason to believe Victor's death wasn't simply an unfortunate accident—well, I think you know what I'm saying."

No fishing expedition, Abigail thought. No assuming Sarakis's unusual interests had a role in his death. A wealthy eccentric with a fascination with the devil drowning in two feet of water—reporters would love that one. The Augustines, who had a business to protect, would understandably want to avoid triggering a media sensation.

She and Bob walked back across the weedy yard to her car. The shade had kept the interior reasonably cool, and she rolled down a window, letting in the warm air.

"Okay," Bob said, "so the devil stuff's weird."

"Something's not right about this man's death, Bob."

"Maybe so. Brief Cambridge PD. Keep digging." He added sardonically, "Of course, that's not an order, since you don't report to me—"

"I appreciate the green light."

"Yellow light. Not green."

Abigail stuck the key in the ignition. Some days, there was no pleasing Bob O'Reilly.

~*Chapter 9*

Beara Peninsula, Southwest Ireland
8:00 p.m., IST
June 21, The Summer Solstice

Keira climbed over a barbed-wire fence—her third fence crossing of the evening—and dropped to the soft, thick grass on the other side, its ankle height suggesting that no cows or sheep fed out here. As far as she could tell, nearly every square inch of the virtually treeless hills around her was marked off for grazing. Sheep, being more nimble than cows, could navigate the rock outcroppings and steep terrain higher up in the mountains.

She hoisted her backpack onto one shoulder. Once again, she'd come prepared, even if it meant a heavy pack. Last night's hike had confirmed more details in Patsy's story and narrowed down the possibilities of where the hermit monk's hut might have been—or might yet still be. Tonight, Keira hoped either to find it or to settle on a spot that would work for the illustrations she had in mind.

With plenty of light left in the long June dusk, she'd be back in her cottage, tucked into her bed, before she needed to resort to her flashlight. The open landscape helped her feel less isolated, less as if she was a little out of her mind, heading off into the Irish hills in search of evidence that an old story told to her in a South Boston kitchen wasn't pure fiction.

She pictured Patsy McCarthy with her wisps of white hair, her bright eyes sparkling as she told the old story.

"The monk, who was a kind and generous man, lived a simple life of prayer in a stone hut he'd built with his own

hands by the spring in the rock-strewn hills above the harbor..."

Keira smiled as she took a moment to regain her bearings. She was still in open pasture, above a stream that had carved a dip in the general upward slope of the hills. She'd left the dirt track a while back. A sharp barb had cut through her pants into her thigh on that first fence-crossing, but she'd bit back a curse of pain, not wanting to alert the bull referred to in the Beware Of Bull sign tacked onto a post just before a small wooden bridge over the stream. The land was owned by Eddie O'Shea's brother Aidan, who had given her permission to go exploring. She'd passed a modern barn and his scatter of well-used farm equipment along the track, but they were out of sight now.

She made her way down the hill, the barren rocks and grass giving way to the trees and undergrowth that flourished along the banks of the stream, the ground wetter now, mushier, the air cooler. All she had to do was climb up the hill and she'd be back out in the open again.

Had her mother come out here on the summer solstice thirty years ago?

"Every year on the summer solstice, the mischief would begin anew."

The stream was one of the distinctive landmarks in the story. The stone circle, the harbor, the position and the shape of the hills—they had all helped pinpoint the village and confirm that the story, however much of it was myth, referred to a real place.

"The monk had no help from his brothers in building his little hut by the spring. He used his own hands, carrying stones up from the village. He didn't mind. He'd always preferred his own company. His solitary life suited him."

Keira crept along the bank of the stream, dodging tree branches, pushing her way through tangles of vines and holly, the lush vegetation creating shifting shadows and a very different mood than out in the pasture. She picked up her pace, wondering how long to give her search tonight.

But even as she formed the thought, she stopped abruptly, half in disbelief.

She was standing at the base of the

remains of what appeared to be an old hut built into the hillside, just as Patsy McCarthy had described, its gray stone visible here and there under a cloak of wild-growing ivy.

Containing her excitement, Keira skirted a large oak tree for a closer look at the ruin.

She could make out a front wall, the remnants of a chimney and a doorway—the door itself probably had been appropriated for another use decades ago. What must have been a thatched roof was gone, replaced now with a natural canopy of vines and debris. She couldn't estimate the structure's age with any accuracy, but she could always ask Eddie O'Shea to put her in touch with someone local who might know. Colm Dermott, a respected scholar, would certainly help.

Abandoned buildings weren't unusual in southwest Ireland, particularly hard hit by the famine years and subsequent mass emigration, but this one fired Keira's imagination. The monk in Patsy's story—or perhaps a monk upon whom he'd been based—could actually have lived here, in this tiny ruin on the hillside above the stream.

"Never mind that the monk was content in his isolation, his brothers thought he needed company—needed them, in fact. They had other ideas about his life."

Keira could hear the gurgling of the stream directly behind her and, in the distance, sheep bleating at irregular intervals, comforting sounds for their familiarity, their normalcy. Whoever had lived out here clearly had maintained a simple existence. It didn't have to be Patsy's monk. For all Keira knew, Patsy's father, or his father, could have wandered out here and decided to add the ruin to their story of the three brothers and make a good story better.

"It wasn't just his brothers with other ideas, either. Oh, no."

Patsy had hesitated at that point in her telling, her reluctance to admit she believed in fairies palpable.

"It was the monk who first discovered the angel, in the ashes by the fire on the evening of the spring equinox. At first, he thought his brothers had put it there. More of their mischief."

Keira heard a rustling sound nearby and sucked in a breath as she looked around her.

Just above her on the hillside, a large black dog paused in front of a hawthorn, drooling, snarling at her.

"Easy, poochie," she said in a low voice. She'd never been particularly good with dogs, and this was no friendly Irish sheepdog. "Easy, now."

The dog growled, his short black hair standing on end on his upper spine.

Keira put some firmness into her tone. "You just stop. There's no need to growl at me."

Panting now, the dog edged down the hill toward her.

She'd prepared for everything, she thought, except mean dogs.

Mud, fallen leaves, ivy, stone and a half-dead tree partially obstructed the door's opening, but she pushed aside a tangle of muck and greenery and slipped inside, hoping the dog wouldn't try to follow her. She reached into her backpack for her emergency whistle. If nothing else, it might scare off the dog should he go on the offensive.

She heard another growl, a sharp yip
and more rustling of brush.

Then, nothing.

Assuming the dog ran off, Keira eased
her backpack off her shoulder and set it
on the mud floor as she surveyed her
surroundings. The hut was very small,
with a tiny window opening high up on
the far end, above a mostly intact loft,
and another window opening over the
doorway—the only entrance, as far as
she could see. The main wooden support beam above her looked to be holding firm, but rafters had caved in on
each other, fallen leaves, branches and
ivy forming their own organic roof. On
the wall opposite the loft stood a largely
intact chimney constructed of more
gray stone.

*"The monk had never seen such a
thing in all his life as the stone angel.
She was so beautiful, he sat by the fire
and stared at her for hours."*

As Keira's eyes adjusted to the semidarkness inside the hut, she got out her
water bottle and plastic bag of snacks—
a couple of energy bars, nuts, an apple.
She tried to imagine the reclusive monk

in Patsy's story, going with the idea that he had existed and had lived here. What would he have look liked? What would his life on this hillside have entailed? It would have been rough, no doubt, dominated by the necessities of getting food and water, staying warm, maintaining even a modest level of hygiene.

In some ways, Keira thought, it would have been similar to her mother's lifestyle in the woods.

Patsy was a mesmerizing storyteller, taking Keira through every twist and turn as the brothers tried to figure out how the stone angel had come to them and what it meant. They all agreed the angel was a harbinger of good fortune. The monk brother believed Saint Ita herself had sent the angel to turn him and his brothers more deeply to lives of prayer, charity and simplicity as a means of bringing them good spiritual fortune. The farmer brother believed the angel would bring the good fortune of a bountiful harvest and productive cows and sheep.

The ne'er-do-well brother, of course, had another idea altogether and believed the angel was meant to help him and his brothers—the entire village, in fact—turn a profit so they could open their own pub.

All three brothers were convinced the angel had Saint Ita's gift of prophecy.

They were still arguing about their predictions three months later—on the night of the summer solstice—when fairies appeared and plucked the angel from the monk's hearth.

Keira smiled, remembering the glee with which Patsy had told that part of the story.

The monk took the theft as a test of his faith and mettle and resolved to get the angel back. For the next three months, he chased the fairies through the hills, until, on the night of the autumnal equinox, the stone angel appeared again on his hearth.

He kept its return a secret from his brothers. When the winter solstice came and went without a visit from the fairies, the monk thought he'd won the contest of wills, that he was right in his interpretation of the meaning of the angel and all would be well.

But his brothers eventually discovered his deception and accused him of lying and hypocrisy.

They continued arguing, but without animosity—arguing was a way of life for them. It was what they were used to, it was what they loved about each other. A good fight offered them a way to be together.

On the next summer solstice, the fairies again came for the angel.

Then on the autumn equinox, the angel reappeared on the hearth.

On it went, the monk arguing with his two brothers and chasing the fairies, the angel disappearing and reappearing on the equinox or the solstice.

In her elaborate telling of the story, Patsy had used just the right descriptive detail, the well-timed pause, the perfect tone to convey frustration, amusement, a sense of mischief. She'd teared up at the ending, when, one day, the angel simply disappeared from the hills for good. No one had it—not the fairies, not the brothers.

Staying close to the hut's doorway, Keira sipped her water and let the memory of Patsy's voice quiet her mind. She could smell the mud and the pungency of the vines and decaying leaves around her in the hut, feel the dampness, making it easy to imagine the monk's excitement at finding a beautiful stone angel on his hearth.

It would be there...by the fire...

"Keira."

She went still, her water bottle suspended in midair.

Was it the wind, or had she just heard someone whisper her name?

Then came a creak, a groan of what sounded like a tree being uprooted— and then the sharp scrape of rock against rock. Dirt and ivy loosened overhead, and decaying leaves and twigs fell onto the mud floor.

Keira lunged for the door, but didn't get far as several rafters collapsed onto each other, sending dirt and debris down in front of her. She heard stones tumbling on the chimney side of the ruin.

No time.

She had to take cover *now.*

She about-faced and dove under the

loft, scrambling into the far corner of the hut, dropping her water bottle and emergency rations into the mud as she covered her head with her arms.

After a few seconds, the rocks and debris stopped falling. Keira held her breath, not daring to move or utter a sound. She waited. A minute passed. Two minutes.

Nothing.

Hoping the worst was over, she lowered her arms from her head and, still not making a sound, peered through the dust to assess her situation.

Who was out there? Who had whispered her name?

She could make out the half-crumbled fireplace and...something. She squinted, blinked, squinted again.

A small stone statue stood in the rubble in front of the fireplace.

An angel.

On the hearth.

Suspicious that her imagination, fueled by adrenaline, had conjured up Patsy's mythical stone angel, Keira expected she'd blink once more and it'd disappear, turn out to be just more ordinary rock.

But it didn't disappear. She could see wings, a beautiful, delicately featured face and, in the angel's arms, a small Celtic harp.

The three brothers in Patsy's story all agreed they'd heard the angel playing a harp.

Saint Ita had lived in Ireland in the sixth century, but there was no way for Keira to tell if the angel was fourteen-hundred or a hundred years old—or if it'd been bought off a garden-store shelf that morning and popped in here as a summer solstice prank. Maybe she wasn't the only one in the area familiar with the story. At this point, she thought, anything was possible.

Just as she proceeded to get a closer look, she heard a loud snap and tucked herself into a tight ball as more of the ruin caved in. Even with her face pressed up against her knees, she could taste dirt and dust from the collapsing stones and mortar. If her side of the old hut gave way, she was doomed.

But she knew it wouldn't.

It just won't, she thought, surprised by her sense of certainty.

Keira remained in her tucked-in position until all she could hear were the gentle sounds of the stream and the breeze blowing through the trees just outside.

She didn't know how long she waited—at least an hour—but when she was as sure as she could be that the hut had collapsed as much as it was going to, she raised her head and coughed in the settling dust as she took in her situation.

A massive pile of stone and debris had fallen just beyond her free space under the loft, blocking her route to the door. She wouldn't be going out the way she'd come in, but that left few options. There was no rear exit, and the tiny windows were too far up for her to reach without a ladder.

Keira picked up her water bottle and her bag of snacks out of the mud, grimacing when she realized that her backpack was buried somewhere in the rubble.

Even with the long Irish June days, it would be fully dark in a few hours.

She didn't need more time to digest her situation. It was obvious to her.

She was trapped.

~Chapter 10

London, England
5:00 p.m., BST
June 22

Simon took his cell phone to a quieter corner of the bustling London hotel bar and asked Owen Garrison to repeat what he'd just said. Something about an artist who'd turned up missing in Ireland.

Keira Sullivan.

The flaxen-haired fairy princess with a penchant for trouble.

"You met her the other night in Boston," Owen said.

"I remember." Simon pictured her

floating into the drawing room in her long skirt. "She was off to Ireland to look into an old story. What's going on?"

"She was supposed to call her uncle this morning from the pub in the village where she's rented a cottage. When he didn't hear from her, he checked with the pub. The barman said he'd expected her to stop in last night, but she didn't, and no one's seen her today. She doesn't have a cell phone, and there's no phone at the cottage she rented."

Simon felt the muscles in the back of his neck tighten. "Why doesn't her uncle ask someone from the pub to go knock on her door?"

"He did. She wasn't there. Her rented car's in the driveway."

"She's an adult. She's in Ireland on her own. How do we know she didn't just jump on the bus and go to Dublin for a few days?"

"We don't. Bob's not panicking, but he's got this thing about the summer solstice. It's bad luck for his family or something. I know it's a lot to ask as a favor, but if you're at a loose end and could take a look, you'd have a cop in Boston in your debt."

"Always a good idea."

"I've e-mailed you a file on Keira. Link to her Web site, directions to her cottage."

Simon was more accustomed to diving into rescue missions following major disasters, not tracking down some flaky creative type who'd taken off into the Irish countryside. As attractive as this one was.

"All right. I'll see what I can do." He started to hang up, but added, "I haven't rescued a damsel in distress in a while."

"Bob said for me to tell you Keira's also a dead shot with a Glock."

"Is she now?" It was obviously a warning from the uncle for Simon to behave, but he was more amused than intimidated. "Even better. And she's pretty."

"Alas," Owen said, "that she is."

Simon also knew—as Owen and Bob O'Reilly would also know—that if something had gone wrong and Keira was in trouble, the sooner they got started looking for her, the better her odds of surviving.

After he disconnected, Simon returned to his stool at the bar next to his latest partner in debate, a London banker he'd just met, also friends with Will Davenport. The banker had ordered another martini and seemed ready to settle in for an evening of putting an upstart American in his place. He was Simon's age but dressed as if he'd just stepped from tea with Edward VIII. If not for the hotel's dress code, Simon would have been in jeans. Instead, he'd opted for black slacks and a charcoal pullover that barely passed muster.

"Sorry, mate," he told the banker. "Duty calls."

"The fake English accent is annoying, Simon."

"That's the idea."

Simon headed up the elevator to the elegant suite where he was supposed to be keeping a low profile while the FBI and other law enforcement entities went after Norman Estabrook and his pals.

Would John March consider taking off to Ireland to check on an artist late for a call to her cop uncle a way of keeping a low profile?

Probably not, Simon thought, turning on his laptop and opening up his e-mail.

"Whoa."

Having met Keira Sullivan, he'd expected pretty, but in the publicity shot on her Web site, she was smiling, with flowers—pink roses and something purple and frothy—in her shining flaxen hair. She had gorgeous, black-lashed blue eyes, and she wore a dark green velvet dress that gave her the look of an elf princess out of Tolkien—one with a very nice cleavage. He couldn't help but notice, although the flowers in her hair had momentarily distracted him.

"Now that can't be a good sign," he muttered, clicking the link to her bio.

She was born in South Boston and raised in southern New Hampshire, but she'd lived all over the place since—New York, Nashville, Sedona, San Diego. She supported herself, apparently, with her increasingly popular illustrations of classic poems and folktales, but she also had an academic background in folklore.

No mention of a husband or kids.

Simon dialed the number for Will's assistant, Josie Goodwin. Josie, who was particular about people, liked Simon because he'd saved Will's life. At least to hear Will tell it. That particular rescue hadn't been an easy one, Simon remembered. Just him, a rope and an ax. He'd pulled Will out of a bombed-out cave in Afghanistan. Will had never explained what he was doing there, and Simon had never asked. Nor had Simon explained his own presence.

He hadn't seen Will yet this trip. Supposedly, he was extending a stay in Scotland to go fishing. But he'd told friends he was in Scotland fishing when he was lying half-dead in the rubble of an Afghan cave.

That was two years ago, before Simon had met Owen Garrison or had even heard of Fast Rescue and its teams of highly trained volunteers.

"I need to get to southwest Ireland," he told Josie.

"When?"

"Now."

"Ah. You do love to present a chal-

lenge." A keyboard clicked in the background. "I can arrange for a flight into
Kerry tonight, but you'll have to hurry. I'll
need to have a car pick you up in ten
minutes."

"I'll be ready." He smiled into the
phone. "Thanks, Moneypenny."

"Fancy yourself a James Bond, do
you? More of a Hulk, I think, or perhaps
a Conan the Barbarian." She clicked
more keys. "But let me arrange for the
car, and you go pack."

"I owe you—"

"No," she said, serious now, "you
don't."

Ten minutes later, he was downstairs,
his car waiting. He'd be at Keira Sullivan's cottage in a few hours.

Then what?

He had no idea, but in his world, a fascination with Irish stories, fairies and
magic didn't bode well.

⁓ Chapter 11

Beara Peninsula, Southwest Ireland
7:00 p.m., IST
June 22

Keira bit into the last of her three energy bars. It was oatmeal raisin and not half-bad, although she'd begun to fantasize about warm rhubarb crumble at Eddie O'Shea's pub. She'd been trapped in her Irish ruin for almost twenty-four hours. She was uncomfortable, dirty and hungry, but as dank and unpleasant as it was in her intact corner under the loft, she was strangely unafraid. She was unhurt, reasonably dry and safe, and she still had food and water. She also had a solid plan for getting out. It was just taking longer to execute than she wanted it to.

Smoky light filtered through the cracks in the cloak of ivy and debris above the rubble beyond the low ceiling of the loft. The half moon had helped last night, but she had to hurry if she didn't want to spend another night in there. Her flashlight was in her buried backpack, along with the rest of her emergency supplies.

"No more breaks," she said aloud, pushing up the sleeves of her sweater as she stood up.

In ducking into the ruin to escape the dog, she must have dislodged a rock or tree root—or even just the ground—and started a chain reaction. Rafters, mud, mortar and stone had fallen between her and the fireplace, blocking any hope of getting out through the door. She didn't dare fool with that mess. She wasn't an engineer—she couldn't take the chance of collapsing the rest of the ruin around her.

That meant that her only practical route of escape was up.

The distance between her and the loft

was too great for her just to step on a rock or jump up. She'd had to build a ladder. In principle, it sounded simple. In practice—it was anything but. Safety and stability were serious concerns, and the task of finding good "steps" for her makeshift ladder and setting them in place took time, energy, muscle and a certain tolerance for bruises, scrapes and wrecked knuckles and fingernails. As impatient as Keira was to get out, she forced herself not to rush and risk injury.

The bottom "rung" was a large, relatively flat rock. No problem there. Two smaller rocks that she'd exhumed from the rubble provided the next steps up. Again, no problem. Then came a hunk of wood—part of an old rafter, she assumed. It was an iffier prospect than the rocks, but she thought it would work reasonably well.

But she still lacked a few feet, and she was eyeing a sapling out toward the main area of freshly fallen rubble, wondering if she could figure out a way to make it work to bridge the gap between her top step and the edge of the loft.

She noticed a fat, black slug oozing along the mud floor and grimaced. She'd seen her first slug at daylight, and her first spider about an hour later. Now that she knew she had company, she couldn't bear the thought of being trapped in her cell-like free space for another night. She had about six square feet to work in. There were no bathroom facilities, but she could make do. It was the slugs, spiders and darkness that got to her. She wanted out.

Her ladder would work. She knew it would. The plan was to be free by nightfall and off to the pub before anyone missed her. She'd need to call her uncle as soon as possible, but it was a workday for him—surely he was too busy to have noticed his grown niece in Ireland hadn't called that morning, as promised.

Bypassing the slug, Keira reached for the sapling. Her emergency whistle was somewhere in the mud and muck, but she wasn't sure she'd have bothered with it, anyway. She much preferred to get out of here on her own and go about her business. Let everyone think she'd gone off gallery hopping in Kenmare and be none the wiser. She'd left a note in her cottage detailing her route in case of mishap, but obviously no one had become sufficiently concerned about her absence to check on her. She'd have heard a search party out on the hills.

Just as well no one was coming to her rescue, she thought, pulling on the sapling carefully, dislodging it an inch at a time. At the first sign of falling rock and debris, she'd duck back into her corner.

She couldn't see the stone angel from her position under the loft—let alone reach it—but once she was free, she'd investigate from outside the ruin. Had the cave-in crushed the angel?

Or had the fairies come for it?

Keira smiled at the thought. Another hour—two hours at most—and she'd be free.

~Chapter 12

Beara Peninsula, Southwest Ireland
8:00 p.m., IST
June 22

Turn onto lane just past pub.

Look for pink roses and a small traditional stone cottage on right.

Owen's directions to Keira Sullivan's rented cottage were minimal, but as he drove into her tiny village on Kenmare Bay, Simon had no reason to believe they were inadequate. Josie Goodwin had arranged a sporty car for him at the Kerry County airport, but he'd paid for it himself. He'd only go so far in accommodating her boss's need to repay Simon for saving his life. Simon wasn't nearly as wealthy as Will Davenport, but he wasn't a pauper, either.

This was a personal favor to Owen, not Fast Rescue business.

Simon had spent a fair amount of time in Ireland, for both business and pleasure, and enjoyed the narrow, twisting roads out to the Beara Peninsula. He recalled someone telling him that birds from North America would occasionally cross the Atlantic by mistake and end up crash-landing on Dursey Island at the tip of the Beara. Having himself occasionally ended up in foreign lands he hadn't realized he'd set out for, Simon could well imagine the lost birds suddenly finding themselves in an Irish sheep pasture instead of on a Brooklyn street.

With only one pub in the village where Keira had set up housekeeping, the lane was easy to find.

Simon slowed as he came to a small, picture-perfect traditional stone cottage with masses of pink roses and wildflowers. It had to be Keira's rental. He pulled into a dirt driveway behind a parked

Micra—presumably her rental—and got out, pausing a moment to get a feel for the place. A fine mist had left water droplets on the grass and flowers. The air was cooler, windier down the peninsula.

The cottage was unlit. As he approached the front door, he saw no sign of anyone home. Just in case, he knocked loudly. "Keira? It's Simon Cahill."

He waited, but the silence continued.

The door was unlocked. Now here, he thought, was a problem.

But it wasn't much of a lock, and an intruder could have gotten inside easily. Still, an unlocked door was an invitation to trouble. He pushed open the door and flipped on a light switch along the inside wall.

An overhead light glowed on the vibrant yellow painted walls of a single main room that combined the living and kitchen areas. Probably helped on dark and dreary days, Simon thought, noting the comfortable furnishings—overstuffed sofa and chair covered in bright flowers, side tables stacked with books, a sturdy-looking pine table with two pine chairs. The table was spread with colored pencils, oil pastels, sharpeners, erasers, pads and sheets of sketch paper.

He opened a medium-size sketchbook, expecting pretty, whimsical scenes of bucolic Ireland. Instead, he found three dark, atmospheric sketches of what he supposed was, or at least was inspired by, the rugged local scenery.

As he started to shut the sketchbook, Simon noticed a tiny, cheerful red gnome sitting on a fence post in the top drawing. He had to smile. This was a touch of the quirky, fair-haired Keira he'd expected to find.

He checked the kitchen. The electric kettle was unplugged, cold and empty. There were no dirty dishes in the sink. No food left out. He opened up the small fridge—no clues there, either. She had a stash of butter, cheese, bread, milk, coffee, half a cucumber, carrots, two apples.

He looked for a note detailing her whereabouts, but found none.

Helping himself to one of the apples, Simon headed for the bedroom. More vibrant paint—fuchsia this time. A double bed, its flowered duvet neatly pulled up over the pillows. Inside the closet were a couple of blouses and one skirt on hangers, a well-worn brocade satchel suitcase, a pair of sport sandals on the floor and a robe—white, silky—on a hook. He supposed his missing illustrator could have another suitcase, a smaller one for quick side trips. But why leave behind her robe?

He pulled open the drawers of the tall pine chest. More clothes, sturdy stuff for hikes in the countryside.

"Well, Keira, where are you?"

Simon gazed out the window at the beautiful, remote landscape. She could have taken the bus to Dublin for a few days, or she could have headed out into the hills for a ramble and slid off a cliff into the Atlantic. Who the hell knew?

Stifling his annoyance at her poor planning, he flipped through a stack of receipts and brochures on top of the dresser. He didn't find any type of note or letter or even doodle indicating where she was—nothing that would help him locate her.

He headed back outside, grabbing his

rain jacket out of his car—one didn't travel to Ireland without rain gear—and ambled off down the lane in the moonlight. Keira had picked herself a spot right out of an Irish fairytale, that was for certain.

The village pub was lit up and lively with food, drink and conversation among a mix of tourists and locals.

Simon eased onto a barstool and ordered coffee. It was getting dark on the peninsula, and he needed to keep a clear head. "My name's Simon Cahill," he told the sandy-haired barman. "I'm trying to locate Keira Sullivan."

The barman—presumably the Eddie O'Shea who'd spoken to her uncle— tilted his head back and eyed Simon with open suspicion. "You've come all the way from America?"

"London." Simon didn't object to O'Shea's obvious protectiveness. "Keira's uncle asked me to look in on her through a mutual friend. You talked to the uncle earlier. Boston detective."

"His name?"

"Bob O'Reilly. To be honest, I don't know him well."

O'Shea seemed satisfied. "Keira sat right where you are two nights ago."

"Did she say she was going anywhere?"

"She said she was looking forward to the summer solstice."

Simon recalled overhearing the old woman in Boston mentioning the summer solstice. It had something to do with her story about the angel, the brothers, the fairies. He wished he'd done a more thorough job of eavesdropping on what all she and Keira had said to each other.

O'Shea filled a coffee press with fresh grounds and hot water and set it and a mug on the bar, then pulled a pitcher of cream from a small refrigerator and plopped it next to the coffee. "Keira likes to roam about the countryside."

Simon pushed down the press, then poured the coffee. It smelled kick-ass strong, and he added as much cream as he could without overflowing the mug. "Has she ruffled any local feathers?"

"Not that I would know. She's only been here a short time, but I can see she's one who goes her own way."

"She left her cottage unlocked."

"Now, why would you care about that? Think someone around here would rob her?"

"You never know."

Eddie O'Shea grew red in the face. "*I* know."

Simon was neither embarrassed nor offended by the barman's strong reaction. "Any idea where she is?"

"There's no telling."

"She give you any hints?"

Calmer now, O'Shea shook his head. "She likes to pull my leg about fairies and leprechauns. I told her I've no use for that nonsense."

"Would you say she's careful, takes normal precautions?"

"I suppose that depends on what you'd call normal, wouldn't it, Mr. Cahill? It's the wet and the cold and the rock I worry about. One slip." O'Shea snapped his fingers. "That'd do it."

It would, indeed, Simon thought.

"I have to say..." O'Shea grabbed Simon's coffee press and set it on the work counter behind him. "Never mind."

Simon waited a moment, but when the

barman didn't go on, he nudged. "What were you going to say, Mr. O'Shea?"

"I don't recall telling you my name."

Simon recognized that he was being tested and decided not to play games with the man. "You didn't. You told Keira's uncle in Boston."

O'Shea sighed, less confrontational. "Keira had something on her mind. She didn't tell me any details, and I didn't ask." He snatched up a white cloth and mopped the spotless, gleaming bar. "For all I know, she's off to kiss the Blarney Stone or some damn thing."

"If necessary, can you help me pull together a search team at first light?"

"I can."

Simon drank a bit more of his coffee and started to pay for it, but O'Shea waved off any money. "Thanks," Simon said quietly, sensing the man's worry. "I'll see what I can find out."

So far, it was proving to be a cheap trip to Ireland. He headed outside, debating his options. He assumed everyone else in the pub had eavesdropped on his conversation with O'Shea and would have volunteered information on Keira if they had any.

Simon noticed a man in simple farmer's clothes smoking a cigarette at a picnic table by the pub entrance. "Your girlie's stirring up things best left alone." His eyes were a piercing shade of blue, and his voice was steady, sober. "There are good spirits and evil spirits. Best to leave all of them be."

"Did Keira talk about these spirits?"

The man smiled a little. "You have the look of an Irishman."

That was all he had to say. He took one last drag on his cigarette, then got up and headed down the quiet street. Simon started to call after him, but before he could get a word out, the man had disappeared into the mist.

As Simon walked back along the quiet lane, fog swept down from the hills, adding to the moodiness and the sense of remoteness of the place. Obviously, his AWOL artist wasn't a fainthearted type, but he had to admit he understood the draw of being out here alone.

And it was the land of her ancestors

and his, which had its own appeal—as well as its own dangers. Easy to get caught up in the romance of a place and think one was safe, protected.

Lights in bungalows along the lane and down toward the harbor suggested life in the little village—families gathered in front of the television, getting cleaned up for the next day, settling in for the night. Simon had seldom known such normalcy himself.

When he returned to Keira's rented cottage, he flipped through another sketchbook, pausing at a hasty-looking pencil drawing of a winding stream amid thick trees and lush undergrowth.

A real place, or a product of her obviously vivid imagination?

Simon turned to the next page. The stream again—this time, curling under a small wooden bridge on a dirt track running through open, rocky pasture.

He tore off the page, folded it and shoved it into his jacket pocket.

If the stream, the dirt track, the fence and the bridge existed, then Keira had drawn enough detail for him to find them—and, with any luck, her.

~Chapter 13

Beacon Hill
Boston, Massachusetts
4:00 p.m., EDT
June 22

Abigail joined Bob O'Reilly on the front steps of the Garrison house while Fiona and her friends practiced in the drawing room. "They're on their millionth run-through of 'Boil the Breakfast Early,'" Bob said. "One more time, and my fillings are going to start falling out."

"I don't know Irish music that well, but I like that song," Abigail said.

"It's a happy tune, at least. The sad

ones make me want to drive straight to the shooting range."

"Ever take music lessons as a kid?"

"Fiddle. Hated it."

"Irish dancing?" she asked.

"I'm taking the Fifth on that one."

"I don't know, Bob, I can see you as this little redheaded kid step dancing—"

"I'm armed, Abigail."

She leaned against the stair railing, feeling the heat and humidity building back in after a couple of dry days. "Any word from Simon?"

Bob shook his head. "You think I'm overreacting."

"I didn't say that."

"Any other time of year—any other place—" He broke off. "Keira's never lived a simple life. A dead man in the Public Garden the other night, and now this."

"Did you check with the Irish police? Any accident reports, unidentified—"

"No. I haven't checked. I'm not going to. She's fine."

Abigail wasn't sure what to say. "I imagine you'll hear something from Simon soon. Owen says he's one of Fast

Rescue's best, and he's a disaster-preparedness consultant."

Bob grunted. "Keira's a damn disaster all by herself."

"You don't mean that, Bob. You're just worried."

Abigail tensed, noticing Charlotte Augustine walking up Beacon Street, clutching a book in one hand.

"What?" Bob asked.

"Never mind. Maybe you should go inside and see Fiona."

He followed her gaze to Charlotte. "Who's that?"

"Victor Sarakis's sister. Look, let me deal with her—"

"What's she doing here?"

"I don't know, Bob," Abigail said testily. "Will you just go inside and—"

"Nope. They're playing a dirge now. I'm in a bad enough mood." He nodded toward the street. "Go ahead. Pretend I'm not here."

She didn't argue with him, just descended the stairs and intercepted Charlotte. "Mrs. Augustine, what can I do for you?"

She was in her late forties, trim and

average-looking except for badly dyed red-brown hair. She wore a crisp, conservative navy skirt suit that Abigail figured had to be hot for late June. They'd met yesterday at her and her husband's house in Newton. It had been a short visit. Abigail still had nothing but gut instinct to indicate Victor Sarakis's death wasn't an accident. She'd left her card for Charlotte—which didn't include the address for the Garrison house.

"I don't mean to intrude, Detective Browning, but I thought I might find you here. I was at our showroom, trying to work. It's difficult..." Her voice faltered. "I can't get over what happened."

Bob descended two steps. "Did Detective Browning ask you to meet her here?"

"Oh, no. No, no." Charlotte's faced reddened. "I just remembered reading about her husband's murder last summer and that he was connected to the Dorothy Garrison Foundation."

"Her husband wasn't killed last summer. Abigail figured out who killed him last summer. He wasn't connected to the foundation, either. The man she's—"

"It doesn't matter," Abigail said, jumping in before Bob explained her whole life to this woman.

Charlotte thrust the book she was carrying at Abigail. "Here's the history of Satan I mentioned yesterday."

Abigail took it from her. "Thanks." It was a weighty, musty tome. She glanced at the title. Sure, enough. *A History of the Devil* was emblazoned on the cover in academic-looking type.

Bob leaned over her. "Not exactly light reading, is it?"

"It's a thorough but basic history," Charlotte said. "Victor—I can't explain why he was so fascinated by the subject. He's the one who gave me the book."

"Birthday present?" Bob asked, neutral.

"No. I think he just wanted me to understand his interest. He liked to remind me that the devil is a single entity. People tend to forget there's only one Satan. One devil. We think of him in multiples these days, though, don't we? He's become generic—a cliché."

"I suppose you're right," Abigail said.

"Mrs. Augustine, do you believe your brother's obsession with the devil played a role in his death?"

Charlotte seemed hardly to hear the question. "I don't know what to believe," she said. "You're a homicide detective. Do you consider most murders the devil's work?"

"I don't," Bob interjected.

"It doesn't matter what we think," Abigail said. "Is that what your brother believed?"

"He never said."

"When was the last time—"

"The last time we discussed the devil?" Charlotte gave a bitter laugh. "It's all we ever talked about. Tell me, if God is all-powerful, why not rid us of Satan? Why not just defeat the devil and free us all of his influence?"

"Or she," Bob said. "The devil could be a she, right?"

Charlotte didn't even crack a smile. "The devil is God's enemy, but he's our enemy, too. Mankind's enemy. He tempts, lures, cajoles, tricks. He takes many forms in order to do his evil. He's always on the search for new minions—fresh and able diabolical followers."

Bob rubbed the side of his mouth with one finger. "That's in the book, right?"

She didn't seem to hear him. "If God can't defeat Satan, how can we mere humans hope to?" She smiled suddenly, as if she'd just realized she was starting to sound like a nut. "I hope you find the book instructive, Detective Browning."

Abigail gave her a tight smile. "I'm sure I will."

"I don't really believe there's a connection between my brother's interest in evil and his death. I just—I don't know. I suppose I'm hoping the book will give you a better appreciation of Victor's interests the way it did me."

"I understand, Mrs. Augustine."

She seemed relieved, smiling again as she nodded toward the drawing room. "The music's wonderful. Irish, isn't it?"

Bob bristled visibly. "I don't know much about music."

"Of course," Charlotte mumbled. "Well, I should be going. Thank you for your time."

Abigail watched her for a moment before turning back to Bob. "I didn't tell her to come here."

"Good thing we were here. I wouldn't want her dropping off a devil book with Fiona. You know, Abigail, it's easier for someone with an anonymous life to be a detective."

She had to admit that lately her life had been anything but anonymous. With her father's high-profile job, it never had been, but people were used to it. They'd already factored in that she was the daughter of the current FBI director. But her husband's shocking death—and the discovery of his murderer last summer—had kept Abigail in the news. Falling for a Garrison and the founder of Fast Rescue had only added to the complications of her life.

Bob sighed at her book. "When the nuns started in on hell, damnation and the devil in catechism class, I'd sneak out to the drugstore and buy comics. You know, good guys, bad guys. Bad guys lose. Good guys win. Simple."

"Nothing about Victor Sarakis strikes me as simple."

"I've been at this job for a lot of years,

and I've never once run into a murder committed by the devil. They've all been committed by human beings. Our job is to figure out which human beings. Period, end of story."

Fiona O'Reilly, in skinny jeans and a baggy Irish rugby shirt, appeared in the doorway behind him. "Dad?"

He turned sharply. "Hey, kid. You guys finished?"

"We're taking a ten-minute break. Dad—who was that?"

"Just a woman who wanted to give Abigail a book."

But Abigail saw that Fiona was pale, even scared. "Fiona, do you know her?"

"No! I just—with your work and all...I was curious. Dad, you don't have to wait for me if there's something you need to do."

Abigail kept the front cover of the book out of Fiona's line of sight, but she hadn't checked the back cover. For all she knew, it was decorated in the flames of hell and red, fork-tongued devils.

One devil, she reminded herself. *The rest would be his minions.*

"There's nothing I need to do," Bob told his daughter. But he eyed her a moment, then said, "Fi, what's up?"

She peered past him at the street. "Did she know the man who drowned?"

"He was her brother," Abigail said.

Bob shot her a look, but Fiona gulped in a breath. "Did he have anything to do with the old woman and the priest who were here?"

"Fiona," her father said. "What old woman and priest?"

His daughter's eyes flickered on him, and color rose in her cheeks. "Nothing. Never mind. I forgot you and Abigail weren't here. You didn't see them—"

Abigail started up the steps. "Fiona, it's okay. You can tell us. If it's nothing, it's nothing. If it's something, we need to know."

"It's nothing—my mistake. Honestly."

She wasn't lying, Abigail decided, but she wasn't telling all she knew, either. Bob had to see it, too. But he said, "Come on, Fi, let's go inside. You and your friends can play a tune and I'll see if I can remember how to dance to it."

Abigail reined in her impatience. "Bob—"

He glared at her over her shoulder. "Go home, Abigail. Read about the devil." Then he gave her a strained grin. "No way am I dancing an Irish jig in front of you."

"If Fiona—"

"Leave my daughter to me."

Abigail sighed, nodding. She saw the worry etched in his face and decided not to push him. "All right. Let me know if you hear from Simon, and I'll do the same."

He didn't respond. As Fiona started back into the elegant house, she turned and glanced down the street, her face pale again, but she said nothing and neither did Abigail.

By the time she was unlocking her car door, she could hear Irish music again and almost peeked into the windows, just to see if Bob O'Reilly was dancing.

~Chapter 14

Beara Peninsula, Southwest Ireland
9:15 p.m., IST
June 22

Keira heard a rustling sound outside the ruin and went still, her upper body on the loft, her hands gripping rafters and ivy. Her feet were balanced precariously on the length of branch she'd propped at the top of her makeshift ladder.

The black dog? A stray sheep?

Whoever had whispered her name last night?

"Keira!"

She was so startled, she nearly lost her footing. This wasn't a creepy whis-

per—someone was obviously out looking for her.

Eddie O'Shea?

"Keira Sullivan—are you out here?"

Not Eddie. A man, though, but obviously an American, his voice steady,
confident—and familiar, somehow.

Her makeshift ladder teetered under
her. It was just a matter of time—
minutes, probably—before it gave way.
When it did, she wanted to be safe on
the loft, not hanging by her fingernails.

"It's Simon. Simon Cahill."

Keira lost her grip for a split second,
catching herself and hanging on as she
swore under her breath. Of all people.
She wasn't so far gone as to have conjured up a search-and-rescue expert,
but did it have to be this one?

"We met the other night in Boston."

Oh, indeed.

His presence meant that her uncle,
for whom she'd long been a mystery if
not a disappointment, had immediately
kicked into worry mode after she'd
missed her call to him. He must have
gotten in touch with Owen, who in turn

had gotten in touch with Simon in London.

But Keira tried to stick to the practicalities of her situation. Simon was a big guy. He knew how to pull people out of rubble. It would be dark soon. And it would be rude and ungrateful to let him wander past her when he'd taken the trouble—for whatever reason—to come out here to look for her.

Never mind any potential gloating on his part or stubborn pride on hers. She could use his help.

"I'm here!" she called. "By the stream—there's a stone ruin..."

"Got it. What's your situation?"

"There was a cave-in, and I got trapped in here. I'm not injured—I'm about to climb out through the loft."

"Have you had food and water?"

"Yes. I'm doing fine."

"Then let's get you out of there." He sounded controlled, capable—and very close now, somewhere on the back side of the hut. "Tell me where you are."

She explained her position. "There's just one door and it's blocked—"

"So I see. How the hell did that happen?"

"Beats me." She didn't want to get into Patsy's story, the black dog, the voice, the angel—the fairies.

She heard a creak and a thud, and in the next second, the ivy and muck a few feet above her gave way, creating a larger opening. Smoky light poured in.

Simon peered down at Keira. "How'd you get up there?" he asked.

"I built a ladder."

"Resourceful."

"I don't know if you can see, but I'm trying to scoot onto a loft. I'm not sure how stable it is."

"Then why don't I pull you out and we call it a night? I'd rather not have to come down there. The place looks as if it has rats."

"No rats. Just spiders and slugs."

"I don't mind spiders, but I'd rather deal with rats than slugs."

Keira guessed that he was deliberately trying to calm her nerves. She started to edge farther onto the loft, but she felt the branch lurch to one side under her. "I feel like Winnie the Pooh stuck in the entrance to the cave. He couldn't go forward, and he couldn't go backward. But if I can just—"

"Hold on, okay? I'm dropping a rope down to you. I want you to grab it and hang on, then tie it around your waist. Can you do that?"

"Happily."

"It's not perfect, but it's the best I can do, unless you want to wait for the local fire department—"

"I don't want to wait."

She could feel his smile more than see it. "I didn't think so."

Simon lowered the rope through the opening, and she caught it, her hands weak and scraped from the hours of hauling, pulling, lifting and digging. "There's a window—if I can reach it, I can crawl out that way."

"Not unless you really are a fairy princess and can change into a bird or a bat. It's too small, probably smaller than you realize from your position."

"I could climb up the rafters—"

"One thing at a time, Keira."

She hung on to the rope. She didn't know how she could tie it around her without further destabilizing the ladder and decided not to risk it. "How did you secure this rope? You're not just holding on to it, are you? I don't want you to hurt your back."

He laughed. "No worries."

This was his show, she thought. Between his succinct, efficient directions and her urgent desire to get out of there, she managed to creep farther up onto the loft.

The ladder started collapsing, and before Keira could react, Simon reached one arm down through the opening and hauled her up and out onto the back wall of the hut, grabbing her around the middle before her momentum took her straight over the edge. Although the hut was wedged into the hill, there was still a drop to the ground.

Simon was solid muscle, a big, broad-shouldered, bruiser of a man. She didn't have to do a thing except breathe.

"Okay?" he asked.

She balanced next to him on ivy and old stone and mortar. "Yes, thanks."

"Hang on one sec, and I'll help you get down from here."

Keira welcomed the feel of the breeze on her face, and she looked at Simon with his thick black hair, his green eyes—a clear, mesmerizing green, she thought. She'd noticed he was good-looking in Boston, but now, at dusk on a long June day, out on the southwest coast of Ireland, she was struck by how sexy he was. Being close to him was enough to make her throat catch.

He looked totally relaxed, as if he'd just wandered up from the village pub.

She quickly thrust the rope at him. "I can jump," she said.

He shook his head. "I don't advise it—"

But she was already springing off the wall, and if he could have stopped her, he didn't. She bent her knees and landed on her feet, letting herself drop onto her forearms into the tall grass at the base of an oak tree.

She leaped to her feet, brushing herself off as she grinned up at Simon. "It's good to be free."

"Lucky you didn't land on a rock."

"I suppose I am."

He hopped down next to her, without

having to drop down onto all fours to break his fall. "Where did you learn how to land like that?"

"Police academy."

He shook his head. "I'm not even going to ask."

"One of my false starts in life. Thank you," she added. "I appreciate the backup."

"Backup?" He seemed amused, but he gave her a quick, professional appraisal. "Should I check you over for injuries—"

"I'm not hurt." Keira imagined his big hands on her and felt a rush of heat, but attributed it to relief and adrenaline and changed the subject. "Did you have any trouble finding me? My directions were okay?"

"What directions?"

"In the note I left at my cottage. I assume you went there first."

"I didn't see a note."

"No? It was on the counter. Maybe the wind blew it onto the floor. How did you find me, then?"

"I used your drawings."

She digested the notion of him going

through her sketchbooks, but decided that, given the circumstances, she had no complaints.

"I found the rope and a flashlight in the kitchen," he said.

"You're good at pulling people out of messes, aren't you?"

"First time I've come to the rescue of an American in Ireland."

He wasn't making fun of her, she realized, dusting herself off and wondering just how awful she looked. Filthy hair and nails and scraped knuckles. She could imagine her face—dirty, smudged, probably pale—and she ached, as much from the tension of her ordeal as hauling rocks and crawling around in the ruin.

"What happened?" Simon asked quietly.

The ruin looked downright eerie in the gathering darkness, and Keira didn't know how she could accurately explain the past twenty-four hours to this feet-flat-on-the-floor man.

"I'm not sure, exactly," she said.

He eyed her, and she could sense his questions, his doubts about her judgment, but he picked up his rope, slung it over his shoulder and didn't press her to explain. "You've had a hell of a time." He nodded up the stream toward open pasture. "Let's get you back to your cottage."

"One quick thing first."

Without waiting for his response, Keira pushed through the tall grass down the slope, then carefully approached the front of the hut. As she'd suspected, the half-dead tree had fallen across the open doorway, either because of the cave-in or the cause of it.

Simon stood next to her and toed a sprawling branch of the tree, its sparse leaves withered. "This tree looks as if it could have given way at any time. Any wind last night?"

"Not really, no."

"You can see the ground's eroded under this corner of the ruin. When the tree fell, it probably triggered this entire section to give way. Lucky the whole thing didn't just come down on top of you."

"I was never afraid," Keira said. "At least not after the first hour."

"Adrenaline'll do that."

"It wasn't just adrenaline."

"Ah. Fairies?"

She was almost relieved at his cheer-ful jibe, because it meant he was no longer keeping an eye on her for signs of injury or mental distress. But she didn't respond as she leaned over the fallen tree and tried to peer into the hut.

"I want to check on something," she said, half to herself, then glanced back at Simon. "Can I borrow your flashlight? Mine's in there with my backpack."

He handed over a small flashlight. "Don't push your luck. I can't save you from a rock falling on your head."

"If a rock falls on my head, it'll be my own fault."

"Only I'll be the one explaining it to your cop uncle back in Boston."

A fair point, but Keira had no intention of going back to her cottage until she checked the fireplace for the angel. She grabbed a small branch of the tree and pulled it away from the door's opening. "I think I can see what I need to without actually having to crawl back in there."

"There's a reason I didn't try to rescue you this way."

"Yes, because I was inside and you

didn't want to make my situation worse. But I'm not inside anymore. As a matter of fact, I was about to get out on my own when you arrived." She smiled at him, hoping she came across at least reasonably sane. "I'm not going to quibble, but 'rescue' isn't the word I'd use."

"What word would you use?"

"I don't know. I'll have to think about it. Are you going to help me?"

He pointed to the hut. "What's in there, Keira?"

She didn't answer right away. She didn't know what to make of this man; even less, her reaction to him. But she'd slept only fitfully last night, and she hadn't had enough to eat or drink, especially given the amount of hard physical labor she'd performed. Her judgment could be off. She knew he was a volunteer with Fast Rescue, but that meant he could be anything. A firefighter, a paramedic, an engineer. He had an easy manner about him, but she wasn't fooled—he was intense, alert and obviously very good at search-and-rescue. He deserved at least an honest response, even if it was incomplete.

"I'm not sure," she said finally. "Let's just say that I saw something I want to have another look at."

She tried to pull back the branch far enough to allow her to shine the flashlight into the ruin, but realized she wasn't going to manage on her own. She'd need three hands, or at least more energy. "Could you help?"

He sighed. "All right." He eased in behind her. "But if I decide the structure's too unstable, that's it. We're done, and we head back to your cottage."

"Fair enough."

He took hold of a larger, thicker branch and lifted it, creating enough of an opening for Keira to squeeze between the branch and the trunk. She planted her middle on the rough bark and switched on the flashlight, directing its beam into the ruin. But it didn't reach the fireplace, and she had to lean farther in over the tree.

As she did so, she was aware that Simon had a perfect view of her butt.

"Why did you come out here alone?" he asked.

She wrestled her way another few

inches over the tree trunk. "Why did you?"

"I had to rescue a pretty damsel in distress."

There was no condemnation in his tone. Not a lot of amusement, either. He sounded as if he was simply stating what he regarded as a fact. But Keira didn't feel like a damsel in distress, and pretty? Not tonight.

"I had something I needed to do," she said. "I took sensible precautions in case I got lost or injured." She scooted forward another inch. Any farther, and she'd go right over the branch and headfirst into the ruin again. "I brought an emergency whistle with me."

"Did you use it?"

"No. It ended up..." But she didn't continue. She went still, her beam of light hitting what looked to be part of the fireplace. "Hold on."

Gingerly edging forward, Keira tried to direct the light toward the hearth where she'd seen the angel. She felt Simon's hand on her hip, steadying her, but pretended it was her imagination. She didn't need any distractions.

The smell of the mud inside the ruin, the taste of it, the thought of slugs and spiders, and the feel of the cool, rough stone against her free hand brought her back to the first moments of the collapse. But she didn't stay there, refused to.

She steadied the flashlight and moved forward another few inches, until just her upper thighs were on the tree trunk. Simon's grip on her tightened.

"Keira," he said, his tone itself a warning.

"One sec."

She squinted at the remains of the fireplace and hearth, picturing the hermit monk out here alone on just such a night, sitting in front of a peat fire, waiting for the fairies as he contemplated the mysteries of the stone angel.

Keira moved the flashlight up and down the fireplace. Maybe the upheaval of the stone and mud and mortar—of trees and ivy and dead leaves—had thrown her off and she had the wrong spot. She'd been inside when she'd spotted the angel, and she was coming at it now from a different angle. She'd only had a few minutes inside the ruin before it had started crashing down on her.

On her third sweep with the flashlight, she was convinced she had the right spot. There was no need to squirm all the way inside for a closer inspection.

It wouldn't change the simple fact that nothing was there.

The stone angel had vanished.

If, Keira thought, it had ever been there.

But it had, and as she withdrew, backing up over the tree trunk and under the branch, she pictured its simple, stunning beauty. She hadn't imagined the statue.

Simon kept his hand on her hip until she was clear of the tree and back up on her feet. He narrowed those amazing green eyes on her. But she saw him tense. "Stand still."

The sharpness of his tone made her heart jump. She followed his gaze to her middle and saw what was wrong.

She was covered in blood.

It was smeared from her breasts to her waist. She could feel it now, more sticky than wet, and she gasped in shock. "Si-mon—I don't—I can't...breathe..."

"Did you cut yourself?"

"I'm okay." She gripped his arm above his elbow, forcing herself to get her emotions under control. "I'm not hurt."

"Keira—"

"It's not my blood."

⁓Chapter 15

Beara Peninsula, Southwest Ireland
10:00 p.m., IST
June 22

Sheep's blood.

Keira tilted her head back and let the hot water of her cottage shower flow through her hair and down her back, her skin red from where she'd scrubbed the blood and mud off her. She'd used a citrus bath gel and shampoo. She breathed in the tangy scent and turned off the water, reaching for a towel as she stepped out of the shower.

She'd resisted the impulse to strip off her clothes after seeing the blood. Simon had remained crisply efficient, showing little reaction when he discovered entrails and bits of sheep's wool in the undergrowth on the chimney side of the hut. Keira had checked out the grisly scene herself and promptly vomited in the grass.

She wasn't embarrassed. Simon had more experience with such sights.

It was getting dark when they headed back to her cottage. She'd broken into a run and made a beeline for the bedroom, grabbing fresh clothes, then for the shower.

All she'd thought about was getting clean.

She wrapped her towel around her and took another for her hair, drying it as best she could and pulling it back into a loose ponytail. She got dressed, welcoming the feel of her clean, dry jeans and sweater.

When she returned to the kitchen, her good-looking rescuer glanced up from his inspection of the side door. "This door's locked. Front door isn't."

"I locked both doors, or at least I tried

to. They're not great locks. Maybe the front-door lock popped open."

"Where's your key?"

"In my backpack in the ruin. There's a spare—I'll get it." She pulled open a utility closet off the kitchen and grabbed a key from a hook above the washer. "There's no sign anyone broke in here. Maybe my note just blew under the refrigerator."

He shrugged. "We could check."

She gave him a cool look. "You don't believe I wrote a note, do you?"

"You've just been through a trauma, Keira. Telling yourself you wrote a note describing your location helped you get through it. There's nothing wrong with that."

"I wrote the note with my favorite drawing pencil. I sketched a little shamrock on the bottom for fun."

He was undeterred. "In your head, you did."

"I also locked both doors."

He stood back from the side door. "All right. First things first. You're done in. Why don't I cook you up something? Toast, eggs—"

"We can get to the pub before it closes. I want lights, people." She took a breath. "And warm rhubarb crumble. All last night, all day today...I kept thinking about warm rhubarb crumble."

"Then let's go see if Eddie O'Shea has some."

As they headed out to the lane, Simon asked if she wanted him to drive her to the pub, but she shook her head. She preferred walking. It was just after sunset on the long June day, the night not yet fully dark. And it was so quiet, she thought. There was barely any wind, and she could hear only the distant bleating of sheep far up in the hills, nothing from the sheep and cows in the pens close by the lane.

Keira wasn't fooled by his silence as he walked beside her. "I know you must have a lot of questions," she said.

"They can wait."

When they reached the pub, he settled at a table with three local men chatting among themselves. They seemed surprised, but when he called for a round of drinks, they warmed right up to him.

Keira eased onto a high stool at the

bar. Eddie O'Shea shook his head at her. "You got yourself into a fix, didn't you?"

"I did, indeed," she said. "Please tell me you have rhubarb crumble, Eddie."

"Fresh this afternoon."

"Perfect. And a shot of Irish whiskey. You pick the brand."

He splashed whiskey in a glass and set it in front of her. "Are you going to tell me what happened?"

"I had a mishap in an old ruin up in the hills above my cottage." She drank some of her whiskey. It burned all the way down, but she welcomed it, none-theless. "I'm sorry if I worried anyone."

"You're safe. That's what matters."

Behind her, Simon adopted a re-markably natural Irish accent and made an inflammatory comment about Irish weather. The men roared, and the good-natured fight was on. He could get away with anything, Keira decided. He was charming and convivial, a hale-and-hearty type who fit right in with the Irish-men. They all sat with their arms crossed on their chests, legs stretched out, comfortable with each other as they laughed and argued.

If it'd been a group of Wall Street investment bankers he had to drink with, Keira had the feeling Simon would have fit in with them, too. He wasn't a chameleon so much as a man at ease with himself.

Eddie placed a plate of steaming crumble on the bar and grinned at her. "Wouldn't have been near as good if one of us'd come to your rescue, now, would it?"

She felt herself blush and tried to blame the whiskey. "I appreciate Simon's help, but I was about to get out of there on my own when he turned up."

"Ha. So you say."

She dipped her spoon into melting vanilla ice cream mixed with the sweet-sour rhubarb crumble and felt her exhaustion, her hunger. Her head spun with images of the past twenty-four hours. She saw Eddie's gaze fix on her scraped knuckles, his frown as he returned to his work.

"Do you know anyone around here who owns a black dog?" she asked.

He had his back to her as he got beer glasses down from a shelf. "What kind of black dog?"

"I don't know. A dog...that's black."

"Short hair, long hair, big dog, little dog?"

"Maybe like a black lab, but not quite that big. A mutt."

He turned back to her and started filling the glasses with beer from a tap. "You're describing half the dogs I shoo out of here every morning and every night."

"What about creepy, scary, mean black dogs?"

"That would be my mother-in-law's dog." His eyes sparked with humor as he set a full glass on a tray. "Or maybe it's my mother-in-law herself."

One of the men at the table hooted at him. "You don't have a mother-in-law, you lying snake."

Eddie nodded to the man, also blue-eyed, sandy-haired and wiry. "That, my dear Keira, is my worthless brother Patrick."

She'd met Aidan O'Shea, the third O'Shea brother, briefly upon her arrival on the Beara Peninsula—he owned the cottage she'd rented as well as the pasture where she'd come upon the ruin. She wondered if any of them would know anything about a bloody, dead sheep. But she didn't ask. She didn't want to think about the sheep right now.

"Deep down, Eddie," she said, taking another bite of crumble, "you believe in fairies, don't you?"

Instead of answering, he moved off to the table with the tray of beers. But as he unloaded them, he gave Keira a sideways glower, which told her that he'd at least heard the question.

As she finished her rhubarb crumble and concentrated on her whiskey, Simon joined her at the bar, remaining on his feet. "I ran into a man outside on the picnic table earlier," he said, addressing Eddie. "Older guy in a wool vest and wellies—right off an Irish postcard. Smoking a cigarette. Did you see him?"

Eddie slipped back behind the bar and grabbed a cleaning cloth. "An old man, you say?"

"He was there one minute and off into the mist the next."

"Is that so, now?" Eddie mopped up a tiny spill. "I must have missed him."

Keira finished her whiskey, remembering her strange encounter two nights ago. It had to be the same man.

Simon stood back from the bar. "That's the way it's going to be, is it?"

Eddie shrugged. "That's the way."

Keira started to speak, but Simon had pulled out his wallet, obviously preparing to pay for the drinks and her crumble. Eddie put up a hand and shook his head. "On the house."

"Thank you," Keira mumbled, her head spinning now with fatigue, sugar and alcohol. As she eased off the stool, it occurred to her she didn't know where Simon planned to spend the night. "We can go. I'm sure you'll want to get back to Cork or Kenmare or wherever you're staying—"

"I'm not going anywhere tonight."

The men at the table all looked at the two Americans—expectant, eager for a sparring match, their eyes twinkling with amusement. Keira figured they'd side with Simon. She couldn't have picked a more appealing rescuer, nor could she blame him and his new Irish friends if they thought her flighty, eccentric and reckless for having ended up trapped in an Irish ruin for the past twenty-four hours.

"Let's go," Simon said quietly.

Eddie slung his cleaning cloth over his shoulder. "Stay safe, Keira," he said.

She nodded. "Thanks."

When she stepped outside, she shivered and tightened her sweater around her in a chilly wind kicking up off the Kenmare. "There's something about this place..." She smelled the lavender in the baskets hanging on the lampposts that lined the quiet street. "It's like a part of my soul is here. I can't explain it."

"You don't have to," Simon said next to her.

She abandoned the thought. She wasn't even sure where it had come from—the whiskey, probably. "If I hadn't told my uncle I'd call this morning, no one would have been the wiser—"

"You have people who care about you enough to worry. Don't be too hard on yourself, Keira. You're only human." Simon grinned back at her. "Well. I think you're only human. Could be you're a fairy princess after all."

"A shape-shifter," she said, starting up the street toward the lane. "At any moment, I might just change into a lizard or a snake—"

"Not a snake. Not while we're in Ireland."

She realized she was as comfortable with him as the men at the pub had been. He rescued people from dire situations, but she wouldn't say he was chivalrous. That suited her; natural charm she could handle—any forced gallantry would just make her feel hemmed in and needy.

"Cold?" he asked her.

"Not really."

"Keira...I'm staying with you tonight. Word of your ordeal is going to spread, and given what you do for a living, and how damn pretty you are, who knows what kind of nutcase it'll bring to your doorstep."

"Probably none at all."

"Well," he said, leaning in closer to her, "you can't always count on your magic and fairies, now, can you?"

"A little brute strength does come in handy on occasion."

He smiled. "And charm."

"Telling me I'm too stupid to live isn't charming."

"Honesty has its place. You're worn out, Keira, and you need to rest. But I want to know what happened up at that ruin. You were up there because of the story that old woman in Boston told you, weren't you?"

She nodded. "It's a wonderful story, Simon. It has mischief, magic, fairies, Irish brothers." She shivered in the wind as they turned onto the lane. "It's not a dark, tragic story."

"Do people around here know it?"

"I haven't had a chance to find out. I asked Colm Dermott about it. He was at the reception in Boston, too. He's an expert in Irish folklore, but he's never heard the story or any recognizable version of it."

Simon slung a big arm over her shoulders. "I'd love to hear this magical story of yours."

"There's no way I can tell it the way Patsy does. I've only known her a few weeks, but my mother and my uncle grew up a couple doors down from her in South Boston. She's a natural story-teller."

"How does it start?"

"With three Irish brothers—a farmer, a hermit monk and a ne'er-do-well."

Keira went on from there, telling the story in truncated form as she and Si-mon continued along the dark, quiet lane.

When she finished, he dropped his arm from her shoulder. "You love this stuff, don't you?"

"I do. Normally I don't care about the literal truth of a story. That's not the point. But this one..." She looked up at the sprinkle of stars against the black-ening sky. "I thought it'd be fun to see if I could find the hermit monk's hut—to see what happened there on the night of the summer solstice."

"So you think the fairies toppled that ruin onto your head?"

"I don't know." But she thought a mo-ment, remembered the eerie whisper of her name and shook her head. "No. I do know. Whether they were there or not isn't for me to say, but—it wasn't fairies that caused the cave-in, Simon."

Keira could feel his eyes on her and took note of his sudden reserve. There was none of his boisterous charm now. He plucked a pink blossom from the massive rosebush that tumbled over the ancient wall in front of her cottage. "Keira..."

"I ducked into the ruin to get away from a dog," she said. "There was this voice. This whisper."

He eased the rose blossom into her hair, then ran one finger along her jaw. "Tell me."

She slowed her pace and told him about last night—about finding the old stone hut, running into the dog, hearing the voice just before the cave-in.

And the angel. Keira told him about that, too.

As she walked up her cottage driveway, she was aware of Simon watching her, studying her, and she turned to him. "You're thinking what I saw was just a hunk of rock that I mistook for the stone angel in the story. And the dog—that it was an ordinary sheepdog, not some big, menacing dog—" She paused, cold now in the wind. "And the whisper was the evening breeze."

"You're imaginative, and you've experienced a trauma. You're also exhausted and spinning on sugar and alcohol."

"But did I get it right about what you're thinking?"

He approached her, snatched the flower just as it fell from behind her ear. "I'm not that good with flowers. I probably should have checked this one for bugs, huh?"

"Simon..."

"You had a close call out here."

"I've had close calls at home."

"Let's see how things look in the morning. I don't like the sheep's blood and entrails. Did you hear anything that in retrospect—"

"Was a sheep in the throes of death? No. I didn't."

He nodded without comment.

"Maybe what happened had nothing to do with me or Patsy's story."

"Do you believe that?"

"It doesn't matter what I believe. What

matters are the facts." She gave a mock shudder and tried to laugh. "Now I sound like my uncle."

"At least you don't look like him."

"We have the same eyes," she said.

"The same color, maybe. Ah, Keira, Keira," Simon said in his exaggerated, fake Irish accent. "You're gutsy. I'll say that for you."

She couldn't help but smile as she unlocked the side door and slipped into her cottage. She looked back at him. "You can come in. I'm not going to make you sleep in your car, and I can tell you're not going anywhere. You can have my bed." She waved a hand toward the living room. "I'll sleep out here on the couch."

Simon entered the kitchen, locking the door behind him. "No, you won't."

"You deserve a good night's sleep after charging to my rescue, and I'll fit on the couch better than you would. I'm beat, Simon. Nothing's going to keep me awake. I just want to curl up under a stack of blankets—"

"I can sleep next to you in your bed without getting personal." He winked, giving her the slightest smile. "I'm disciplined."

She stared at him. "You're serious!"

"You should have thought of the consequences before you took off into the hills."

"I did think of them. And you've no room to talk. You went looking for me by yourself. You're unfamiliar with the area."

"Rocks, grass, sheep. What else is there to know?"

"There's a mean bull—"

He laughed. "I always make allowances for mean bulls. Plus, I had Owen waiting to hear from me, and I had a working cell phone—and I was prepared."

"You had a rope and a flashlight. That's not prepared."

"I had a jackknife, too."

He was irreverent, confident but not quite cocky—a man most anyone would find hard to stay mad at for long. Keira appreciated his straightforward opinion of her escapade. She hated being coddled. But she wasn't ready to give in. "If you're in my bed with me, I'll never get any sleep."

She winced at how her words sounded and, suddenly feeling hot, ran into the bedroom, whisked an extra blanket off the foot of the bed, then headed back into the living room.

Simon, merrily whistling some Irish tune, retreated to the bathroom.

She dropped onto the couch and pulled the blanket up over her front. She didn't have the energy to go back for a pillow.

She really did need a bed.

"This is insane," she muttered, dragging the blanket with her back into the bedroom.

Skipping her usual nightgown, she changed into sweatpants and a T-shirt and climbed into the bed, pulling the duvet up to her chin. As a volunteer for Fast Rescue, Simon would be accustomed to rough conditions. A too-short couch wouldn't be a problem for him.

She heard the shower.

No. Don't picture him naked...

She just wanted to close her eyes and go to sleep and forget the past twenty-four hours until morning. With a good night's sleep, she'd be rested enough to climb back up the dirt track, over the fences and through the steep pasture in order to check out the ruin in daylight.

But she was still wide awake when the shower stopped, and Simon walked into the bedroom wearing a Guinness T-shirt and shorts. He smelled not of her citrus bath gel but the plain soap that had come with the cottage. She noticed the thick muscles in his legs and arms and thought of his hand on her hip while she'd wormed her way into the hut's entrance to check on the stone angel.

He yanked back the duvet on the opposite side of the bed and climbed in. "Cozy," he said, pulling the duvet over him. "I figure if you didn't really want me here, you'd have stretched out in the middle and not left any room."

"I'd never get any sleep on the couch." She scooted another two inches toward the edge of the bed. "Pretend there's an invisible electric fence between us."

He adjusted his pillow. "Will do."

"Black dogs often appear in stories as supernatural shape-shifters."

"You might not want to think about that right now."

"Their purpose can be for good or for evil," she said.

"Why don't you picture that painting of yours I bid on in Boston?"

She shut her eyes. "It's a half real, half imagined place," she said. "The dog was real. I didn't imagine him."

"Maybe not." Simon's voice was surprisingly close, gentle. "Get some sleep, Keira."

"You, too."

"I will as soon as you stop talking about shape-shifting black dogs."

She smiled. "Sweet dreams."

"Yeah. Sweet dreams."

~Chapter 16

South Boston, Massachusetts
8:00 p.m., EDT
June 22

Bob O'Reilly rang the doorbell to Patsy McCarthy's single-family house on the tidy South Boston street where he and his sister had grown up. He'd made a practice of not dwelling on Deirdre's murder thirty years ago, but he thought of her now, running out onto the street as a young teenager, always more attractive than she'd realized. He'd never met anyone like her.

It was hot and late, and he didn't want to be here.

But Patsy opened the door, and when she saw him, she put her hand to her mouth and gave a small gasp. "Nothing's happened—"

"No," he said. "Everything's fine."

"You've got that cop look of yours." She relaxed slightly, dropping her hand back to her side. "I remember when you were a little boy, and you'd come here with that same look on your face. Your mother and I knew you'd become a police officer."

"Mrs. McCarthy, what did you tell Keira?"

"What do you mean?"

"You went to see her the other night— the night before she left for Ireland."

Patsy opened the door wider and stepped out onto the stoop, pulling her sweater more tightly, despite the heat. Bob could see into her front hall, where she had a wall covered with postcards of Ireland and stickers of shamrocks and leprechaun hats. It'd been that way forever. She never went anywhere herself, but she'd ask people she knew to send her postcards from their trips. Even back when Eileen took off to study in Ireland at nineteen, Patsy had asked her to send postcards for her wall.

"I didn't tell Keira about Deirdre," she said, her expression hardening. "If that's what you're asking."

Bob didn't mince words. "It is."

"It's not my place to tell her."

He heard that subtext—that it was his place to tell his niece, and presumably his three daughters, about his murdered childhood neighbor. But he didn't go there. "What did you tell her, then?"

"Old family stories."

"The one about the Irish brothers and the stone angel?"

Her mood seemed to lighten. "You remember it?"

"Sure. Yeah, of course. Patsy, you know you've opened up a can of worms telling Keira that story. Telling her that her mother looked for the village where it was set when she went to Ireland before Keira was born."

"Oh, Bob." Patsy waved her bony fingers at him. "So what if I did? Maybe Keira will be the one to find the angel. Wouldn't that be something?"

Bob gave an inward groan. Yeah, hell,

he thought, it'd be something. After he'd dragged out of Fiona what she'd over-heard Patsy telling Keira at the Garrison house, he'd known what to expect, but the confirmation hit him in the gut. His sister had gone off in search of that stu-pid angel thirty years ago. He didn't know the details—Eileen had never told him—but he'd long suspected that little adventure of hers had everything to do with how she'd come home from Ireland pregnant.

No question, Keira was retracing her mother's footsteps. Bob didn't want to think about what would have happened if Simon Cahill hadn't pulled her out of that ruin when he did.

Not that Bob was all that sure about Cahill. Big brute of a guy, good-looking, charming.

Bob ground his teeth together. All three of his daughters looked up to Keira. He loved her to death, but having her right there in Boston was a lot differ-ent than having her in San Diego or the other places she'd lived in the past few years. Fiona already was bugging him about going on adventures of her own.

"Bob?"

"It's okay, Patsy," he said. "You haven't done anything wrong. When did you and Keira hook up?"

"It's been a couple of months. I have all her books. She's so talented, Bob, isn't she?"

"That she is. Did she get in touch with you or you with her?"

"I e-mailed her. I'm handy with a computer, I'll have you know. I heard about the Irish project and went to her Web site—"

"How'd you hear about the project?"

"Billie and Jeanette Murphy told me about it. You remember them, don't you, Bob?"

Bob nodded. They were a few years ahead of him in school, and they'd made a fortune in Boston real estate. They lived in a high-priced waterfront condominium that was technically in South Boston, although not exactly part of the old neighborhood, and they owned the land on which his sister had built her cabin.

"Who else did you tell that story to?" he asked Patsy.

"I've told it for years to anyone and everyone. Why shouldn't I?"

"Didn't say you shouldn't."

"Then what's wrong with you? Why are you here?"

He sighed. "Keira ran into a little trouble in Ireland. She's fine—I just let myself get worked up over it. Because of Eileen, I guess. That summer."

Patsy clutched his hand, digging her bony fingers into his palm. "You're sure Keira's all right?"

"I'm sure. Don't worry, okay? She's got someone with her."

"I told her three or four stories my grandfather used to tell me. Keira seemed to enjoy them, but she especially liked the one about the three brothers. It was Deirdre's favorite, too. She wanted Eileen to look for the stone angel when she was in Ireland. Bob, you remember how excited Deirdre was about Eileen's trip, don't you?"

He pried Patsy's small hand from his and squeezed it gently, then kissed her on the cheek. "I remember every minute I spent with Deirdre. She was the best.

You okay? Anything you're not telling me?"

"You're a good boy, Bob. You always have been."

It wasn't a direct answer. "Nah. I'm not that good." He tried to relax but couldn't, and he slipped one of his cards into her palm. "You hold on to that. It's got all my phone numbers on it. If you think of anything you want to tell me—anything unusual happens—you call. Better safe than sorry, right?"

She nodded.

But he knew he didn't have her full trust. He hadn't kept up with her the way he probably should have, but he'd known her forever and felt her restraint, her resistance. "Patsy..."

"I'll call you if I think of anything else," she said, then smiled, letting go of his hand. "Don't worry so much."

He grinned at her. "Now you sound like one of my ex-wives. It's good to see you, Patsy. The priest from your church drove you to see Keira? I don't know him."

"He's been at Saint Ita's for a little more than a year. Father Palermo. He came up with the idea to have a church bazaar with an angel theme. I brought in my entire angel collection to display. We had such a wonderful time."

He heard her native Ireland in her voice now. "Sorry I missed it."

She gave him an impish grin. "No, you're not."

"I should come by more often."

"You should."

"You can tell me that story again. It's perfect for Keira's new book."

"I think so, too. That would be wonderful, wouldn't it?" She looked happier, more at ease. "I'm so glad to see you, Bob. Come back soon."

"I will." He started down the steps, then turned and pointed at her. "You'll call, right? Anytime. I'm available 24/7."

She rolled her eyes. "You really do worry too much."

He probably did, Bob thought, returning to his car, unable to shake his uneasiness. He wanted to blame the summer solstice and his general pessimism, but he knew that wasn't all—it was the body in the Public Garden, the dead man's devil room and now Keira's mess in Ireland.

And Fiona. His daughter hadn't told him everything, either.

He debated trying again with Patsy, but he knew it wouldn't do him any good. She was a sweet soul, but she was also stubborn and secretive. In her own way, she was hard as nails. He remembered taking her out to the waterfront where Deirdre's body had washed ashore and how she'd talked about ways to fight the devil. If anyone could do it, it was Patsy McCarthy.

After Bob left, Patsy changed into her housecoat and slippers and poured herself just the tiniest bit of Irish whiskey to take with her into the dining room. She knew she'd have a hard time sleeping tonight. She was accustomed to keeping her own company, and she wasn't afraid in her own house—that wasn't it, she thought as she stood in front of the curio cabinet where she kept the best of Deirdre's angels.

You should have invited Bob in for tea. He'd have come—she could tell he

suspected she hadn't told him everything that was on her mind. He'd have
used tea as a way to get her to open up
to him, and she wasn't going to.

She sat at the table, sipping her
whiskey and gazing at the angels.

Finally, she started up to bed, but a
noise drew her into the kitchen. She
flipped on her back-porch light, hoping
it was a cat in her wind chimes. She had
only the one set left. She used to have a
half dozen, but one of her neighbors, a
young hotel events coordinator who'd
"discovered" the east side of South
Boston and moved next door, had com-
plained about them. Patsy would never
have said a word over such a thing herself. Her neighbor had no such com-
punctions and had demanded that even
this last set of chimes go, too. Off to a
white-elephant sale with it, the woman
had suggested.

"If there's not an ordinance against
wind chimes," she'd said, "there should
be."

How could someone deny an old
woman the pleasure of one lonely set of
wind chimes?

Patsy used to know all her neighbors, but maybe it was just as well she didn't even know this one's name. She'd told Patsy she was attracted to their street for its proximity to downtown Boston and the waterfront. No mention of family, friends, anything of the sort. She talked about "gentrification," a word Patsy loathed.

"No gentry here," she muttered, peering out her kitchen window.

If it was a cat in her wind chimes, she resolved not to take her irritation out on an innocent animal. That would be wrong, although she had no doubt her neighbor wouldn't resist if similarly provoked.

How different it was now from when Deirdre was growing up and would bring her friends to the house. Patsy had loved baking for them, telling them stories. She'd hoped to have five or six children, but it hadn't worked out that way. She'd had just Deirdre.

Patsy opened the back door, comfortable in her slippers and cotton housecoat. But she didn't see a cat, and her wind chimes were quiet in the still, humid air.

She paused, frowning. Did she hear music now?

"Oh, my goodness," she whispered. "I do!"

It wasn't her wind chimes, either, or her imagination. She wasn't losing her mind. No—it was music she heard, sweet, mournful music. She didn't recognize the melody, but it had an Irish sound. Where was it coming from?

Was it a tipsy neighbor, humming as he staggered home after over imbibing at a nearby pub?

Kids?

The music stopped. The wind chimes stirred, clinking pleasantly in the summer night. Patsy didn't know what had started them dancing. There was no breeze that she could feel.

As she turned to check the wind chimes, she saw a stone statue of an angel standing on the broad porch railing.

She grabbed the front of her housecoat with one hand, as a way to steady herself, and stepped out onto the porch, thinking maybe she'd drunk more whiskey than she'd realized. But she could see the statue clearly—it was definitely an angel, about two feet tall and constructed of gray stone, with wings, an Irish harp in one arm and a face that was so loving and peaceful, Patsy thought of her daughter.

How did the statue get here? Was it a gift for her collection?

She reached for the back of a metal porch chair. Surely the music hadn't come from this captivating statue. It couldn't have, unless it was some kind of elaborate music box.

Had someone left it as a prank, then?

Real angels, Patsy remembered, appeared before those who were worthy.

I'm not worthy.

They also fought demons.

I'm a sinner...I'm not a demon.

And this was a statue—a beautiful statue. It wasn't a real angel.

She'd call Bob. She'd ask him to come back here. She'd tell him everything. All she knew, all she suspected.

She left the angel on the porch and

returned to her kitchen, locking the door behind her.

"Patsy..."

The voice came from the dining room.

"Patricia Brigid McCarthy..."

Whoever was whispering her name was with her in the house. Patsy reached for Bob's card on the counter, but she knew she was too late. There was no more time.

The devil had come for her.

As she dove for her telephone, she began to pray.

⌒*Chapter 17*

Beara Peninsula, Southwest Ireland
5:30 a.m., IST
June 23

Keira flopped an arm down on Simon's stomach in her sleep. He was wide awake and had been for some time. So much, he thought, for her invisible electric fence. Not that he minded. He felt her warmth next to him. The early-morning sunlight streaming in through the window landed on his bedmate's long, pale hair and fair, smooth skin, and he figured if someone saw her lying here there'd be a new story to tell by the fire.

But she was in a troubled sleep,

moaning to herself, thrashing. He felt her entire body tense, and she made a fist, clutching his T-shirt and a good hunk of flesh. Her nails were cut short, and there were nicks and scrapes on her knuckles and wrist from the hours she'd spent trapped. It was a strong hand, and yet delicate, and Simon imagined her slender fingers skimming over him.

Just kill me now.

He wondered how much Keira hadn't told him about her trip to Ireland.

She was self-sufficient and obviously not one to panic, but he wouldn't be surprised if she'd come out to the southwest coast of Ireland thinking fairies would protect her. Who knew, maybe they had kept her safe in that ruin. From the outside, it looked as if no one could have lived through the cave-in, but not only did Keira live, she'd come through her ordeal relatively un-scathed.

Simon had to admit that if he hadn't come along, she probably would have managed to climb out of there on her own. But he wasn't sure what she'd have done if he hadn't been there when she'd stood up, covered in blood.

She cried out in her sleep and dug her fingers into his chest. He felt her knee coming at him but deflected the blow, just as her other hand went for his head.

Time to wake her up. In the close quarters his work often required, he had witnessed his share of teammates having nightmares. Usually he'd just toss his watch or a water bottle at the person and say, "Hey, pal, wake up. You're having a nightmare." But he was reluctant to be that perfunctory with Keira, not so much because he wanted to be gentle with her—he wanted her to be gentle with *him*. They were in the same bed, and she was in good shape. One well-placed blow would ruin his day.

And they were in a tricky mustn't-touch situation that another well-placed blow could make even trickier.

He placed his hand on hers—the one that had a grip on his shirt and some skin and hair he wanted to keep. "Keira."

She bolted upright, holding on to his hand, clearly not awake. She was breathing hard, close to the point of hyperventilating, and looked repulsed and terrified, haunted by whatever images were assaulting her in her sleep.

"Keira, you're having a nightmare."

Her eyes focused on him, widened, and she dropped his hand and rolled back to her side of the bed. Simon didn't know what had her more distressed—her nightmare, or waking up half on top of him.

"I was..." She raked a hand through her hair and inched a bit farther from him. "Spiders and slugs were crawling on me."

Simon leaned back against his pillows. "Nasty."

She blew out a breath, shivering. "It was awful."

"Nightmares are normal after a trauma."

She lifted her gaze to the window. The shade was up, and the lace curtains were pulled back, providing a view of a small sheep pen across the yard. "Do you have nightmares?" she asked without looking at him.

"Sometimes."

"Your work with Fast Rescue—"

"I've had a lot of training to help me learn to process what I experience. There's no training for what you went through in that ruin."

Her very blue eyes shifted to him. "Did I hurt you?"

"Not at all." He grinned at her. "It's not a bad way to wake up, as a matter of fact. If I'd stayed in London, I'd have woken up in a big, elegant, empty bed. This is cozy, the two of us—"

"I'll go into the other room. You can go back to sleep."

"I'm good. Wide awake." He threw off the duvet and got up. "Take your time. I'll make coffee."

"That'd be great. I'm still—" She waved her hand. "I'm still fighting off spiders and slugs."

Her hair was tangled, and her shirt was askew. Now that she was safe, Simon knew, her mind—consciously or subconsciously—could indulge in the fear, revulsion, claustrophobia and whatever other emotions it hadn't let her access during the hours she was trapped.

And he'd be a slug himself if he took

advantage of her waking up from a stress-induced nightmare.

He retreated to the kitchen and filled the electric kettle with water, turned it on and headed for the bathroom, changing into jeans and a sweater. His own hair was a mess. He wet his hands and ran them over his head, gave up and went back into the kitchen. He heaped grounds into a coffee press and poured on what looked like the right amount of water.

While the coffee steeped, he got down two mugs, and he imagined being here with Keira on an ordinary morning, making coffee, planning their day. He wouldn't have jumped right out of bed after she'd clawed at him while having a nightmare, that was for damn sure.

Simon indulged in those images for about five seconds before he pushed them far to the back of his mind, filled his mug with the strong, steaming coffee and headed outside. A dozen or so sheep stirred in the pasture on the other side of the fence. The sun dipped in and out of gray clouds, and the air was brisk, scented with roses, the damp grass and, he swore, the sea.

Keira joined him with her mug of coffee, and he nodded to the dramatic hills that swept up into the heart of the peninsula. "It's beautiful country, but six weeks is a long time to be out here alone."

"I have a lot of work to do—and exploring," she said with an unembarrassed smile. "I won't be alone the entire time. I have friends from San Diego who're vacationing in Ireland in a few weeks and plan to stop by, and Colm Dermott will be here in late July with his family. And being on my own gives me a chance to get to know some of the local people."

Simon eyed her. "Keira, I've called the Irish police to come have a look at the ruin. They're on their way."

"When did you call?"

"Early. You were still dreaming about slugs and spiders."

"I suppose it makes sense, bringing in the police." But she quickly sipped her coffee and winced. "Strong, isn't it?"

"I just eyeballed the measurements."

"It's good—thank you."

She'd put on jeans and an oversize rugby shirt and combed the tangles out of her hair, but Simon had to admit his heart had skipped a few beats at the sight of her. He figured half the men she met probably fell a little in love with her within seconds of setting eyes on her. So why the hell wasn't she here with a man? He considered the prudence of asking her, then figured why not, "No boyfriend to take off with to Ireland?"

She didn't avert her eyes from him even a millimeter. "No. As I said, I plan to get a lot of work done while I'm here."

"A man would just get in the way?"

"That's not what I said."

She walked over to the fence and cupped her mug in both hands as she sipped her coffee and stared out at the pasture. Simon watched her, aware that she wasn't fully there with him. She was either still in her nightmare or, more likely, back in the ruin. He stayed quiet, giving her time, recognizing that he wanted to dive into whatever world she was trapped in and rescue her. Slay her demons, if need be. It was kind of mad, but he'd be dishonest if he didn't acknowledge the protective impulse, understand it for what it was. But Keira was a woman who went her own way, not out of defiance so much as disposition. It was just who she was.

His father had been like that, and he'd ended up dead.

She took her coffee down the driveway to the roses and mishmash of wildflowers. Across the lane and down the hill, the harbor glistened in the early morning sun. She seemed to soak in the scenery, the life and movement of the new day. She had an unpretentiousness and clarity about her that Simon could appreciate, and hell if he didn't want to scoop her up and carry her back inside for the rest of the day. Let the weather turn bad. What would they care?

"I don't really know you at all," she said abruptly, then turned to him.

Not a subject he wanted to get into. "What's to know?"

"You're a volunteer with Fast Rescue. Unless you're independently wealthy, that must mean you have a job. What do you do that you can drop everything to respond to a disaster anywhere in the world, live on a boat, go off to London—"

"I have my own business." It was true, as far as it went. "I work with various corporations and individuals on disaster preparedness and response planning. I also do some training. Some guide work."

"Guide work?"

He leveled his gaze on her. "If an artistic type wants to search for a mysterious ruin on a remote Irish peninsula on the night of the summer solstice, I can get her there and back safely."

"It wasn't night. Sunset isn't until ten o'clock here in June."

"Let's leave out night, then. Keira, you haven't told me everything about why you're here—"

"How did you end up as a Fast Rescue volunteer?"

He sighed. Obviously, she intended for them to do this her way. "A friend of a friend put me in touch with Owen."

But it wasn't that simple. That friend was John March, who'd put Simon in touch with Owen eighteen months ago simply because Fast Rescue needed search-and-rescue experts, and Simon, in the middle of sorting out what was supposed to be his post-FBI life, was one. At the time, March knew Owen only as the Maine summer neighbor of March's murdered FBI agent son-in-law. Owen hadn't yet fallen for Abigail, Chris Browning's widow, March's daughter.

By then, Simon was back in the FBI fold, working undercover and going after Norman Estabrook. Owen, who was thorough and protective of Fast Rescue and had extensive contacts of his own, figured out Simon's personal history with March, his undercover status, that his mission likely involved Norman Estabrook.

With the imminent takedown of Estabrook and the dismantling of his network, Owen was left in the unenviable position of not being able to tell the woman he loved what he knew about Simon, her father, their friendship. That information was all on a need-to-know basis, and Abigail didn't need to know.

Neither, Simon thought, did Keira Sullivan.

A brown cow meandered up to the fence in the enclosure across the lane. Simon walked over to her and patted her. She pushed her head against his hand, obviously enjoying the attention. "So, Miss Cow, what did you see the other day? Did you see Keira here go off into the hills? Did you see someone sneak into her cottage and steal her note?" He lowered his ear to the cow, pretending he was listening to what she had to say. "Ah. Fairies. I see. It was the summer solstice, and you saw fairies dancing." He glanced back at Keira. "Don't you wish cows could talk?"

"All right, all right." Keira laughed, dumping out the last of her coffee into the grass. "Let's go meet the guards."

⁓Chapter 18

Beara Peninsula, Southwest Ireland
6:30 a.m., IST
June 23

Coffee and sunlight had Keira feeling more like herself as she tried to keep up with Simon as they crossed the open pasture in the general direction of the ruin. "Slow down," she said. "I'm tall, but your lope is still my run, and I can't keep up with you, especially after my nightmare from hell."

He glanced sideways at her, the wind catching the ends of his black hair. "I thought my coffee would put some zip in your step."

"It did. I'd be crawling otherwise."

Threatening clouds pushed down onto the hills. The wind was picking up, but Keira welcomed the brisk air and hoped it would help clear her head, stop her from thinking about waking up from her nightmare and finding herself more or less in Simon's arms. Common sense warned her not to get too caught up in her physical attraction to him. He'd be on his way back to London soon. He lived a very different life from hers, and even if a one-night stand would have been fun, she wasn't the type and never had been.

When they came to another fence, Simon hopped over it, then turned and offered her a hand. She took it, resisted the impulse just to jump into his arms. But he caught her around the middle and lifted her down to the ground, giving her a quick, irreverent smile. "You were about to land in sheep manure."

She glanced down, and sure enough, he wasn't kidding. "I see that your search-and-rescue skills are highly adaptable."

"Helps to know I'm dealing with someone who doesn't look over her shoulder for trouble."

Simon started down the hill to the muddy, thick undergrowth along the stream. Keira matched his pace, not letting him get too far ahead of her. "I'm not paranoid. I'm not going to sit home because something bad might happen if I go out."

"I can see that." He came to the stream and pushed back the low branch of an oak that dipped almost down to the water. "If the angel wasn't just another hunk of Irish rock, how did it get onto the hearth? Why hasn't anyone around here found it and sold it to a museum or put it on eBay by now?"

"I don't know."

"More important, where did it go?"

Keira shivered, wishing she'd worn a coat instead of just throwing a sweater on over her rugby shirt. "I don't know that, either."

Instead of putting her on the defensive, his questions—fired at her ever since they'd started the hike back up to the ruin—had helped her to focus on the specifics of her ordeal and remember them with greater clarity.

"Tell me about the fairies in this story," he said, thrashing along the edge of the stream. "Are we talking about a solitary fairy—a banshee or a leprechaun or something—or a fairy troop?"

"You know Irish folklore?"

"Not much. Enough to ask you a question."

"And to spark a good argument in an Irish pub, I imagine. It's a fairy troop, at least according to Patsy. They're determined and relentless. They believe they're entitled to the statue—"

"Because they insist it's one of their own who's been turned to stone."

Keira smiled. "So you were paying attention last night."

He winked at her. "Hard to resist a magical story told on a dark Irish night."

"It's easy to see out here how Ireland's strong oral tradition took root, isn't it? In any case, the fairies won't take no for an answer. They want the statue back."

"Patsy McCarthy obviously believes the statue exists, or at least wants to believe it." Simon pushed back another low-hanging branch along the stream. "I didn't overhear everything she said to you, but I gather she's with the brothers and thinks the angel can bring good fortune."

"She asked me to look for it on the summer solstice," Keira said.

"Because of the story itself—the angel first appears on the hearth on the night of the summer solstice. Someone else familiar with the story would know that."

"And therefore could have picked the same night as I did to be out here."

Just ahead, Keira spotted the ivy-enshrouded ruin through the trees, the cave-in making it easier not to miss. She stifled a sudden sense of dread, noticing that Simon hadn't slackened his pace at all.

But he paused just then and glanced back at her. "You okay?"

She nodded, ignoring a tightening in her throat and chest. *Concentrate on figuring this thing out.* "I've been thinking," she said, continuing on up the hill. "And I suspect the collapse itself might have exposed the angel. What if it was buried in the ruin?"

"Then the question is what caused the cave-in at that precise moment?"

"Someone poking around the same as me. But," she said, standing just below the tree that had fallen across the ruin's only door, "why leave me out here trapped inside the rubble?"

Simon's eyes darkened. "Good question. Have you told the story to anyone besides Professor Dermott?"

She shook her head. "I can't speak for Patsy, though."

"Who all knows you were coming out here to research an Irish story?"

"I've made no secret of it, but I haven't given the details to many people. The location of my cottage, for instance. I'm aware I'm here on my own."

As she tried to get a better look at a heap of rubble, Keira almost stepped on a tuft of sheep's wool in the tall grass. She repressed a sudden wave of the revulsion she'd felt last night when she'd realized she was covered in blood.

"Keira?"

"Just getting my bearings," she said, choking back the memory.

Simon eased closer to her, coming

within an inch of his arm brushing against hers. "Do you remember any details now that you're back here?"

With her back to the ruin, Keira looked at the stream, sunlight and shade dancing on the clear, shallow water. "It's an enchanting spot, isn't it?" But when he didn't answer, she turned again, squinting at the dead tree, the partially-collapsed chimney. "I didn't sneak out here—I wasn't singing or anything, but I wasn't worried about anyone hearing me, either. Once I saw the dog, I was preoccupied with him. I certainly made enough noise if someone else was out here and didn't want to be seen. As for the sheep..." She grimaced. "It wasn't an act of nature that killed that poor animal."

"We don't have enough to go on to say for sure. Let's let the police get out here and see what they say."

She stared at the remains of the tiny hut. "It wasn't my imagination that started this place collapsing on top of me."

"No, it was probably your crawling around in an unstable structure without

the proper knowledge or equipment."
Simon's tone was more matter of fact
than critical. "You were worried about
the dog and not paying attention."

"That doesn't explain the angel.
Maybe someone purposely started the
cave-in to trap me, then figured I was
dead or at least incapacitated and stole
the angel. If it's an authentic early Celtic
statue, it's valuable."

"And if it's solid rock, it's also heavy."

"It's only about two feet tall. I doubt it's
that heavy."

"So this 'someone,' whoever it is,
crawls into the hut after it collapsed,
grabs the angel and—"

Keira shook her head. "Not *after* the
cave-in, while it was happening. I saw
the angel during a brief lull in the collapse. After it started up again, I
couldn't see much—I was huddled under the loft trying to keep rocks and
rafters from falling on my head. Someone could have grabbed the angel and
crawled out in the middle of the action."

"Risky," Simon commented.

"Opportunistic, too." She gestured to
the tree blocking the door. "I'll bet he—

or she—toppled the tree, deliberately or accidentally, on the way out, then headed for my cottage and stole my note to delay my rescue or the discovery of my body."

"Any candidates?"

"No."

She was aware of Simon watching her and turned toward him, noticing that his eyes were as green as the vegetation on their lush hillside. She felt a drop of rain on her hair. The wind was picking up. She could hear it howling up on the exposed hills. The police would be here soon, and she'd have to go through it all again—why she'd come out here, what had happened, every detail of the past two days.

Her gaze fell on a smear of dried blood in the disturbed ground by the fallen tree, and she turned abruptly and ran, thrashing up the hillside through the mass of trees and undergrowth. She came to a barbed-wire fence, barely breaking her stride as she clambered over it.

The wind was fierce out in the open. She could hear sheep bleating nearby, and as she stood on a rock jutting out of the ground, she could see the harbor far below, fishing boats, a pricey-looking sailboat. Crossing her arms in a gust of wind, she squinted out at the jagged MacGillicuddy Reeks across the bay, soon, no doubt, to be consumed in gray clouds and fog.

Simon stood next to her. "We'll wait here for the guards," he said calmly.

The Garda, Keira thought. The Irish police. *"A Garda Siochana,"* she said, half to herself. "I'm butchering the pronunciation, but it means Guardians of the Peace. I like that."

"Keira…"

"I'm okay. I had a mini panic attack." She stepped off her rock, wishing again for warmer attire. "I have to go back to Boston. At least for a few days. I want to check with Patsy to make sure she didn't leave out a part of the story that might help me make sense of what happened here, and I want to talk to Colm Dermott. I can't—" She broke off, then resumed. "I have to figure out what happened at that ruin, Simon. I can't stay here for six more weeks without knowing."

"All right. I'll get you back to Boston. Today, if you'd like."

She nodded. "I would. Thank you. I'm not as rested today as I'd hoped I'd be."

Her fatigue wasn't just due to the aftereffects of her experience in the ruin or her nightmare. It was also due to her night in bed with him, waking up in his arms—even if she'd been clawing imagined slugs and spiders off him. She'd come within a split second of asking him to make love to her.

Another reason, she thought, to head to Boston.

Simon took a breath. "Hell, Keira."

She didn't know whether she made the first move or he did, but suddenly she was in his arms. His mouth found hers, and she let go of all her tension and threw her arms around his neck, deepening their kiss. She loved the taste of him, the feel of his hard body against hers, the warmth of him in the cold, damp wind.

He lifted her off her feet. The hem of her shirt rode up, and he spread his hands on the bare skin of her lower back, sending a jolt of pure desire straight through her. She pressed herself into him, was sure she heard him give a moan of a yearning as wild and uncontrolled as her own.

A gust of wind blew down from the hills, and more sprinkles fell, the combination of the cold air and water with the heat of their kiss setting every nerve in her body on fire. Sensations coursed through her. She'd never responded to anyone the way she did Simon. She wanted to run her hands through his hair, taste every part of him, feel him inside her. And it wasn't just adrenaline, or being out on an Irish hill—she'd had a strong reaction to him the moment she'd spotted him in Boston.

"I'd love to go back to the cottage," she said between kisses. "A storm's brewing. We could forget all this mess..."

But even as she spoke, he was lowering her back onto the cool, damp ground, and she steadied herself and caught her breath as she adjusted her shirt and looked out across the barren landscape.

Just as well they'd stopped when they

did, Keira thought, because now she could see two men walking toward the ruin.

"The guards have arrived," Simon said with a hint of amusement.

"In the nick of time, wouldn't you say?"

"Hardly." And, as if to make his point, he gave her a fast, fierce kiss. "We'll pick up where we left off another time. We're not finished."

Keira didn't respond, just ran toward the two Irish police officers and waved to them, hoping they'd have answers. Perhaps they'd tell her they'd just arrested someone who'd been out killing sheep and terrorizing tourists.

But she knew that was unlikely, because the answers weren't in Ireland.

They were in Boston.

~Chapter 19

Jamaica Plain, Massachusetts
10:00 a.m., EDT
June 23

Using a screwdriver she'd borrowed from Bob O'Reilly, Abigail opened a gallon can of blue paint she'd put on newspaper in her bedroom. A grainy black-and-white picture of Victor Sarakis stared up at her, as if to remind her that the investigation into his death was not yet finished.

She tried to focus on the paint. "Do you like the color?" she asked Owen, who watched her from the doorway.

"It's a nice shade."

He didn't give a damn about paint. She knew he didn't, but she still had to ask. She wanted him to like it, to have some role—however small—in its selection. He'd arrived back in Boston last night from Austin. Her gaze drifted to the double bed—anything larger wouldn't fit in the tiny room. She hadn't bothered to make it. The sheets were tangled from their lovemaking.

"If you want a different color," she said, "now's the time to speak up."

"Blue's good. I can help—"

"It's so small in here, we'd just bump into each other and get paint all over everything." She lifted off the lid, set it on Victor's face and put down the screwdriver, picking up the wood stirrer that came with the paint. "I'm not kicking you out."

"I know you're not."

Did he? She wasn't sure anymore. "I'm preoccupied with a case." She dipped the stick into the paint and smiled, or tried to. "I've got the devil on my mind."

She'd been reading Charlotte Augustine's book on the history of the devil last night when Owen had arrived. "It's your day off," he said. "You could sit in a lounge chair, drink wine and read Jane Austen."

"Sounds tempting." There were a thousand things she could do besides paint the bedroom.

"Simon's on his way back here with Keira," Owen said.

"Bob told me when I went out for the paper. He's been beside himself. I guess I don't blame him. It's weird, Keira coming on the body in the Public Garden and now this mess in Ireland." Abigail shoved the stick into the paint. "I don't like coincidences."

"Is there any reason to think the two are connected?"

"No."

When she didn't go on, Owen drew himself up straight from the door frame. "There are a couple of things I need do at the foundation. Nothing important. Fiona O'Reilly and her friends are coming back to practice. If you want to, stop by later." He smiled. "We can dance an Irish jig."

Abigail felt a little of the tension go out of her. "Do you know how?"

"No, but maybe Bob could teach us."

"That I'd like to see."

She stirred the paint. It was such a great color. She'd picked it out while Owen was out of town. He could afford decorators, but she couldn't, not on a detective's salary. And she didn't want to. She'd had visions of redecorating the bedroom together, but it wasn't working out that way.

Without looking at him, she continued. "Bob's annoyed with me. I sat outside last night reading a history of Satan while I waited for you. The man who drowned the other night was obsessed with devil imagery."

"Bob thinks you're wasting your time?"

"I'm bucking him and everyone else I work with. We're all under pressure to improve our percentage of solved cases, and this one—it's not even a case at this point, really. The preliminary work's done. I should wait for the full autopsy report. It could be a couple more weeks."

"You think you should wait, or everyone else thinks you should?"

"Both." She lifted the stirring stick out

of the paint and scraped the excess off on the edge of the can. "Something's not right about this man's death, Owen."

"In other words, as the lead detective, you don't believe waiting for the autopsy report is in the best interests of your investigation."

"That's a better way to put it than to tell me I'm just being difficult." She looked up at him from her paint can. "I love you, Owen. You know that, don't you?"

"Never a doubt. Abigail—"

She jumped in before he could finish. "The color will darken when it dries."

"It'll be perfect. But you're not going to paint today, are you?"

She rolled back onto her heels, not responding right away. One of the many things she loved about him was his insight—she didn't have to constantly explain herself. "I haven't decided. I admit I'm preoccupied. I can't shake this Sarakis thing. I keep thinking I'm missing something, and someone's going to end up hurt if I don't figure out what."

"Do what you have to do today, Abigail."

"We're grilling tonight. Keira and Simon will be here by then, won't they?"

Owen nodded. "I'm picking them up at the airport."

"I don't like this, Owen. I'm glad to know the Irish police are investigating. What if some nut followed Keira to Ireland and tried to kill her? It could all be a bizarre mix of accident, coincidence and her imagination. But I'd want to know more if I were an Irish detective."

"You want to know more as a Boston detective."

She sighed. "I guess I do. Can't help it."

"Simon's on the case. He's got contacts even I don't know about." Owen stepped into the room and kissed her softly. "You know you could paint this room chartreuse for all I care, don't you? I'm not looking at the walls when I'm in here."

She laughed. "I should call that bluff and exchange my pretty blue for a really ugly chartreuse and see how you like it."

He left, and thirty seconds later, Abigail did exactly as he predicted and gave up on painting. She placed the top back on the can, tapped it down tight and got to her feet, part of her wishing he'd kicked over the paint can and swept her off to the beach for the day. They could be in southern Maine in less than two hours, depending on traffic.

Getting out of her way, going off to Beacon Hill, had nothing to do with painting the bedroom or her preoccupation with the drowning in the Public Garden. Owen was simply giving her room to figure out what was going on with her.

And wasn't that part of why she'd fallen in love with him?

She headed through her small, IKEA-decorated kitchen out to the backyard. Hers was the first-floor and the smallest of the three apartments in the Jamaica Plain triple-decker she'd bought with Bob and Scoop Wisdom, an internal affairs detective. Abigail had heard Scoop leave early for work and thought Bob had gone off, too, but she found him out back drinking coffee and cleaning the grill.

"I just saw Owen," Bob said. "Why aren't you with him?"

"I'm painting the bedroom."

"No, you're not. You're messing with that accidental drowning."

She knew he'd said "accidental" deliberately to get under her skin. "You know damn well it hasn't been determined—"

"Officially it hasn't." He dug his grill scraper into a baked-on hunk of black gunk. "I don't know what's going on with you and Owen, but you two need to talk before someone besides me notices it's affecting your work."

"Nothing's going on with Owen and me, and my work's fine. Since when are you the relationship expert, anyway?"

He ignored her, flipping the black glob onto a paper towel. He wore shorts, a Red Sox T-shirt and sports sandals—not an outfit he'd wear to work. "Take it from someone whose had two marriages go sour on him. It's worse when you're lying in bed alone again, and you know you should have just let it out, talked. Maybe it would have helped save things, maybe it wouldn't have, but you'd know you'd done everything you could."

Abigail didn't want to talk to him about

relationships. "You're not going in to-day?"

"Nope. Abigail, you need to listen to me." He pointed his grill-cleaning brush at her. "You were on your own for seven years. You spent those years focused on becoming a detective and finding your husband's killer."

"I lived my life, Bob," she said quietly, knowing he wasn't going to quit until she said something.

"Yeah, but your life revolved around finding Chris's killer. Everything else came second. You know it did. You got your answers last summer, but you didn't have a chance to absorb them before you and Owen fell like bags of rocks for each other." Bob attacked the grill again. "I don't think you know if you want to stay a detective."

"That's insane. What else would I do?"

"Wrong question. Ask yourself if being a detective matters to you today as much as it did last summer before you got that tip that sent you to Maine."

To Mount Desert Island, she thought, where her husband had been born and raised. Where he'd died on his honeymoon, on the rocky coastline between his childhood home and Owen's summer home. Chris's killer had lain in wait for him, shot him, left him to die. Owen found his dead friend the next morning. Now, eight years later, Abigail had what people called—awkwardly, inadequately—closure.

"I'm not asking myself anything," she told Bob.

"Then you've been hanging around me too long. This job doesn't make it easy to talk. We get used to just not going there. To bottling it up." He managed a grudging grin. "Only, I'm not that deep. Nothing to bottle up."

"Owen and I are fine," Abigail said, feeling her prickliness return. "I'm almost finished with the book Charlotte Augustine loaned me. You know, Lucifer is a fallen angel."

Bob glared at her. "So?"

"Keira went to Ireland to investigate an old story about a stone angel twenty-four hours after finding Victor Sarakis—"

"You want to jerk my chain, fine," Bob said, dropping his wire brush onto the grill. "But you just remember. I'm a senior detective who can kick your ass from here to Bunker Hill if you don't straighten out."

Abigail didn't back down. "My gut tells me there's a connection between Victor Sarakis's death and what happened to Keira in Ireland. Your gut would, too, if you weren't emotionally involved."

She knew questioning his judgment and instincts—telling him outright that he was, in fact, emotionally involved in her case—would set him off, and it did. He glared at her, his entire face turning red. "I'm getting you pulled off this investigation."

"Just try it. See what I do."

He turned purple, swore under his breath and thundered up the outside stairs to his third-floor apartment.

Abigail exhaled, feeling lousy. Bob was her friend, and he'd had a rough couple of days. She had no business baiting him that way.

She debated following him upstairs to apologize, but rejected the idea. They'd just end up in a bigger fight.

Neither one of them could get along with anyone these days.

She went back inside, grabbed her car keys and headed out.

Jay and Charlotte Augustine's Back Bay showroom was located above an upscale health club with lots of sweating, intense, skinny people on treadmills, stair-climbers, elliptical machines, exercise balls. The treadmills had their own televisions, and most of the machines were placed in front of tall windows that overlooked the street. Abigail used the BPD gym. It wasn't bad, but it was perfunctory.

She took a claustrophobic little elevator up to the renovated brick building's third floor. It let her out into a reception area that consisted of an oak rolltop desk, an unoccupied ergonomic swivel chair and a library table that held a telephone, computer and crates of manila files. Behind the desk was a floor-to-ceiling partition and a locked door that, presumably, led to the main room.

The door opened, and Liam Butler, Victor Sarakis's graduate student assistant, poked his head out. "Hey, Detective," he said. "I thought I heard the elevator. What's up?"

"I wanted to stop by and thank Mrs. Augustine for a book she gave me."

"I know the one—I suggested it. Fascinating, isn't it? Believe it or not, there are entire college courses on the devil. Victor could have taught one—he was that knowledgeable on the subject."

"What about you?"

"I'm not that wild about it, to be honest. I had nightmares when I first started working for him, but I got over my resistance after a while. Victor understood. He said it was natural to be reluctant to confront evil, even on an intellectual basis. Part of the deal, really."

"A defense mechanism," Abigail said casually, then nodded to the open door. "Mind if I have a look in there?"

"If I said no, you'd need a warrant, right?"

"If you said no, I'd leave."

"Gee, don't tempt me. But it'd be provocative, wouldn't it? If I just told you to get lost?"

She didn't answer. She'd need more

time with Liam Butler, she decided, to have a better sense of him. The outfit he had on looked like the same one he'd worn the other day, but she couldn't tell for sure. His hair was greasier—she doubted he'd showered. She didn't know if that was the norm for him or if the sudden death of his landlord, friend and employer had yanked him out of his routines. He seemed as easygoing as he had been at their first encounter with Jay Augustine in Victor's devil room. Abigail knew from personal as well as professional experience that not everyone handled loss in the same way. From what she'd seen so far, Liam's behavior—even tweaking her over a search warrant—wasn't entirely out of the ordinary.

"I have a key, in case you're wondering," he said. "I check on the place when Jay and Charlotte are out of town—once or twice a week, at most."

"They don't have employees?"

"Sometimes they hire a tempt to sit at the front desk, but that's only if paying customers are coming by and they need the extra help. They don't keep regular hours. Most of the people who come here have appointments."

"Do the Augustines know you're here now?"

He shrugged. "I don't know. I haven't seen them. I guess we're all still trying to get our heads around what's happened." He held open the door and motioned with one arm. "Care to have a look around? I was only joking around about the warrant. No one's got anything to hide, Detective."

Abigail entered a room that looked as if it took up all or most of the third floor of the narrow building. Larger items—furniture, statues, trunks—were arranged on the floor in what looked to be an orderly fashion. She peeked at deep shelves filled with colorful pottery vases, small statues of animals and naked warriors, an ornately carved box and an ancient-looking bronze falcon.

"Jay and Charlotte keep good records," Liam said. "They know everything in here, right down to the mice turds."

Abigail smiled at his infectious humor. "Do they have a specialty?"

"They have to be pragmatic, but

they'd deal exclusively in Classical and early Medieval works if they could."

"European?"

"Ideally, I guess."

She wandered between stacks of wooden crates. "Give me some examples."

"I don't know—I have a hard enough time keeping track of Victor's collections. Jay and Charlotte don't keep their really good stuff here. I know that much. A lot of it's museum quality, and they just don't have that level of security in this showroom. Their most valuable items are specially handled and go right from the seller to the buyer. They're known for being knowledgeable and trustworthy."

"Do they do a good business?"

"They make most of their money on a handful of deals a year—according to Victor, at least."

Abigail had no reason to doubt Liam's information. "The history I read says that anthropomorphic images of Satan didn't take hold until around the sixth century. Would the Augustines be interested—"

"They aren't into the devil the way Victor was. Most of their customers aren't, either."

"So a Medieval statue of Lucifer wouldn't interest them?"

"I doubt it, but I guess it'd depend. There are alternative religious subjects—happier ones. They deal in a lot of jewelry and household items." Liam gave an irreverent grin. "You'd be surprised how popular chamber pots are."

Abigail heard the elevator open.

"Oops," Liam said. "Guess you're caught. The pesky detective returns with more questions."

She ignored him, and he followed her back out to the reception area.

Both Augustines looked startled to see her, but Jay recovered first, greeting Abigail politely. "Detective Browning, it's good to see you. What can we do for you?"

She didn't give him a direct answer. "It's an interesting business you have. Do you deal in Irish-Celtic pieces?"

"When we can get them," Charlotte said, obviously awkward.

Abigail doubted Charlotte had told her husband about giving the detective investigating her brother's death a book on the devil. Clearly, it would be simpler for the Augustines if Victor's death were ruled an accident.

"Any Celtic work is in high demand," her husband added.

Abigail didn't pursue the subject and guiltily wondered if she would have if Bob had been with her. "Could Mr. Sarakis have stopped by here—"

"The night he died?" Charlotte asked, gulping in a breath. "No, I don't think so."

"Did he have his own key?" Abigail asked.

Liam shook his head. "Not on him. I had it."

Jay sat at the rolltop desk and spun the chair around, turning on the computer. "Anything else, Detective? Please feel free to look around as much as you'd like, but if you don't mind, we have work to do."

"I'm done for now."

"Where's your partner?" Charlotte asked.

Jay tapped the computer keyboard. "She's here on her own," he said, giving

Abigail a cool look. "Aren't you, Detective?"

She didn't answer. "If you think of anything else, you know how to reach me."

When she headed back down the elevator, Abigail checked with the health club to ask a few questions. The manager wasn't in, but she left her card with a skinny kid at the front desk. "Please ask him to call me." She pointed to the computer. "Do people who use the club sign in and out?"

"Just in," he said.

"You keep the records?"

"Uh-huh. They're all on computer."

"Do the Augustines belong to the club?"

The kid nodded. "Mrs. Augustine comes in more than her husband. When he does, though—man, he goes at it like you wouldn't believe. Uses every machine in here."

Abigail couldn't help but smile. "Thanks for your help."

"You bet."

As she left, he gave her a little salute. She laughed and headed out to her car, realizing she'd just accomplished ex-

actly nothing. She drove the few blocks
to Beacon Street and parked in front of
the Garrison house. When she opened
her car door, she heard Irish music and
remembered it was her day off. She
didn't have to be talking about devils
and Medieval art and health club proce-
dures. She could be dancing with Owen,
even if neither of them could dance.

Before she could get out of her car, her
cell phone rang, and a man with a heavy
Irish accent identified himself as Seamus Harrigan, a detective with the Irish
Garda. "I'm returning your call, Detective Browning. What can I do for you?"

Abigail remained behind the wheel and
shut the car door. "I'd like to talk to you
about a case on the Beara Peninsula."
She hesitated a fraction of a second. "It
involves an American named Keira Sullivan."

~Chapter 20

Beara Peninsula, Southwest Ireland
8:00 p.m., IST
June 23

Eddie O'Shea hunched his shoulders against the fierce wind and lashing rain. A proper gale had kicked up since the guards and the Americans had left. How poetic, he thought, holding his cap on his head as he pushed on up the dirt track. He'd left his pub in his brother Patrick's hands, but there wouldn't be a crowd—surely he wouldn't manage to burn the place down before Eddie could get back.

Rain pelted his face with such force it

might have been hundreds of tiny needles. The landscape was all gray and green. It seemed fine and normal to him, but he expected that Keira Sullivan would have found a way to capture it in a painting and make it feel special. Eddie had lived on this land his entire life. His ancestors went back a thousand years or more on the Beara, or so his mother had insisted—and who was he to argue?

A Yank with Irish blood coming to the village because of an old story about fairies and other such nonsense wasn't all that unusual. Eddie didn't pay attention to such things, typically.

But this story, and this Yank, were different.

He came to a dip in the upward sweep of the hills and crossed a wooden bridge over a winding stream, just as he had ever since he'd first sneaked off from his mother the first time at three years old.

He paused at the fence and caught his breath, shifting to keep the wind at his back. The grass and the rocks would be slick. The ground would be muddy.

There'd be manure piles to navigate. Eddie had no illusions that he'd have ever made a good farmer.

I don't want to go into the pasture.

But he knew he had to, if any measure of peace of mind was to be his.

The guards, Keira and the big man—Simon Cahill—had crawled around in the old ruin without finding a thing except the bloody remains of a dead sheep. Eddie had pried at least some of the details from Seamus Harrigan, a regional detective with the Garda who'd stopped by the pub for a bowl of soup. Harrigan didn't know what to make of the American folklorist and her tale, but they hadn't found her backpack in the rubble—or, he'd said, any Irish artifacts. Nothing. Harrigan had said "artifacts" with a scowl. But he didn't disbelieve her. He'd told Eddie that Keira had been sincere—and quite beautiful. He just didn't know what was fact and what was imagination.

Harrigan had liked Cahill, too. Everyone did.

Eddie frowned at the fence. He'd stalled long enough. He'd have been over it by now as a boy. He stood on a rock to give him more height, and felt a pull in his thigh as he climbed over the fence, catching his trousers on a sharp barb. He could just hear his brother snorting with laughter—not Patrick, the brother minding the pub. He was an aimless, jobless ne'er-do-well if there'd ever been one, but always cheerful, not a bad word to say about anyone. Eddie couldn't say that about Aidan, a farmer and the eldest of the O'Shea brothers.

Three of them—just as in the old story their grandmother had told their mother and she had told her sons.

The same story that had lured Keira Sullivan to Ireland, and her mother before her.

Has to be. It's all that makes sense.

Eddie's boot sank two inches into the muck and manure on the opposite side of the fence, but he managed not to fall. He preferred to stay in the pub on such days. Whip up a mutton stew, sweep the floors or just sit with a pint and con- template his life.

More by instinct than memory, he found his old boyhood trail that ran across the open pasture above the stream. He and his brothers had taken it a thousand times. There were several more fences to cross and more wind and rain to brave. When Eddie started down into the trees, he felt a mix of trepidation and excitement. He was out of the worst of the gale now, and he could see matted grass where Keira, Simon and the guards had come through.

Eddie had known they wouldn't find anything.

Thirty years ago, Keira's mother had gone exploring out in this same spot. She took the bus from Dublin and camped in the hills by herself, and Eddie and his brothers, just teenagers themselves, hadn't bothered her. These were the days before Ireland's economic boom—long before the Beara Way, the nearly two-hundred-kilometer mix of marked trails, lanes and roads that snaked down one side of the peninsula and back up again. It was popular with walkers and bikers, and Eddie had seen a boost in business, thanks to its proximity to his pub. But the isolation and remoteness of the Beara hadn't seemed to bother Eileen O'Reilly.

She hadn't been pretty—certainly not the striking beauty her daughter was—but Eddie remembered she'd had a nice manner about her. She'd talked to his mother about the story of the three brothers and their dance with the fairies over the stone angel. Even then, his mother was apparently the only one left in the village who'd ever heard of the tale. She believed, as Eileen did, that the back-and-forth between the brothers and the fairies would resume if the angel were ever found. That it was meant to be.

Eddie had never spent so much as two seconds of his life looking for the thing.

He didn't believe the stone angel existed, and he didn't believe in fairies, either.

So why are you here instead of in your warm, dry pub?

Disgusted with himself, Eddie crept through the wet grass and undergrowth to the ruin, as gray as the sky above him. The place was no secret to him. No great discovery. He and his brothers had

come out here many times. If there'd
been an ancient angel to find, surely
they'd have found it. But he hadn't been
out to the ruin in years, and he knew his
brothers hadn't.

In her last hours, his mother had
begged Eddie to tell her the story she'd
told him and her mother had told her.
*"The one about the farmer, the hermit
monk and the ne'er-do-well. Tell me that
one, Eddie, my good boy."*

He'd sat on a wood stool by the fire
and told it to her over and over as he
watched her fade away.

*"I'm going to the angels, Eddie...I can
see Saint Ita now..."*

His mother had been a faithful church-
goer and believed in angels, and in
fairies, too. None of it mattered to Eddie.

She died two days after Eileen O'Reilly
had gone home to Boston.

The rain eased, and Eddie walked
closer to the ruin. A fallen tree lay half in
the stream—Seamus Harrigan had described how he and Simon had dragged
it there from in front of the hut's open
doorway. They'd discovered the re-

mains of the ladder Keira had built for her escape, but nothing else.

Eddie felt terrible that she'd been up here, trapped and frightened, and he'd been none the wiser. He and his brothers would have gladly come to her rescue. But that was another part of her tale that Harrigan had found both amusing and curious—Keira's insistence that for most of the night and day she was stuck in the ruin, she was unafraid, confident of her ability to get out of there on her own.

Having known her just a short time, Eddie was nonetheless unsurprised by her strength and determination, never mind how those same qualities could also lead her astray.

He approached the entrance to the old hut and saw clearly how the hillside had eroded under the front corner on the chimney side. Keira had been lucky, indeed, not to be killed or seriously injured.

But what was this?

Eddie frowned, gingerly making his way to the spot where the uprooted tree had been. A holly tree grew up the hill close to the chimney—or what remained of it—and there, leaning into its waxy leaves and healthy branches was a shovel, as if a farmer had abandoned it moments ago.

Had the guards used it to dig in the ruin when they'd looked around here this morning?

But no, Eddie thought, rubbing his fingertips over the top of the shovel's sturdy wooden handle. It wasn't left here by a farmer or the guards. He couldn't say who'd left it, but he knew it had been left for him, put there against the holly tree as if whoever had done it had known he would come and figured he'd be fool enough to miss it if it wasn't right there under his nose.

Rain ran off the end of Eddie's cap as he squatted for a closer look. Bits of gray mortar were stuck to the blade and there were fresh nicks, indicating the shovel had been used recently.

There you have it.

Eddie rose and pulled off his cap, smelling the wet wool as he ran his forearm across the top of his head. Someone had been digging here. And the digging had caused the old hut to cave in while Keira was inside, escaping her black dog.

Digging for what?

But Eddie knew the answer to that question.

Digging for the stone angel in his mother's story.

He remembered how Eileen O'Reilly had returned to the village that fall, and never mind the wool cape she wore, it was easy enough to see she was expecting a baby. She'd stayed for a week that time, roaming the hills in every manner of weather, speaking to no one. Eddie had wanted to help her, but what could he do? He and his brothers had just buried their mother.

"Ach," he said aloud, "that was a long time ago."

Eddie picked up the shovel and placed it on his shoulder. If it'd been left for him, then it was up to him to figure out what to do with it, wasn't it?

When Eddie was within a few yards of the dirt track, something by the rocks on a steep incline above him drew his eye.

The rain was pounding again. The wind howled, and fog surged down from the hills like a live thing. He pictured himself back at the pub with a mug of coffee laced with whiskey and whatever Patrick had prepared for supper—it wouldn't be any good, whatever it was, but it'd be hot.

Wiping rain off his face with cold fingers, Eddie tried to make out what was up there on the hill. Whatever it was, it didn't belong there or he wouldn't have noticed it.

Dread tightened in his chest.

I don't want to go up there.

But even as he formed the thought, he was on his way. The hill grew steeper, and he lowered the shovel and used it as a walking stick, although he knew he'd be destroying any trace evidence on it. He watched the detective shows. He knew about such things.

He was panting now from the exertion, and the rain was coming down so hard, whenever he took a breath he'd get a mouthful. Rocks abounded, big enough to serve as places to sit and look out at the landscape, in fairer weather and if he ever had a mind for gazing at the scenery.

He didn't see anything but rock, grass, sheep and sheep dung. He leaned on the shovel, ready to give up—eager to believe whatever he'd seen had been a trick of his imagination.

As he stood up straight, he felt his heart skip and his chest tighten further, so that his breaths came only in shallow gasps, as if his body was responding already to what his mind couldn't grasp.

Slumped amid the rocks was a dead sheep—or what was left of her. Her woolly coat soaked up the rain. Even from where he stood, Eddie could see she'd been dead for at least a few days.

She hadn't died of natural causes.

He saw that, too. Saw that some evil bastard had brutalized the poor creature, tortured her without mercy until she breathed her last.

He'd never seen such a sight in all his life.

Eddie made a sign of the cross, grabbed the shovel and ran, slipping on wet rock and grass, stepping in dung and mud as he tried to keep his footing on the steep slope.

He had to get the guards, call Seamus Harrigan and tell him what he'd just seen.

And he had to get that image out of his mind, he thought desperately, although he knew he never would.

The image of that sorry, innocent beast would be with him until his dying day.

Eddie arrived at his pub soaked to the bone, with the shovel heavy on his shoulder and his heart still racing from fear and horror. The rain had stopped, and he decided he'd get warm and dry before he called the guards.

As he lowered the shovel from his shoulder, he automatically glanced at the picnic table next to the pub entrance to see if Patrick hadn't cleaned up out here. It would be just like him to forget. Even with the rain, people would come outside for a smoke.

Eddie noticed a backpack on the table's back bench. It wasn't the first time a hiker or cyclist had left one behind. He set the shovel down and had a look, unzipping the main compartment, welcoming the chance to do something ordinary—something to take his mind, even for a moment, off the shovel, the dead sheep...his deep uneasiness about what was to come.

He found a flashlight, a compact emergency blanket, a Boston Red Sox cap.

His heart thumping, Eddie dug deeper into the backpack and pulled out a sketchpad and a plastic bag of artist's pencils.

He stood up straight, shocked down to his toes and no longer cold or hungry.

It was Keira's missing backpack, sitting out here in front of his pub as big as life.

~Chapter 21

Boston, Massachusetts
4:00 p.m., EDT
June 23

A part of Keira knew she was dreaming again. Another part was convinced that Simon was making love to her. That the feel of his hands on her was real. His mouth, his tongue. They'd come together in the sunlight—somewhere. She didn't know where, but it didn't matter. He was unrelenting, caring, so incredibly sexy. He thrust deeply into her, and she gave herself up to a thousand different sensations, a want that was as emotional as it was physical.

A noise jolted her awake.

"We're landing," Simon said next to her.

Keira sat up straight, still aroused. He was working a Sudoku puzzle. He gave no indication she'd cried out in orgasmic ecstasy in her sleep—which meant she hadn't, because otherwise, he'd have said so.

"Dreaming?" he asked.

"Not about slugs and spiders." She noticed he'd nearly erased a hole in one of the squares on his puzzle. "You're not supposed to guess, you know. It just messes you up more."

"I didn't guess. I just was wrong."

"Well, it's a seven."

He glanced at her. "You can't know that in two seconds."

"No, I can. Look. There's a seven in the box above and a seven in the box below and—"

"Right. It's a seven." He smiled at her. "I hate this game."

In ten minutes, they were on the ground. Keira set her watch back on Eastern Daylight Time. She hadn't been in Ireland long enough for her body to adapt to Irish Summer Time, but it wasn't on Boston time, either. Two flights across the Atlantic in one week— never mind the rest of what she'd experienced—had taken a toll.

So had sitting thigh-to-thigh with Simon on a plane for seven hours. Every nerve ending in her body seemed electrified. He, on the other hand, struck her as completely unaffected by their proximity.

Suddenly hot, she slipped off her sweater. "I hope you and Owen have Fast Rescue business you can discuss. I wouldn't want you making this trip for nothing."

He shrugged. "I'm not that involved with Fast Rescue business."

"What about your job?"

"I'm between assignments."

"Do you have a family you could visit?" She grabbed her bag from under the seat, trying to stave off a sudden sense of panic at having Simon attach himself to her. "A father, mother, brothers, sisters, ex-wives, pets, estranged children—someone?"

He shut his Sudoku book. "None of the above."

"You're not all alone in the world, are you?"

"I didn't say that."

"What about girlfriends, a fiancée, an ex-fiancée you owe money?"

His vivid green eyes sparked with amusement. "Panicked at the idea of having me around, are you, Keira?"

"I don't need a bodyguard, and I'm sure you have better things to do—"

"Not today I don't." He got to his feet, easing into the center aisle. As big as he was, he moved gracefully. "Relax. It's not unusual for someone to bond with their rescuer."

"You didn't rescue me."

"Did I or did I not pull you out of that place?"

"You did, and I'm grateful, but I'm sticking to my story that I would have gotten out of there on my own."

"Tell it to your grandkids."

He didn't relent as they got off the plane. By the time they went through customs and met Owen, Keira had let go the last of her erotic dream. But she still made sure that Simon sat up front with Owen and not in the backseat with her.

"Your uncle's invited you to dinner," Owen said.

"Summoned or invited?" Keira asked.

"Is there a difference with him?" Owen merged into a line of traffic exiting the airport. "He won't say so, but he's glad you got out of Ireland in one piece."

"I was never in any real danger."

Neither man in the front seat responded, and Keira sat back, jet lag and erratic sleep gnawing at her. And nerves, she admitted. She was accustomed to being on her own, not having anyone fretting about her. She could be smart, stupid, reckless, cowardly—who would care? She had friends and colleagues, but no one who'd even think to sound the alarm when she didn't call from Ireland as promised. Having Bob O'Reilly as an uncle when she lived in San Diego was very different now that she was in the same city with him.

And men, she thought, noticing the black waves of Simon's hair in the late-afternoon east-coast light. She recalled the sensation of running her fingers through his hair as if it'd been real and not just an adrenaline-generated dream. She'd hardly dated since moving to Boston. Before that—the truth was, there'd never been anyone remotely like Simon in her life. Which threw her more than the idea that her intense reaction to him was natural, expected even, under the circumstances. Falling for him just wasn't going to get her anywhere.

Simon looked relaxed, not the least bit torn about having kissed her. "So, Owen," he said casually, "have you and Ab set a wedding date?"

Owen didn't answer right away, then said simply, "No."

"What's the delay?"

Keira raised her eyebrows at Simon's bluntness, but Owen kept his tone even. "There's no delay. Abigail's preoccupied with her work right now. She can have all the time she needs. I'm patient."

"Don't let her mistake patience for indifference."

"Words of wisdom from Simon Cahill?"

"Damn straight. Marriage will change your lives. You'll want kids, right? You've got places here, in Austin, in Maine. You come and go as you please right now. Ab dives into a case. She's a dog-with-a-bone sort of detective."

"Simon, you're giving me a headache."

"Ab's got all this on her mind, Owen. Mark my words."

"She hates being called Ab."

"What about Abby?"

"Hates that, too."

Simon grinned. "Good to know."

Abigail was pacing in her kitchen when Owen arrived with Keira and Simon. Despite Owen's warning, Keira was surprised at how preoccupied and agitated the BPD detective looked.

Simon, undeterred, walked up to Abigail and slung a big arm over her shoulder. "Hey, Ab, when's the wedding?"

She gave him a dark look and slid out from under his arm. "Don't think I can't take you on, Cahill, because I can."

"Did I just get deleted from the wedding guest list?"

"You were never on it." Her expression softened as she turned to Keira. "Bob's out back waiting for you. I'm waiting for a call."

They all took the hint and headed out to the small backyard.

Scoop Wisdom was on his knees in his tidy vegetable garden. "Hey, Keira," he said, rising with a metal colander of fresh-picked peas tucked under one well-muscled arm. He was a compact, bulldog of a man with a shaved head and a take-no-prisoners demeanor. "Welcome home. Good flight?"

"It was long."

He glanced at Simon and grinned. "I'll bet."

Bob O'Reilly thumped down the stairs from his third-floor apartment and sighed at Keira. "You look like you just got plucked from an Irish ruin in the nick of time. Scare the hell out of me, why don't you?"

"I'm sorry I worried you."

He grunted. "You've been going off like that since you were a little kid. You'd think I'd be used to it."

"I've also been very good at taking care of myself since I was a little kid."

"No choice, seeing how your mother

was in another world half the time. A good thing you grew up in the country. When you were four years old, Eileen called me in a panic because she couldn't find you. One minute, you're drawing pictures on the back porch. Next minute, you're off in the woods. Packed yourself a couple of slices of bread and went in search of fairies or some damn thing."

"Frogs," Keira said. "I remember."

Simon, looking amused, sat at the round plastic table and stretched out his legs, his hands folded on his stomach as he watched her and her cop uncle. She was too restless to sit. "I'm not four anymore, Bob," she said.

"Twenty-nine doesn't seem so old to me, either." He nodded to Simon. "Thanks for rescuing her."

Simon leaned back deeper into his chair. "Not a problem."

"I know Keira insists she was three seconds from getting out of there on her own—"

"More like three minutes," she said.

Her uncle pointed a thick finger at her. "Don't think you're not like your mother, because you are. Instead of copying Bible verses on goatskin and living alone in the woods, you paint pictures of fairies and thistle and go off to the wilds of Ireland by yourself. No damn difference."

"She doesn't use goatskin—she uses a beautiful cotton paper. The true illuminated manuscripts were done on vellum made from the skins of cows, goats or sheep, but the real thing is hard to come by these days and very expensive."

"You're pushing my buttons, Keira."

Scoop stepped out of his tiny garden with his colander of peas. "What's this about your sister, Bob?"

"Nothing." He snatched up a can of charcoal lighter fluid, squirting it over the heap of charcoal. "Forget it."

Keira noticed Simon's eyes narrowed on her as if he'd just penetrated a secret corner of her life. She shifted her attention to Scoop. "My mother is a religious hermit. She lives alone in a cabin in southern New Hampshire."

"Since when?"

"Last summer. It's one reason I returned to Boston."

Scoop's shock was evident. Keira thought she understood. The younger detective had known her uncle for years. They'd worked cases together. But Bob had obviously never mentioned that his sister had become a religious hermit. "Is she—you know..."

"Mentally stable? Yes, she is," Keira said. "She's a kind, good person. I drove out to see her before I left for Ireland. She's doing well—she's working on an illuminated manuscript, a mix of calligraphy and illustrations of Bible passages. The true illuminated manuscripts are centuries-old—"

"Before printing presses," Scoop said, pragmatic.

Abigail emerged from her apartment, her expression tight as she pinned her gaze on Keira. "I just got off the phone with the Irish Garda detective you and Simon met this morning—"

"Seamus Harrigan." Keira sank onto a chair at the round table. "What's going on?"

"The village barman, Eddie O'Shea, came upon the carcass of the sheep that presumably was the source of the blood at the ruin where you were trapped."

"Had the dog—"

"No," Simon said, serious now, as he got up and stood behind Keira, putting a hand on her shoulder. "It wasn't the dog, was it?"

Abigail shook her head. "No. Someone deliberately brutalized the sheep. It was a female—she was carved up pretty bad." Abigail looked away a moment, staring at the ground as if she didn't want to make eye contact with anyone in the yard. "I guess it was a gruesome sight."

"The poor animal," Keira said, her stomach lurching as she thought of the blood, the entrails, the bits of wool at the ruin. She met her uncle's eyes, but he didn't say a word, and she shifted back to Abigail. "How's Eddie?"

Abigail gave a curt sigh. "Shaken up, according to Harrigan. O'Shea's been around sheep all his life, and he's never seen anything like this."

"Where was the sheep in relation to the ruin?" Simon asked.

"About three hundred yards above it. It

was on a steep hill among a lot of rock, I gather. After you and Keira and the police all left, O'Shea went up to see the ruin for himself. He took a different route on the way back and spotted the sheep."

"So whoever it was—" Keira paused, picturing the beautiful, rugged landscape. "Whoever mutilated the sheep either gathered blood and entrails and took them down to the ruin or dragged the body up the hill."

"It's possible," Abigail said, "that this person was using the ruin as a hideout, or even a base for his games. Harrigan said they're looking for other mutilated animals and checking for any reports of similar acts elsewhere Ireland. But they're keeping an open mind. They have to."

"Did Eddie see anyone?" Keira asked.

"Not that he's told the police, no. If you mean fairies—"

"I don't mean anything or anyone."

But even as Keira resisted Abigail's sudden scrutiny, Bob picked up a bag of charcoal and dumped a heap into the grill. "So, Abigail," he said, his tone deceptively mild. "What were you doing talking to our friends in the Garda?"

"Harrigan called."

"How'd he get your number?"

"I called and left it. I didn't know Harrigan would be the one to call me back. At first I had trouble understanding his accent, but hearing it just makes me want to check out Ireland one of these days."

"Abigail."

"I wanted to know what was going on, and I called. Simple."

"There's no connection between your drowning in the Public Garden and a bloody sheep carcass in Ireland."

Abigail ignored him and turned to Keira. "Would you mind taking us through what happened in Ireland? I know you've already spoken to Seamus Harrigan—"

"I don't have a problem going through it again," Keira said.

She expected her uncle to comment, but he didn't. Simon dropped into a chair next to her. Abigail, still visibly tense, sat in an Adirondack chair next to Owen, whose focus was almost entirely on her. Keira couldn't help but notice just how much he was in love with Abigail—and she with him. She'd automatically gravitated toward him. But her difficult mood was impossible to miss. She was just a year or two older than Keira but had pursued a single-minded dedication to law enforcement since the murder of her husband on their honeymoon eight years ago. Keira had never experienced such tragedy and violence in her own life.

Scoop settled at the table with his colander and, using his fingers, snapped off the ends of the peas one by one. Bob lit the coals and stood back, watching his grill, listening. Keira was most aware of Simon, sitting as still as he had throughout their flight, watching her as she told the story of how she'd ended up trapped in a ruin on a stretch of windswept Irish coast.

She kept to the facts and didn't elaborate, left out her emotions and questions. If she'd learned nothing else during her brief stay at the police academy, she'd learned how to talk to cops.

When she finished, Scoop, halfway

through his colander, shook his head. "I don't see how this ruin spontaneously collapsed. It must have had help."

"Maybe the fairies did it," Bob interjected.

Keira noticed a change in Abigail's expression. "There's more, isn't there?"

Abigail nodded. "I wanted to hear your story first. The barman says he found an old shovel at the ruin—before he ran across the sheep."

Simon sat forward. "Where?"

"Propped up against a tree where he couldn't miss it. Harrigan says it wasn't there this morning, or he'd have seen it."

"It wasn't there last night, either," Simon said.

Keira felt the late-day sun hot on the back of her neck. "I didn't see it. Do the police think someone went out to the ruin after we left this morning, before Eddie got there?"

"Possibly," Abigail said.

"I'm not going to get worked up over a shovel," Bob said, then glared at Abigail. "You're chewing on something else. What is it?"

She settled back in her Adirondack chair and addressed Keira. "Eddie O'Shea also discovered your backpack on a picnic table outside his pub."

This news got to Keira. "How did it end up at the pub? It was in the ruin—it got caught in the collapse. I don't know if it was buried in rubble or not. The police tried to look around inside this morning, but they didn't get far. Too risky."

"You'd just been through a difficult twenty-four hours," Abigail said, "and you were focused on the stone angel and then on the sheep's blood. Is it possible the backpack was within easy reach of the entrance, even with the collapse?"

"I don't know." Keira jumped to her feet, restless, more shaken than she wanted to admit. "The key to my rented cottage was in my backpack."

Abigail gave an almost imperceptible shake of her head. "It's not there now."

Scoop tossed the last of his snap peas in the colander. "That probably explains the unlocked door and missing note. Our guy lets himself in, finds the note, gets rid of it and forgets to lock up on his way out. He dumps the backpack, and some hiker finds it and leaves it at the pub."

"Maybe," Keira said. "But there was no way anyone could have known I wrote that note, and I didn't notice anything else missing."

"Harrigan plans to talk to Eddie O'Shea again tomorrow," Abigail said. "He'll go back up to the ruin and take another look."

Bob sighed at Keira. "I can't believe you went to Ireland chasing a fairy story."

"It's a great story, and I went to Ireland to do my work. You investigate homicides. I investigate old stories." Not investigate, precisely, but she'd made her point.

Her uncle stood back from the flames. "When I investigate a homicide, I'm never thinking fairies did it. You're not a detective, Keira. You don't think like one. You don't have the training."

"I didn't get trapped because I was trying to be something I'm not."

"No, I guess not." When he looked at her this time, his eyes were filled with pain and worry. "How bad was it in that place?"

Her throat caught. "Pretty bad." She attempted a smile. "There were slugs."

Scoop made a face. "I hate slugs." He nodded to his garden. "I had to go on the warpath against them during a rainy spell earlier this month. They were eating everything. What kind of slugs were in the ruin with you?"

"Black ones, about six inches—"

He shuddered. "Stop. I can't take it."

Even Abigail managed to grin at the prospect of Scoop Wisdom getting the creeps over slugs. "How did you learn about this story about the brothers and the fairies?"

Bob lifted a package of preformed hamburger patties out of a cooler. "What difference does it make?" He ripped open the package and started laying patties on the grill. "Scoop, you got enough peas for all of us?"

"More than enough," he said.

Abigail didn't relent. "The story, Keira?"

"Drop it," Bob said.

"I'm just asking a question, Bob. It's not an interrogation."

But it was, Keira thought with sudden clarity. Abigail was in detective mode, and it was irritating Bob. His reaction struck Keira as out of proportion to the offense, and she suspected it had something to do with her mother's trip to Ireland thirty years ago.

"Never mind," Abigail said quietly. "I'm sorry, Keira. You've had a long day—"

"A woman who lives on the street where my uncle and mother grew up told me the story. Supposedly my mother looked for the village when she was in Ireland before I was born."

Her uncle was seething. "She went to a lot of places when she was in Ireland, and it was thirty years ago. Leave her alone."

Keira turned to Simon and tried to lighten the mood. "Now I could use rescuing."

"Nah." He gave her a reassuring smile. "You're three minutes from crawling out of this one on your own, too."

"Can you sketch this angel for us?" Abigail asked. "The dog, the ruin?"

Keira didn't bother to hide her relief at the slight change in subject. "I can try."

"I'll see what I can scrounge up for drawing materials." Abigail retreated into her apartment, returning in a few moments with a stack of printer paper and a mug of colored pencils, crayons and markers. "I know these aren't the kind of supplies you're used to—"

"They're fine. Thanks."

"It'll help us visualize your experience, and it could jog your memory, produce some detail you haven't thought of."

Keira picked through the mug, choosing a black fine-point felt-tip pen. "I don't know if I can capture the moody beauty of that evening. My ancestors are from Ireland," she said. "My great-great-grandfather O'Reilly came over during the famine years in the late 1840s. My grandmother was born in Ireland."

"But this wasn't your first trip?" Abigail asked.

"My fourth. Eddie O'Shea and his brothers have lived on the Beara Peninsula their entire lives. Their family goes back there hundreds of years. Being a basic tumbleweed myself, I'm drawn to that sense of place—that continuity of home."

Simon leaned forward over the table without crowding her. "Is Patsy McCarthy from the Beara Peninsula?"

"No—another village in West Cork. Her grandfather worked in the copper mines. The copper veins drew ancient settlers—the ruin is up in the hills above a megalithic stone circle. Some people believe that's fairy ground."

She stared at the blank page a moment, visualizing the Irish landscape, the hidden ruin, the ivy, the snarling dog. *Had* the dog snarled? Had he meant to harm her? Or was he just reacting to the dead sheep?

"The sheep's blood wasn't there," she whispered. "Not when I arrived."

No one spoke, and she let her instincts lead her pen to the right spot on the paper. She drew quickly, but carefully, trying to get the details right without overfocusing on them.

She put the pen down. She was aware of the burgers sizzling on the grill. Scoop had gone upstairs with his colander. Abigail was leaned back in her chair,

Owen next to her, Bob still at the grill. Simon hadn't moved.

"I can't believe I felt safe when someone was smearing the blood of a murdered sheep a few yards from me." Keira looked at the two detectives and the two search-and-rescue experts. "Someone was there. I didn't imagine the voice."

"But you still felt safe," her uncle said, all the ferocity gone out of his voice now.

"Afterward. Not at first. But afterward—in the dark." She appraised her sketch. The basics were there. Dog, stream, gray stone, debris. The dead tree. At least a sense of the moody light. "Yes. I felt safe."

"What about the angel?" Abigail asked. "Can you draw it?"

"Not as easily. I can draw what I saw— what I remember. It won't have the kind of detail you're probably looking for." It took several false starts, several different pencils and markers, before she managed to draw an angel that even came close to what she'd seen that night. "I can't..." She sighed. "It was more beautiful than this. Truly a work of art."

Bob leaned over her shoulder. "Patsy's always liked her angels," he said.

Something in his voice made Keira look up, but he quickly returned to the grill. Scoop came down the back stairs with a bowl of steamed peas, and Abigail and Owen went inside and brought out a platter of paper plates, condiments, buns and a bowl overflowing with a green salad—a well-practiced ritual, Keira realized.

"Jet-lagged?" Simon asked, close to her.

She remembered the feel of his thick thighs against her on the long flight across the Atlantic. "Very. The sheep is disturbing, Simon. Eddie O'Shea didn't deserve to find such a horror. If I attracted whoever killed that poor animal to the village—"

"You're not responsible for what someone else does."

His clear, succinct words helped center her, but they didn't chase away all her sense of guilt at Eddie's grisly discovery. "It's not a coincidence," she said. "The story, my presence, the dead sheep."

"I don't think so, either."

And the man who'd drowned, she thought. Was his death not a coincidence, either?

"I'm going to see Patsy in the morning," she said abruptly.

Her uncle's eyes were half-closed. "She's an old woman, Keira."

"I know. I'll be careful what I tell her. I don't want to upset her. I just want to know if there's some part of this story—some tidbit her grandfather told her that she hasn't thought about in years—that could help make sense of things. Then I'll talk to Colm Dermott."

"Are you planning to go back to Ireland?" Abigail asked.

"I certainly hope to, but I'm not wild about staying in my cottage alone until I have a better fix on what's going on. Maybe the Irish police will trace the dead sheep back to some hiker who has nothing to do with me."

Her comment was met with silence, which Keira took as skepticism—they all believed the poor mutilated sheep had everything to do with her own ordeal.

With a sudden burst of energy, she reached for a bright green marker and drew a cheeky leprechaun on one of her discarded sheets.

Scoop Wisdom gave a mock shudder. "I don't know, Keira. I think I'd rather run into a mean black dog coming out of the Irish mist than that little sucker."

Everyone laughed, but when dinner was served, Keira didn't eat a bite.

~*Chapter 22*

Beacon Hill
Boston, Massachusetts
9:00 p.m., EDT
June 23

As soon as Owen pulled in front of the Garrison house on Beacon Street, Keira grabbed her brocade bag from next to her on the backseat and leaped out, shutting the door behind her. Simon watched her charge for the front door. "She's got a lot of energy for someone who's been through what she has in the past few days."

"She could just be anxious to put

some distance between you and her," Owen said.

"True enough."

"Simon—" Owen sighed, threw the car into Park. "What the hell's going on?"

"I wish I knew."

Simon kept his eyes on Keira as she set her bag on the step and dug out her keys. If she locked him out, he could always ask Owen to let him in. It had been a torturous flight. He'd done one damn Sudoku puzzle after another to stay awake. Whenever he'd dozed off, he'd ended up dreaming about making love to the woman next to him.

He acknowledged he was restless. He was accustomed to search-and-rescue missions and changing time zones—to long flights, as well.

So it had to be Keira. The mess she was in.

Kissing her out in the windswept Irish countryside.

"What about John March?" Owen asked.

An image of the FBI director's face wasn't exactly how Simon wanted his memory of kissing Keira interrupted, but nothing he could do now. "What about him?"

"Does he know you're here?"

"I left a message for him before I left London. Said I was off to rescue a damsel in distress." Simon shrugged. "He hasn't called back. The less you know about my business with March, Owen, the better. It hasn't followed me back here, if that's what you're asking."

"I don't know if I should have called you in London after all."

Simon summoned his sense of humor from deep inside. "And spared me a night in an Irish cottage with our flaxen-haired fairy princess?"

"Simon...I swear..." Owen sighed again. "Do you know what you're doing?"

"I'm about to carry my bag upstairs. How many flights up to the attic apartment with no phone?"

"Three. The last one's steep and narrow." Owen added dryly, "Don't trip."

Simon grabbed his own bag from the backseat, thanked Owen for the ride and, with a fresh burst of energy, headed for the elegant brick house, run-

ning up the steps and catching the front
door just before it could shut tight.

Keira had a decent jump on him. He
started after her, taking the stairs two
and three at a time, but dropped his
pace down to one. Owen hadn't been
kidding. The last flight of stairs in particular was steep and narrow, clearly not
built for someone Simon's size.

When he reached the attic, he noted
that Keira had left the front door slightly
ajar. He took that as a positive sign.

"You can come in," she said, "but
watch your head."

He had to duck to get through the
door. The apartment had low, slanted
ceilings, its open floor plan easing any
sense of claustrophobia. A pine table
doubled as a work space, an arrangement she'd duplicated at her Irish cottage. One edge of the table was lined
with art supplies. Open shelves held
books and additional supplies, and a
desktop computer with a massive flat
screen sat on a rickety-looking cart.

A couch, a chair and a coffee table
formed a small seating area in front of

three windows that looked out on Boston Common.

Simon plopped his bag onto the scuffed hardwood floor.

Keira's eyes were on him, serious. "I appreciate everything you've done for me, Simon. I know I've had a bad time of it, but I don't want to take advantage of your generosity."

"Tell me you want to stay here alone tonight in a way that I'll believe."

"I didn't—" She paused, obviously fighting to hang on to her self-control. "I didn't expect the sheep. I keep thinking about that blood. And the shovel—my backpack. I feel terrible for Eddie."

"He strikes me as a man who's seen a thing or two in his day."

"And he has his brothers and all those guys at the pub." The thought seemed to cheer her somewhat. "My backpack turning up is odd. Maybe Scoop's right and a hiker found it and just dropped it off at the pub and went on his way. But maybe it was someone who knew exactly what it was and left it for Eddie—someone who wanted to remain anonymous. Last night, Simon, you mentioned a man you saw—"

"You saw him, too, didn't you?"

She nodded. "I had a strange conversation with him the night before I was trapped. Nothing ominous—just unusual. Like he knew things about me."

"A fairy prince?" Simon's tone was only half lighthearted.

"A hard-bitten looking one, if he is," Keira said, almost managing a smile. "I'm not suggesting he's involved, certainly not that he'd brutalize a sheep."

"Seamus Harrigan seems competent. He'll investigate—"

"You're right."

"It's been a long day," Simon said simply.

She averted her eyes, and he could see that they'd filled with tears.

His heart nearly stopped. "Keira..."

"There's one more piece of this—I don't know where it fits, or even if it does fit. My mother came home from Ireland pregnant with me. She dropped out of college. She's never talked about what happened. When I ask her about my father, she just—" Keira sucked in a breath, turned to him. "She tells me that my father was John Michael Sullivan. And he was. I know that. He adopted me after he and my mother were married when I was a year old. He died in a car accident when I was three, and I barely remember him."

"I'm sorry, Keira."

"By all accounts, he was a wonderful man. My uncle thought the world of him. He was an electrician—salt of the earth. The rock my mother needed."

"You went to Ireland in search of your birth father?"

"Yes and no." All the tension and fear of the past few days seemed to have welled up inside her to the point of bursting. But she exhaled, blinking back any remaining tears. "I went because of Patsy's story—the book I'm doing. But also because I thought I might find some answers, or at least make my peace with not having them. I had a happy childhood, Simon. My mother's a loving, open woman, deeply committed to her faith. But over the past few years, she's pulled further and further away from everyone and everything she knows."

"And you blame yourself?"

"If this is what she wants, I can accept that. I just..." Keira raked her fingers through her hair, suddenly looking exhausted. "I keep thinking if I'd stayed closer to home, if I'd shown more interest in her life—"

"Keira, don't. You're not responsible for your mother's happiness."

"It's one thing to know that—it's another to feel it in your gut. The truth is, I'm not even sure she actually got pregnant when she was in Ireland."

"The monk in your story's a hermit. Do you think he inspired your mother in some way?"

She lifted her shoulders and let them fall in an exaggerated shrug. "Who knows?"

"So, I'm trying to picture your mother," Simon said. "Does she look more like her brother or more like you?"

Keira stared at him, and he thought he might have gone too far—but then he saw the spark in her eyes, the crack of a smile. "You're impossible, Simon. You know that, don't you?"

"Laugh hard, live long—or at least well."

He went over to her microscopic kitchenette and pulled two glasses and a bottle of Jameson's whiskey off an open shelf. Keira didn't need him there. She had all those cops she could call on in a pinch, and she was smart, capable and resourceful—not such a flake after all.

Maybe telling himself she was a flake was his own way of keeping his distance.

Not that he was doing a good job of it, he thought as he set the glasses on the foot of counter space and opened the whiskey, splashed some into the glasses.

He handed her a glass, watched her take a sip. "Keira, I want you to know that I don't make a habit of kissing someone I've just rescued. Never mind if that someone quibbles about who did the rescuing. This morning—"

"It seems like a million years ago, doesn't it?"

"Actually, no."

Color rose in her cheeks, but he decided it wasn't from embarrassment. She was remembering their kiss, too.

"Simon, I know you're doing a favor for Owen—"

"It's gone beyond that, Keira."

"I suppose it has. I don't even know that much about you, and—well, here we are." She spun over to the table with her glass of whiskey, but didn't sit down. "How did you get into search-and-rescue work?"

"I started picking up skills in high school and college." It was the truth as far as it went. "My father died when I was fourteen. Learning how to survive and to help other people in extreme conditions gave me something to do."

"What happened to your father?"

"He was killed in the line of duty. He was a DEA agent."

"How awful. Do you have any brothers and sisters?"

He shook his head. "Cousins, and my mother remarried not long after—a guy with three kids from a previous marriage." He walked over to the table and picked up a book with a beautifully illustrated cover of a girl running into a magical forest. He immediately recognized Keira's distinctive style. A collection of fairytales. Her photo with the flowers in her hair was on the back. "Is this a recent book?"

"Last year. Normally I don't keep my books out in the open—I prefer to focus on current projects. But I looked up a poem before I left for Ireland—"The Fairies," by William Allingham. '*Up the airy mountain, Down the rushy glen...*'"

"'*We daren't go a-hunting for fear of little men.*'"

Keira smiled, obviously pleased. "You know it?"

"My father taught it to me."

"It's a fun one. Some believe Irish fairies are angels who aren't good enough to be saved nor bad enough to be damned. Others believe they're the remnants of the old Irish pagan gods and heroes who went underground to live. I'm not trying to prove or disprove Patsy's story on any level—I just want to record it accurately. That comes first. Then I want to come up with illustrations that will capture its essence."

"Your personal connection?"

"I don't know for sure I really have a personal connection. I went to see my mother the afternoon before the auction, and she wouldn't tell me a thing."

Simon could see his comment had triggered Keira's tension again and shifted the subject. "Do you need quiet and solitude to work?"

"It depends." She pulled off her sweater and tossed it onto the back of a chair, looking more relaxed. "Sometimes I lose myself in what I'm doing and nothing distracts me. I could be anywhere, and it wouldn't matter. Other times I need total peace and quiet. I know I have an attic apartment, but I'm not exactly the artist-in-the-garret type."

"What about the cottage you rented in Ireland?"

"I expected to get a mix of time to myself as well as time with other people."

"You were also on a mission," he said.

She nodded. "I had personal as well as professional reasons to go to Ireland. I should have told you about the personal reasons." She took two quick sips of her drink and set the glass down, then pointed to her couch. "It's a pull-out."

"Unlike the couch at your Irish cottage," he said. "What'll you do if you have nightmares about slugs and spiders again tonight?"

"Trust me, I won't. I'll fetch some linens." She eyed him with a frankness he found both unsettling and sexy. "I can see you're not going to your boat."

She retreated into her bedroom. Simon sat on the sofa and put his feet up on the coffee table—it looked as if that was okay to do—and flipped through Keira's fairytale book. Her work, which clearly appealed to both adults and children, had heart, imagination and a style that was uniquely hers. Even the art snob at the auction had been captivated by the two paintings she'd donated, although he'd probably never admit it.

But she still didn't own a phone, Simon thought, getting to his feet when she returned with an armload of linens. He took them from her. "Go on to bed," he said. "I'll take it from here."

"I can help."

Watching Keira shake out sheets was

more than he could take right now if
what she wanted was sleep. "I can handle it."

"You've been at my side since you
yanked me out of the ruin," she said,
touching his arm. "Thank you."

"You're welcome. Now, that's it, right?
No more gratitude." He set the bedding
on a chair. "It gets in the way after a
while."

But she didn't take her hand from his
arm, and he knew it didn't have a damn
thing to do with gratitude. He was tired,
she was tired. Simon knew he should
just send her to bed and tell her to put a
chair in front of her side of the door and
he'd do the same on his side. So they
wouldn't be tempted.

He'd just never been one always to do
what he thought made sense.

He whispered her name, and it was
enough. They were kissing before he
knew he'd even moved. The taste of her,
the feel of her slim body against him,
were just what he'd imagined during the
long trip across the Atlantic.

Need ripped through him, immediate,
hot. He wanted to be inside her, now.

She opened her mouth to their kiss and pressed herself hard against him, as if she'd been thinking about this moment, practicing it in her mind.

"I dreamed about this on the plane," she said between kisses. "For all those hours. It was worse than my nightmare, I swear."

She laughed, and it was sexy and a little wild and good to hear. Simon relished the spark in her eyes, the flush in her cheeks as the trauma of the past two days receded. He scooped her up and laid her on the couch. She was slim and lithe and had long, graceful limbs that tantalized his imagination. The rugby shirt and jeans had to go. He wanted to feel her smooth skin in his hands. He wanted to taste every inch of her and make her ache for him.

Something in his expression must have alerted her, because she draped her arms around his neck, skimmed her fingers up into his hair, then locked her eyes with his. "Make love to me, Simon. Let me make love to you. It's right. I know it is."

"You trust your instincts."

"It's not just instincts." She lifted herself to him, kissed him. "Remember, I
brought water and food and a flashlight
with me out to the ruin."

"No rope," he said.

"If I'd had a rope, I'd have climbed out
of there in time to make that call to Bob,
and you'd still be in London. And, anyway, who goes hiking with a rope?"

He kissed her again, and it was all he
could do not to rip off all their clothes.
She slipped her hands under his shirt,
placing her palms on the small of his
back, and he caught the hem of her
shirt. He heard her breathe, give a small
gasp of awareness of what came next.
But he had her shirt off in seconds. He
cast it aside.

She lay back on the couch, and now
he saw a touch of self-consciousness in
her. He didn't look away. He gazed at
her, her skin creamy, almost translucent.

"You're beautiful," he said.

Her hands trembled, but not with
nervousness, he decided, as she went
to unfasten her bra. "I can't get
it...damn..."

Simon tried the clasp, couldn't get it

either, and just ripped it. "I'll buy you a new one," he said, tossing it onto the floor with her shirt. But she didn't say anything, and he wasn't sure she could. "I didn't do all those damn Sudoku puzzles on the plane for no reason."

He skimmed his hands over the swell of her breasts. She moaned softly, lying back onto a lacy pillow. He went with her, lost in the taste of her, the feel of her pulse quickening under his touch.

She started to wriggle out of her jeans, and he helped her, drawing them down her slender legs, adding them to the pile on the floor.

"I don't..." She fought for a breath. "I've never..."

"Never, what, Keira?"

"It's so fast. You, me."

"But it's right," he whispered, slipping his hand between her legs, felt her response, saw the same want and need in her eyes that were in him. "Tell me if you want me to stop."

"No. Oh, no." She smiled, moved against him as he eased his fingers into her. "Don't stop."

"Good," he said, and he circled,

probed and thrust, until finally she grabbed at his shirt.

"Your turn," she said raggedly, clawing at him.

They dispensed with his clothes, and she drew him back to her, drifting her fingers over his flesh just as he'd dreamed last night and again on the plane, but reality was ever so much better.

"Now," she said, guiding him to her. "Simon...please..."

He didn't hold back, and they joined together in a frenzied haze of desire, heat and hunger. His body was ahead of his mind, responding, giving, taking, never doubting. He felt her body shudder and quake beneath him, her fingers digging into his upper arms as she came and came, then came again. Finally, he let go, thrusting fast and deep and hard, aware of her clutching his hips now, drawing him into her, taking him with her as they rose to the next peak together.

In the stillness that followed, he felt her heart racing and smiled. "It's a wonder we didn't fall off this little couch."

"We managed to fit."

"Oh, yes," he said. "We certainly did."

He saw the flush in her cheeks, and she slipped out from under him, gathered up her clothes, pulled on her rugby shirt and underwear. Her blond hair shone in the city lights pouring through the small windows. Her eyes gleamed with that gorgeous cornflower blue. If she couldn't believe what they'd just done, she didn't show it.

She waved a hand at the bedding. "If you need help with the sofa bed, just let me know. It's still early, I know—my body's not on Irish time or Boston time. I'm beat."

"Keira."

"Don't say anything. Please. This was perfect. No regrets. I just..." She adjusted her shirt, pushed back her hair. "We both need to get some sleep."

"Not going to trust your invisible electric fence tonight?"

She grinned at him. "Not a chance," she said, heading into her bedroom and shutting the door firmly behind her.

Simon noticed a light under her door. Well, he thought, she had to be tired.

And he supposed part of her was thinking she needed to figure out what was going on before she got in over her head with him.

Part of him was thinking he should get a flight back to London in the morning.

But regrets?

No regrets, whatsoever, he thought, pulling open the sofa bed. The mattress was hellishly thin, but he'd endured worse conditions than an artist's garret on Beacon Hill. He shook out the sheets and a summer-weight blanket. A white lace sachet fell out, filled with some kind of scented herb. Lavender, he suspected.

And the lace would be Irish.

Of course.

⌐Chapter 23

Jamaica Plain, Massachusetts
9:30 p.m., EDT
June 23

Abigail brought a glass of white wine outside, thinking she'd be alone, but Bob was at the table with a beer, and Scoop was weeding his garden in the semidarkness of the long June night. Owen was back from dropping Keira and Simon off, but he was inside on a call from a training team in Hawaii.

Scoop stood up from his tomato plants. "Oh, my aching back," he said with a grin.

Bob grunted. "Do you even feel pain?"

"Only when I have to. This thing with Keira—I don't know. I'll be around to-morrow if you need any help."

"Thanks," Bob said, unusually somber.

But Scoop didn't respond, and Abigail could see they were all troubled by the news from Ireland. The mutilated sheep raised the stakes. She'd heard the con-cern in Seamus Harrigan's voice when he'd relayed Eddie O'Shea's discoveries to her, a marked change from when they'd talked earlier in the day. Clearly, the Irish detective didn't know just what they were confronting.

"I should be the one talking to this Irish cop," Bob said.

Abigail shook her head. "No, you shouldn't be."

He started to say something, but Scoop nodded toward the back steps. "Hey—look who's here."

Fiona O'Reilly jumped off the steps into the yard. "Hi, guys. Owen says he'll be out in a sec." She cheerfully kissed her father on the cheek. "How're you doing, Dad? You look grumpy."

"Hi, kid," Bob said, obviously strug-gling to dismiss his somber mood.

"What're you doing out running around in the middle of the night?"

"It's not even ten o'clock. I told Colm Dermott I was stopping by here, and he asked me to give this to Abigail." Fiona handed a file folder to Abigail. "I went to a lecture he gave at BU tonight on Irish folklore and the sea. It was amazing. I'm seriously considering switching my major to Irish studies."

"There are no more jobs for someone with a degree in Irish studies than a degree in harp," Bob said, teasing her, but he nodded to the folder. "What's that all about?"

Fiona shrugged. "I don't know. Colm didn't say."

"Shouldn't you be calling him Professor Dermott?"

"He said Colm is fine. He and Keira are friends— I love to talk about Irish music with him." She turned to Abigail and Scoop. "I'm majoring in classical harp, but I'm totally into Irish music right now. I still want to visit Keira in Ireland."

"Don't count on it," Bob said.

Fiona rolled her eyes. "I'm nineteen,

Dad. I have a passport. I can buy my own ticket and go."

"You're a student. You don't have any money. Besides, Keira's back in Boston, at least for a couple days."

"She is? Why? What happened?"

"Nothing you need to worry about. You have a ride back to your apartment?"

"Yeah," Fiona said, clearly distracted by news of her cousin's sudden return. "I just wanted to drop off the folder. Dad…"

Bob looked up at her. "Is your ride a he?"

"It's a friend."

"The fiddle player in your band?"

Abigail recalled a very cute fiddler the other night at the auction and noticed Fiona blush as she answered her father. "As a matter of fact."

"Why didn't he come in? What's he doing, sitting out in his car waiting for you?"

"Yes—"

"I'll walk you out," Bob said, but he reached over and tapped the folder. "Well?"

Abigail sighed, annoyed. "It's the guest

list for the auction at the Garrison house. I ran into Colm earlier today and asked him for it."

"You didn't run into him. You looked him up. Why?"

"You know why, Bob."

A muscle in his jaw worked. Scoop blew out a breath but said nothing.

Fiona frowned. "What's going on? Why's Keira back in Boston? What does this list—" She stopped, then winced. "Oh. I get it. You want to know if the man who died in the Public Garden was on his way to the auction. To see Keira? Is that what you think?"

"Abigail's speculating," Bob said, making it sound like an accusation.

Abigail tried not to let her irritation with him get to her. "It's an informal, incomplete list. Colm says they're not that sophisticated an operation."

Bob got to his feet. "You want to waste your time, fine." He turned to Fiona. "Let's go meet your fiddle player."

"Dad…"

"Did I ever tell you I took fiddle lessons as a kid?" he asked her.

That obviously piqued Fiona's interest,

but as she headed out with her father, she glanced back at Abigail with a worried look.

With O'Reilly father and daughter gone, Scoop shook his head at Abigail. "You're playing with fire. We're talking about Bob's family."

"I'm just doing my job." She flopped back in her chair. "I didn't mean for Colm to give these names to Fiona."

"That's the risk you took. Turn the Sarakis case over to someone else, Abigail."

Since Scoop never interfered with her conduct on the job or off, clearly he thought she was seriously out of line. Abigail drank some of her wine. "I'm not on a fishing expedition, and I'm not trying to provoke Bob. You tell me what you'd do, Scoop, under the circumstances."

"I just told you. I'd turn the case over to someone else."

"No, you wouldn't." She paused, feeling a twinge of guilt. "I didn't have a clue about his sister. Makes you wonder what else he hasn't told us, doesn't it?"

"Don't go there."

Abigail didn't back off. "Come on, Scoop. You don't like this situation any more than I do. Bob's sister is a religious hermit, and his niece goes off to Ireland to investigate an old story about a stone angel and is damn near killed—and I've got a dead guy who was obsessed with the devil."

"Would he have been interested in this missing angel?"

"Possibly. His sister and brother-in-law are dealers in fine art and antiques. They have a particular interest in Classical and Medieval works. I don't know where this angel falls—"

"Keira said it could be from Wal-Mart for all she knows."

"Someone messing with her head?"

"Maybe it was part of an animal sacrifice. Grab an angel statue, torture a sheep."

"That's sick," Abigail said. "From what I can gather, Victor Sarakis's interest in evil and the devil was intellectual—I don't see him having anything to do with that sheep."

"Carving up a sheep like that is pretty

damn evil, if you ask me," Scoop said. "But angels, devils. Not the same thing."

"Lucifer is a fallen angel. He was an archangel—the highest order of angels."

"Gabriel, Michael. Those guys are archangels, right?"

Abigail smiled. Scoop had a remarkable ability to change the mood of a conversation, depending on what he wanted to accomplish. "Right. Lucifer couldn't accept that he was a creation of God—he wanted to be an autonomous power. He rebelled against God, and God threw him out of heaven."

"Rough," Scoop said.

"In a nutshell, Lucifer becomes Satan. The devil. He's in a perpetual fight with God for supremacy. He recruits others to acts of rebellion against God's will. He demands loyalty above all else, but he doesn't care about being loved or feared—his overriding emotion is hatred, specifically, hatred of God."

Scoop, eminently practical, nodded. "So the rest of us have to choose between God and Satan."

"That's fundamental to the understanding of the devil and evil—we choose. Satan will do anything to get us to choose the path of evil, and therefore him." Abigail thought back to the book Charlotte Augustine had loaned her. "There's a lot more to this subject, but so much hangs on this basic concept."

"I can imagine," Scoop said, then gave Abigail an incisive look. "Do you think your guy's interest in Lucifer had a hand in his death?"

"I don't know."

"A lot of people believe in angels and the devil, Abigail."

"But not everyone has a room filled with flame-spewing, fork-tongued devils," Bob said as he rejoined them, picking up his empty beer bottle off the table with a calm that Abigail found unsettling. "That's what Abigail here is fixed on, Scoop."

She forced herself not to respond, and Scoop just shrugged.

Bob continued. "Keira paints pretty pictures of folktales and flowers. No devils. Her only interest in angels is the one in this crazy story."

"All right," Scoop said, starting for the

back steps to his second-floor apartment. "I've had enough. I'm going on up. You two can fight it out."

Abigail didn't blame him. In his place, she'd have fled inside a long time ago.

She opened the folder Fiona had delivered and peeked at the printout of names. Victor Sarakis's name was no secret. Colm could easily have figured out what she was up to and checked the list, deleted names if he'd wanted to. Not that he had any reason, but she realized she hadn't been all that clever in asking him for the list.

"You weren't aware of Keira's reasons for going to Ireland, were you?"

Bob remained on his feet, but he seemed uncertain, which wasn't like him. Finally, he sighed, shaking his head. "Keira doesn't confide in me or anyone else. She's an O'Reilly, after all. She does what she needs to do." He returned to his chair at the table. "That was you last summer in Maine, Abigail. You had to check out that tip on your own. You shut out Scoop, me, your father, the Maine police. It's just that you're not used to shutting people out, and Keira is."

"Maybe she doesn't want to be used to it."

"I don't know about that. She wants to do things, see the world, draw, paint, talk to people. But deep down I think she's worried she's going to end up a recluse like her mother."

"Does she blame herself for her mother's decision to become a religious hermit?"

Bob didn't answer and seemed to stare out at nothing.

"Bob," Abigail said, "do you blame yourself?"

She half expected him to tell her to mind her own business, but he didn't. "Eileen came home from Ireland pregnant with Keira. She was nineteen—quit college. She's never talked about what went on in Ireland. Not to me, not to our folks. As far as I know, she never told a friend. I don't even think she told her husband. He was a great guy. He adopted Keira, loved both of them—" Bob paused, raked his forearm over the top of his head. "Hell of a thing, his death. Freak accident in the Callahan Tunnel. They happen, you know. Freak accidents."

Abigail ignored the jibe. "Do you think Keira latched on to this old story because her mother looked for the village when she was in Ireland and hoped it'd lead her to her father?"

"John Michael Sullivan was her father. Keira missed him like crazy when he died. She was just this little tyke, but you could see it. She kept wanting her mother to read her stories and poems. One after another. Eileen loved it. Helped her, too. They moved to southern New Hampshire, and she opened an art supply store. I got out there when I could." He looked up at the darkening sky. "I don't know what more I could have done."

"Bob, it's not your fault."

He shifted his gaze back to her. "What, that my sister's abandoned her family, her friends, the whole damn world to live by herself in a cabin with no running water, no electricity? Keira doesn't have a phone, but her nutty mother..." He stopped himself. "I respect Eileen's religious convictions, but this life—it isn't her, Abigail. Her choice isn't easy on the rest of us, but we could live with it if we thought it was her. It's not. She's never married again, but she's always been social—lots of friends, all that. Now she sits in the woods and doesn't see anyone for days on end."

"What about Keira? It must feel as if her mother's rejected her, even if that wasn't her intention."

"We haven't talked that much about it. My opinion, she's not trying to talk Eileen out of the woods so much as trying to figure out what it means about who she is. Keira's pretty as hell, but she—well, you've seen her. She marches to the beat of her own drummer."

"Sounds like an O'Reilly to me," Abigail said with a smile. "Except the pretty part. You're not pretty, Bob."

He grinned at her. "I hope to hell not. You know why Keira went to the police academy? Because she figured that was what an O'Reilly would do."

"She thinks you're disappointed in her for not becoming a police officer?"

"Nah. That's not it. She's pissed she

wasted her time at the academy when she could have been drawing pictures of fairies and researching crazy old stories."

"Not everyone figures out what they want to do in life at age five. You did. A lot of us take a winding road."

"You're a good detective, Abigail."

His praise caught her off guard. "Thanks."

"I'm sorry you came to the job the way you did, but you'd have found your way to it, eventually."

"I don't believe that. I'd have finished law school if Chris hadn't died. My life changed because of his death."

"What are you doing, Abigail?" he asked suddenly. "If you have a legitimate reason to think your drowning case ties back to Keira, you could turn it over to someone else. But you don't want to, do you? You latched on to it because you wanted to pick a fight with me. Why?"

"I didn't want to pick a fight with you, Bob. I'm just—"

"Just doing your job? That's crap. You've been prickly for a while now, looking for distractions. Something. What's going on?"

"Nothing."

It was true as far as it went. Abigail hadn't spent much time exploring her feelings, but she had to admit that she'd been out of sorts for several weeks.

"Everything okay with you and Owen?"

"Everything's fine. We have unusual lives, that's all."

"Afraid of losing him?"

She shook her head. That wasn't it, she thought. Not even close, but she couldn't put her finger on exactly what was troubling her, either. "I'm not afraid of anything, Bob. Really."

"We're all afraid of something," he said.

"I meant in terms of Owen and me. What are you afraid of?"

He gave her an irreverent grin. "Marriage. All right. I guess I shouldn't give you advice on your relationship with Owen seeing how I have two ex-wives."

But for once, Abigail didn't let him use humor to pull back from a conversation about his emotions. "You got married thinking it'd be forever, didn't you?"

He surprised her by answering. "The first time." He shrugged. "The second time I had a feeling I was biting off more than I could chew, but I did it, anyway."

Abigail knew Bob's first wife—the mother of his three daughters—better, but she'd met his second wife, and she could see his point. His two wives had been polar opposites of each other. He'd overcompensated with the second for what he regarded, as only Bob could, as mistakes with the first.

"You did too hot and too cold," Abigail said. "Now you need to find your Goldilocks woman. The one who's just right."

He snorted. "She's going to have to find me, because I'm not looking. I'm spending my money on a new sound system. Scoop and I are buying a boat." Bob exhaled at the now dark sky. "Abigail...I wish I knew what the hell went on with Keira in Ireland."

"I know, Bob. I do, too."

"This Simon character's a bruiser. Looks as if he's not going anywhere. He'll figure out what to do if Keira's stuck her hand in fire. And she's always been good at taking care of herself." He looked at Abigail, his eyes focused now, alert, sharp. "If you had information that Keira was in trouble, you'd tell me, wouldn't you?"

"Yes. If I had anything. I don't."

"You didn't bite my head off, Abigail. Why not?"

"Scoop reminded me we're talking about your family. Your niece, your sister. Even your daughter."

But Bob responded to her serious tone with a victorious snort. "That's it. I'll be damned. I've got it now." He slapped the table, obviously excited about whatever he'd just figured out. "You're not afraid you won't have kids. You're afraid of what happens if you *do* have kids."

Abigail jumped to her feet, grabbed Colm's folder and her wineglass. She wasn't having this conversation with Bob, not now—not even as a way for him to keep from thinking about his own problems.

He didn't take the hint and kept going. "You're afraid of what kids will mean to you and Owen, your lives. He's on the go all the time, you chew on a case night and day. Kids would change that. You're worried he won't—"

"Good night, Bob."

He waited until she was on the back steps before calling to her. "I'm right."

She ignored him and went inside. She set the wineglass in the sink and opened the folder on the counter, telling herself she was just doing her job and not looking for a distraction. She didn't want to think about Bob's comment. He was good at reading people. Had he just read her?

She scanned the printout of Colm's database, saw that the list was alphabetical by last names. She didn't see a Sarakis or an Augustine. There was one Butler, but not Liam.

Bob had regarded her asking for the names not as thoroughness on her part but as a deliberate thumb in his eye. He didn't want there to be a connection between the auction and Victor Sarakis's death, and Abigail couldn't blame him.

She headed for the bedroom, just wanted to forget about everything.

Owen had the paint can open at his

feet. "What's up?" she asked, easing beside him in the doorway.

"I don't know about the color after all. This shade isn't my favorite." He slipped an arm around her waist. "If you love it, I can live with it. Blue's fine."

"Meaning you hate it," she said.

He kissed the top of her head. "That would be one way to put it."

She laughed. "Then let's pick out a color we both like, okay? Owen, honestly—I consider this place as much yours as mine. I want you to speak up and not just go along with me."

"Fair enough." He nodded toward the backyard. "How's Bob?"

"Worried. Hey, did you notice the way Simon and Keira looked at each other tonight?"

"No."

She elbowed him playfully. "You did, too. I don't know that much about Simon. He's okay, though?"

"If you'd seen him in Armenia—" Owen stopped, nodded. "I'd trust him with my life."

"You're careful about who becomes a Fast Rescue volunteer, right?"

"Absolutely. Simon's one of our best."

"I'm still wide awake." She slid out of Owen's embrace and set the top back on the paint can. "Since we're not going to be painting tonight, why don't you tell me what you know about our man to the rescue."

"I have a better idea," Owen said, grabbing her up into his arms and carrying her to the bed.

Abigail didn't object. Given what Owen clearly had in mind, she could definitely wait until morning to talk to him about Simon Cahill.

∼Chapter 24

Beacon Hill
Boston, Massachusetts
7:00 a.m., EDT
June 24

Dying for coffee, Keira listened for sounds of life in the next room. She didn't know why she should be self-conscious now, but she was. She pressed her ear to her bedroom door. She couldn't hear breathing, a running faucet, the drip of a coffeepot—nothing. She cracked open the door. She didn't want to wake Simon, but, even more, she didn't want to catch him stretched out temptingly on her sofa bed.

"It's safe to come out," he said with a note of irony in his voice.

She threw open the door. "I'm trying to be polite."

He was dressed—lightweight pants and a dark polo shirt—and sitting at the table with a classic collection of Irish folktales, the sofa bed put away, the linens folded and stacked on a chair. He looked freshly showered and shaved, but she hadn't heard the shower.

"No nightmares?"

She shook her head. "How was your night?"

"I dreamed about fairy princesses."

Keira wasn't going near that one.

He set his book on the table. "These are addictive."

"Aren't they? Sean O'Sullivan put together that collection. He was the chief archivist of the Irish Folklore Commission during its entire existence in the mid-twentieth century. It was a nation-wide effort to gather and preserve folk-tales. Its work is now part of the National Folklore Collection at University College Dublin—literally millions of pages of transcripts, tens of thousands of photographs and audio and video recordings. It's incredible, really."

"Quite an undertaking."

"Sean O'Sullivan was from the Beara Peninsula."

But Simon rose. "Let's go see your storyteller."

Keira grabbed her various sketches as she and Simon headed out, fetching her car and stopping for coffee and muffins on the way to South Boston. She called Patsy on his cell phone, but didn't get an answer. "She goes to church most mornings. My grandmother did, too, especially in the last few years before she died."

"Did your grandparents always live in South Boston?" Simon asked.

She shook her head. "No, they moved to Florida when my grandfather retired from the police department. He's still there." She smiled, thinking about him. "He keeps trying to get me to learn golf. He loves the weather in Florida—he can play year-round. I've told him I've seen golfers playing in gale-force winds in Ireland."

"If you wait for perfect weather, you wouldn't play much."

Keira enjoyed the normalcy of their conversation. She pointed out the simple duplex where her grandparents had raised her mother and uncle, imagined them on just such a warm early summer morning.

They parked in front of Patsy's house, one of only a handful of single-family houses in the neighborhood, and Keira rang the doorbell. During their first visit, Patsy had explained that she'd managed to keep her home after she was widowed at a young age because her husband had insisted on having good life insurance. She'd worked various office jobs over the years, but it was that insurance that had made the difference—she'd wanted Keira to know.

When there was no answer, she knocked. Again, no response from inside the house. "She should be home from church by now—it's just up the street."

"Maybe she's out back," Simon said.

They headed up the sidewalk and pulled open an unlocked, rickety white wooden gate between Patsy's house and the looming triple-decker next door, making their way back to a tiny, fenced-in yard crammed with bird feeders, bird-houses, leprechauns and gnomes. But Patsy wasn't there, either.

Keira climbed the steps onto the back porch, where a lone wind chime dinged once in the slight stir of a breeze. She raised her hand to knock on the back door, but saw that it wasn't latched all the way. "Simon..."

He touched her hand. "Let me go first." He opened the door. "Mrs. McCarthy? My name's Simon Cahill. I'm with Keira Sullivan."

"Hi, Mrs. McCarthy," Keira called, trying to sound cheerful.

She followed Simon into the kitchen, half expecting to find Patsy at the table with a cup of tea. Instead, her teapot, decorated with green shamrocks, sat on the counter. Magnets of American flags held an array of postcards of Irish scenes to her refrigerator. In their hand-ful of meetings, Keira had enjoyed Patsy's sense of humor. Patsy was com-fortable with her romanticized view of an

Ireland she knew more now from memory and stories than from experience.

"Her bedroom's upstairs?" Simon asked.

"I think so." Keira nodded to the hall door. "That'll take us to the dining room and living room. There's a small study, too. The stairs are in the front entry."

Simon gave a curt nod. "Stay close, okay?"

Halfway down the hall, he stopped in the open doorway to the dining room, and when she stood next to him, Keira saw why. Scores of angels were set out on Patsy's lace-covered oval table, all facing the door as though to greet whoever walked in. They ranged in size from barely an inch to two feet tall and were constructed of a variety of materials—porcelain, pottery, silver, copper, gold, wood, glass, wax and origami paper.

Three silver-framed photographs of a pretty blond-haired girl stood among the angels. One appeared to be at her First Communion. In another, she was teetering on roller-skates at about age twelve.

In the third, she was standing next to a teenage Bob O'Reilly, both dressed to the nines for what had to be a high school prom.

Simon pointed to a prayer card propped up against a multicolored glass angel.

Deirdre Ita McCarthy.

"She must be Patsy's daughter. Oh, Simon. She was just nineteen when she died. I had no idea. Patsy never said a word."

"Were these angels and pictures here when you visited her?"

"No—none of them."

"We need to find her," Simon said.

Keira took shallow breaths, her tension mounting as they moved down the hall. When they reached the study, Simon swore and spun around quickly, grabbing her around the waist, stopping her. "Keira, don't look, sweetheart."

She clutched his arms. "Simon, what is it?"

"Your friend's dead."

"Oh, no...no..." Keira cried out, lunging toward the study, but Simon kept his arms tight around her. She saw blood spattered on the white woodwork. Her eyes filled with tears. "Are you sure—"

"I'm sure. There's nothing we can do for her, Keira. She's been dead at least a day." He kissed the top of her head. "I'm so sorry."

"Simon, the blood..." She forced herself not to hyperventilate. "It wasn't a heart attack, was it?"

"No."

"I have to see."

"Yeah. I know." He eased his hold on her. "Just stay out here in the hall. It's best we don't contaminate the scene, and it's a tough sight. A lot of blood. We need to call the police."

Her fingers digging into his arms, Keira peered past him into the study and saw Patsy sprawled on the floor in the middle of a hooked rug, her pastel pink sweater drenched in blood.

"Was it—can you tell—" She gulped in air, pulling herself together as she loosened her grip on Simon. "Can you tell if she suffered? If she was tortured, like the sheep..."

"She wasn't tortured."

"There was time for whoever killed the

sheep to get back here and..." Keira broke off, unable to finish the thought. "There's a phone in the kitchen."

But he was already dialing 911 on his cell phone, his arm dropping to her waist as they returned to the kitchen. Keira was reeling, her head spinning as he provided a crisp, detailed report to the dispatcher. She remembered the dead man in the Public Garden just a few days ago, pictured the blood and entrails at the ruin and ran out to the back porch, half tripping down the steps to the yard.

The priest from the other night in Boston was there, white-faced and motionless. "Father Palermo," Keira whispered, choking back tears.

She could see he knew something horrible had happened. "Mrs. McCarthy didn't come to mass this morning. I walked over here to check on her. It's the second morning in a row she's missed mass. It's not—" His voice faltered. "It's not like her. Miss Sullivan..."

"I'm sorry, Father. I'm afraid Patsy's dead."

Keira realized how blunt her words sounded. She didn't know if she should

have told him even that much. She realized the police would want to talk to
him, and, in any case, she didn't want to
be the one to describe the scene.

He gaped at her, obviously trying to
absorb the news. "What—"

But Fiona appeared on the concrete
alley-like walk to Patsy's backyard. Her
blond hair was pulled back neatly, and
she had her Irish harp with her, tucked
under one arm as she stared, clearly in
dread, at Father Palermo and then her
older cousin.

"Fiona," Keira said, "what are you doing here?"

Her eyes—that O'Reilly cornflower
blue—widened in obvious fear, and she
about-faced and took off back out to
the street.

Keira could hear police sirens in the
distance as she turned to the priest. "I
have to go."

He nodded, and she charged after her
cousin.

~Chapter 25

South Boston, Massachusetts
9:30 a.m., EDT
June 24

Abigail jumped out of her car just down the street from Patsy McCarthy's house and raced up the sidewalk, intercepting Bob before he could get to the door. She leaped in front of him. "You can't, Bob," she said. "You know you can't go in there—"

His eyes were blue steel. "Get out of my way, Abigail."

She didn't budge. He was a senior BPD detective. If he wanted to see the scene, the BPD officers posted outside would let him in. But it wasn't a good idea. Abigail had been at her desk at BPD Headquarters, doing paperwork to mollify her partner and get her head screwed back on straight, when word spread that a seventy-nine-year-old woman had been knifed to death in South Boston. That kind of outrage always got to everyone. She'd known instantly, in her gut, that it was Keira Sullivan's storyteller.

Then came the news that Bob's niece was the one who'd found the body.

And his eldest daughter was there.

Even her partner was shaken. Tom Yarborough was an ambitious SOB. Twenty-nine, and he thought he should be running the department. But he'd understood when Abigail had abandoned her computer and charged out to the scene.

Police vehicles crowded the street. Some of Patsy McCarthy's neighbors had ventured out in front of their houses in shock.

"Bob," Abigail said, "you can't investigate this one. Stay out of it. You'd be telling me the same thing—"

"Where's my daughter?" His eyes

didn't change, remained hard, flinty. "Where's Keira?"

"Let me find out, okay? I imagine they're with the responding officers."

He looked past her to the simple house. "What the hell was Fiona doing here?"

"I don't know, Bob," Abigail said, feeling his anguish despite his rigid self-control. "I just got here myself."

"I'm going in there, Abigail. Going to try and stop me?"

Abigail sighed, stepping away from him. "No."

In his position, she'd do the same. She'd done the same eight years ago when she'd flung herself at her dead husband's body.

She followed him past the patrol officers posted at the door who didn't, as she'd expected, question his presence. No one would.

They worked their way back to the study, where Patsy McCarthy's tiny body lay on a blood-soaked rug. "She hooked that rug herself thirty years ago," Bob said in a near whisper. "Look

at it. It's like new. It's a scene from Ireland—a farm, a couple of sheep."

"Bob..." Abigail had to push back a
rush of emotion. "I'm sorry."

"Not your fault. You didn't kill her."

The grim-faced lead detectives—experienced men Bob and Abigail both
knew well—said it looked as if she'd
been stabbed twice.

Once for the blood. Once for the kill.

"This was no way for an old woman to
die," Bob said softly. "For anyone."

He continued down the hall, and Abigail was struck by his easy familiarity
with the house. She pictured him running through there as a kid and couldn't
imagine his pain now. But he stopped at
the dining room, and Abigail grimaced.
More detectives were in the room, carefully documenting the strange scene.

"Damn, Bob," Abigail whispered, her
eyes fixed on one of a trio of pictures in
the middle of dozens and dozens of angel figurines on the table. "That's you.
The girl—"

"Patsy didn't set up this stuff. Her killer
did."

He turned around and stalked back up the hall.

Abigail charged after him, her heart racing.

Out on the street, Bob stood under a scraggly maple tree and stuffed a stick of gum into his mouth. "Patsy believed in fairies." He didn't look at Abigail as she stood next to him in the thin shade. "She wouldn't admit it, but she did. Told me she'd hear the cry of a banshee just before someone close to her died. She said the first time she could remember hearing one was when as a little girl in Ireland when her kid sister died of some dread disease."

"I could do without hearing a banshee," Abigail said.

"Yeah. Patsy told me that quaint little story when I was nine or ten. Scared the living hell out of me." Bob chewed hard on his gum. "She was a simple woman, Abigail. She never asked for much out of life. She never got much, either."

"We'll find out what happened. Who did this to her."

"You know how many unsolved homicides are stacked up on my desk? There are no guarantees. Save the platitudes for someone who doesn't know any better." He looked back toward the house, lace curtains in the front windows. "Sorry. I didn't mean to bite your head off."

"Forget it."

"I'm going to find Fiona and Keira."

"If there's anything I can do—"

"I'll let you know."

Abigail saw his daughter and his niece coming around from the backyard and left Bob to them. She returned to the house and made her way to the kitchen, where she found Simon Cahill chatting with a couple of patrol officers. He struck her as remarkably self-possessed for someone who'd just found an old woman murdered in her own home. Then again, she thought, she'd observed that same control in Owen. She didn't know if their search-and-rescue work developed such composure, or if they could do that work because they were naturally that way. A little of both, maybe.

"You must be wishing you'd stayed in London," she said.

"No sense wasting time wishing for

something that can't happen. Bob O'Reilly's here?"

"Outside with Fiona and Keira."

Simon waited a half beat, then said, "You and O'Reilly are right up to the line separating personal and professional business."

"I'm up to it," she said. "Bob's crossed it."

His very green eyes leveled on her. Then he flipped a business-size card at her. "This was under Patsy's teapot." He nodded to the counter behind him. "There."

Abigail winced when she saw it was one of Bob's cards.

"I figured I'd give it to you," Simon said.

She regarded him with new insight. It wasn't everyone who'd notice a business card under a teapot with a dead woman in the next room, much less think to pocket it and give it to her. "Simon," she said, "do you mind telling me who the hell you are?"

"Stewing about me isn't going to help find whoever killed Patsy McCarthy."

He headed out through the back door.

Abigail started to follow him and make him talk, but two more detectives came down the hall. She debated giving them Bob's card. Had he given it to Patsy? Did his daughter have one, and had she given it to her? Keira?

Abigail knew they weren't her questions to ask or answer.

If she'd been one of the detectives walking toward her right now, she'd want the card. Period. No games from a colleague.

But she tucked the card into her pocket. "You guys need to talk to Bob," she told the detectives. "Ask him when he last saw the victim."

"Abigail—"

"Just do it," she said and walked past them up the hall.

Fiona was still crying, her nose red, her cheeks raw, a tearstained tissue squished in her hand. She'd wiped her eyes, cried some more, wiped her eyes again. "Don't leave me, Keira," she said, sniffling as her father approached them. "Dad's going to—he's not going to understand."

"Give him a chance, but don't worry. I'm not going anywhere."

Her uncle was stoic, but Keira had learned to read the little signs and could see he was shaken—and furious, she thought. Apoplectic under his outward calm. A woman he'd known all his life murdered in her own home. His daughter and niece on the scene. He was a cop—an experienced detective—and he'd feel as if it was his fault, somehow, that he could have done something, stepped in before some maniac slipped into Patsy's house and killed her.

Keira could identify with such guilt. She couldn't shake the feeling that she'd set into motion the events that had led to the horror in the house behind her.

But her uncle held his emotions in check as he greeted his daughter. "Hey, kid." His tone was gentle, even kind. "How're you doing?"

"Oh, Dad. I feel so bad."

"I know. It's an awful thing."

Fiona nodded, tears welling in her eyes. "I liked her so much. She reminded me of Grandma with her Irish accent."

"They both were something. Should have seen them when we were kids, the two of them standing out here on the street laughing over little things. The weather, a new recipe. They'd argue, too. Remember how your grandma could argue?"

"She hated to lose," Fiona said, sniffling as she tried to smile.

"Patsy was the same way. We'll get you down to Florida, and your grandpa can tell you stories about the two of them. He thought Patsy was a loon, but he liked her."

Fiona continued to cry, and when Bob touched her shoulder, she fell into his arms and sobbed into his chest. He glared over the top of her head at Keira. "You want to tell me what the hell's going on? Did you introduce Patsy and Fiona—"

"No, Dad," Fiona said. "It wasn't Keira."

But her cousin sank against Keira's car, shaking with silent sobs. Keira stuffed her own grief down deep and explained what she knew, what she herself had just learned from Fiona. "Fiona's taking Irish music lessons a couple of blocks from here. She started after college let out for the summer. She walked over one day to see where you grew up and ran into Patsy at her church. Patsy reminded her of Gran— she wasn't hiding anything from you—"

"I didn't know about the lessons," Bob said, cutting her off. "I didn't know about Patsy. In my book, that's hiding something."

Fiona stood up straight, her face red from crying. "Dad—"

"You recognized Patsy when you saw her with Keira the other night in Boston."

"I never said I didn't."

He pointed a finger at her. "Don't bullshit me, Fi. Not now. I'm sorry she's dead. I'm sorry you're upset. But what you have to do right now is make sure you've told me every damn thing you know. Everything. Don't leave out anything, no matter how small or stupid or embarrassing you think it is. Understood?"

Fiona nodded, but instead of her father's stern words beating her down, they seemed to strengthen her. "I can't get my head around what was done to her, Dad. It's—it's beyond comprehension."

"Yeah. It is." He turned to Keira, his gaze unrelenting, like nothing she'd ever seen in him before. "What about you and Simon? When did you get here?"

"Around eight-thirty. I tried calling, I rang the doorbell. When I didn't get an answer, we went around back—"

"Hell, Keira. The body in the Public Garden, the mess in Ireland—and now this."

"I don't like it, either," Keira said.

Fiona sobbed, lifted her head. "Mrs. McCarthy was the sweetest woman, Dad. How could anyone hurt her?"

"I don't know, Fi, but it doesn't matter if she was sweet or a pain in the neck, she didn't deserve to die this way."

"I didn't see her, Dad. Mrs. McCarthy. Keira stopped me before I—"

"One good thing, anyway. Was it always just the two of you when you vis-

ited, Fi? No plumber, electrician, mail-
man, neighbor?"

"It was always just the two of us. I saw
her maybe a half-dozen times, usually
after my lesson, sometimes before—I'd
catch her on her way home from church.
That's what I was hoping to do this
morning. She liked to talk, and if I had
somewhere else I needed to be..."
Fiona's eyes filled with fresh tears.
"That's awful of me, isn't it, Dad?"

"No, it's not awful, Fi. Patsy would
understand. She was nineteen once
herself."

Fat tears spilled down Fiona's cheeks.
"I walked over here one day after my
lesson to see your old neighborhood. I
went past Saint Ita's—your old church—
and some of the church women were
setting up for a bazaar in the parish
hall. An angel bazaar. They had angel
everything—food, decorations, knitted
items, music." Fiona talked at a lightning speed, as if she needed to get
everything out in one breath. "Patsy and
some of the other women were display-
ing their collections of angel figurines.

Patsy's was the best by far. Have you seen it, Dad? It's unbelievable."

"She collected angels for a long time."

"Father Palermo said some of them might be valuable. I hope... Dad, you don't think someone was trying to rob her, do you?"

"Too early to say. Did you go to this bazaar?"

Fiona nodded, perking up slightly. "I bought two handmade angel Christmas ornaments for presents, and I had a piece of angel food cake with green frosting."

Her father gave a half hearted grin. "Gross."

"It wasn't that bad. Dad, Patsy had all of Keira's books—she loved them." Fiona went pale again. "I can't believe what's happened."

"I know, kid. It's a tough one." Bob turned to Keira, his expression showing more of his anguish now and less of his fury. "Were you already in touch with Patsy when Fiona got to know her?"

Keira nodded. "Patsy e-mailed me around the same time, but she never mentioned she knew Fiona." Keira hesi-

tated, then added, "She never mentioned she had a daughter, either. Bob,
the angels, your prom picture—"

"I need to get Fi out of here," he said.

Keira gave up on trying to pry information out of him. Now wasn't the time.
Fiona pulled away from her father, some
color returning to her cheeks. "I'm meeting my friends at the Garrison house for
a practice session. Dad, I just want to
play my music right now. Please…"

"No problem, kid. I'll drop you off.
Keira?"

"I'll wait for Simon."

"Thought you might." But his attempt
at humor—normalcy—faltered, and he
said, "I know this is hard, Keira. I'm
sorry you have to deal with it. We'll talk
later, okay?"

"Sure."

"You know how to reach me if you
need me."

"Yeah. Thanks."

Keira watched him walk up the street
with Fiona. He was the one rock of her
life—her tight-lipped, emotionally repressed uncle who'd never told her he'd
taken his neighbor's long-dead daughter

to their high school prom. What, Keira wondered, had happened to Deirdre McCarthy?

Her head ached, and she was wiped out and yet, at the same time, still keyed up, replaying in her mind walking through Patsy's house, finding her body, then going out into the yard and seeing Fiona and Father Palermo. Waiting for the police to arrive. Noticing how Simon, who'd dealt with countless disaster scenes in his search-and-rescue work, had met the responding officers with such calm and professionalism.

She looked around for him now, but saw only cops, crime scene technicians and a few reporters setting up, trying to figure out what was going on and whether it merited full coverage.

The detective who'd taken her statement earlier joined her in the shade. He was a tall, gray-haired, serious man she didn't recognize from any social gatherings at her uncle's place. "I just spoke to Detective Browning," he said, nodding back toward Patsy's house. "She told me you ran into trouble in Ireland. Mind telling me what happened?"

As if it mattered if she did mind. Nonetheless, she appreciated the gesture. "Not at all. Can I ask you a quick question first? I didn't realize Patsy McCarthy had a daughter until this morning. Do you know how she died?"

"You're an O'Reilly, all right. You like to ask the questions."

"Does that mean you're not going to give me an answer?"

He sighed. "I don't know how she died, Ms. Sullivan. It's one of the things we're looking into."

Because of the prom picture and the prayer card, she thought, but before she could ask a follow-up question, the detective—Boucher was his name, she remembered now—steered her back to the subject at hand. Ireland, and what had happened there.

~Chapter 26

South Boston, Massachusetts
10:30 a.m., EDT
June 24

Simon found the priest walking from one colorful gnome and leprechaun to another in Patsy McCarthy's backyard, as if they had the power to tell him who had killed their owner. "I encouraged her to share her angels with the rest of the congregation," he said, more to himself than to Simon. "We had a bazaar a few weeks ago—it was my idea. I helped her get all her angels out, pack them up, haul them to the church, unpack them, pack them up again..."

He sighed, looked up, his face shiny with tears and sweat. "It was a chore, Mr. Cahill. I don't understand why she'd go to the trouble of taking them out again. The police asked me—I didn't know what to say."

"We don't know that it was her," Simon said.

"Ah. I see what you're suggesting." His skin turned even more ashen. "You mean her killer could have done it."

"I mean her killer almost certainly did do it."

"That's..." Palermo swallowed visibly. "That's hard to accept, Mr. Cahill, isn't it?"

"When did Mrs. McCarthy start collecting angels?"

"Her daughter started the collection as a little girl. After Deirdre's death, Patsy kept adding to it as a way to stay close to her daughter. I wasn't here then, of course, but she told me. She loved all her angels, but the ones original to Deirdre's collection were her particular favorites." Palermo patted the head of a three-foot-tall gnome and tried to smile. "Did you ever wonder who actually buys these things and puts them in their gardens? Patsy had such a sense of mischief about her."

"That's what I understand," Simon said.

But the priest's eyes filled with tears, and he turned away. "We all enjoyed the bazaar. It was a fine day. Patsy made Irish bread and apple crumble. It was as if...I'm not sure I can explain. It was as if her daughter was there with her."

"Father—"

"Deirdre was murdered, Mr. Cahill."

Somehow, Simon wasn't surprised.

"It's a horrible story. Patsy never told me. I looked it up. Deirdre was kidnapped on her way home from work. She was missing for several weeks—her body washed ashore not far from here." Palermo moved on to a small figure of a lithe pink fairy. "She was tortured and sexually assaulted."

"Her killer?"

"A road worker named Stuart Fuller. He'd moved in a few blocks from here not long before he kidnapped Deirdre— he didn't grow up in the neighborhood."

"He was caught, then?"

Palermo shook his head. "No. As it turns out, he committed suicide before the police could arrest him. Patsy didn't like to talk about what happened, except to say she believed with all her heart and soul that Deirdre is an angel."

"Did she tell you she was in touch with Keira Sullivan?"

"Patsy adored Keira's illustrations and couldn't wait to meet her." He smiled suddenly, some of his color returning. "She loved the idea of being part of one of Keira's books. I think she enjoyed the attention, to be honest."

"She never discussed her daughter's murder with Keira, either."

"That doesn't surprise me, frankly," Palermo said. "Patsy believed Deirdre had the gift of prophecy—that angels spoke to her and guided her throughout her short life. There's a famous story about Saint Ita—Deirdre's namesake—and Saint Brendan, another famous Irish saint. Do you know it, Mr. Cahill?"

Simon shook his head, and he noticed Keira on the concrete walk, motionless.

"Brendan was one of Saint Ita's students—he came to her convent in Ireland as a tiny boy. She was like a foster mother to him. Even after he left, he would come back to visit and ask her advice. He was an explorer. Some say he came to North America a thousand years before Columbus." Palermo choked up, then smiled through his tears. He seemed unaware of Keira's presence. "He's known as Brendan the Navigator. Doesn't that have a nice sound to it?"

"My father's name was Brendan," Simon said, just to break some of the priest's tension. "He was something of a wanderer himself."

"Was he?" Palermo took a breath, got hold of himself. "Brendan once asked Ita what were the three things that most pleased God, and she told him a pure heart, a simple life and generosity."

"Not a bad answer."

Palermo smiled suddenly. "Yes, indeed. Then Brendan asked what three things most displeased God, and Ita said a hateful tongue, a love of evil and greed."

"What do you think, Father?"

"I think that Saint Ita was a wise woman, but I hope she never knew the kind of person who could do what was done to Patsy, or to Patsy's daughter that terrible summer thirty years ago. How can we even comprehend such acts of depravity and evil?" But he didn't wait for a response. "I haven't been in this parish that long, but sometimes I feel as if I knew Deirdre myself. Her murder lingers in the lives of the people she knew, but so does her spirit."

Simon saw Keira turn pale and knew she'd put it all together—that Deirdre McCarthy was murdered the summer Eileen O'Reilly came home from Ireland pregnant.

He started to go her, but Keira bolted back toward the street.

Simon turned to Palermo. "Excuse me, Father—"

"Of course," Palermo said. "Please tell Keira how sorry I am."

"I will."

By the time Simon reached the street, Keira had jumped into her car and sped away. He dug out his cell phone. Abigail Browning and Bob O'Reilly had left, and no way was Simon asking one of the other cops for a lift.

He called Owen. "I could use a ride."

"I heard about Patsy McCarthy. Simon, Abigail called—"

"She's onto me, I know. She won't care that I'm in law enforcement or that I work for her father. She'll care that I've been like a son to him since I was a kid and he never told her, and she'll care that you've known for eighteen months and, likewise, haven't told her."

"She's not just suspicious, Simon," Owen said calmly. "She knows."

Simon tried to smile. "Not one to underestimate, that Abigail. All the more reason to set your wedding date. Get her thinking about picking out flowers instead of whether or not she should trust you."

"She can trust me. That's not an issue. None of this is anything you need to worry about right now. What about her father?"

"No worries. I'll deal with Director March. Just come pick me up."

"Where are you?"

Simon told him and disconnected,

then dialed Will Davenport in London. "Up for a trip to Ireland?"

"I can leave in ten minutes."

"You didn't even ask what's going on."

"All right. What's going on?"

Simon gave him the short version. "When you get to Ireland, talk to a Garda detective named Seamus Harrigan. Find Eddie O'Shea. Do this, Will, and we're even. I mean it."

"This Keira Sullivan—"

"Don't go there."

"I looked up her Web site. Very pretty. You can always use my place in Scotland for the wedding."

Will's place in Scotland was a castle. "Keep me posted on what you find out in Ireland."

Simon tucked his cell phone back in his pocket. His calls were done.

Now it was time to learn more about the murder of Deirdre McCarthy thirty years ago.

~Chapter 27

Back Bay
Boston, Massachusetts
11:00 a.m., EDT
June 24

Keira ran up the three flights of narrow stairs to Colm Dermott's office in an ivy-covered Back Bay building overlooking the Charles River. His door was open, and she burst in, set the Ireland sketches on the corner of his desk and forced back tears. "I'll explain everything," she said, "but first I need to borrow your phone."

"Keira, dear heaven—"

"Patsy McCarthy's been murdered.

Colm..." She was breathing hard after running up the stairs. "It's bad."

"Here." He thrust his cell phone at her. "Call whoever you need to."

She went to the window, watching a lone sculler on the river as she dialed Simon's number. He'd insisted on giving it to her as they'd waited for the police to arrive at Patsy's house, never mind that she didn't own a phone herself.

He picked up on the first ring, but she spoke before he could. "I can come get you."

"Too late," he said. "Owen beat you to it. I dropped him off on Beacon Street and borrowed his car. I figure if you and I are going to be hanging out together, it's easier if I have my own car."

"I'm sorry I took off—"

"Don't," he said, surprising her with his intensity. "I just want to know you're okay."

"I am. I'm at Colm's office." She noticed the sculler lift his oars out of the water and sit back, coasting a moment, as if he just wanted to enjoy the perfect Boston June morning. "I didn't know about Patsy's daughter."

"So I gathered."

"She was killed the summer my mother went to Ireland. They were the same age. My uncle took Patsy's daughter to the prom. They all grew up together, Simon, and I never had a clue. I didn't know Deirdre McCarthy even existed."

"It sounds as if it was a particularly horrific murder," Simon said, as if that explained thirty years of silence.

Keira turned away from the window. Colm nervously held the sketch of the black dog in midair, but he was looking at her, as if she might suddenly crack into little pieces. She tried to relax some of the tension in her muscles as she continued speaking to Simon. "I keep thinking there's a subtext to everything Patsy told me over the past few weeks. Something I've missed. I videotaped her telling the story—Colm has a copy."

"The police will want it," Simon said.

"I brought the original with me to Ireland. I don't know if this is on the tape, but I remember Patsy saying she was worried she was talking too much, trusting too easily. I didn't think anything of it at the time. I assumed she meant me and just had the jitters over being taped. That's natural—it all seems so exciting until someone sticks a camera in your face." Keira looked down again at the river, but her sculler was out of sight. "Simon, what if Patsy was talking about someone else?"

"Keira, just tell the police everything, and let them do their job. You've done all you can at this point."

"I know, but what if Patsy told someone else that story—someone who decided to look for the ruin and the angel, and then turned around and killed her?"

Simon didn't answer.

"You've thought about this, too," Keira said. "If it's the same person who killed that sheep in Ireland, left me trapped in the ruin—maybe even tried to kill me—and took the stone angel, then Patsy would have known who it was. Murdering her kept her from telling anyone."

"Whoever was responsible obviously wanted a lot of blood," Simon said.

Keira felt her mouth go dry. "Just like with the sheep."

"I'll tell the police here and in Ireland about the tape—"

"Where are you right now? At the Garrison house?"

A half-beat's pause. "I'm at BPD Headquarters."

"You're looking into Deirdre McCarthy's murder. How—" But she stopped herself, then sighed. "I'll be damned. You're a cop, aren't you? What are you—a fed, right? ATF, FBI, the marshals?"

"It's complicated."

"Are you a spook? What would happen if I Googled you? Would my computer blow up? Would I end up on some watch list?" But Simon didn't answer, and she knew he wasn't going to. "You know the FBI director is Abigail's father, right?"

"Yes. I know."

His tone told her everything. "Oh. I get it now. You're an FBI agent. Do Owen and Abigail know?"

"Focus on your own situation. We'll talk later."

She pictured his vivid green eyes and could almost feel her fingers in his hair. She'd made love to him with such abandon last night. But as close as she'd felt to him then—even now—she realized she didn't know Simon at all. He was charming, good-looking and very sexy, but also controlled—and he was a federal agent.

"You have secrets, Simon."

"Everyone has secrets."

She thought of her mother, her uncle—Patsy. And a teenage girl murdered thirty years ago. "I'm driving out to see my mother after I talk to Colm. Simon, I'm sorry you had to be there this morning, but I can't imagine having had to find Patsy without you."

"Keira..." But he didn't go on.

"Good disaster planner that you are," she said, "I figure you'll want directions to my mother's cabin."

He sighed softly. "I could fall in love with you, you know."

Her heart jumped, and she smiled, even as she bit back more tears. "I'd like that," she said, and gave him directions to her mother's cabin.

When she hung up, Colm exhaled and rushed to her, hugged her fiercely, then stood back. "Keira," he said, his voice cracking. "Dear heaven, tell me every-thing."

He listened intently, without interruption, as she filled him in.

When she finished, he shook his head with obvious emotion. "I'm so sorry. What a grisly business. Of course I'll find the tape of Patsy telling the story. I haven't watched it yet myself, but I'll get it to the police straight away."

She jotted down her uncle's phone number, then added Simon's. "If you need anything, call my uncle or Simon, okay? I don't have Abigail Browning's number, but feel free to get in touch with her, too—"

"I will, indeed. And I'll take a closer look at your sketches," Colm said, then added briskly, "If I can be of any assistance at all in finding this bloody bastard—"

"I just don't want anyone else to get hurt. If I'm responsible in any way—"

"Don't do this to yourself, Keira," Colm said. "Let the police sort out what's going on. You've done all you can. Just be with your family and friends now and remember the good times you had with Patsy."

She smiled at him. "I like hearing you say her name with your Irish accent."

He kissed her on the cheek. "Happier times are ahead, Keira."

"It's hard to believe that right now. Well, I should go. I need to see my mother and tell her about Patsy."

Colm grabbed his cell phone and tucked it into her hand. "Take it." His eyes sparked, and he winked at her. "I remember this Simon Cahill from the auction, and I have a feeling you'd be wise to stay in touch with him."

Keira felt a rush of heat. "Probably so. Thank you for the phone."

Colm gave her a quick grin. "I'll be taking up a collection for you for a phone of your own."

"I don't blame you. You're a good friend, Colm."

She ran down the stairs and out to the street, jumping in her car and heading out to Storrow Drive and onto Route 2. In less than two hours, she'd be at her mother's cabin.

~Chapter 28

Boston Police Department Headquarters
Roxbury, Massachusetts
11:25 a.m., EDT
June 24

Simon stood in a small, hot room in the sprawling headquarters of the Boston Police Department with the file of Deirdre McCarthy's murder in front of him and Norman Estabrook, soon to be in federal custody, on the phone.

"You're a dead man, Cahill," Estabrook said.

Simon didn't have time to listen to threats. "Yeah, whatever."

"I trusted you."

That was a lie. Estabrook didn't trust anyone. Simon didn't care.

Abigail Browning materialized in the doorway of the room where the BPD had led him, her arms crossed, her re-markable self-control firmly in place. He doubted now was the time to tell her how much she reminded him of her fa-ther.

Estabrook wasn't finished. "I have feds swarming over me right now because of you."

"Trust me now, Norm." Estabrook hated being called Norm. "Give yourself up peacefully, or they'll kill you."

"I didn't get to be a billionaire by giving up. You're dead, Cahill."

"How'd you find out about me?"

"Process of elimination. *You* trust *me* now. You're dead. Dead, dead, dead."

Estabrook could be remarkably petu-lant, but he typically wasn't one for empty threats. He was a portly, bland-looking, dangerous forty-year-old who thrived on risk and beating the odds. But Simon wasn't worried. After months of helping Estabrook plan, execute and survive his adventures—of insinuating himself into Estabrook's life—Simon was glad to be rid of him. Estabrook had decided to cross the line from ultrarich thrill seeker to international criminal. No one had done it to him.

"First I kill John March," Estabrook said. "Then I kill you."

"Send me a postcard from prison. It'll be your biggest adventure ever."

Estabrook sputtered, and Simon disconnected. He'd had enough.

John March's daughter walked into the room. "Well, Special Agent Cahill, should I ask what that was all about?" But she just nodded to the file. "I see you and I are here for the same reason. What do we have?"

"An ugly murder, Detective."

She picked up Deirdre McCarthy's high school graduation picture. "Sweet-looking kid, wasn't she? No wonder she ended up collecting angels."

Simon nodded. Deirdre was pretty, but it was her kindness that people who knew her had told police most defined her. If there were demon-fighting angels, Deirdre McCarthy wouldn't have been one.

Her mother, on the other hand...Patsy McCarthy had calmly predicted to more than one investigator that she would die fighting the devil with her bare hands. Simon thought of the tiny, crumpled body on the hooked rug and wondered if her premonition had come to fruition.

Abigail set the picture back down. "I see you're armed," she said.

"I had to look like a proper FBI agent before I came in here." But Simon couldn't pull off irreverence. He'd read the summary of the exhaustive investigation into Deirdre's kidnapping, torture, rape and murder. Now her mother was dead, slain in her own home. He looked again at Deirdre's picture, taken on a day when kids thought about their lives ahead of them. And a year later, she was dead. "Her killer stalked her for at least two weeks before he grabbed her. He took pictures of her—police found them in his apartment afterward."

"Deirdre didn't know she was being stalked?"

"She never filed a police report or said anything to her mother."

"Would she have?"

Simon didn't hesitate. "She'd have told her mother. It was just the two of them. She was a sweet kid who told her mother everything."

"Nobody tells anyone everything." Abigail swallowed visibly as she continued to flip through the file. "She was kidnapped on the summer solstice. No wonder Bob hates this time of year. I had no idea about this poor girl—not a damn inkling. He never said a word."

"He wouldn't. It's not how he's wired."

She sucked in a sharp breath but didn't argue. "How long did this monster have her?"

"Three weeks. You don't need to read the file to know what he did to her."

"No, I imagine I don't."

"Killing her was an afterthought. Either he just got tired of her, or he knew she couldn't live much longer. He slit her throat and dumped her body in Boston Harbor."

"Bob never even hinted..." Abigail's expression tightened as she came to the photographs taken after Deirdre's body had washed ashore. "Eight years I've worked here, and I've never heard of this case." She shut the file. "The killer—Stuart Fuller. Who was he?"

"A twenty-four-year-old road worker. He wasn't on the radar—no record. He grew up in a rough family. The father was in and out of prison and beat the hell out of his wife, and she beat the hell out of their kids. They lived all over the place. Stuart moved to South Boston to get away from his family two months before he kidnapped Deirdre."

Abigail had no visible reaction. "How did the police find him?"

"They didn't. He set himself on fire and jumped in Boston Harbor a week after Deirdre's body turned up."

"It was the right guy?"

"Police found overwhelming evidence—"

"That's not what I asked."

Simon had known it wasn't, but he didn't give her an answer.

She folded her arms on her chest again, pacing in the small room. "For seven years, I didn't know who killed my husband. Why, what happened. Any of it. I met Bob when I was still a recruit. He wasn't easy to win over."

"I can imagine," Simon said.

She didn't seem to hear him. "He's taught me so much."

"Abigail, that hasn't changed—"

"I believed I was teaching Bob what it's like to lose someone close to you to violence, when all the time, he knew and just never said anything."

"Some people bury something like that down deep and learn just not to go there."

"You had it right. Bob doesn't need a reason to be emotionally repressed. It's natural for him." She stalked to the door, but turned to Simon, her expression softening slightly. "Where's Owen?"

"I dropped him off on Beacon Hill. Fiona O'Reilly's at the Garrison house practicing with her friends." Simon tried to smile. "We could hear the Irish music all the way out on the street."

"I hope it's therapeutic for her."

"Yeah. Hope so. Today's been a tough one."

She gave a curt nod. "Bob?"

"He took off two seconds after Owen and I got there."

"Did he say where—"

"No. He didn't say a word to either of us."

"He's got the bit in his teeth, then."

Simon nodded. "I expect so."

"We don't need Bob O'Reilly going off half-cocked. One more question for you, Simon, before I leave." Her dark eyes leveled on him. "Just how well do you know my father?"

"As I said, some people learn to bury the bad and just don't go there."

John March had lost a friend and undoubtedly blamed himself for Brendan Cahill's execution, and to tell his daughter required confronting those feelings—that reality—in a way that keeping silent didn't.

Abigail took in Simon's nonanswer. "I have to be somewhere right now, but we're not finished."

"Hope not." He grinned at her. "I like weddings."

She scowled at him. "You're even less invited than you were last night."

But he saw some of the tension go out of her, if only for a moment, and she left, shutting the door behind her.

Simon opened Deirdre McCarthy's file

again and turned to the last page Abigail had looked at.

It was a report on the Fuller family submitted by a BPD detective sergeant named John March.

Speaking of people who buried their emotions. Abigail had to have seen her father's name. She didn't miss anything.

According to everyone who knew him back in his BPD days, March had been hardworking, hard-driving and ambitious, putting himself through law school at night, figuring out how he could advance his career and still be a decent husband and father.

And friend, Simon thought, visualizing his own father's execution. What did John March owe the memory of the friend whose son he believed he'd helped orphan?

Simon knew the answer, because John March had lived it.

He set the file on the table and left. He wanted to be with Keira—now, not later. Deirdre McCarthy's murder had hung over Keira's life since the summer she was conceived, but no one—not her mother, her uncle, her grandparents or

Patsy herself—had told her or her younger cousins about the girl next door, the friend who'd lost her life to violence.

And yet Simon understood why they hadn't.

Once he was on the road, navigating the busy urban streets, he called March's private number, barely letting the FBI director get out a greeting. "Do you care that Norman Estabrook just threatened to kill you?"

"No."

"I didn't think so. How long before you take him down?"

"Hours. He's still in Montana. We have him under surveillance. He's not going anywhere." March paused, then added, "We're monitoring his calls."

Simon had assumed as much.

"You're not calling to tell me Norman Estabrook hates me," March said. "You're in the middle of a mess that could explode in both our faces."

"You heard about Patsy McCarthy."

"Yes, I did," March said, a crack of emotion in his voice.

"You remember her, then."

"Her daughter's murder was one of the toughest cases I ever worked on, Simon. If I could forget it—well, I'm not sure I would. It's a reminder of what some people in this world are capable of doing."

"How'd you find out about the mother's murder? Who're you keeping tabs on, me or Abigail? Or have you been keeping tabs on Patsy McCarthy all these years?" March didn't give an answer, and Simon gritted his teeth. "All of the above, probably."

"Is Abigail—"

"She's in the thick of things, which is what you'd expect, isn't it?"

"Then she knows I worked on Deirdre McCarthy's murder investigation," March said. "That's not what's important now. Finding her mother's killer is. Simon, you need to walk away from this. It's not your fight. Go back to London, go fishing in Scotland with your friend Sir Will."

"Will's in Ireland."

"Of course. I should have known. The two of you are too independent for your own good. Dare I ask about Keira Sullivan?"

It was Simon's turn to avoid answering.

He heard March's soft sigh. "You do know how to complicate your life. There's no going back once we move forward with Estabrook, Simon. You have no illusions about that, I hope."

"My cover's pretty much blown as it is, and there's never any going back in life, anyway."

"I guess there isn't," March said with a note of melancholy that took Simon by surprise. "You've been clear-eyed and full-throttle since you were fourteen years old."

"Maybe so. Director March—John." Simon kept his eyes on the busy Boston street. "Did the right guy set himself on fire and jump into Boston Harbor thirty years ago?"

"Yes." There wasn't a hint of doubt. "Stay in touch," the FBI director said and hung up.

Simon tossed his phone onto the passenger seat. John March was as professional, honest and decent a man as there was, but he'd also kept his friendship with his dead friend's son secret from his daughter for twenty years. But Simon knew all about keeping secrets.

He hit the gas pedal, picking up speed.

"I was having the adventure of my life in Ireland while my best friend, the best person I've ever known, was in the hands of that monster."

Nineteen-year-old Eileen O'Reilly's words from Deirdre's case history had jumped off the page at Simon. Who could blame her for not telling her daughter about Deirdre's murder? And who could blame Keira, now, for wanting to understand her mother?

Simon gripped the wheel, half wishing Norman Estabrook would call and threaten to kill him again.

It would be a long drive out to the woods of southern New Hampshire.

He peeked at the speedometer.

Never mind, he thought—he'd get there in less than two hours.

Way less.

～*Chapter 29*

Back Bay
Boston, Massachusetts
Noon, EDT
June 24

The lunch crowd was descending on the busy, upscale health club under the Augustines' showroom on Clarendon Street. Abigail watched men and women with lives very different from her own burst into the locker rooms, jump onto treadmills, each with its own built-in little television, and climb onto weight machines. Several stretched on mats. One older guy crunched abs on an exercise ball. He looked as if he'd crunched about two million abs in his day.

All in all, Abigail would have preferred to strap on her iPod and go for a run along the Charles River, pump up her endorphins and just not think about an old woman killed in her home among the angel figurines her murdered daughter had collected—not think about the brilliant, honorable, frustratingly secretive man who was her father. She'd tried calling him on her way out to Clarendon Street, but she only got his voice mail. She didn't leave a message. She figured he was avoiding her or talking to Simon—maybe both.

She didn't call Owen. He knew about Simon, she realized. Owen was thorough in everything he did, but especially in his work with Fast Rescue.

She expected lies and secrets in her work. They came with the territory—part of her job was to peel them back to get to the truth.

Secrets and lies weren't supposed to be part of her personal life.

But she was determined not to think about that for a while.

Instead, she was standing next to a stack of freshly folded white towels on the health club's front desk.

A lean, tanned man in a black tracksuit emerged from a back room. He was about Bob's age but in a lot better shape. "Thank you for waiting, Detective Browning," he said. "We spoke on the phone earlier. I've been expecting you. I'm Ron Zytka—I manage the health club. It's okay to talk here?"

"No problem."

"Charlotte and Jay Augustine stopped by just before you called. They're still very shaken up about Charlotte's brother." Zytka grabbed a perfectly folded towel from the top of the pile, shook it out and spread it out on the desktop, preparing to refold it. "Understandably."

"Did you know Victor?"

"Not really." He carefully folded the towel lengthwise into thirds. "I ran into him with Charlotte a few times, and she introduced us. I could pick him out of a crowd, but that's it. He wasn't a member here—not the type."

Zytka finished folding the towel and set it back on top of the pile. As far as Abigail could see, the towel looked exactly the same. She'd called him that morning before news of Patsy McCarthy's murder had reached her. Now she didn't know what difference the Augustines' exercise habits made. But she persisted. "I notice you check people in. You must keep a record—"

"We do, and I already checked to see if Charlotte and Jay were in the day Victor drowned, because I figured you'd ask. They weren't, but the kid who works for them was. I think he's actually the brother's employee. The poor man who drowned."

"Liam Butler was here?"

"That's right. He could use the club as a guest of the Augustines. We offer a limited number of day passes to people in the building. But he was here on his own—he has a six-month membership." Zytka pointed to a line of treadmills in front of a floor-to-ceiling window. "He always uses one of the treadmills over there."

Given the placement of those particular treadmills, Abigail noticed, Liam could watch people come and go into the building with little concern they would see him. "You're sure it was the same day—"

"Yes, Detective," Zytka said. "It was the day of the drowning. I can show you the log if you want."

"What time was he here?"

"Liam signed in just before six that evening." Zytka's hands shook as he lifted the refolded towel and took the one underneath it.

"Did Liam's behavior strike you as unusual?" Abigail asked.

Zytka licked his lips and averted his eyes, not because he was hiding something, she thought, but because he was uncomfortable, even afraid—but of what? He was an officious sort. He could simply be worried that one of the health club patrons would overhear him and question his discretion as a manager.

But Abigail suspected Zytka's nervousness had more to do with Victor Sarakis's death and Liam Butler's behavior that night. "We can talk in your office if you'd like—"

"I checked the log, Detective Browning," he said without looking at her as he unfolded the towel. "Liam Butler took out a membership two months ago. I can give you the exact date if you want. Since then, he comes several times a week, sometimes twice in the same day."

"If he was helping out upstairs—"

"He shows up here on days he doesn't work. I checked with my staff, and they've noticed. My opinion?" Zytka sucked in a breath and plunged ahead. "I think he's been spying on the Augustines."

"He couldn't just be training for a marathon?"

"No. I know the difference."

Abigail stood back a moment. "Mr. Zytka, did Liam Butler or the Augustines ever discuss angels or devils or evil with you?"

Zytka was so startled, his elbow jerked and struck the tower of towels, toppling several of them. He caught them as they fell and shook his head. "No—no, nothing like that. Detective, what—"

"Listen, thanks for your time," Abigail said, leaving her card for him on the counter. "If you think of anything else, call me, okay?"

"I will." He rubbed the back of his lean neck and suddenly seemed less sure of himself. "Listen, I don't want to get Liam into trouble if he just—you know. If he didn't do anything. I'm not accusing him..."

Abigail thanked him again for his time, and left.

When she got back out to her car, she called Tom Yarborough. She'd avoided him when she'd seen Simon. "Can you meet me at Victor Sarakis's house?"

"What's going on?"

"Sarakis's assistant was at a health club down the street from the Public Garden the night he drowned. Liam Butler. He hasn't told the truth."

"Give me the address," Yarborough said. "I'll get in touch with Cambridge PD and meet you there."

~Chapter 30

Eileen Sullivan belted out the words to one Irish song after another as she stacked wood in front of her cabin. She could hear the Clancy Brothers in her mind, although she couldn't remember the last time she'd played a CD, listened to a radio. Her voice was terrible—Keira couldn't sing a note, either. They weren't the ones in the family with the musical talent.

A cool wind kicked up, and for a moment, Eileen let herself think it was a breeze off Kenmare Bay on her face. She shut her eyes and pictured herself dancing in an ancient stone circle above a quiet, gray harbor on the Beara Peninsula, and she hugged a log to her chest as if somehow it could bring her there—back to Ireland, back in time.

Before Deirdre's death.

That monster had Deirdre when I danced that night.

Eileen opened her eyes. She tried to sing again, but the words didn't come. She'd hoped singing and sweating and praying would finally chase away the demons that had been crawling over her since Keira's visit. Her distress wasn't Keira's fault—none of it was her fault. How could it be, when she didn't even know about Deirdre?

I should have told Keira about her.

About Deirdre's awful death, yes, but, even more so, about her life.

"You'll go to Ireland and have adventures. Oh, Eileen! I know you'll have the adventures of your life there. You'll

have to tell me everything when you get home."

They'd laughed and planned some of the adventures Eileen would have—seeing the Cliffs of Mohr, kissing the Blarney Stone, finding long-lost cousins. Tracking down the village where Patsy McCarthy's story of the three brothers and the stone angel was to be Eileen's biggest adventure.

"You have to go alone. You know you do, Eileen. You'll never find the hermit monk's ruin if you don't. That'll be half the fun of it, going alone will. You can feel it's the thing to do, can't you?"

Deirdre had always had a gift of knowing. Not true prophecy in the way Eileen had been taught its meaning, but simply of knowing—of understanding people, opening herself to see into their hearts. Her intuition in those weeks before Eileen had left for Ireland had been keen, unrelenting.

"If something happens to me while you're in Ireland, promise me you won't regret a thing. Please, Eileen. Promise me."

Eileen blinked back tears, remembering how she'd refused that one request on the grounds that such a promise would somehow jinx Deirdre. In the years since her death, Eileen had come to see that Deirdre hadn't had a premonition about her imminent murder. She hadn't known she was being stalked. It was just Deirdre being Deirdre—she was a nurse's aide, and she'd lost her father as a teenager, knew her mother had lost a sister young. Every day was to be treasured.

She also had known Eileen, how hard she could be on herself—how undeserving she often felt. That was *her* nature, and Deirdre, with her uncanny ability to look into people's hearts, had only wanted her friend to have a good time in Ireland. To trust herself to let go and come home with no regrets.

What had Deirdre seen when she'd looked into her killer's heart?

"Stuart Fuller."

Eileen spoke his name aloud to remind herself of his humanity. A supernatural creature hadn't murdered Deirdre. A man had made the deliberate choice to stalk her, kidnap her, torture, rape and kill her.

Tears spilling down her cheeks, Eileen set the log on her woodpile. She needed to get back to work on the illuminated manuscript. She'd decided to shift to another, happier passage and leave aside serpents for the moment. For most of the past week, she'd been pre-occupied with finding the perfect one to illustrate the Fall of Adam and Eve.

No wonder I keep thinking about demons. Eileen brushed her tears with her sleeve. Seeing an ordinary snake curled up on a sunny rock that morning had helped perk her up. It was a part of the natural order of life out on her wooded hillside.

She looked at the beautiful landscape, focusing on a robin perched on a hem-lock branch. She found comfort in her solitude, in her routines and rituals. They quieted her mind and eased her soul.

To a point, anyway.

"You have to look for the village, Eileen. Imagine if you find the angel! How happy Mum would be."

Eileen smiled now, shaking off her melancholy as she thought of her daughter in Ireland, having adventures of her own.

She stacked the last of the wood and propped her splitter against the chopping block, then headed back into her cabin. She'd clean up, and then she'd sketch angels. She didn't have Keira's artistic gifts—her spark, her joy of drawing, painting, creating. It was all hard work for Eileen, but that wouldn't have bothered her if the results were what she wanted. But they never were. She would put her heart and soul into this one illuminated manuscript, and that would be it. No more.

She peeled off her zip-front sweatshirt and tossed it on the back of her work stool.

A sound distracted her.

She went still, listening.

Music...

The sound of a harp, playing a melody so sweet it seemed to pierce her straight to her soul, floated through her tiny cabin.

Eileen placed a hand on her worktable, steadying herself.

She heard a whisper now.

"Deirdre Ita...she died for your sins, Eileen...you know she did..."

And she turned, she gasped.

A stone statue stood on the hearth of her woodstove.

An angel.

~Chapter 31

Kenmare, Southwest Ireland
5:35 p.m., IST
June 24

Eddie O'Shea waited impatiently for Mary Feeney, his cousin Joe's wife, to finish checking a middle-aged American couple into the midpriced inn right in the heart of Kenmare. It wasn't as fancy as the busy town's five-star hotels, but, with its sleek modern furnishings, it was fancy enough. Eddie liked Kenmare all right but couldn't wait to finish his business there and get back home.

The couple went merrily off to their room, and he stepped forward to Mary's desk and gave her his friendliest smile. "Do you believe in fate, Mary?"

"No."

She was just twenty-nine and had the prettiest red hair Eddie had ever seen, but she'd always been a bit of a shrew as far as he was concerned. "Well, I do, and it's fate that brings me here. I've never asked anything of you, have I? And I wouldn't now, except I've no choice. The guards'll be coming for me before sundown if I don't figure something out."

She raised her pale blue eyes to him. "I hope they throw away the key."

He grinned in an attempt to soften her up a little. "Oh, come, Mary, what would you do without family?"

"Enjoy my life," she said, then sighed behind her elegant desk. "What can I do for you, Eddie?"

"Look up an American who was here on the summer solstice."

"Name?"

"I don't have a name."

"Then I can't help you."

"At least I think it's a man we're looking for—"

"*You're* looking for," Mary said.

True enough. "He wore a black sweater with a zipper, and he stayed here by himself. He ate dinner in your restaurant. I have the receipt—"

"You do? Well, then—"

"Part of the receipt, I should say. It's been torn." By a mysterious black dog...but Eddie wasn't going into that with someone as without imagination as Mary Feeney. "There's no credit-card number or room number."

Mary rolled her eyes in clear disgust. "Eddie, I'm not a miracle worker. I can't be expected to remember a man because of his sweater."

But Eddie was determined, and he smiled big for her. "What if I told you he lost his wallet and there'll be a reward?"

"It sounds as if he lost his sweater."

She could cover for her shrewish nature with wit and humor when it suited her. The sweater wasn't lost, Eddie thought. It'd been ripped off its wearer by Keira Sullivan's black dog, who'd bolted out of the roses in front of her cottage not three hours ago and dropped the sweater at Eddie's feet. It was torn and bloody, and Eddie wasn't taking any chances by giving it to the guards and getting himself locked up. He'd collected Patrick and Aidan, and they'd smuggled him off to Kenmare.

"If it was a wallet your man lost," Mary said, all superior and sarcastic, "you wouldn't need me to find out his name and address for you, now, would you?"

"I've never been a good liar."

"Your only charm, Eddie." She faced her computer monitor and clicked keys, her lips pursed in that sour way of hers. "In any event, this man's not the sort who'd offer a reward for anything."

"Ah. You do remember him."

"I do, indeed," she said softly, then eyed Eddie, a gray look to her fair skin now. "You'll stand here all night if I don't help you."

"You have a bad feeling about him, don't you, Mary?"

Before she could answer, a lean, fairhaired man walked up to Mary's desk. She blushed, and, married woman or not, Eddie couldn't blame her. The man was good-looking and obviously belonged in one of the five-star hotels, not Mary's little inn.

Instead of greeting Mary, he turned to Eddie. "My name's Will Davenport," he said, his accent identifying him as an upper-class Brit. "Simon Cahill sent me."

Eddie wasn't as shocked as he might have been at mention of the big, black-haired Yank who'd come to Keira's rescue.

"You're Eddie O'Shea, aren't you?" Davenport asked.

Eddie tried not to gape at the man. "How did you—"

"You and your brothers are too honest not to leave a trail."

Somewhere in Will Davenport's words was a compliment, Eddie thought, but no matter. At least he was getting no more argument from Mary.

"How do I know you're telling the truth?" Eddie asked.

Davenport didn't hesitate or look miffed. "Simon got into an argument about Irish weather when he was at your pub the other night. He says everyone liked him, regardless."

That sounded like Keira Sullivan's black-haired rescuer, but Eddie was still wary.

"All right, then," Davenport said. "Seamus Harrigan is the name of the Garda inspector looking into what happened in your village."

"That's not hard to find out."

The Brit's hazel eyes narrowed, and Eddie detected a seriousness about him—a competence that went beyond getting his brothers to rat him out. Davenport said quietly, "The woman who told Keira Sullivan the story that brought her to Ireland was found murdered this morning in Boston."

Mary gasped, and Eddie, an awful sickness in his stomach, stood up straight, and put out his hand. "It's good to meet you, Will Davenport. I could use any help you have to offer before this devil strikes again."

~Chapter 32

Cambridge, Massachusetts
12:40 p.m., EDT
June 24

As Abigail mounted the front steps to Victor Sarakis's Cambridge house, she was struck by how abandoned the place looked. The grass was taller. Dandelions blew in the afternoon breeze. He was just a week dead, and his home looked more than merely neglected. It looked as if he'd died without anyone in the world who'd cared about him.

Liam Butler's car was in the driveway, but obviously he hadn't worked up the energy or focus—or whatever it would take—to get out the lawn mower.

Or shut the door, Abigail thought, noticing that it was slightly ajar.

She rang the doorbell and waited a few seconds. When there was no answer, she knocked, the door swinging open about a foot.

But as she started to announce herself, she heard music coming from the direction of the devil room.

Irish music.

It was a kick-up-your-heels tune that sounded familiar but she couldn't name.

Why would Irish music be playing in Victor Sarakis's house?

The music paused, and Abigail could hear laughter and talking now—kids.

"It's just not there yet. Let's go through it one more time, okay, guys?"

Fiona.

Abigail stifled a gasp, recognizing the voices of Fiona O'Reilly and her musician friends.

A tape?

Drawing her weapon, Abigail stepped into the foyer. Yarborough and the Cambridge PD would be here any minute.

The music started again, and she noticed the pocket doors to the devil room were wide open. She couldn't see anyone...it had to be a recording.

But where? And why?

Pushing back an image of Bob if he'd been with her, she followed the music into the room with its disturbing collection of devil imagery. On the far wall, the door to the climate-controlled room stood partially open like an invitation—a temptation.

Fiona shrieked with laughter, she and her friends finding delight in having just messed up the piece they were practicing.

Abigail stepped into a small, dark, windowless room. With her free hand, she felt the side wall and switched on an overhead light. The room was obviously once a large closet that had been converted into this climate-controlled space. Floor-to-ceiling shelves were crammed with more items that reflected Victor Sarakis's interests.

The music and the voices of Fiona O'Reilly and her friends were coming from a tape recorder set up on an oak desk. It was a trick, Abigail thought. A mind game by someone who'd expected her, who wanted to unnerve her.

Oh, God.

Photographs—a dozen of them, at least, tacked to a bulletin board propped against the leg of a desk.

Fiona...Madeleine O'Reilly, Jayne O'Reilly.

Bob's daughters.

There was blond-haired Fiona in front of the Garrison house on Beacon Street.

Red-headed Madeleine at soccer practice.

Little blond Jayne eating an ice cream cone in Lexington with her friends.

Abigail steadied herself. Where the hell was Liam Butler?

She headed back out into the main room and reached for her cell phone with her free hand, dialing Scoop. "I need to put you in charge of finding Bob's daughters. All three of them. Owen's with Fiona on Beacon Hill. I have no idea where Madeleine and Jayne are."

"What about Keira?"

"Find her, too." There were no pictures of Keira on the bulletin board, but Abigail wasn't taking any chances. As unemotionally as possible, she described the scene at Sarakis's house. "Yarborough's on the way with the Cambridge guys."

Scoop swore under his breath. "What else can I do?"

"I haven't told Bob yet." It'd be tough, telling Bob, and she needed to stay focused on what she was doing. "Find him, Scoop. Find him now. Tell him."

"It's done."

She stepped out into the main hall, her gun still drawn. "Scoop, I don't know what's real and what's a mind game. This creep—"

"Doesn't matter right now. We cover all the bases until we know what's going on. Be careful, Abigail. Wait for Yarborough."

But she saw blood smeared on the hardwood floor and heard a moan down the hall. Butler? One of the O'Reilly girls? "I can't wait."

⌒Chapter 33

South Boston, Massachusetts
12:50 p.m., EDT
June 24

Bob O'Reilly walked from his old street to Saint Ita's, his boyhood church, just as he had so many times growing up. His colleagues were still processing the scene of Patsy's murder. They'd be at it a while. He couldn't stand the thought of her dying the way she had, but how many times had she told him she'd die fighting the devil with her bare hands? And it had been a quick, if bloody, death. Her killer hadn't toyed with her the way Deirdre's had.

The lead detective, a guy Bob had helped train, had pulled him aside and said they believed Patsy's killer had set up the angels and the pictures in the dining room after she was already dead.

That was something, anyway.

Saint Ita's was a white sided building that looked as if it belonged on a New England town green. He almost ran into a sobbing white-haired woman on the front walk. She identified herself as a friend of Patsy's and told him the priest was in the attached parish hall. Bob was relieved. He hadn't stepped foot in Saint Ita's since Deirdre's funeral all those years ago, and now, at least, he could avoid the sanctuary.

He found Father Palermo sitting on an old pew pushed up against the wall for extra seating. In his open palm was a delicate white porcelain angel, a small Irish harp in her arms that Bob recognized immediately.

"That was one of Deirdre McCarthy's favorites," Bob said. "It wasn't a gift. She picked it out herself."

Palermo nodded without looking up.

"Patsy gave it to you?"

"Yes. At our angel bazaar a few weeks ago."

"Interesting that of all her angels, she parted with that one."

Bob glanced at the empty room, imagined it filled with tables and displays of angels, imagined Patsy beaming proudly, because hers would have been the best collection there—and because it would reflect well on Deirdre's memory.

Palermo didn't respond, and Bob said, "So, Father, if I dug into your background, would I discover your real name isn't Michael Palermo?"

The priest raised his dark eyes to Bob, but he didn't try to read them. If he was right, Palermo had practiced for this moment.

When Palermo still didn't speak, Bob continued. "Stuart Fuller had a younger brother. Nice kid, apparently. I never met him. He was just fourteen when Deirdre was killed. Lousy family. Abusive parents, lots of sudden moves, lots of different schools. So you know what the kid did?"

Palermo lowered his eyes again to his

angel. "He found an escape—a way out of the darkness."

"He created a fantasy world for himself. He filled one notebook after another with *National Geographic* articles on islands in the Mediterranean."

"How did you learn about these notebooks, Detective O'Reilly?"

There was no sharpness in Palermo's tone, no bitterness, just curiosity—as if he'd played out the different ways this all would end and hadn't come up with this one. "My father was a cop," Bob said.

Palermo shook his head. "Your father didn't tell you about the notebooks. He was a regular beat cop—the people here say he loved being on the street."

Bob shrugged. "He never wanted to be a detective. He knew I did—everyone did. People said things in front of me. I paid attention. It's not in the file on Deirdre's murder, about this kid and his notebooks. I doubt anyone's around anymore who'd remember."

Not true. John March remembered. He had worked the investigation as a young BPD detective, and Bob had talked to him just before heading over to Saint Ita's, asking the FBI director if there was anything he could think of about the people Stuart Fuller had left behind. Mother, father, brothers, sisters, friends.

March told him about the notebooks.

When Palermo didn't say anything, Bob resumed. "Palermo's the capital of Sicily, the largest island in the Mediterranean. I heard the brother turned to religion after Stuart's death. Funny how these things work out, isn't it?"

Palermo didn't answer right away. "Maybe so, Detective O'Reilly. Maybe so."

"Patsy figured out who you were, didn't she?"

"We never discussed it."

"She figured it out, Father. Trust me. I grew up a couple of doors down from her. I helped her bury her only daughter. Giving you that angel was Patsy's way of telling you she didn't blame you for what your brother did."

Palermo looked up, and this time his eyes brimmed with tears. "She didn't deserve to lose Deirdre. She didn't deserve what my brother did."

"No, she didn't."

Palermo sank back against the pew, but he kept a tight grip on the angel figurine. "Patsy asked me to drive her to Beacon Hill to see Keira Sullivan before she left for Ireland—and I realized then that she knew I was Stuart's brother. It wasn't anything she said. But there's no doubt in my mind that she had me pegged."

"Did she kill your brother, Father?"

His expression softened, and Bob could see how the members of his church had come to love him as their priest. That was the word from the detectives back at Patsy's house—that she and everyone else adored Father Palermo. "You know in your heart she didn't kill Stuart," Palermo said. "After Deirdre's body turned up, Patsy figured out where Stuart had taken her. Where he killed her. Where he was hiding. She didn't tell the police."

"How did she figure it out?"

"She told me an angel came to her. I am a priest, Detective O'Reilly. That part's not a lie. But I don't believe she meant, literally, that an angel told her."

"Stuart called her," Bob said, seeing it now.

"He told her that he wanted to ask her forgiveness."

"Patsy didn't believe that line, did he?"

"No. She knew he was manipulating her. He wanted to relish her pain. My brother fed off other people's suffering, Detective O'Reilly. Patsy's grief and horror were as satisfying to him in their own way as what he did to her daughter." Palermo got heavily to his feet. "Stuart lured Patsy out to the boat where he was hiding. He set himself on fire in front of her. She blamed herself for not stopping him."

"Could she have?"

"Who's to say? I doubt it, personally. She was glad he couldn't hurt anyone else, and she was glad he'd suffered. She didn't regret that she didn't tell the police that Stuart had called her. She knew they'd stop her from going out to him—"

"Damn straight," Bob said.

Palermo hesitated before he continued. "I'm convinced Stuart planned that call to Patsy right from the beginning. He wanted to make them both suffer. Patsy and Deirdre. Mother and daughter."

Bob grimaced, but he said, "Unusual for someone like that to commit suicide."

Palermo didn't comment. He looked tired, ashen, but he attempted a smile. "Patsy was so happy when Keira came into her life." He gave a small laugh. "She was someone else Patsy could tell her stories to."

"She was quite a storyteller."

"The best. She loved Keira's work—a lot of the people in the church do. She has quite a following here."

"That's nice," Bob said tightly, uncomfortable with mention of his niece.

"Patsy believed good things would happen if the stone angel in the story of hers was ever found—she loved the idea of it as much as anything. Detective O'Reilly, I never meant..." Palermo shook his head, his eyes filling again with tears. "It doesn't matter what I meant.

My brother played a terrible, twisted game with her, but what have I done?"

"Did you ever think she was in danger?"

"No. I saw no danger, Detective. I felt none."

"The only person responsible for the violence against Patsy is the one who committed it. Period. The same with Deirdre."

"Life isn't that black-and-white, is it?"

"Some things aren't. This is."

Bob thought of Abigail and her investigation into the drowning in the Public Garden. He'd been so impatient with her. He wasn't the only one, but how many times in the past years had he told her not to hold back just because she was taking heat? If she had a legitimate reason to pursue a line of questioning, a theory, then she should do it.

"Did you know Victor Sarakis, Father?"

"Just his name. He's the man who drowned the night I drove Patsy into Boston to see Keira."

"Liam Butler, Charlotte and Jay Augustine?"

He shook his head. "No." Palermo

pulled open the outer door and bright sunshine streamed into the hall. "If you think of any other questions, Detective O'Reilly, I'll be here."

"I have to report what I know about you, Father."

"Yes. Of course you do. I'm sorry I lied about who I am. And I'm sorry about Patsy, Detective. I only knew her a relatively short time, but I was very fond of her."

"I didn't stay in touch with her the way I should have."

"From what I saw, she found a way to carry on with her life. We were all affected by what my brother did thirty years ago. Your sister's new life, I'm sure, is partly a result of—"

Bob stopped abruptly in the doorway. "What do you know about my sister?"

Palermo reddened. "Just what everyone else in the parish knows. She came to mass from time to time before she finished building her cabin. People here like her and appreciate her commitment to her faith, but they're surprised she chose this life. They're not being critical of her. They just didn't expect it because she's such a people person."

"Eileen's always been hard on herself."

"That's not the purpose of the life she's chosen."

"It's hers."

Palermo said nothing.

"Has Keira talked to anyone else in the church about their old family stories?" Bob asked.

"Not specifically, no, but word has gone out that she wants to talk to people who emigrated from Ireland in the last century."

"Anyone you know who's involved in this Boston-Cork conference?"

Palermo shook his head.

"What about people who collect Irish art and whatnot?"

"That's a broad group—"

"Someone who'd know Patsy, my sister, my niece," Bob said.

"Well, the Murphys, of course. They're avid collectors. I heard they bid on one of your niece's paintings at the auction, but I don't believe they were actually there."

Bob knew the Murphys. "Did you tell the detectives about them?"

"No—"

"Do. Go on up to Patsy's house and tell them. They'll want to know." Bob felt his cell phone vibrate. "I have to go. Be where we can find you."

Palermo nodded, clutching the angel and looking pale and shaken as Bob headed back outside. He glanced at the readout on his cell phone and sighed as he saw Scoop Wisdom's name and answered. "I hope to hell you're not calling to talk to me about compost piles."

"Everyone's okay, Bob," Scoop said. "I'm on my way to the Garrison house. Owen's there with Fiona. The Lexington police have Madeleine and Jayne. They're okay. They're all okay."

Bob had to lock his knees to keep them from going out from under him. "Bring me up-to-date. What the hell are you talking about?"

Bob stood in the summer sun on the sidewalk of his youth. Scoop described the pictures and tape Abigail had discovered at the Cambridge house of her drowning victim. Victor Sarakis. The man whose death Bob had insisted was an accident unrelated to the auction on Beacon Street that night. To Keira. To his family.

He pushed back the guilt. "What about Keira?" he asked when Scoop had finished.

"She's on her way to see her mother—"

Bob swore, cutting Scoop off, and looked back at the parish hall. Killing Patsy may have been expedient, but it also had been part of the plan. Setting up the angels, the pictures, the prayer card. Finishing Stuart Fuller's work. Mother and daughter were both dead now. Patsy, Deirdre.

Bob thought of the devils in Victor Sarakis's house.

They were chasing a devil. That was for damn sure.

Billie and Jeanette Murphy, longtime members of Saint Ita's, had let Eileen build her cabin on their land in southern New Hampshire. They'd bid on one of Keira's paintings. They collected Irish art.

Patsy had told Keira her Irish stories.

And someone had watched, plotted, manipulated and, finally, taken action.

"He wanted to make them both suffer. Patsy and Deirdre. Mother and daughter."

Bob felt the hairs on the back of his neck stand on end. "Scoop, it's Eileen and Keira. They're this bastard's target. They're the main event for this devil."

"How the hell—never mind. We'll get the state and local guys out to your sister's place. Can you can give them directions?"

"Follow the bread-crumb trail through the ferns—no, I can't give them directions. I've never been out there. We need to find the Murphys. They own the land. They'll know."

"I'm on it, Bob."

He gave Scoop their names, where to find them. "Cahill's on his way to New Hampshire," Scoop said. "He's FBI— Keira must have given him directions."

"FBI?" Bob tried to smile; gallows humor had always been his defense. "Can't wait to see Keira when she figures out she's fallen for a Fed."

"Think she's fallen for him?"

"Hard and fast. It's the only way she does things." Bob's chest felt tight. "Scoop...I can't lose them."

"You won't. I have to get moving, Bob."

"Yeah, go. I'm on my way to Cambridge. Scoop—" Bob choked up. "Thanks."

But Scoop had already hung up.

~Chapter 34

Near Mount Monadnock
Southern New Hampshire
1:00 p.m., EDT
June 24

The city and suburbs of Boston gave way to rolling hills, woods and farmland as Keira drove west and then north into New Hampshire, but the picturesque scenery gave her no sense of relief as she pulled over to the side of the quiet secondary road just before the turn for her mother's cabin. Colm Dermott was on the phone, and she didn't want to risk losing service before he could finish what he'd called to tell her.

Jeanette and Billie Murphy—the couple who owned the land on which her mother had built her cabin—had purchased the second painting she had donated to the auction.

"I didn't see them, but I arrived late—"

"They weren't there." Normally so cheerful, Colm sounded tense, strained. "They bought the painting through a third party. Keira, this is troubling—Jay and Charlotte Augustine acted as intermediaries for the Murphys. They're fine art and antiques dealers in Boston. Charlotte Augustine is Victor Sarakis's sister."

"But Colm—he's the man who drowned."

"Yes," he said.

Keira tried to contain her shock. She rolled her window down, her heart racing as she listened to the stream that ran alongside the road. She was all alone out here. There were no other cars, no houses, no people in sight.

"The Augustines telephoned the bid on behalf of the Murphys," Colm said. "I'm trying to find the volunteer who took the call. I'm positive the Augustines didn't attend the auction. Their names aren't in the database of people we invited or on any of the sign-in sheets. Not everyone signed in, of course, but I don't remember meeting them. I would think I would have. I made a point of greeting everyone who attended, and I have a good head for names. Keira," he said, increasingly breathless, "the police will want this information, won't they?"

"Yes, absolutely they will, Colm. Have you heard of the Augustines? Do you know anything about them?"

"I looked them up on the Internet. They seem to be respected and knowledgeable dealers."

"Do they specialize in Irish works?"

"Not that I can see, no."

"I'm not thinking of my painting—I can't imagine it's what the Augustines are into." She felt a warm breeze, heard crows in the distance. "I'm thinking of Patsy McCarthy's stone angel. Would that interest them, assuming it's Celtic or even Celtic Revival?"

"It would interest a lot of people, Keira."

She sighed. "I can't imagine some

high-class Boston dealers crawling around in an Irish ruin for a statute they'd have no reason to believe exists." Keira paused, suddenly feeling isolated on the quiet road. Her throat tightened with emotion. "But I can't imagine someone killing an old woman in her own home, either."

"That surely was a terrible thing," Colm said.

"Has anyone picked up the Murphys' painting?"

"Not yet."

"Colm—you've been incredible. I'll lose cell coverage any minute, so I can't call the police myself—"

"I have the numbers you left me right here. I'll try your uncle first. Keira... please, be careful. This is worrying."

"I don't have far to go. I'll be at my mother's cabin soon."

After they disconnected, Keira drove another mile before turning onto a narrow dirt road that took her deeper into the woods and finally dead-ended in a small circle. She got out and stood a moment, catching her breath amid the pine trees and sugar maples. Just a week ago, she'd come out here to talk to her mother about her trip to Ireland. Despite her ambivalence over her mother's new life, Keira had looked forward to seeing her. The prospect of finding out about her birth father had intrigued her, but it was the story of the three Irish brothers and their battle with the fairies over possession of a stone angel—the possibilities it presented to her as both an artist and a folklorist—that had fired her imagination.

She located the trail that led to her mother's cabin just as a stiff, sudden gust of wind blew strands of her hair in her face. She hadn't even thought to pin up her hair that morning. She'd been in a hurry to see Patsy and to get her black-haired search-and-rescue expert out of her apartment before anything else happened between them.

Except he was also an FBI agent.

Keira doubted that was Simon Cahill's only secret. He was a charmer if ever there was one, but he was also a man of many layers.

Another breeze stirred. She picked up her pace, navigating tree roots, rocks and low-hanging tree branches, pushing through the tall ferns that flanked the narrow trail. Ordinarily, she would have enjoyed the hike, especially on such a beautiful summer day, but today she felt only dread at the prospect of facing her mother, telling her about Patsy and pleading with her to talk—about Ireland and her long-dead friend.

And if she couldn't talk, at least engage with her daughter the way she used to, if only for a few minutes. Listen. Be there. Was that so selfish to want?

Keira forced herself to dismiss any need on her part. She'd only known Patsy for a matter of weeks. Her mother had known her all her life.

Why not turn around and go back to Boston? Why even tell her?

Keira tripped on an exposed rock, but regained her balance before she fell. The stumble brought her out of her thoughts, and she focused again on her surroundings. For the entire drive, she'd debated whether to leave her mother in blissful ignorance. Let her pray and work in her isolated world. Wasn't that what she wanted? But Keira had kept driving, and now she kept walking, because she didn't have a choice. She had only to envision Patsy's body, and the angels and pictures on the dining room table, and she knew she couldn't turn back.

As she came to the rustic cabin, Keira was struck by the similarities of the site she'd chosen to that of the ruin in Ireland. Although the landscape was more thickly wooded here than the open countryside on the Beara Peninsula, and there were no sheep or ancient stone circles in the area, the hill dipping down to a stream and the remoteness of the spot brought Keira back to her search for the ruin of Patsy's hermit monk hut on the evening of the summer solstice.

She gave an exaggerated shudder to rein in her active imagination and stepped up to the cabin's back door, calling through the screen. When there was no answer, she didn't hesitate, just pulled open the door and poked her head inside. "Hey, Mum—it's me, Keira."

But still there was no answer. She

hadn't considered that her mother might be at the spring fetching water or checking on the Murphys' country house—or even just out in the woods listening to the birds.

She went inside, calling again as she headed through the rustic kitchen into the cabin's main room. Her mother had left a series of sketches of various serpents on her worktable.

She must have gone outside for a break, Keira thought, venturing out the front door.

She noticed the faint smell of sawdust and several freshly split logs awaiting their addition to the neatly stacked woodpile. With the woodstove her mother's only source of heat, the work to keep it stocked was never ending. Keira would have helped, but that wasn't an option in the new rules her mother adopted for her life.

The fenced-in garden was quiet in the afternoon sun. It included flowers as well as vegetables, which Keira had taken as a positive sign that this isolated existence really was what made her mother happy.

She heard a muffled sound down toward the stream.

A moan.

Her heart jumped, even as she saw a wet, dark smear on the tree stump her mother used as a chopping block, and it was as if she were back at the ruin in Ireland, standing up from the fallen tree covered in sheep's blood.

Except this wasn't sheep's blood.

Mum—where are you?

A splitter was propped against the chopping block. Keira took it in both hands, but there was no blood on the metal head.

The wind gusted through the trees, and she could hear the stream tumbling over rocks below her on the hillside.

She pictured him peering down at her in the rubble of the ruin, so calm, so competent. She didn't care that he'd obviously thought she'd been reckless, or that she'd worked for hours in grueling conditions to construct her makeshift ladder. That didn't matter—she couldn't think of anyone she'd rather have at her side right now.

She steadied herself. She'd chopped

wood with her mother as a kid. She could wield a splitter if she had to.

She saw a shadow—a movement—among the hemlocks on the hillside.

It wasn't a squirrel or a wild turkey, or even the wind.

Someone was there.

~Chapter 35

Near Mount Monadnock
Southern New Hampshire
1:25 p.m., EDT
June 24

Simon's cell phone rang a few miles after he'd crossed into New Hampshire from Massachusetts. Before he could speak, Will Davenport said, "I have information, Simon."

"Are you having trouble getting to Ireland?"

"I'm here in Kenmare."

"Even our Moneypenny couldn't get you there this fast. Helicopter, Will, or were you already there when I called?"

"I anticipated you'd need my assistance."

Simon tensed, hearing the note of seriousness in his friend's voice. "Go ahead, Will. What's up?"

"An American named Jay Augustine arrived in Shannon on a flight from Boston on the morning of June twenty-first," Will said. "He rented a car at the airport and stayed in Kenmare that night. He returned to Boston the next day on a flight out of Shannon. He would have arrived midafternoon."

Given Will's extensive sources inside and outside government, Simon wasn't surprised at how much his friend had managed to discover in such a short time.

Will was also thorough, and he had a labyrinthine, suspicious mind.

"The timing fits," Simon said. "Who is he?"

"Jay Augustine is the brother-in-law of the man your Keira found dead in Boston before she left for Ireland herself."

Simon swore. He was keeping an eye out for the turn onto the dirt road that would take him to Eileen Sullivan's cabin. At the speed he'd been going, he figured he couldn't be too far behind Keira. "Go on," he said tightly. "There's more, isn't there?"

Will continued with his grim report. "Physical evidence—a blood-stained sweater—places Augustine at Keira's ruin on the Beara Peninsula. He and his wife are fine art and antique dealers in Boston, Simon. They would know the value of an ancient Irish artifact and have access to potential buyers."

"Money could explain wanting to beat Keira to the angel and make off with it. It also could explain leaving her in the rubble of that ruin. But the sheep, Will..." Simon broke off, controlling his anger. Keira had gone to Ireland to research an innocent story of mischief and magic, hoping to understand her mother and learn more about her birth father—perhaps, in a way, both her fathers. The one who'd given her life and the one who'd adopted her.

Simon saw his turn, took it and realized he was losing cell coverage.

"Simon?"

"I'm about to lose you, Will. I'm in the woods, on my way to Keira and her mother. Augustine didn't do much to cover his tracks."

"That means he has an escape plan," Will said. "What do you want me to do?"

"Inform the Irish police—"

"Are you kidding? They're on my elbow right now." But Will's touch of humor faded almost immediately. "This man's a cold, calculating predator, Simon."

"Yeah," Simon said, but he knew his phone had died.

The road was narrow and dotted with potholes, but he drove faster. Will and the Irish police would get word to Boston law enforcement about Jay Augustine. In the meantime, Simon would find Keira and her mother.

He rolled down his window, heard birds and felt the breeze. He could understand the appeal of building a cabin out in the woods. He lived on a boat himself, although for most of the past eighty-plus miles, he'd pictured Keira on his boat with him. If she didn't know about boats, he could teach her. If she did, he could just watch her paint Irish fairies and rainbows.

An image of Patsy McCarthy interrupted Simon's visions of sailing the seven seas—any sea—with his fairy princess.

He kept driving.

⁓*Chapter 36*

Cambridge, Massachusetts
1:30 p.m., EDT
June 24

Charlotte Augustine shrieked on the
front walk to her brother's house. "You
can't stop me! I have a right to be here.
I'm Victor's next of kin." She pushed at
the Cambridge PD officer restraining
her. "Let me go, damn you!"

Abigail stepped out of the house and
ducked under the yellow tape two officers were still unfurling to mark off the
crime scene. Two Cambridge detectives, who reminded her of Bob, glow-
ered at her, but they didn't impede her.

Tom Yarborough fell in behind her. He was fair-haired, driven and absolutely the most cynical law enforcement officer Abigail had ever met, and she'd met plenty. He hadn't let her out of his sight since he'd arrived twenty minutes ago, finding her on her knees in a pool of blood as she tried to save Liam Butler's life. The Cambridge police and paramedics had since descended.

"Actually, they can stop you," Abigail told Charlotte.

"What's happened? My husband—Liam—"

"Liam's in tough shape. He's been stabbed repeatedly." But deliberately left alive, if barely so, Abigail thought. In order to suffer or to distract police, at least for a little while. Maybe both. "I found him in the sunroom. I did what I could. Paramedics are with him now."

"Will he..." Charlotte trembled, unsteady on her feet. "He'll live, won't he?"

"I don't know."

She put a hand to her mouth. "Oh, no...no."

"Where's your husband, Charlotte?" Abigail asked quietly.

"Did Liam—did he tell you who did attacked him?"

It was a question Abigail had no intention of answering. Liam had been at best semiconscious, unable to respond to any of her questions or instructions—finally, she'd just applied pressure to the worst of his wounds and waited for medical help to arrive.

"Mrs. Augustine—"

"I don't know where Jay is."

"Did you know that Liam was spying on you and your husband?"

Charlotte wobbled and took in shallow breaths. "I have no idea what you're talking about."

Abigail shook her head. "I think you do, Charlotte."

"Go to hell. You have no right to tell me what I know and what I don't know."

Yarborough moved slightly behind Abigail, but he said nothing. She noticed the dandelions going to seed in the unkempt yard and remembered the traditional, expensive clothes Victor Sarakis had been wearing the night he drowned.

A man of contradictions, but wasn't everyone? Charlotte herself wore a female version of her brother's attire—light-colored khakis, a dark pink polo shirt, tennis shoes, simple gold jewelry. Nothing antique, nothing Celtic—nothing to indicate she had an interest in Irish artifacts.

"Mrs. Augustine," Abigail said, "when's the last time you were in your brother's climate-controlled room?"

Her hand dropped from her mouth. "What? Why?"

Abigail debated, then answered. "There's a bulletin board in there that's covered with photographs of the daughters of another detective—"

"They're not Victor's doing!"

"I believe we're dealing with a serial killer, Charlotte. You can help us stop him by telling us what you know."

She sagged, taking a step backward toward the street. She looked as if she might faint, but she rallied, even as tears streamed down her cheeks. "The spying—it was Victor's doing. He asked Liam to help him. He—they—" Charlotte faltered, wiped her tears with her finger-tips. "They were trying to help me."

"How?" Abigail asked.

"Everything's happening so fast..."

"Just stick to the facts. You can sort out all the emotions later. Okay? How did your brother think he was helping you by spying on you and your husband?"

"I wanted a divorce," she blurted, then waved a hand dismissively. "Jay travels so much. That's where he is now. Traveling."

"Traveling where?"

"I don't know. He didn't tell me. He often doesn't. He's on the road a lot because of his work. Our work, I mean." She squinted at Yarborough, then at Abigail. Except for her red cheeks, there was no sign of tears now. "Jay is...remote."

"Have you told him you want a divorce?"

"No. No, I haven't." She wrapped her arms around herself, hugging herself as if she was cold. "I'd hoped Victor's death was an accident. If he was murdered—can you imagine what that'll do to my life?"

Abigail stiffened and gave Yarborough a sideways glance, saw that Charlotte's comment had hit a wrong note with him, too. Never mind cooperating with the police and, if her brother had been murdered, finding his killer—making sure no one else got hurt.

But Charlotte Augustine didn't seem to think there was anything off-putting about her remark. "Detective Browning, I know you have to explore all the possibilities, but I don't see how these photographs of the detective's daughters or the attack on Liam have anything to do with me or my husband. What if Liam's the one responsible for the bulletin board, and this detective found out and attacked him?"

"That didn't happen," Yarborough said.

Charlotte went ashen. "I'm sorry, I..." Fresh tears welled. "I want to help if I can. Go ahead. Please. Ask me any questions you want to."

"Keira Sullivan," Abigail said. "Do you know her?"

A flicker of recognition.

Yarborough took a half step forward. "The truth, Mrs. Augustine."

She tightened her hug on herself and looked toward the house as the door opened and paramedics carried out Liam Butler on a stretcher. "Oh, Liam," she whispered.

"Charlotte," Abigail said, "how do you know Keira Sullivan?"

"I don't. We—we've never met. I just know her name. Her work. Victor showed me one of her illustrated books the day he drowned. That afternoon. I didn't tell you. He came out to the house..." She bit on her lower lip. "It was the last time I saw him."

Abigail could see that Charlotte wasn't finished and didn't interrupt her pause.

"I only remember because I liked the illustrations. They're so original—so cheerful. I was surprised Victor liked them, considering his obsession with the devil and evil."

"Why did your brother show you Keira's book?" Abigail asked.

"I don't know!"

But that wasn't the truth, and Yarborough, clearly losing patience, shook his head. Instead of pouncing on Charlotte for her obvious dissembling, he spoke quietly to her. "You have a lot bottled up inside you, Mrs. Augustine. You just lost your brother. It's tough. We know that." His tone was reassuring, friendly. "It'd do you good to finally let it all out. Tell us everything. Let us decide what helps and what doesn't. Don't censor yourself."

She dropped her arms to her sides. "It has been hard. So hard. I wish now I'd pushed Victor to give me more information, but I didn't. And now it's too late."

"There was an event on Beacon Hill the night he drowned," Abigail said. "A benefit for a folklore conference. Keira Sullivan was there. So was one of the girls whose pictures are on the bulletin board. Did Victor—"

"He wasn't invited. Jay and I weren't, either."

"Charlotte—"

"I don't know why Victor showed me that damn book! He was *spying* on me, Detective Browning. He was trying to help, but still." She suddenly kicked the top off a dandelion, sending little white seeds floating into the air. "He didn't like Jay."

Her tone had changed, and Abigail resisted the temptation to jump in with another question. Yarborough remained impassive at her side.

Charlotte squashed what was left of her dandelion with her toe. "I want this all to go away. But it won't, will it?" She raised her gaze to Abigail. "Liam didn't know why Victor was having him spy on Jay and me. Victor didn't tell him. There was no need to tell me—I saw for myself what was going on with Jay. I just didn't want to admit it."

"But Victor did tell you," Abigail said.

Charlotte nodded. She wasn't shaking now. "He said there were times when he'd look at Jay and think he was looking into the eyes of the devil. I wanted to believe it was an exaggeration. I didn't want to believe Jay was that bad."

"He is, though," Yarborough said. "Isn't he?"

"I think so," Charlotte said, hugging herself again.

Out on the street, Abigail saw Bob

O'Reilly pull up to the curb, jump out of his car and show his badge to a Cambridge police officer, who didn't stop him.

Abigail didn't contain herself. "Bob—your daughters—"

"They're safe. They're with Scoop, Owen and the Lexington police." But he didn't look even marginally relieved as he narrowed his eyes on Charlotte Augustine. "Jeanette and Billie Murphy."

She gasped as if he'd stuck her with a needle and she lunged for the street, but Abigail and Yarborough both grabbed her before she could get a half step. Charlotte calmed down, and they let her wriggle free.

Bob hadn't moved. "You acted on behalf of the Murphys and bought one of my niece's paintings at the auction the night your brother drowned."

"I told Detective Browning already that my husband and I weren't there."

"You phoned in the bid. I just talked to the Irish professor who's heading up the conference—"

"He's wrong."

"The Murphys are your clients. They're

into their Irish heritage." Bob was steady, focused. "They'd love to get their hands on an Irish Celtic stone angel like the one in Patsy McCarthy's story."

Charlotte turned to Yarborough, as if he could help her, but he just stepped back from her. She started shaking again. "Please—the Murphys aren't involved in any of this. I didn't tell you about the painting because I knew you'd jump to the wrong conclusion."

Bob remained icy. "You picked up the painting this morning."

"No—"

"Charlotte," Abigail said without sympathy, "no more lies and half truths."

She stared down at the ground. Some of the fight seemed to go out of her. "I delivered the painting to Billie Murphy's office in Boston. He wasn't there. I left it with his receptionist."

"Whose idea was it to bid on it?" Bob asked.

Charlotte clamped her mouth shut and refused to answer.

Even Yarborough gave a little hiss—no more playing the nice, patient police officer—but Bob remained calm to the point of scary. He rocked back on his heels. "Mrs. Augustine," he said, "you're going to tell us what you know."

Abigail glanced at the paramedics sliding the stretcher into the back of an ambulance. Liam Butler was fighting for his life, and this woman was playing games. "You need to stop thinking about how this situation is going to affect your business and your social life."

"The Murphys are new clients," Charlotte said weakly. "They're from working-class South Boston, but they have a spectacular home now on the waterfront. They're wonderful people. They have exquisite taste—"

Bob cut her off. "I grew up with them. I know who the hell they are. They looked after a woman who was just found knifed to death in her own house. The Murphys were good to her. They own the land in New Hampshire where my sister built a cabin. How did you meet them, Mrs. Augustine?"

"My husband. Jay—I don't know how he met them."

"He insinuated himself into the Murphys' lives, Patsy McCarthy's life—*my* life." Bob's tone hardened even more. "Where is Jay now?"

"I told Detective Browning—he's traveling."

"He's not traveling."

"No," Charlotte mumbled. "Please."

"My sister's name is Eileen Sullivan. She's a religious ascetic. She—"

Charlotte was sobbing quietly now. "I know. I don't know her, but we— Jay and I have been out to the Murphys' house in New Hampshire."

Bob didn't say a word, but Abigail could feel her own knees going unsteady under her. Jay Augustine knew how to get to Eileen Sullivan's cabin. She was there. Keira was on her way.

"Bob..."

He turned and walked back out to the street.

Yarborough nodded to Abigail. "Go. I'll see to Mrs. Augustine and fill in the Cambridge guys."

"Tom—"

"It's Bob's family, Abigail. Go."

She tried to smile. "I might have to revise my opinion of you."

He ignored her, and she ran to join Bob. She didn't know what she could do to help, but he didn't have to be alone.

～*Chapter 37*

Near Mount Monadnock
Southern New Hampshire
1:45 p.m., EDT
June 24

Keira sank onto her knees on the bank of the stream in front of her mother, whose moan of pain had been the sound she'd heard. Her mother sat with her knees tucked under her chin in the shade of a white pine, her hands and feet bound tightly with blood-soaked rope.

She was bleeding from a dozen slashes on her arms and shoulders. Superficial wounds, Keira thought. Designed to elicit pain and a lot of blood, not to kill. Not yet, at least.

"I can feel the Irish wind on my face," her mother whispered, her lips cracked and bloodied from where she'd bit down during her torture. "Oh, I can see the green—such a green. Deirdre won't fly. She would love to see her mother's birth place and meet her Irish relatives, but she's too afraid to get on a plane."

"Mum...it's Keira." She had to fight to keep herself from sobbing. "You're in New England. Be with me now, okay?"

Her mother's eyes flickered, and she tried to sit up straighter. "Keira, please tell me you understand. I didn't tell you about Deirdre because I couldn't. She was—she was the best of us, and she was taken from us..."

"I know, Mum. I understand."

A few feet from them, the stone angel stood among the ferns at the edge of the stream, as beautiful as the night of the summer solstice when Keira had spotted it on the hearth of the collapsing ruin.

"Run, Keira." Her mother groaned in pain. "Leave me. *Please*."

"Don't talk. Save your strength."

"We can't let him kill again."

He was there, Keira realized. In the trees, just as he'd been in Ireland. Lurking, enjoying the fear and suffering he was causing.

Jay Augustine.

Using the edge of the splitter, she managed to whack through the rope on her mother's ankles. The rope on her wrists, yanked tight and soaked with blood, would be impossible to cut with any precision—she'd need a sharp knife.

"Can you walk?" she asked her mother.

"Yes...but, Keira, take the splitter. Run as fast as you can. Let him amuse himself with me—I'll buy you as much time as I can."

"I'm not leaving you."

Keira rose, slipping in the mud as she hung on to the splitter and, with her free hand, helped her mother up. *Distract and disrupt.* It was one commandment she remembered from her police academy days for just such a situation. She didn't have to take on Jay Augustine.

She simply had to distract him and disrupt his plans, get her and her mother away from him if she could.

"He's evil, Keira," her mother said. "He's not insane. He's chosen this path."

"I know, Mum."

Her mother was reasonably steady on her feet despite the blood, her bound wrists. "He doesn't believe in angels or saints—or fairies and magic. Or the devil himself. He just wants to commit violence and play his games. Feel his own power."

"What does he have for weapons?"

"Knives. Two that I saw. And fear. He uses fear as a weapon."

At least if he didn't have a gun, Keira thought, he couldn't just shoot them from the bushes. She had no doubt he was watching, taking pleasure in her reaction to her mother's condition—plotting his next move. If the splitter deterred him, it wouldn't be for long. He'd think of some way around it.

Her mother faltered, shivering not with cold, Keira realized, but with the agony of her wounds—with her own fear. "He killed Patsy. He told me. She told him that story of hers. He manipulated her, too. It's not your fault. It's not her fault. Oh, Keira."

Keira focused on taking the next step, paying attention to any movement, any sound in the nearby trees and undergrowth. "Let's just keep moving."

Her mother sobbed, then nodded, as if summoning her resolve.

A crunching sound came from the hill above them. "Keira, Keira." A man's voice, chiding her as if she were a recalcitrant child. "Don't you see? Your mother wants to suffer for the sins of her past. She needs to suffer."

Keira maintained her hold on the splitter.

The man stepped out from the cover of several small hemlocks. He was middle-aged, trim, dressed neatly in slacks and a button-down shirt and lightweight jacket. But she saw spots of blood on his slacks, his knuckles, one cheek, and his eyes shone with an excitement that struck her as sexual, physical.

Keira pushed back her own fear. "Jay Augustine, right?"

He seemed momentarily surprised, then gave her a mock bow. "I did anticipate that my identity would be discovered. Part of the fun, in fact." But before Keira or her mother could speak, he continued. "While your saintly mother was cavorting in Ireland, indulging in fairies and magic and sins of the flesh, her best friend was being tortured and raped. She never told you, did she, Keira?"

"Why would she tell me? Any mother would want to protect her child—"

"I'm offering your mother redemption. I left her alive deliberately so she can watch me brutalize you, just as Deirdre's killer did her. You, the daughter conceived in sin—your mother can suffer the worst pain she's ever known, and thus be free."

Keep him talking, Keira thought. "You don't care about redemption—"

"I offered Patsy redemption. She set her daughter's killer on fire."

Keira's mother shook her head. "No. Not Patsy. She didn't kill Stuart. I'd have if I'd known where to find him, but Patsy didn't kill him."

"She wanted to—she let it happen. She always knew she'd have to pay for what she did. When I came for her, she knew her moment had come. I could see it in her eyes."

Keira scoffed at him. "You killed Patsy because she could identify you to the police. You wormed your way into her life, and she told you the story about the stone angel. With what happened in Ireland, you knew she'd figure out your role, and you killed her to protect yourself. Everything else is a narrative you've established for your own amusement."

He ignored her, his arrogance almost palpable. "Do you really think you can take me on with that ridiculous ax?"

Only if I have no choice, Keira thought. "Killing that poor sheep in Ireland wasn't about redemption."

"Practice, my dear Keira." He held up a double-edged assault knife covered in what Keira assumed was her mother's blood. Perhaps Patsy's, too. He smiled. "Practice."

She did her best to hide her revulsion.

"You won't stop with me or my mother. You'll always want more, and you'll pay for it. Someone will make you pay."

"Not you, though, or your mother. And not today."

"Why didn't you kill me in Ireland?" Keira asked quickly, trying to distract him from his knife.

For the first time, he looked uncomfortable.

"You didn't expect me to find the ruin, did you?" She kept any fear out of her tone. "You thought you'd beat me to it. You're a planner—you're not spontaneous. You had to think on your feet when I showed up. Did you assume I'd die there?"

"I didn't want you to." He sounded sincere, as if the thought of her death had troubled him. "I wanted you here, now. I wasn't meant to kill you in Ireland. That way."

"The dog...he wasn't yours. He threw you off your game."

"Too late to help you. The ruin started to collapse and exposed the angel." He gestured with his knife at the simple, mesmerizing statue. "Look at her, Keira.

Her beauty and grace. Have you seen Deidre's picture? They look so alike."

"How did you meet Patsy?" Keira asked, hoping his ego would lull him into lowering his guard, give her an opening, or just keep him talking until Simon could get there.

"We met the day she displayed her silly angels at the church. Most were junk, but a few were of value." He raised his knife to eye level. "I've enjoyed the chitchat, but don't think you're in control. You're not tough, Keira. Don't pretend you are. I can end your mother's suffering in an instant. I can kill you in an instant. It's my choice."

He was almost spitting his words now, but not because of exertion and fatigue, Keira realized. The thrill and anticipation of what he had planned were getting to him. Her pulse throbbed in her ears, and her hands felt clammy as she gripped the heavy splitter, edging closer to him. If he wanted to keep talking, she'd talk, but she knew she had to be prepared to defend herself and her mother.

"If I know about you," Keira said, "the police do, too."

That seemed to throw him off, but only for a moment. "Drop the ax," he said.

Keira knew she'd gone as far with him as she could. He was done talking. "Technically, it's not an ax," she said. "It's a splitter."

With an unexpected surge of energy, her mother stomped on his instep, and Keira whipped the splitter at him. He ducked away from the sharp edge, and she caught him in the midsection with the back of the metal head. He yelped in pain and stumbled, dropping his knife, charging into the woods.

"The police will catch up with him," Keira said, reaching an arm around her mother's waist and helping her to a boulder. She picked up Augustine's knife.

Her mother shook her head. "He'll come back. He's obsessed—he wants to do Deirdre's killer one better. Stuart Fuller enjoyed Patsy's suffering almost as much as he did Deirdre's. Mother and daughter..."

"Maybe, but Augustine's also an art dealer. He'll want to profit from the angel. Does he have a buyer? Did he tell you?"

"The Murphys. They think he's legitimate—"

"They won't for long."

Keira cut the ropes on her mother's wrists.

"It stops here, Keira," her mother said, wincing as she eased her bloody hands in front of her. "We can't let this man kill again."

"We won't, Mum. Simon's on his way. He'll be here soon. He'll help us find this bastard."

"Keira—Simon? Ah, the way you say his name. Did you meet him in Ireland?"

"Boston, actually." She managed a smile. "But I fell for him in Ireland."

Simon slowed his pace on the trail out to Eileen Sullivan's cabin in the woods, thinking he'd heard singing up ahead.

It *was* singing.

Really bad singing, he thought. He recognized "Irish Rover," a song his father used to belt out in the shower a long time ago, but this version had a desperate, half delirious sound to it. A warning? A distraction?

Simon stepped off the trail into knee-high ferns, ducking behind a thick oak tree for cover as a middle-aged man plunged down the trail, both arms out for balance as he negotiated a sharp turn.

He was panting, sweating.

He had to be Jay Augustine.

Simon jumped out onto the trail in front of him. "Stop—FBI. Keep your hands where I can see them—"

Augustine ignored him, turned and bolted into the woods on the opposite side of the trail. Simon raced after him, tackled him and dropped him facedown onto the ground. Hard, right into the middle of a low, thorny bush. Augustine moaned and tried to get up, but Simon held him down.

Moving fast, he got his knee into the middle of Augustine's back and, his eyes on Augustine's hands, cuffed him in about three seconds flat, then patted him down. He found an assault knife in a sheath on Augustine's belt. There was a second, empty sheath.

"Where's Keira?" Simon kept his knee in place. "Where's her mother?"

"Let me go, and I'll tell you."

"You look a little worse for the wear. Keira nail your ass?"

"She'll bleed to death," Augustine said, spitting his words. "So will her mother. Slowly, painfully. You know I can make it happen."

"That wasn't you singing, so I'm guessing they're okay."

Just then, Keira swooped down through the trees with a wood splitter held high.

"Whoa," Simon said. "Easy, there."

She lowered the splitter, breathing hard, hair flying in her face, eyes shining with fury as she focused on Augustine. "Your only way out now is to turn yourself into a bat or a snake, you bastard," she said, "and I'll bet you can't do that."

Augustine raised his chin and grinned at her, enjoying her anger—her hatred—as if he'd accomplished something. Simon didn't ease up on him at all.

A woman who had to be Keira's mother staggered down the nearby trail, bloody, holding an assault knife in one trembling hand. She stepped closer, and Simon couldn't tell if she planned on shoving the knife in Augustine's heart. If she tried, he'd have to stop her.

"That was you singing, Mrs. Sullivan?" he asked her.

She nodded, staring at Augustine. "I thought it would help cover Keira's running and perhaps throw him off, and keep me from having to..." She didn't finish her thought, instead lowering her knife. "I didn't want to scream. I didn't want to give him the satisfaction. I love that song, and I didn't know what else to do."

"We'll belt out some Irish songs together sometime," Simon said, then winked at her. "You, me and the Clancy Brothers."

Keira started toward her mother. "Mum..."

But Eileen Sullivan raised her bloodshot eyes to Simon. "Is your voice better than mine?"

He grinned at her. "A wee bit, ma'am," he said in his best Irish accent.

Sirens sounded in the distance. The local and state police would be arriving soon, and Simon wouldn't be surprised if a few Boston cops were thrown into the mix for good measure.

He saw a glimmer of a smile from Eileen Sullivan as she turned to Keira. "I like his wit," she said, then fainted in her daughter's arms.

~*Chapter 38*

Cambridge, Massachusetts
8:00 p.m., EDT
June 24

Abigail showed her badge to the police officer posted at Liam Butler's hospital room. Prosecutors were still debating whether to charge him with anything, but she doubted they would.

It was late in the evening, the end of a very long day.

Liam looked as if he was sleeping. The worst gash was in his abdomen, but no vital organs were seriously affected. The paramedics and doctors had intervened in time. They'd stopped the bleeding, given him blood and stitched him up. He was on pain medication, but what he needed most now, they said, was time to heal. He'd have scars from his ordeal, but otherwise he'd make a full recovery.

Emotionally, Abigail didn't know. He'd endured a horror few people had ever survived.

And he'd made a lot of mistakes.

Only he wasn't alone when it came to mistakes.

What promised to be a thorough, painstaking investigation had begun. Authorities in Boston, Cambridge and Ireland had already begun retracing Jay Augustine's steps over the past few weeks and months, when he'd gone from being a respected fine art and antiques dealer to a killer handcuffed in the New Hampshire woods.

Charlotte Augustine had already hired a lawyer and a spokesperson to manage media inquiries and to portray her as another of her husband's victims.

Maybe she was, but she hadn't told the truth to the police, either.

Abigail couldn't tell if Liam was aware of her presence. His parents and brother would be arriving soon from Chicago. "Hey, Liam," she said. "It's Abigail Browning. Are you awake?"

"I'm sorry," he mumbled without opening his eyes.

She hadn't expected any response. "Your folks will be here soon," she said.

This time he didn't respond.

Bob O'Reilly entered the room, jerking a thumb back toward the nurses' station. "The nurses are worse than the Cambridge cops. I thought they were going to frisk me before they let me in here."

Abigail was heartened by the return of his wry sense of humor.

He stood next to her at Liam's bed. "Cambridge PD's annoyed with you for not telling them about the devil room," he said.

"You didn't tell them, either."

Bob shrugged. "Hell, I thought your guy tripped on his shoelaces."

"We're still not sure he didn't, figuratively speaking—I realize he was wearing loafers. But it still could have been a freak accident."

"You don't believe that."

She shook her head. "No, I don't. Maybe we'll learn more when the rest of the autopsy results come in. The medical examiner's already taking a closer look at the preliminary results. You'd think there'd have been some obvious sign of a struggle."

"Maybe Victor thought he was up against a devil and didn't struggle."

"Not *a* devil, Bob. *The* devil or one of his minions. There's a distinction—"

"One you don't need to make." Bob grimaced at the sight of the thin, bandaged kid in the bed. "At least Augustine didn't slice and dice his brother-in-law the way he did that sheep in Ireland. What he had in mind for Keira and Eileen..."

"Bob—"

"It worked out," he said. "That's what counts."

"How's your sister?"

"She'll be okay. The bastard didn't lay a finger on Keira. She and that ax." He shook his head. "She's tougher than she looks, that one."

"And your daughters—"

"I think Fi's got a crush on Scoop. Something new to keep me awake nights."

Abigail smiled at Bob's bravado. As far as she could see, there wasn't an O'Reilly who wasn't tough.

"Augustine told people he was in New York the day Victor drowned."

"Yes, well, supposedly he was in New York when he was in Ireland, too."

"He wanted that angel—wanted to beat Keira to it. He knew he could get the Murphys to pay him a fortune for it. Figured he could always take the money and disappear. Start up again under a new name."

"He and Charlotte have only been married two years," Abigail said. "Who knows what we'll find when we dig deeper into his past?"

"Charlotte told Yarborough that she and Jay met after he found some of the pieces for her brother's devil collection. Didn't mention that tidbit to you, did she?"

Abigail shook her head. "Jay told us that day at Victor's that he and Charlotte met over a Renaissance tapestry he'd helped Victor find. Did he hook up with Patsy through the Murphys, or vice versa?"

Bob rubbed the back of his thick neck, his fatigue evident. Today had shaken him, Abigail thought. But she knew he wouldn't stop until he had a solid sense of the time line of the past few weeks. What Jay Augustine had done. When. Why. How. All of it.

"He turned up for the angel bazaar at Saint Ita's," Bob said. "I just came from there. Showed Father Palermo a picture of this maniac. Several dealers stopped by the bazaar looking for bargains— some figurine some poor old lady had squirreled away for years and didn't realize was valuable. Palermo remembers Patsy and Augustine taking a shine to each other."

"He's a manipulative son of a bitch," Abigail said.

"He befriended the Murphys. He and Charlotte are legitimate dealers—Billie and Jeanette had no reason to suspect that anything was wrong. Patsy eventually figured out he was no good." Bob dropped his hand from his neck and looked at Abigail, his cornflower-blue eyes filled with pain. "In the end, she knew."

"He loved it all. Patsy's story and the possibility of finding a valuable Irish Celtic artifact. The tragedy of her daughter's death. Her killer's bizarre death." Abigail bit down on her lower lip to control a wave of emotion. "Keira. Her mother."

"Yeah," Bob said. "He loved it all."

"Keira knows she had nothing to do with bringing him into Patsy's life, doesn't she?"

"She knows. I'm just not sure how much that helps."

Liam's eyes, swollen from his ordeal, opened, focused on the two detectives. "I should have told you..."

Bob sighed at him. "Life's full of should haves, kid." He spoke as if he was just laying out an obvious truth. "Get used to it. You have a lot more mistakes ahead of you."

"Geez, Bob," Abigail said, "remind me not to have you come visit if I'm ever in the hospital."

He glanced at her, obviously mystified.

"What?" But he turned back to Liam. "Detective Browning and I are experienced investigators, and we took a house tour with Augustine. I should have known something was wrong when that twisted son of a bitch didn't get the creeps in the devil room."

"Me, too," Liam mumbled. "But Victor..."

"Weird guy, but he was okay, huh?"

Liam stirred, more conscious now. "Victor figured it out. He knew what Jay was. I thought Jay was just hiding money and stealing from Charlotte. I got his log-in information for his accounts. Bank, credit card. Victor—he checked them out. He must have found something."

"Receipts for Jay's tickets to Ireland, maybe," Abigail said.

"He didn't tell me. That day..." Liam's eyes closed, and he was clearly fading again. "He said he had the devil on his heels. I didn't...I thought it was just... you know, Victor being Victor."

"Rest up, kid," Bob said. "You'll need your energy for when you look for a new job. Nothing involving devils this time, okay?"

Liam's mouth twitched with humor. "Thanks."

Bob didn't speak again until he and Abigail had exited the hospital and were outside in the warm, clear, beautiful June evening. "Yarborough's still annoyed with you for being right about your drowning. Me, I'm getting used to the idea."

"No, you aren't, and I don't care. I wish I'd been wrong."

"Better to die tripping on a crack in the sidewalk than believing you're being chased by the devil."

"We'll prove Augustine was in Boston that night," Abigail said.

"Yeah, but the bastard had me beat," Bob said, matter of fact. "Keira and Eileen are alive because of what they and Simon did, not because of what I did. I let my assumptions drive my conclusions."

"Augustine had us both beat," Abigail said.

"I don't know, though. Go back through the time line. We'd have had to be damn lucky to get ahead of Augustine any sooner than we did. Even if Butler had told us what he and Victor had been up to, he didn't know that Augustine was a killer. We're just a couple of detectives, Abigail. And we didn't kill anyone."

She walked out to her car. Bob had parked right behind her. She got out her keys but didn't step off the curb. "My father worked on the Deirdre McCarthy murder investigation."

"Yes, he did. Abigail—" He broke off, seemed to try to find the right words. "Deirdre's death is something I got used to not talking about."

It was as close to an apology as she'd ever get from Bob O'Reilly. "You I can understand. You were just a kid yourself thirty years ago. But my father..."

"He's not that much older than me. It was a tough investigation. I didn't know him that well, but you were a toddler when Deirdre was killed, Abigail." Bob took a pack of gum from his pants pocket, tapped out a piece and gave it to her, then tapped one out for himself. "Why would your father tell you about an unspeakable act of violence that happened when you were still in diapers?"

Abigail supposed he had a point, but she didn't want to get into it. He'd had a hard enough day without taking on defending her father. "Not me, Bob. I was out of diapers by then."

"No kidding? I thought my girls would be going to kindergarten in diapers." He headed for his car, but stopped after a few yards and called back to her. "You'll be a good mother, Abigail."

She pushed back a tug of emotion. "Yeah. I think so."

Two minutes later, she was in her car, tossing Bob's stick of gum into her little trash bag. She didn't chew gum that wasn't sugar free, and he didn't chew gum that was.

She stuck her key in the ignition, pushing back her fatigue. She was on her way to the triple-decker she shared with Bob and Scoop—and Owen, she thought.

Her eyes teared up, and suddenly she couldn't wait to be home.

~Chapter 39

Jamaica Plain, Massachusetts
9:00 p.m., EDT
June 24

Keira laid a handful of loose-leaf lettuce in Scoop's dented colander. "I must really look like hell for you to let me in your garden."

He was picking lettuce a few feet down the row from her. The garden was his turf. He'd all but posted No Trespassing signs. He smiled at her. "Tough for you to look like hell, Keira."

"It's been a long day," she said without further explanation.

"Yeah. But working in the garden

helps, doesn't it? Puts life into perspective. I'll wash the lettuce, toss it with this nice balsamic vinaigrette I whipped up." He rolled back onto his heels. "Feeling better already, aren't you?"

"I am," she said, standing up. "Thanks, Scoop. Thanks for everything."

"You're welcome, but I didn't do a damn thing except listen to Fiona O'Reilly play harp for a couple hours—"

"You got Madeleine and Jayne into protective custody, and you were the one who had to tell Bob about the pictures."

"Yeah. There was that."

The thought of the pictures—the thought of Jay Augustine stalking her cousins—made Keira sick to her stomach. She could only imagine how her uncle felt. But they were a ruse, a part of Augustine's game. Fiona, Madeleine and Jayne were never his targets.

"I didn't ask enough questions around here," Scoop said. "Bob and Abigail needed an objective voice, and I wasn't there. They weren't letting anyone in, given their crappy moods, but I should have forced myself in."

"We all did our best." Keira brushed dirt off her hands as she got to her feet. "I guess that's all we can ask of ourselves."

Scoop rose next to her with his colander. "Let this guy Cahill in, Keira. The two of you. It's new, but it's for real. That's not one of the things I missed the past week."

His words took her by surprise. "Scoop—"

But he'd already bolted for the stairs up to his apartment. Keira stepped out of the garden, carefully avoiding tramping on any of his tender plants. Scoop wasn't easy to figure out, but none of them was—him, her uncle, Abigail.

And Simon, she thought. He'd stayed at her side after he'd tackled Jay Augustine. The police had arrived within minutes. Augustine had gone silent by then, but Keira knew his cold stare would stay in her mind forever. But he was in police custody now. He couldn't hurt anyone else.

Simon was in Abigail's kitchen with her and Bob. Talking cop talk, probably. Keira wanted to stay close to her mother, who'd given in to her brother's wishes not to go back to her cabin. She'd had her wounds stitched up at a local hospital.

Augustine was, indeed, very good with knives.

She was half asleep in an Adirondack chair now. It was her first visit to the triple-decker Bob had bought with his two colleagues.

"Doing okay, Mum?" Keira asked her.

She managed a small, reassuring smile. "Never better."

Owen walked out into the tiny yard with two tall glasses of iced tea, handing one to Keira and the other to her mother.

Keira relished the normalcy of drinking iced tea on a warm summer night. "You knew Simon was FBI?"

Owen nodded without hesitation. "I did."

"For how long?"

"Eighteen months."

"And you didn't tell Abigail," Keira said, making it a statement.

"It turned into a bigger deal than it should have. Simon and I didn't really become friends until recently. The Armenian earthquake in particular—he's tireless. He's also one of the bravest men I've ever known."

Keira smiled. "Scary almost, isn't it?" But she couldn't sustain any real humor and instead dropped into a chair at the table, drinking some of her tea. "In other words, you never expected for you and Simon and Abigail to become friends."

"Fast Rescue has a lot of volunteers."

"Do you know what he does with the FBI?"

Owen looked uncomfortable. "Keira…"

"I'm guessing he's used his disaster-preparedness consulting as cover. I imagine he's had to tell the BPD and state detectives who he is by now, if not the details. Is that going to cause him problems?"

"Nothing he can't handle, or so he tells me." Owen pulled out a chair next to her and sat down. He could be exacting and intense, but he was also one of the kindest men Keira had ever met. "Simon's status was a confidence, not a secret."

"A distinction without a difference if you're the one in the dark. I'm not talking about myself. I'm just getting to know Simon." Never mind last night, she thought with a welcome surge of heat. "Abigail, though. Yikes. She must not be real pleased."

Owen shrugged, obviously not worried. "That's one way to put it. I've known Simon long enough to say this, Keira. He's the same man whether or not he's wearing his badge."

She knew what he was saying—that there'd been no pretending this week. The man she'd met—the man she'd made love to, had fallen for so hard and fast—wasn't part of an act.

But she'd known that. "Badge, hell, Owen. I'm just glad he showed up when he did this afternoon. Otherwise I'd have had to do serious bodily harm to that cretin."

"I heard about your ax," Owen said with a smile.

"Splitter. Now *that's* a distinction with a difference. An ax has a proper blade. If I'd had to tackle Augustine myself—" She stopped herself, not wanting to dive too deep into the bottomless ocean of might-have-beens. "It doesn't matter. I'm just relieved I didn't have to do more than I did."

"Which was enough."

"That whole deadly force thing is what bit me at the police academy. There's usually one thing in particular that gets people who don't make it through train-ing, and that was mine."

"You dropped out. You didn't flunk out—"

"Another distinction without a differ-ence."

"Maybe so. I'm not in law enforce-ment, but I know that the purpose of deadly force is to stop, not to kill."

She leveled her eyes on him. "There you go."

Simon had been gentle with her mother and professional with the police, but Keira knew he'd have used deadly force on Jay Augustine if he'd had to. He didn't just have handcuffs on him— he had a 9 mm Sig Sauer. Of course, he'd made wisecracks once the imme-diate danger had passed. He had an uncanny ability to sense when people were at their breaking point and knew how to ease their tension, to make them smile in spite of themselves, to remind them that life was too damn short to be serious all the time, even over serious matters.

And yet all the while, Keira knew he had other things on his mind—the life and work he'd dropped to check on her in Ireland.

The long June day was slowly giving way to darkness when Fiona arrived with her two younger sisters, and Bob emerged from Abigail's apartment, his emotion palpable as he took all three daughters into his arms. "Kiss your aunt," he said, nodding to his bandaged sister. "She's lucky to be alive with this crazy bastard come to cut her into ribbons."

Keira watched her cousins surround her mother, crying, hugging. Her mother's reserve, the inevitable result of living alone for so many months, lifted, and she let Jayne, the youngest, sit on the arm of her chair.

Without any warning, Bob broke into an Irish song as he lit the grill.

He had an amazing voice. Keira and her young cousins gaped at him, and he grinned. "What, haven't you ever heard me sing?"

"Not like *that,* Dad," Fiona said, obviously impressed.

Simon walked out into the yard, and Keira's heart jumped at the sight of him with his black curls, his green eyes, his confident manner. He winked at her, then joined in the singing, his voice just as amazing as her uncle's. The two of them adopted Irish accents, and Fiona got up, inserting herself between the two men and hooking one arm with each, the three of them step dancing merrily as they sang.

The tears came next as they belted out a sad song. Fiona, her sisters, Bob and his sister all cried openly. Keira couldn't stop herself from sobbing, but she noticed that Simon remained dry-eyed, just kept singing with that beautiful voice. When they switched to a jauntier tune, he scooped her up and spun her across the clipped grass. She didn't know any of the moves, but he showed her, holding her close, his eyes sparking with humor, and, she thought, desire as he sang and danced with her.

He tightened his arms around her. "Just don't you and your mother start singing," he said, and with one smooth move, swept Keira up and off her feet.

She shrieked in surprise and started to laugh, and she couldn't imagine anywhere else she'd rather be.

The dissecting of events began over dinner, just as Keira had known it would.

Colm Dermott joined the crowd as Abigail, tense and quiet, set the table, refusing help from anyone. He placed a computer disk in the middle. "The police have the original, but I'd copied it onto my computer and burned it onto a disk. I'm quite handy, I'll have you know." But he sighed, his humor not taking hold as he tapped the disk case with one finger. "Patsy doesn't say a word about this bloody bastard. It's just her telling her tale. What a tale it is, too! She was a fine storyteller, Keira."

"Here's my theory," Bob said, breaking the uncomfortable silence that had descended over the table. He glanced at his daughters, and Keira half-expected him to send them upstairs. But he didn't, and continued. "We're talking about Deirdre now. I don't doubt Michael Fuller—now known as Father Michael Palermo—was telling the truth when he said his brother called Patsy and got her out to his boat just as he jumped into the harbor in flames."

Eleven-year-old Jayne O'Reilly scrunched up her face. "That's gross, Dad."

"Yeah. It is." He winked at her. "Not everyone's as loving and wonderful as your dad, right, kid? Okay. Back to my theory. Let's say our fourteen-year-old Michael Fuller knows what his big brother has done and what a monster he's become."

Abigail sat across from Owen, not looking at him as she spoke. "Hadn't Stuart moved out by then?"

"Yeah, but he stayed in touch with Michael. Who knows, maybe he knew his little brother was on to him. Stuart didn't leave much of a trail. Nowadays, it's harder not to, but thirty years ago..." Bob shrugged. "So Michael's caught between a rock and a hard place. He doesn't have enough evidence—at least in his own mind—to take to the police. He's worried his brother's going to get wind of his suspicions and disappear, and who knows how many girls like Deirdre he'd kill before police caught up with him."

"This is an awful scenario, Bob," Abigail said. "This kid had no one he felt he could trust."

Bob didn't respond right away. He winked at Madeleine and Jayne, as if to remind them they were safe, and he stood behind Fiona, who sat between Owen and Scoop, and patted her on the shoulder, then gave his sister a nod. "Eileen, you okay? You hanging in there?"

"Keep going," she said in a tight whisper.

Keira watched her uncle move back over to the grill and pick up a barbecue fork. She had no idea if he was offering a theory that he'd just come up with, or if it was one he'd contemplated on and off over the past thirty years.

He stirred the coals and continued.

"Michael figures his only way out is to take matters into his own hands. By now, Deirdre's body has washed up on shore. The police are searching for her killer. Michael knows who the killer is, where he is—but he makes up his mind not to tell the police. Instead, he waits until Stuart passes out from drinking, douses him with gasoline and sets him on fire."

Madeleine gasped, but Fiona and Jayne listened silently, wide-eyed. Keira pictured her uncle at twenty, learning the fate of the monster who'd so brutally and terribly slain his friend. The girl he'd taken to the prom. Patsy's daughter.

"There were less violent options," Abigail said.

Scoop shook his head. "Kid didn't want a less violent option."

"That's right," Bob said. "Michael wanted his big brother to burn for what he'd done. To suffer, here on earth. He wanted him to have a chance to ask forgiveness for his evil acts and save his eternal soul."

"Did it work out that way?" Fiona asked.

"Witnesses say Stuart was on fire when he leaped into the harbor."

"Did his younger brother watch?" Keira asked, then added, "At least according to your theory."

"There's no evidence putting Michael on the scene," her uncle said.

Abigail tilted her chair back. "Whatever he did or didn't do, I can't imagine knowing your brother's a killer and believing you're the only one who can stop him."

Simon stretched out his long legs. "Maybe your theory is off just a little, Bob. Maybe Stuart Fuller actually thought he was the devil, and he set himself on fire, thinking he'd survive."

Bob made a face. "That's creepy, Cahill. I've got freaking goose bumps now thinking about it."

Colm Dermott shuddered. "Aye," he said. "I do, too."

Keira shared their revulsion, but her mother leaned forward, wincing in pain. "It's also possible that Stuart Fuller really was Satan."

Her brother snorted. "Well, if he was Satan, he's a dead Satan, because I saw his body. In fact, Abigail, your father showed it to me. Hell. That was a long time ago."

Fiona got to her feet and hugged her father. "I'm sorry about your friend, Dad."

"Yeah, kid. Thanks."

But Owen rose and invited her and her sisters into Abigail's apartment for ice cream. Keira saw how good he was with the girls and wondered if Abigail noticed.

"Maybe I should have kept my mouth shut," Bob said, returning to the table.

"No," Abigail said, staring at the retreating O'Reilly girls. "They'll remember that you leveled with them and didn't shut them out. But it can be tough, seeing what we see in our work and then thinking about bringing kids into the world. If I could wave my magic wand and rid the world of violence, I'd do it. I'd put us right out of business."

"I know you would, kid, but if it's magic wands you need—talk to Keira."

Bob grinned, then laughed, and Abigail groaned and threw a plastic spoon at him.

Simon put a hand on Keira's thigh and leaned close to her. "Something's come up with my work," he said in a low voice. "I have to go."

"Your consulting work or your FBI work?"

"It could take some time."

"That's not an answer, Simon."

"You won't be able to reach me for a while, but don't worry." He squeezed her thigh and smiled. "I'll find you."

After Simon left, Abigail and Scoop retreated to their apartments, and Colm bid everyone good-night, whispering to Keira on his way out that Patsy's story was, indeed, perfect for her new book. "She wouldn't want that devil to ruin it," he said, "and she'd be so proud."

Her uncle closed up the grill. His daughters had come back out with their ice cream and watched as if they were seeing a side of him they'd never seen before. He pretended not to notice, but Keira thought he did.

"Looks as if it'll be me and the womenfolk tonight," he said. "I don't have enough beds, but I want you all to stay. Keira, Eileen—you, too. It'll be a crowd, but it's been a hell of a day. For a while there..." He shook off whatever he'd started to say. "Eileen, it'll be like the old days. Remember when we thought it was a big deal to sleep on blankets on the living room floor?"

She smiled. "We thought we were living large, didn't we?"

He pulled out his wallet and took out a cracked picture. "I've never shown you kids my prom picture." He held it in front of the citronella candle lit on the table as the girls gathered around him. "This is me. And this—" He paused to clear his throat and pointed gently to the pretty blond girl with him. "This is Deirdre Ita."

Fiona touched his arm. "Dad..."

"She was named for an Irish saint, and she loved angels and a good story."

"Oh, she did, Bob," his sister said.

As Keira listened to her mother and uncle talk and laugh, one story spinning into another about the friend they'd lost so long ago, she wondered if Simon had known this was coming, and that was at least part of the reason he'd chosen that particular moment to make his exit.

When they blew out the candles for the night, her uncle tucked an arm over her shoulder. "Well, kid, where's your fairy prince?"

"Simon, you mean? He had to leave. I think he might object to being called a fairy prince—"

"Do you, now? Interesting character. On my way back here from Cambridge, I got a call from a state detective I know. Your by-the-book type. Worse than Abigail's partner, that prig Yarborough. In a nutshell, this guy said they didn't find any damn stone angel by the stream, and we all should shut the hell up about one before we get carted to the loony bin."

"But, Bob," Keira said. "I saw it myself."

"You saw a rock. So did your mother. The woods out there are full of rocks. They don't call New Hampshire the Granite State for nothing." He yawned, dropping his arm back to his side.

"Stress can do weird things to your mind."

"Then as far as the police are concerned, there's no stone angel?"

"No stone angel," her uncle said. "Of course, that's not what I told the State guy. I told him maybe the fairies took it. He threatened to come out here and shoot me himself. No sense of humor. But, who knows? I keep thinking about your backpack showing up at that Irish pub, and that scrap of sweater the barman in Ireland says he found."

Keira gave him a sharp look. "Bob, I didn't know you believed in fairies—"

"I don't. I just keep an open mind."

"Well," she said, "there was an old man in Ireland..."

"What old man, Keira?"

"I shouldn't say old. He was probably about your age—"

He grinned at her. "That's definitely not old."

As they all headed upstairs, Keira related her encounter with the man at the picnic table the night before the summer solstice, and her uncle listened, amused, curious. When she finished, he said, "I think you should go back to Ireland."

"I do, too."

Bob had a bedroom for his daughter, but they'd already made mats on the floor out of blankets, their aunt stretched out among them, saying she didn't want the couch. "Will you be staying?" she asked Keira.

"Yes, Mum. I'd love to stay."

She didn't want the couch, either, and settled on the floor with her mother and cousins. Bob put on the DVD Colm had brought.

Patsy was at her kitchen table with a pot of tea and a plate of brown bread, and she had on a pastel blue sweater, her eyes bright and filled with life. "Once upon a time," she said in her Irish lilt, "there were three brothers who lived on the southwest coast of Ireland…"

Keira bit back tears and felt her mother take her hand. "This is how Patsy would want to be remembered," she whispered. "For telling a good story."

It was true, Keira thought. And she knew what she had to do. She'd camp out here tonight with her family, and tomorrow she'd head back to Ireland. There was unfinished business there, although she couldn't put her finger on what it was.

And there was Simon.

She would trust him to find her.

⁓Chapter 40

East Boston, Massachusetts
10:00 p.m., EDT
June 24

Simon had his feet up on the table on the top deck of his boat and didn't rise to greet John March, who seemed to have come out to the Boston Harbor pier alone—although that was unlikely if not impossible.

The FBI director's presence was not unexpected. He'd warned Simon he was on his way.

"My voice is hoarse," Simon said. "I've been singing Irish songs."

"You always could sing."

"Maybe that could be my new job."

"Hell of a day, Simon."

"Yeah."

March looked out at the harbor, the city lights glistening on the dark, still water. "I wonder what would have happened if I'd remained a Boston cop. Deirdre McCarthy's murder is one of those cases that stays with you, eats at you forever. I know that from a law enforcement point of view, it doesn't matter if the victim of a crime—a brutal murder—is a good person or a bad person. We have a job to do, regardless. But Deirdre..." The FBI director shook his head with emotion. "Deirdre was a good person."

"You wanted out of BPD before her murder. You were always ambitious."

"Her murder helped me to understand why. Abigail can do that work in a way I never could." He sighed at Simon. "You've complicated my life. You know that, don't you?"

Simon shrugged. "You can handle it."

"Reporters are already calling to ask me what I remember about Deirdre's murder. They know Abigail's my daughter." He gave a grim smile. "Wait until they find out about you, Simon."

"You're not just talking about my FBI status."

"That's right. There's also your father."

"Yes. There's my father."

"Someone will start digging and find out we were friends and that he died the way he did. Maybe it's time I talked about him. Brendan Cahill was a dedicated Federal agent. He deserves better than my silence."

"You have nothing to hide," Simon said.

"That's not the point, is it? Talking reminds me of my own failings, but that part doesn't get me so much. I wish I could have saved him, Simon. That's the truth of it." But March didn't linger on the thought and smiled suddenly. "Your father could sing, too. Do you remember?"

"He's the one who taught me my first Irish drinking song."

Simon thought of Keira and how much she still didn't know about him. Then again, she was nosy by nature—curious, she'd say. It was how she could sit in an old woman's kitchen and get her telling stories, and it was why she was interested in the first place. That curiosity—that sensibility—showed up in her artwork. She could go off to Ireland by herself for six weeks, but she wasn't a loner.

"Simon?"

He gave himself a mental shake. "What's going on with Estabrook?"

"We're making our move now. He's still in Montana—I'm expecting a call in few minutes. It'll be a big story. Simon, you need to drop out of sight for a few weeks."

He'd figured as much. "I'm on my way to Scotland. Will's castle. He wants me to play golf."

"And if Fast Rescue needs you?"

"Owen's up to speed on the situation. I'll be back in action as soon as possible."

"You're good, Simon. You don't crack under pressure."

"I don't know. I've fallen for a folklorist who paints pictures of Irish fairies."

March cracked a smile. "I hear she's also quite capable of defending herself.

Sounds as if she's a woman right up your alley."

"It's going to take her a while to put this week behind her. She'll do it her own way, just as you did.... Stuart Fuller?"

"I was sitting in Patsy's kitchen eating brown bread and drinking tea when he called her. She knew what we were up against before we did. She believed he was the devil—not that he thought he was the devil. That he was, in fact, Satan."

"Did she tell you?"

March shook his head. "No. I figured it out later. She should have told me, but she didn't. Not for Fuller's sake, Simon. But she shouldn't have had to witness what he did to himself."

"So he did kill himself?"

"Yes, but that wasn't his intention. He believed he could survive the flames."

Simon took a moment to digest that one. A twenty-four-year-old killer luring the mother of a victim of his violence to watch him set himself on fire. "Figured he'd burn a while, prove how evil he was, then, what, set Patsy on fire?"

"Probably." March got heavily to his

feet. "I promised your father I'd look after you if anything happened to him—"

"You have, John." Simon rose and put out his hand. "Thank you."

The two men shook, then March surprised Simon by embracing him. "Brendan would be proud of you."

"Tell Abigail about him." Simon stood back and smiled, remembering his father on a summer night just like this one. "He was named after an Irish saint. Brendan the Navigator."

"That tape of his execution..."

"Letting me see it was the right thing to do. Maybe not with another kid, but with me—it's when I knew you understood me. It's when I started listening to you. If you hadn't come along when you did, done what you did—" Simon gave the FBI director a broad grin. "I'd probably just be getting out of prison right about now."

And for the first time in many visits, and most likely many days, John March threw back his head and laughed.

⁓ Chapter 41

Jamaica Plain, Massachusetts
11:30 p.m., EDT
June 24

Abigail couldn't contain her surprise and delight when she entered her living room and saw Keira Sullivan's painting of the Irish cottage that had caught her eye at the auction. She'd never been to Ireland and wasn't Irish, but it didn't matter. Something about the painting—about Keira's work—had captivated her.

"Owen," she said, turning to him, "where did this come from?"

"Simon left it for you. For us, really, but it's more for you. He says if you're happy, I'm happy, and this'll make you happy."

"It does. It's beautiful."

"He wants to know if he's back on the guest list for the wedding."

"Now we'll have to invite him, assuming..." She didn't go on.

"There'll be a wedding, Abigail," Owen said, slipping an arm around her. "Sooner rather than later, I hope."

"It's complicated."

"Only because we're making it complicated. We're lucky. We have friends, family, resources, work we love—and we have each other. I love you, Abigail. I want to spend the rest of my life with you. I'm patient, but only to a point. Let's get married."

"We don't have everything figured out."

"We don't need to."

It sounded so simple when he said it. "I've been launching myself into the future. I haven't done that in a long time. Before Chris was killed, I had so many plans. Then I didn't. I focused on making detective and finding his killer. That was it. Nothing else. For seven years."

Owen kissed her softly. "We can plan together," he said. "You don't have to figure everything out by yourself."

"I keep thinking about Bob bottling up that poor girl's murder for all these years. Owen, I don't want us to shut each other out. Bob's one of the best men I know. I'd trust him with my life without hesitation. He's a great detective. But I'll bet you he never told either woman he married about Deirdre McCarthy."

"He's protective."

"Yes, but I think Simon got it right. He said Bob learned just not to go there—he put a wall up around that part of his past. I was never that way with Chris's death. I went there every day."

"Because his murder was unsolved," Owen said.

"I don't go there every day anymore. Owen—I love you so much. I love thinking about you, and I do. I think about you every day." She looked at the painting. "Our first wedding present. It's incredibly generous of Simon. Now we owe him—"

"He'd disagree. Hates having people owe him."

She just saw the card. *"'Dear Ab','"* she read aloud. *"'Enjoy the painting. Let me know when you pick a wedding date. I think of you as a long-lost sister, even if you're not Irish.'"* She shook her head at Owen and smiled. "Simon does have a way about him. He's cheeky, though, isn't he?"

But there was a loud knock on the back door, and Abigail wasn't surprised when she found Bob and Scoop there with yellow pads and sharpened pencils. "The girls and my sister and niece are asleep," Bob said, "but I need to go through it all again."

"I'm not asleep," Keira said, appearing behind Bob and Scoop. "I'm not a cop, but can I join you?"

Abigail looked back at Owen, but he was already clearing off the kitchen table. It'd be a long night. Then a knock came at the front door, and as she headed down the hall, she couldn't even imagine who it'd be. Yarborough? The mayor? Reporters?

But it was her father, standing by himself on the welcome mat. "Hello, Abigail."

Her breath caught. "Dad. Tell me nothing's happened to Simon—"

"Nothing's happened to him," her father said. "He's fine."

"Cahill's a fun guy," Bob said from behind her in the hall, "but I have a feeling a lot of people want to kill him."

"One in particular at the moment."

"Norman Estabrook," Scoop said, then shrugged at the surprised looks. "I made a few calls."

Abigail noticed her father's slight smile. He was adept at keeping his emotions under tight wraps, but she could tell he had a genuine fondness for Simon. He stepped inside her small apartment, shrugged off his suit jacket. "I wouldn't worry," he said. "The people who want to kill Simon always end up dead or in prison."

Bob, Scoop and Owen obviously liked and understood that answer, but Abigail saw Keira's pale look. Keira knew little about Simon, but she was clearly in love with him. *We could be friends,* Abigail thought, and sat at the small kitchen table between her and Owen.

"May I join you?" her father asked.

Abigail nodded. "I'd love it," she said.

Before he sat down, he put an arm around Keira. "You can trust Simon," he said.

His tone gave Abigail a jolt, and she realized that Simon hadn't been kidding in his note. He *was* like a long-lost brother, because the way her father had just spoken about him...it was as if he were talking about a son.

~Chapter 42

Keira walked down the lane from her cottage with her Irish sweater pulled tight against her in the chill of the wind and damp evening air. She'd begun to notice the days getting shorter, dawn coming a little later, night a little sooner, on the southwest Irish coast. She imagined life in the village before electricity, and it was easy to understand how telling stories by the fire had taken hold here.

As she turned the corner onto the

main village street, she could hear an uproar at the pub. Laughter, arguing, hoots of protest. Her step faltered.

Simon.

She picked up her pace, breaking into a run. She hadn't pinned up her hair, and she could feel it tangling in the wind. A cold, damp mist swept up from the harbor. It was a good night for a warm pub, an even better night to be back with Simon.

When she pulled open the pub door, she forced herself to calm down, not look as if she'd just been chased by ghosts or wild dogs—although there'd been none of that in her weeks at her cottage. There'd been a lightness, tranquility, on her quiet lane. She liked to think Patsy's wish had been fulfilled and the stone angel was back where it belonged—somehow, some way.

Keira tucked back some wild strands of hair and caught her breath.

She wasn't wrong. It was Simon who'd caused the uproar in the pub.

He stopped midargument and stood up from his stool at the bar. He had on an Irish sweater, and his black hair was a little longer, curling into the wool. His eyes, as green as the hills outside the pub door, sparked, and he smiled. "I had a feeling it'd be easier to find you this visit."

Eddie O'Shea polished a beer glass behind the bar. "Ah, Keira. You didn't have to get yourself into a pickle this time, now, did you?"

The local men gathered at the tables exchanged amused glances. None admitted to believing she'd seen the stone angel up at the ruin, or that the black dog had been anything but a stray, or that they knew anything about an old man in wellies or how her backpack and that shovel had ended up for Eddie to find.

They believed in the devil, though, who'd killed the sheep that awful night, who'd killed Patsy McCarthy in South Boston and had tried to kill Keira and her mother in the woods of southern New Hampshire.

But in the weeks since Keira had returned to the cottage, the horror of those days had receded. She'd worked tirelessly on her collection of tales from

Irish-born American immigrants, taking time to roam the hills and play tourist, buying a pottery vase in Adrigole, riding Ireland's one cable car from the tip of the Beara Peninsula to Dursey Island, crawling through castle ruins. Colm Dermott had visited her with his wife and four children, and she'd hooked her laptop up to the Internet.

Seamus Harrigan had stopped by to tie up any loose ends of Jay Augustine's havoc in Ireland. The Irish detective had his own theories. For starters, he believed that killing the sheep had been opportunistic—of the moment, when the poor beast wandered in front of Augustine on his search for the ruin. Harrigan's team had found a bucket Augustine had undoubtedly used to carry the blood and entrails off with him.

A grisly thought that disturbed even Harrigan, an experienced detective.

Once Augustine found the ruin and started digging, the dog attacked him, and he hid in the trees. Then Keira turned up and ducked into the ruin, thinking the dog was after her.

Augustine, still nervous about the dog,

decided he had to take action. The ruin was already showing signs of collapsing. He whispered her name and triggered a bigger collapse, then grabbed Keira's backpack and ran.

But before leaving the ruin, he dumped his bucket of blood and entrails.

On his way out of town, he slipped into Keira's cottage and stole her copy of the tape of Patsy telling her story—and, when he saw the note on the counter detailing her whereabouts, he snatched that, too.

As for the angel—Harrigan had his doubts there'd ever been a stone angel in the ruin. "But if you want to believe there was, Keira," he'd said, with a flash of his very blue eyes, "you go right ahead."

And Keira had decided, who was she to argue with an Irish detective?

Harrigan, who had relatives in the village, said he had a story or two he'd like to tell her one of these days, and he spoke to her as if he knew she'd be back.

A few of the locals had pulled her aside to entertain her with tales of their own. None admitted to knowing the story about the three Irish brothers and the stone angel.

But throughout her weeks in the village, Keira had dreamed of this moment.

Simon set down his glass. "Sorry, fellas. Another time. We'll pick up where we left off."

He walked over to Keira and whisked her up into his arms, and the men all hooted and laughed as he carried her effortlessly out to the street. He didn't set her down until he reached the lane that led down to the harbor.

"A boat," she said. "I should have known."

"It's borrowed."

"Someone else who owes you his life?"

"The same person."

"Will Davenport," she said. "Eddie told me about him."

"Will's fishing in Scotland, but he wants to meet you. It's the flowers in your hair on your Web site."

"I suspect it's because he's your friend, and he knows I'm smitten."

"Smitten?" Simon grinned at her. "A word for a fairy princess, don't you think?"

She laughed, and he led her along the pier, fitting in with the Irish fishermen. But he was a man who could fit in anywhere. When they reached the boat, he scooped her up again, carrying her below, as if he'd been thinking about this moment for days.

He laid her on the bed, and she threw her arms over her head, sinking into the soft, warm sheets and taking in the welcome shock of being with him.

"Keira..." He stared into her eyes. "We're a couple of wanderers."

"At least for now." She threaded her fingers into his hair. "Let's wander together."

He quieted her up with a kiss. "Keira, Keira," he whispered, kissing her again and again. "I've missed you."

The next kiss lasted a long time, and all she wanted was it to go on forever. She smoothed her palms down his neck and over his shoulders, loving the feel of his warm sweater, his firm muscles. When he deepened their kiss, tasting her, she sank even deeper into the soft bed, feeling the want spread through her.

"I've dreamed about you," she said. "I knew you'd find me. I never doubted—"

He slipped his hands under her shirt, lifting his mouth from hers and smiling. "I thought that might get your attention."

"You were right." She relished the feel of him on her bare skin. "Simon...I'm not just falling in love with you any longer. I am in love."

"I've thought about you saying that for all these weeks. Keira," he whispered, skimming his hands up her sides, "I love you."

He curved his palms over her breasts, and she couldn't talk, just let herself take in that he was finally here, with her, making love to her. In seconds he had her clothes off, and his, and all she wanted was to give herself up to the feel of him. She couldn't get enough of him. Not now, not ever.

He pulled back the covers, holding her in his arms. "Are you cold?" he asked.

She smiled, running her hands up his strong back. "Not for long, I imagine."

His mouth found hers again, a deep, lingering, erotic kiss that fired her skin and her soul. She could feel his focus—his purpose. He could pluck survivors out of rubble because of his ability to zero in on a mission. She was more out of control.

A challenge, she thought. A distraction.

"We belong here," she said. "Right now, this moment..."

He kissed a trail lower and found her nipple, and she cried out in surprise and pleasure at the feel of his tongue. She heard the Irish wind howling outside. Appropriate, somehow. They'd met in Boston, Keira thought, but it was Ireland that had brought them together. She'd have fallen for him if they'd met over a pint at Eddie O'Shea's pub.

"Keira," he said, "stop thinking."

And he touched her, licked her, forcing all thought right out of her brain.

She drew her legs apart, and he raised up and drove into her, slowly, deeply, warmth as well as hunger in his green eyes. She responded, savoring every thrust, every inch of him, her pulse quickening, her skin tingling. Her release came suddenly, as the wind beat against the small boat and Simon cried out her name, and she knew they were where they were meant to be.

Afterward, they made their way back out to the pier, bundled in wool sweaters as the wind died down again. Keira looked up toward the barren hills, and against the stars and the moon, she saw the silhouette of a man in an Irish cap and wellies up among the rocks and sheep. He was trailed by a troop of dancing shadows—fairies, she thought, and whether they were real or imagined, she didn't care.

Simon slipped an arm around her, and she knew he'd seen them, too.

"My father's home village is up the coast," he said. "I've heard there are stories there of farmers, fishermen, fairies and magic."

Keira leaned against him, welcoming his warmth and strength. "I can't think of anything I'd rather do than sail the Irish coast with you."

"Up for an adventure, are you?"

She smiled. "Always."

~Epilogue

Beara Peninsula, Southwest Ireland
7:00 p.m., IST
August 6

Bob O'Reilly entered the toasty pub and noticed that no one seemed to care that he was soaked to the bone and dripping on the floor. He'd walked down the lane from the cottage his crazy niece had rented for another month. She'd arranged for a cot in the living room and sent him and her mother tickets to Ireland.

What could he do? A free trip to Ireland. He had to go.

He peeled off his rain jacket and hung

it on a coat tree with a lot of others just as faded and worn.

The barman, Eddie O'Shea, eyed him as he filled a beer glass from the tap. "Well, Detective, did you have a good walk?" He said "detective" as if he thought it was pretty funny Bob was a cop.

Bob shook some of the rainwater off his head. "The weather's lousy, and the air smells like wet sheep."

"Ah, but you love it, don't you?"

"I'm not saying."

He eased onto a high stool next to his sister. The scenery on the Beara Peninsula reminded him of some of the postcards Patsy McCarthy had tacked to the wall in her front hall.

And it reminded him of stories his mother used to tell.

He'd stay a week in Ireland. Then he had to get back to work.

He didn't know about Eileen. She might just stay forever. She'd finished her illuminated manuscript before heading to Ireland. Colm Dermott had hired her to help work on the Boston-Cork conference. Bob figured she'd have to find a place to live that at least had flush toilets. But she was already loving the idea of the job. Billie and Jeanette Murphy, horrified at how Jay Augustine had manipulated them, had set up a scholarship in Patsy's name and were sending the first recipient to the conference.

It'd be weeks yet before the Augustine investigation was wrapped up. Bob wasn't in charge of it—he wasn't even part of it, except as a witness. He didn't like that, but what could he do? The rest of the autopsy results were back on Victor Sarakis. Still no smoking gun on how he'd drowned in two feet of water, but the medical examiner had taken a closer look at Victor's body. He'd taken a solid hit on his left temple, undoubtedly when he struck the concrete edge of the pond. It wouldn't have killed him or probably even knocked him out, but it could have rung his bell enough to disorient him. And there was a bruise on Victor's back that could have been from his brother-in-law standing on him.

One or the other, or both, could have prevented Victor from fighting off that devil.

Jay Augustine's actions weren't arbitrary or nuts, Bob thought. Augustine'd had a mission. It just hadn't included grabbing a BPD detective's daughter off the street. He'd wanted a mother and daughter. A religious ascetic who lived in the woods and a pretty artist and folklorist.

Eileen and Keira...

Bob let the thought go. The bastard was behind bars where he belonged.

And I'm on vacation.

On his first day in Ireland, and Eileen's first day back in thirty years, they'd walked up to the ruin where Keira had nearly met her end on the summer solstice and all that bit about a dog and an angel and fairies had occurred. Maybe it was the old hut of the hermit monk from Patsy's story. Maybe it wasn't. It didn't matter—it was definitely the place where his sister had holed up for three days in a gale all those years ago.

But maybe, ultimately, that didn't matter, either.

"Keira called before you got to the pub," Eileen said. "She wants to arrange for us to spend Christmas in Ireland.

You, me, the girls. We'll stay in fancy places in Dublin and Kenmare. Can you imagine, Bob?"

"I can imagine how much it'd cost."

"Her illustrations have caught on, and she's never been a big spender."

"What about Simon?"

"Oh, he'll be there, too," Eileen said. "I know he will, don't you?"

"At least I won't be the only male. That's what I know."

But he could imagine Fiona's excitement in particular at the prospect of spending Christmas in Ireland. She'd drag him to pubs to listen to music. Probably make him sing. She was getting her younger sisters into Irish music—Madeleine had taken right to the fiddle. Jayne was more like him and not that enthralled.

Eileen's cheeks were flushed with the anticipation of it all. "You can see it, can't you, Bob? All of us together for Christmas."

"Oh, yeah. I can see me in some damn five-star hotel with those girls of mine."

Eddie sighed with amusement. "You

Yanks," he said, setting a pint of Guinness in front of Bob.

"American as apple pie," Bob said, raising his glass to Eddie with a wink.

"If you think the weather's bad now, wait until you're here at Christmas. The damp will sink into your bones."

"You keep the pub open?"

"All but Christmas Day."

"Good. I'll talk Keira out of putting us up in a five-star hotel."

Eddie laughed, but when he set a pot of tea and a small plate of steaming brown bread in front of Eileen, Bob saw her eyes film with tears. She was thinking of Patsy, he knew. And maybe Deirdre. He drank some of his Guinness and didn't speak.

"Ah, Eileen," Eddie said with a twinkle in his eyes, "sitting there you don't look a day over twenty."

She smiled through her tears. "Well, aren't you a big liar."

He laughed. "You've been missed all these years."

"I have a story to tell," she said with a catch in her voice. "A true story. Some of it's sad, and some of it's not. I can keep it to myself if you'd like."

Bob kept his mouth shut, but Eddie said, "No, tell it. It's a rainy, windy night, a good one for a story. Tell it start to finish, and don't leave out a word."

He closed the pub for the night. Several of the local men stayed, gathered at the small tables, nursing beers and coffee as the weather roared outside.

Eileen started tentatively, with her and Bob and Deirdre growing up together on the same street. She covered it all, from then until now, and Bob hadn't realized what a storyteller his sister was. All those months by herself in that cabin, chopping wood, hauling water, fending for herself—and praying, of course. She still prayed a lot. He didn't mind. He hoped now and then she put in a good word or two for him.

As she wrapped up, she said, "Deirdre always wanted to see Ireland. She truly was an angel."

"She still is, then," Eddie said, a little choked up himself.

"We used to talk about running off to

Ireland and having adventures and ro-
mances."

"And here you are, back again."

"Because of Keira. Deirdre would be
pleased at her happiness."

"And yours."

Eileen smiled. "Yes. Mine, too. I don't
know who Keira's father was— I just
know I was trapped in that ruin for three
days in a proper Irish gale, and I loved
hard and well for that time."

"But John Michael Sullivan," Eddie
said with some emotion. "He was the
love of your life, wasn't he, Eileen?"

She bit back tears. "Eddie…"

"If you hadn't come home from Ireland
expecting, you'd never have let yourself
look at him. You were the college girl.
He was the boy from the neighborhood."

In the past thirty years, Bob had never
thought of Eileen's relationship with her
husband that way, but he saw her blush
and had a sudden appreciation for the
barman's wisdom.

"We loved each other," Eileen mur-
mured.

Eddie O'Shea leaned over the bar, his

eyes intense now, certain. "You didn't lose Deirdre or John Michael because of anything you did here. Your daughter's a blessing."

Bob couldn't take anymore. "I don't know about that. She's off sailing the Irish coast with some black-haired rake of an Irish fairy prince, drawing pictures of leprechauns and thistle and sticking me here in the back end of nowhere—"

He didn't get to finish—the locals were on him. He bought a round of drinks, and they laughed and argued and talked politics and sheep and fairies. Eileen didn't take part, but that was okay. Bob could tell she was listening, and she was happy, in the company of friends. He could feel all her anguish and guilt fall away. A mad affair that was meant to be was long over, and she knew what she knew about her daughter's father and that was all.

Not everything in life needed to be explained.

When they finally headed back to the cottage, the rain had stopped, and Eddie O'Shea joined them on the walk up the lane. His two brothers fell in beside him. It was a night for mischief, they said—and the three of them headed up the dirt track off into the dark Irish hills.

Bob stood with his sister in front of the pretty stone cottage with its pink roses, and they looked out at the starlit sky and the eerie mist above the harbor.

"We're in the company of angels, Bob," Eileen said softly.

"Yeah, sis." He slung an arm over her shoulders and thought of Deirdre and Patsy and John Michael, and he felt them all with him now in the Irish wind. "We surely are."